SHADOWS

By Jennifer N. Bogle

Prologue

Terra ran.

It was behind her and it was gaining fast.

She misstepped on the soft forest floor and nearly went down. Correcting herself she hung a sharp left and kept going.

She didn't know how far ahead she was but she didn't want to stop and find out. She had to get away and get back to the cave and to him. She had save him. He would be asleep by now and if the shadows were coming for her they were coming for him.

Another sharp left and past a few trees and suddenly Terra, princess of the Kingdom of Sol, found herself standing in a clearing filled with wild red flowers and a stream that flowed directly through the middle of it.

Terra came to a halt, slipping on the rain slicked wild grass.

She knew the shadow was closing in behind her but it didn't matter now.

Standing in the field before her, larger than she'd ever seen it, was the monster that haunted her dreams every night. The monster that had destroyed her life.

It stood, leering at her as the shadow behind her finally closed the distance between them.

Chapter 1

Terra crept forward slowly; watching carefully for the rafters she knew would creek under her weight. When she found the vantage point she was looking for she lowered her slim fifteen year old body down and watched in wonder at what was going on in the room below her.

Diana stood, crouched and ready. Her arms were up and the defensive spell her teacher wanted her to use was on her lips and could be unleashed at a moment's notice. Her blue eyes scanned the room, waiting to see where the shadow would appear. Carefully she scanned each corner, trying to memorize where the sunlight streamed through the door ways and windows, and where the shadows in the corners stretched out to the middle of the room. There was no furniture to worry about, so the only shadows came from the walls themselves. She would get it this time, she knew she would.

Terra watched her sister slowly spin in a circle. She could tell by her posture what spell she would use against. It was a new spell Master Bell had taught her yesterday. Diana had bragged to her all last night after dinner. Terra, not being allowed to study magic, didn't understand all of the logistics of the spell, but she could tell from up here that Diana wasn't doing right. Something in the way she had her hands raised didn't feel right to Terra. Often when Diana was showing her a new spell she learned, Terra would get a feeling when it was right and when it wasn't.

She had one of those feelings now.

Diana, sensing something in the corner behind her spun around lightning fast and tried to fire the spell off her fingers. It sputtered for a moment, like blue and gold fire on her hands, and then fizzled out into nothing. A small amount of the spell had managed to leave her hands but all it succeeded in doing was blackening a small section of the wall in front of her.

There was no shadow there.

"Ugh!" Diana exclaimed when she saw the burnt wall. "Why must they hide like children? Shadows in the real world don't hide. They spring out of nowhere and try to trap you in their darkness. They

3

don't play children's games!" Diana was screaming and had stopped paying attention the room around her.

A shadow, smaller than Terra had seen before, silently crept up behind her. Knowing better than to look it in the eyes, she kept her gaze focused on the misty semi-solid base of the creature. She knew that if called out to warn Diana she would get a lashing from her mother for sneaking into another one of sister's classes. So she sat silently on the rafter willing Diana to turn around.

Diana did turn around, but much too late. She spun, sensing something behind her to find the shadow less than two feet away. Even knowing what she knew, Diana still looked up straight into the creatures eyes.

She froze, unable to move or speak. Slowly those silvery eyes came down and locked onto the princess. It raised itself up suddenly, six or seven feet tall to tower over Diana, who at sixteen years old only stood five feet four inches tall. Just as quickly as it had grown taller the shadow suddenly grew wider and wider, more than wide enough to swallow up Diana where she stood.

Just before the shadow could make its next and final move, a blast of deep green and silver magic tore through the creature. It screeched a sorrowful and unearthly sound before it dissipated into nothingness leaving a small wisp of black smoke in its wake.

Once the creature was gone Diana came out of her trance and looked around baffled. "What happened?" She demanded.

Master Bell stepped forward, hands folded behind his back and a look of impatience on his handsome well cut face. His deep blue eyes took in Diana's recovered state and her sudden explosion of anger. He reached one hand up and swept a lock of his jet black hair off his face and sighed.

"Diana, what have I told you about the eyes?" He asked. His face was impassive now but his voice showed just a hint of his true impatience.

4

"I know about the eyes!" She exploded, frustrated.

"One look into the silver eyes of a shadow and you're doomed. Shadows don't exist fully in any one plane of existence, and since they float in and out of different places, they can't lock onto any one person or place. That's why shadow attacks are always so random and impossible to predict.

"However, once you look into a shadow's eyes, they can suddenly sense that you're there. Some people believe they can feel your soul through your gaze. They lock onto you and never stop chasing until they get you. They somehow anchor themselves to your soul. No matter where you go or what you do they can find you. The only way to be safe is to find a city or a hold that's been protected against them and pray they let you in."

"We've been through this over and over again Diana," Master Bell said with a sigh.

"I know about the shadows," Diana complained, "You've told me about it more times than I can count. I was just surprised is all."

"In the real world princess you won't have any warning of danger. When you fight the evil the stalks this land, you'll be on your own. There will be no help for you then."

"Do you think I don't *know* that?" Diana exploded, "I am only sixteen years old. Sixteen! And every day since before I can remember people have been telling me about *my* destiny! I know I have to save everyone, I know I'm the only one who can defeat the Shadow King and his army of shadows!"

Diana was really angry now. Her face had gone all red and her eyes were kind of bulging from her face. Terra shrank back on the rafter, hidden but still afraid of her sister's wrath. Knowing how angry her sister was now gave her the advantage of being able to hide later to avoid having that anger directed at her.

"Diana," Master Bell said a warning in his voice.

"It's Your Highness and I'll remind you to not forget that again," Diana said acidly. She gathered her silken skirts in her hand, turned on her heel and marched out of the class room. Terra watched her go with a kind of distant admiration. She could just march out of the room and everyone around let her. No one stopped her or told her where to go. If she showed up to class it was because she decided she wanted to, not because she had to.

People didn't tell Terra what to do unless they saw her. People didn't much think of her. They certainly didn't respect her enough to let her walk out of room, head held high. Terra doubted she would ever command such respect from anyone.

"You can come down now," Master Bell said, not turning to face the young princess, but clearly addressing her.

Smiling at Bell's ability to always know when she was around, Terra lowered herself down by her hands and then dropped silently to the floor.

"How do you always know?" she asked.

Bell smiled and turned to face the second princess. "As I've told you before highness, you have a very particular energy. One that is, in fact, quite easy to feel."

"Please Master Bell, Terra. I feel strange when people call me highness."

"Why do you suppose that is?" Master Bell asked a smile on his face.

"Well, I suppose because I don't feel very high."

Bell let out a boisterous laugh at the thought of a princess not feeling very high. "You truly are a unique person highn . . . I mean princess. Now may I ask you a question?"

"Of course Master Bell," Terra said, excited at the prospect of being taught a little something.

"Why do you hide in the rafters during your sisters lessons? You know if you're caught again the Queen will be most displeased with you. I seem to recall a very sound lashing after the last time."

Afraid that Master Bell might suddenly change his mind and tell the Queen, Terra stepped back just a fraction, making herself ready to run if it came to that.

"Well," she stammered, "Ever since Diana started taking lessons all those years ago, I've wanted to learn what she was learning. Not for fighting or anything like that."

"Then why?"

"It's hard to explain," she said feeling around for the right words. "I get this feeling when I see her doing magic."

"A good feeling or a bad feeling," Bell asked. He was still smiling politely but there was less friendly curiosity behind his words and more of a hard edge.

"It's a good feeling when she's doing it right, and a bad feeling when she's doing it wrong."

Now his smile was completely gone, "you can tell when your sister is doing the spell wrong?"

"Usually," she replied offhandedly, checking the door again.

"Terra can *you* do the spell your sister was trying to do?"

"I'm not sure," she said, biting her lip, "she only showed me once. But I could try."

"Please, do." Bell stepped back a few paces and watched the young princess with growing sense of curiosity. He had heard of people with this particular kind of gift before. A kind of understanding and familiarity with magic that couldn't be taught. In his many years of training he had only known two people to possess such a gift before. One was the Master Wizard of the Moon Kingdom to the north, and the other was the man who trained him, the former Mater Wizard of the Sol Kingdom. If what the princess said was true than she might well be the princess worth teaching.

Terra took a deep breath and calmed herself down. She raised her hands and assumed the position Diana had showed her last night. With her mind she reached down inside herself to where her power lived. Eleven years ago, when Diana had first started her lessons, Terra had watched from the rafters as time after time her sister failed to grasp what her teacher was telling her.

He had said that all our power lives in the very center of our being. If ever we have a need of that power we have to reach into ourselves and open the "door". Not a real door of course but a door within ourselves that held back our magic until we needed it.

Terra opened that door now and felt as the magic spread from her center and covered her until it had become like a shall she had wrapped herself in. Not sure of the words to the spell, Terra focused instead on what she wanted the magic to do. She moved, her hands open, and directed the magic at the wall in front of her. It burst from her fingertips in a wave of purple laced with silver.

The master wizard reached out ran his fingers through the purple and silver magic as it sped past him. Terra was spot on. Every element of the spell was perfect. It should have taken several one on one lessons for her to even get close to that level of perfection. Not to mention the silver threads in her magic.

Everyone's magic manifested in different colors. A primary color and an accent color. Each color spoke to the nature of the person. Anytime the color silver manifested in a person's magic it always meant a true mastery of magic. The silver in his magic he had only recently obtained. Originally the deep green of his magic was accompanied by a dark purple accent. For Terra to have silver in her magic already was something Bell had never seen before.

"Terra," he asked, "how did you do that?"

She took a deep breath and pulled her hands back in, stopping the flow of magic. She exhaled and turned to Master Bell. "I don't know," she said thinking, "I listened to what Diana said you told her and then I watched her try and then I watched you do it and I knew how."

"Princess, that's incredible."

"Not really," she said with a shrug, "I forgot the words." She smiled sheepishly; checking the door again to make sure her sister wasn't going to barge back in for the last word.

Master Bell's mouth hung open. He had gotten so caught up in Terra's effortless mastery of the spell that he hadn't even noticed her silence. Diana had been learning from him for over ten years and fire was the only spell she could do without using the words.

"Terra, how did you get the magic to do what you wanted without the words?" Bell asked.

"What do you mean?" Terra could tell by Master Bell's face that the question he was asking was important, but she didn't understand why.

"Ok, let me explain it to you this way. In the very center of our being is where our power sits, waiting and dormant. When we need to use that power, to defend, to heal, or even to attack, we reach down inside ourselves and open the "door"".

"The door to our power!" Terra shouted excitedly. She knew the answer from the earliest lessons with Diana.

"That's right," Bell said, pleased that Terra was following along. "With some people they can bypass the door. These gifted individuals wear their magic around themselves as an aura. Their magic lives around them and can't be contained like normal magic. Now, when you first lean how to use magic it is very hard to control. That's why beginners need to use the words to help them mold the magic and help it better understand what they want."

Terra nodded. "Ok, so me not using words was a good thing?"

"A very good thing," Bell said smiling. "Now run along before your mother or sister finds you down here."

"Ok! Thank you Master Bell," Terra called as she slipped out the door and down the hallway, as quick and as quiet as a shadow. Even the way she walked seemed to echo some kind of grace or power. Bell was unsure why he hadn't noticed it before. Although the Queen was very good at keeping her in the shadow of her sister, a role she played into as well.

With a quick check of the room Bell decided to head to his room and meditate on the issue of Terra. Had he known all those years ago how gifted she was, he would have made quite a push to have her trained.

Terra ran from the room more than pleased that Bell had praised her. She was so happy about the kind words he had spoken to her that she didn't notice her sister hiding in the shadows of the hall until it was too late.

Diana reached out and grabbed Terra by the arm.

"Hello little sister," she said grinning at the look of shock on her sisters face. "What took you so long?"

"I'm sorry Diana," her sister said looking like a mouse that'd been caught by a cat. "Master Bell knew I was watching and he was asking me questions."

"What kind of questions," Diana asked. She narrowed her eyes at Terra and began dragging her down the nearby hallway.

"Well," she started, "he asked what I was doing there."

"And you said?"

"That I was just curious. I didn't say anything about you sister I swear."

"You had better not."

Six years ago Diana had caught her sister sneaking into her magic lessons for the first time. She had been about to run to her mother with the information when a thought had struck her. If Terra snuck into her lessons and watched what Bell taught her, then maybe she could be used to better Diana's own mastery of magic.

Besides, practicing on something live would be far more entertaining.

"I wouldn't Diana," Terra said earnestly. "You know I value our practice time too highly to risk it."

"Very well then," Diana said pushing her sister off. "Be sure to come tonight. I have to perfect my energy spells for tomorrow."

"I will Diana, thank you." Terra took off, running like some common girl through the hall, long hair braided and flapping behind her. Diana scoffed at her foolishness and headed to her next lesson.

It was a very late that night as Terra stood in her sisters' room breathing hard. She and Diana were going over the lesson she had learned a few days ago from Master Bell. He was teaching her about pulling energy from an enemy. It was a difficult spell and Diana was not grasping it well.

Bell had taught her to take only what energy was necessary to survive and no more. But Diana couldn't regulate how much she was taking, not to mention she still had to be in contact with her sister to take anything at all. Terra was exhausted, it was late and her energy was being sapped by Diana at an alarming rate.

"Alright I think I have this now Terra, just once more should do it," Diana said. She was smiling from ear to ear and almost bouncing where she stood. She had absorbed so much energy from her sister that she felt she could go on for days without sleep.

"I don't know if I can handle much more Diana," she replied breathlessly. "I feel like I might pass out at this rate."

Diana scowled down at her sister. Why did she have to be so selfish right now? Diana needed help to learn this spell before Bell came back tomorrow and quizzed her on it. The last thing she needed was for that sad excuse of a master wizard to come back to the castle and humiliate her again. She was learning as fast as she could, but she had other problems to deal with.

"Terra you know I can't go to lessons tomorrow without being able to do this from a distance. Bell will scold me and tell mother that I'm not learning at the right pace. Do you really want to go through that again?"

Terra thought for a moment. The last time Diana had gotten scolded by their mother about not applying herself enough to her studies she had taken it out on Terra quite mercilessly. It had been one of the worst weeks of her life.

"Alright Diana, you're right of course. Let me show you one more time how to spread the aura from your fingers and out past your body."

Diana eyed her sister suspiciously but decided that she needed to see how it was done at least one more time. "Alright fine," she said. "But don't take too much. I can't be exhausted tomorrow for my exam."

"Of course sister," Terra said smiling, "now the key is to concentrate. Feel the door to your power, nestled deep down inside. Open it and let the magic flow free until it wraps itself around you. Picture your colors form the aura around you.

"Now in your mind see those colors swirl into one concentrated place, your hand is the best place but do whatever works. Then send that aura out from you. See the colors flow from your body toward your target." As she spoke Terra pictured the purple and silver of her magic swirl away from her and toward her sister.

When it reached her, Terra used her mind to tell her magic to pull energy from her sister. At once the energy came flowing back to her in waves. She went from being completely exhausted to feeling only a little tired. She stopped the magic before it could take too much from her sister.

"Now you try," she said smiling confidently.

Diana opened her mouth to say something but a commotion outside drew their attention. Without a word both girls ran to the large window across the room and pushed it open wide so they could stick their heads out.

"What's going on out there?" Terra asked.

"I don't know," Diana replied, "It's too hard to see with all the light in here."

"You're right." Without turning from the window Terra sent out her magic and in a matter of seconds only one fire remained burning in the room and it had died down to almost embers. Diana took notice of her sister's power but chose to say nothing. There was something going on outside that was much more interesting.

With the lights all the way dimmed the princesses could see down to the courtyard with ease. There was a large wagon pulled all the way up to the gates of the castle. People were rushing around trying to get the gate open as fast as they could. Terra recognized the man leading the others by the gate; it was her father the King.

King Sol stood shouting orders to the men around him to get the gate open as quickly as they could. He knew that there was no time to waste. With a bang the double doors came crashing open. Glancing around quickly the King ascertained that no one was around to see what was going on.

As the doors flew open the men on the wagon rushed forward stopping just short of the King. Each man placed his fist over his heart before bowing to the King. The Captain of the Guard jumped down from the driver's bench.

"Majesty," he said with a nod. "We've done it. We have captured the monster as you ordered!"

"Captain Reynolds," the King said, taken back, "could you truly have done such a thing?"

"We have majesty. Behold!" Captain Reynolds moved to the back of the wagon where something large and square sat covered under a huge patchwork of blankets. Lifting one corner the Captain ushered the King to see.

"By the creator you've done it." The King stared at the creature trapped behind the enchanted glass of its prison. "I had almost begun to believe it couldn't be done."

"We *have* done it King Sol. It was a long and arduous battle. Many men were lost to the cause, but in the end we emerged triumphant." Captain Reynolds looked grim at the mentioning of his lost men but he eyes still held the sparkle of victory when he looked to his King.

Slowly the few remaining men from the Captains party shambled in, bleeding, broken and near dead, they still saluted their

King. Each man knowing that their lives would have been a small price to pay for such a victory.

King Sol stepped back from the wagon and Captain Reynolds lowered the patchwork cloth down again. He silently sent up a prayer for the men who had died to provide the kingdom with this most deadly prisoner. "See these men are properly attended too," the King called to a man guarding the gate.

"Where shall we put him Majesty?" Captain Reynolds asked. "The hour is late and I don't relish being stuck in the dark with cargo such as this."

"We've had a room established for some time now," King Sol said. "We must take the wagon around the castle to the kitchens."

"To the kitchens, Majesty?" Captain Reynolds asked.

"Yes," the King replied, "the kitchens have the largest doors aside from the main entrance. And this is not something we want to take through the main door. The fewer people who know about this the better." He gave the Captain a very meaningful look.

"Of course you're Highness," Captain Reynolds said, "I'll see to it that no one outside this party knows of the cargo we've brought this night."

"See that you do," King Sol said. "Now let's get this wagon moved before anyone has the good sense to question us."

Captain Reynolds and his men nodded and thumped their fists over their hearts again before climbing back onto the wagon. King Sol, knowing that his wife was waiting for news jumped onto his horse again and rode like the wind toward the main doors of the castle.

Seeing the King approaching the guards threw the door open as he rode up the steps and through the front door. He jumped off his horse and threw the reigns to one of the guards standing nearby. "Take my horse to the stables and see to it that he's fed and watered. Then go to the kitchens and help Captain Reynolds and his men," King Sol ordered running for the stairs.

Both guards thumped their fists to their hearts and bowed to the King before running off to do as he had commanded.

14

"What do you think is in the box?" Terra asked, as their father disappeared through the front door of the castle.

"I don't know," Diana said thinking. "But I intend to find out."

Without another word Diana ran to her large wardrobe and pulled out a dark blue cloak and threw it around her shoulders. She glanced back at her sister and then rummaged around in the back before producing a dark green cloak from last winter. "Put this on and follow me. Your dress is so bright a blind man could see it. Do as I say and whatever you do don't make a sound."

Terra nodded and threw the cloak on. It was still lovely and soft. It warmed her the second she tied it on. Following her sisters lead she pulled the generous hood up over her head and slipped out the door.

Together, quick and quiet as the shadows themselves, the princesses slipped down the servants stairs. They went down three levels before the sounds of voices halted them in their tracks. Diana put a hand on Terra's shoulders to stop her. Quietly they listened to the voices and the footsteps get closer.

Seconds before the owners of the voices appeared Diana pulled open the door directly to her right and threw Terra in. She followed quickly and pulled the door nearly closed just as three men came into view. She tiptoed over to her sister and put her finger to her lips.

Terra nodded, she would be quiet.

"Captain Reynolds ordered the room sealed. No one but himself or the King, the Queen, and the Master Wizard are to be permitted to enter," one voice said.

"What about Princess Diana?" Another asked.

"If the princess wants in is it really alright for us to tell her no? She's the princess in the prophecy. I wouldn't want to upset her," a third voice replied uneasily.

Diana smiled at the notes of fear in the man's voice. It pleased her to be able to command that kind of a response from a stranger at only sixteen.

"I'm not sure," the first voice answered clearly uneasy about the prospect of having to deny Diana something. "When I see Captain Reynolds again I'll ask him. For now let's just hope the princess doesn't find out about the prisoner."

All the voices agreed as they walked past the door the princesses were hiding behind. Terra held her breath, worried about being caught out of her room this late at night. Not just sneaking out but eavesdropping on the soldiers. Her mother would be furious if she knew.

Once the voices and footsteps had faded out of earshot Diana crept over to the door and pushed it open slightly. She stuck her head out and scanned the hallway. She could see the group of soldiers moving down at the far end of the hall getting ready to turn the corner, most likely headed toward the barracks for the King's personal guard that sat directly to the right of the castles main door. Diana finished scanning the hallway. Once she was satisfied that no one was coming she motioned for her sister to follow her out into the hall.

Terra followed, somewhat nervously, behind her sister.

"Where are we going?" She asked as she and Diana crept down the hall in the opposite direction of the soldiers. She started to move them toward the main corridor on the floor.

"You saw the size of that box didn't you?" Diana asked. When Terra nodded she said, "a box that size is going to take over a dozen men to move and there's no way they're going to be able to move that thing up a flight of stairs. So it has to be on the bottom floor somewhere."

Terra understood what her sister was saying but still didn't understand why they had left the relative safety of the servant's stairs. In all her years she had never seen her mother use any other stairs than the main grand stairway that was at the front of the castle.

Fearing her sister wrath more than her mother's anger Terra kept silent and followed Diana down the hall. They passed by a number of the servant's quarters, and then passed the servants chapel and finally to the end of the hall that turned into a small wide staircase that leads down to the kitchens. Without hesitation Diana slid quietly down the stairs and into the dark empty kitchen.

Terra followed without a word. With the fires in the kitchen out, the stairway was completely dark. She put her hand on the smooth stone wall and carefully felt her way down. Each stone step she took had been worn smooth by the many shoes that traveled up and down them each day for the past several hundred years. It made traversing them in the dark very dangerous.

She reached the bottom and was pleased to see the kitchen windows were letting in at least a little moon light to see by. She stepped forward next to Diana and looked around. The large kitchen doors were closed and bolted as they were every night. None of the wall sconces had been lit and as far as Terra could tell, no one had been down here since the kitchen maids had closed it down after dinner had been cleaned up.

"Damn," Diana cursed under her breath. "They've been through here already."

"How can you tell?"

"Do you see the bolt on the door?" Diana asked. She nodded. "It's not locked properly. The bolt is old and has to be handled in a certain way or it won't close properly. That bolt is only halfway through the lock."

"How do you know all that?" Terra asked disbelievingly.

"If you snuck out of the castle as much as I do, you'd know too." Diana flashed Terra her wicked smile before she started moving off to the other side of the kitchen. Still mildly alarmed at the thought of Diana sneaking out unguarded, Terra followed.

A sudden sound from the stairs behind them froze both girls in their tracks. Diana shot a look to Terra who shook her head. Whoever it was, they were too far off for her to tell yet. Best case scenario it

17

was just a maid coming down to fetch something, worst case scenario it was another guard on his way down to help with whatever was brought in. Either way the princesses could not be seen wandering the halls at night, alone.

Not wasting any time, Terra grabbed Diana by the hand and ran behind the table used for making bread. It was a very large table with curtains running along all four sides. The top was almost completely white after years of having flour ground into it. Seeing as how there was no one making bread at this hour, Terra lifted the curtain and motioned to Diana.

"We'll hide down here until they pass," she whispered to her sister. "Let's just hope they aren't in the mood for making bread at this hour."

Diana did as her younger sister had bid her and ducked under the table. Terra was about to join her when a light at the bottom of the stairs stopped her cold. Standing at the bottom of the staircase holding a magelight torch over his head was Captain Reynolds.

"C . . . Captain," Terra stammered, racking her brain for an excuse to be down in the kitchens at this hour. As far as she could tell, Diana had been hidden before the table had come into his view. Meaning that for the moment, her sister was safe.

"Princess," he said, sounding as equally shocked. He placed his fist over his heart and bowed. "What are you doing down here?"

"I . . . um . . . I was just going out for some fresh air," she lied badly.

Captain Reynolds smiled at her. He was nearing his twenty-fifth birthday if Terra remembered correctly. He had risen in the ranks rather quickly. Her father often spoke of his bravery and cunning. He would sometimes remark that the young man would make general before he was thirty. Even the Queen loved him. He was young and handsome, not to mention dedicated. He had sharp green eyes like hers but lighter and thick brown hair he kept tied back in a ponytail. The fact that he was nearly twenty-five and unmarried was the only thing people ever complained about when it came to him.

"Fresh air?" Captain Reynolds said smiling. "Does your window not provide you with that?"

"It does, normally," Terra said, knowing the Captain didn't believe her. "But I believe my fireplace is clogged. The smoke just billows around my room and doesn't go up and out like it should. I put the fire out but the room is still quite smoky. So I opened my windows and came down here to slip out the back and get some fresh air while it clears." Terra had said the last part in a rush as she ran out of air. She sucked in a deep breath and cursed herself mentally for not being a better liar.

"Well we'll have to send someone up first thing in the morning to check on your fireplace then," Capt. Reynolds said with a smile. "Until then would you allow me to escort you out to get your fresh air? The world's not safe enough for a princess to go wandering around alone."

Terra stared at the Captain dumfounded. She was a *very* bad liar, almost hilariously bad. She couldn't believe he had believed her story. She certainly couldn't go wandering around outside with the man. Captain or not there was something strange in the castle and Terra needed to know what.

"You are very kind of offer Captain," Terra said, "But I couldn't possibly accept."

Diana reached out from under the table and pinched her sister hard on the leg. Terra had to bite the inside of her cheek to keep from crying out in pain. She shot a look down to Diana who waved her off and silently mouthed 'GO' to her.

"I mean to say I couldn't possible accept without knowing that I'm not taking you away from some other pressing matter," she lied again.

Capt. Reynolds smiled at the princess again and said, "There are no matters more pressing than your safety princess."

Terra quickly stepped around the table so the captain wouldn't notice her sister tucked underneath. She met him on the other side of the kitchen, closer to the doors. "Eager to get outside are we?" He asked with a laugh.

"Can you blame a girl?" Terra asked, not sure how much longer she could keep the lie up.

"Not at all." He offered Terra his arm. She accepted and together they walked to the kitchen doors and slipping the bolt, Capt. Reynolds held the door open as she walked through.

Once Diana heard the doors close she slid out from the bottom of the table. She stood and brushed the flour from her cloak. "Idiot," she muttered under her breath about her sister. To get caught up in a weak lie like that, and by a Captain no less! Diana would never be caught consorting with someone so far below her station. It was ridiculous. Creator help her if their father finds her out there with a man. Her prospects would disappear and she would be ruined. He could be a general and it wouldn't matter. No man should be alone with a princess without an escort or two.

For a moment Diana considered going to their father and telling him that she'd woken to find Terra gone. She could lie and say that she'd searcher for her and found her outside with the Captain. She would be ruined, completely and utterly ruined.

It would be delicious to see.

However, when it came to Terra and to the Captain, the King seemed to have a weak spot for them. If Terra buckled and told him the truth it could back fire on Diana. Then not only would she be exposed in the lie but people would get a good look at her real character. That was something the princess was unwilling to risk. All the dark thoughts in her heart and her mind were her biggest secret. No amount of her sisters suffering was worth the possibility of her being exposed.

With a sigh at the missed opportunity Diana turned back to the door that exited into the grand dining hall. At least she could find out what her father had been up to that night. Keeping close to the wall, she crept on.

The grand dining hall was dark and cold. In stark opposite of the way it normally was. Usually all the fires were lit and the large fireplace was roaring with life. It seemed that the room itself hummed with life during the day. People were always coming and going getting things ready for the next meal. Now it stood dark, quiet and lifeless.

Diana preferred it this way.

As she approached the end of the dining hall she had several options of how to go forward. There was a door that led to a rounded hallway that cut through the back of the castle and ended in the queen's private garden. Then there was another door half hidden behind a tapestry by the large raised dais where Diana and her family ate dinner. That particular door led to the network of secret passages that snaked through the walls of the castle. Diana had managed to explore some of the passages and tunnels but had nearly gotten lost on more than one occasion.

Finally there were the large doors that lead to an ornately decorated hallway where guests can sit and wait for dinner to be ready. From there that hallway branched off into more than half a dozen places. Some lead to servant's quarters, others to the armory, then others to the barracks, and then more lead to the main hall of the palace and at least one hallway took you to the throne room.

Diana cursed under her breath at having been held up by Terra's incompetence for so long. Her father and his mysterious box could be anywhere in the castle by now. For a moment she contemplated searching everywhere possible for the box. Terra had, however, taken a good deal of her energy with that last spell and the princess was starting to feel the hour.

With a defeated sigh she turned around and headed back across the empty dining hall. When she reached the kitchen she pulled the doors closed and made sure no one would be suspicious if they woke up to find things amiss.

Diana walked slowly over to the stairs and then stopped. She couldn't tell her father what Terra was up too, but she could certainly make things more difficult for her sister. Walking back to the kitchen

21

doors Diana pressed her shoulder against the left door and slid the bolt all the way home. With this door locked she would have no choice but to go around and use the main entrance to get back in.

Scoffing one more time at her sister's idiocy, Diana turned and disappeared up the stairs. She tiptoed down the hall and then slipped into the servant's stairs again. She was back in the safety of her room in less than two minutes. She changed out of her dress into her dressing gown and settled in for bed, still smiling at the thought of Terra returning to find a locked door.

Terra stepped outside ahead of Capt. Reynolds and waited as he closed the door behind them. It was a beautiful summer evening. It was cool without being cold and there were more stars in the sky than Terra thought she could count in a lifetime. The forest that surrounded the back part of the grounds was alight with fireflies and the sounds of crickets. Through the trees the sound of the nearby river could be heard flowing over rocks and tree roots.

All in all it was an absolutely beautiful night.

"Beautiful isn't in?" Capt. Reynolds asked stepping up beside Terra.

She nodded, still taking in their surroundings. "Look!" she said suddenly grabbing the captain's arm, "Look at all the fireflies! Their beautiful don't you think?"

Capt. Reynolds smiled, "You know I've always had penchant for fireflies."

"Really?" She asked, pleased that this adult didn't find her love of these simple beauties silly or childish.

"Really," he said. "When I was younger I used to want to fly one."

"Fly one?" She asked.

"Yup. I would be wondering through the forest and find the biggest firefly ever. It would recognize me as a friend and let me ride it."

22

"Wow," Terra said smiling at the thought of flying a firefly. "That's . . ."

"Foolish?" Capt. Reynolds asked, cutting her off.

"I was going to say adorable," she said pulling a face.

"Well that's better than foolish," he said with a smile. "Shall we?"

Terra nodded, accepting the captain's arm again. Together they walked across the grass toward the edge of the forest and the castle grounds. The night was peaceful and yet simultaneously full of life. Terra tried to nonchalantly scan for the wagon she and Diana had seen from the window, but there was no sign of it now aside from the fresh ruts the wagon had cut in the dirt near the door.

"So do you want to tell me why you were really down in the kitchen this late?" Capt. Reynolds asked after a few moments of silence had passed.

Terra froze. She knew she wasn't a great liar but she thought she'd fooled the Captain with the story about her fireplace. Still, she should have known better. You don't get promoted to captain of the Guard if you're foolish enough to fall for the lies of a fifteen year old.

Capt. Reynolds stopped when Terra did. He kept his gaze up at the stars and was still smiling when she looked up at him. Literally up, the captain stood nearly a head taller than herself.

When Terra could think of nothing to say the captain started walking again. "Had your room, in fact, been filled with smoke I would have been called immediately. So while I commend your efforts and your attempt to hide your sister, I was fooled by neither."

"I'm sorry," Terra said hanging her head. She let her arm fall from the captains as she stopped walking and stood feeling more than ashamed. She had lied to the captain of the guard and had been foolish enough to think that he had actually fallen for it. She was sure he would report to her father as soon as he ascertained why she had been in the kitchen with her sister so late. Not only would she be severely scolded for being out so late but Diana would be nothing

23

short of murderous when she found out that it was Terra's shortcomings that had landed her in trouble with the King and Queen.

Just the thought of Diana's rage made Terra quiver in her shoes. Before she could stop them, tears began to flow down her cheeks.

"Princess?" Capt. Reynolds asked, turning to see why she'd stopped walking. He nearly fell over when he caught sight of Princess Terra. Her head was down and she was shaking. Despite the lack of light the captain could see the tears streaking down her cheeks. They seemed to almost light up in the moonlight, looking more like silver streams running from her eyes instead of tears.

"I'm so sorry Captain!" Terra exclaimed jerking her head up suddenly. "I didn't want to deceive you but I didn't know what else to do. I know it was wrong but please, I beg you, don't tell my father. I wouldn't be able to stand it if Diana got in trouble because of me!"

Capt. Reynolds stumbled back a step. While the princess had stood there pleading her case so passionately, the moon had come out from behind a rouge cloud and lit Terra's face like a pale torch. In that moment, eyes full of tears, hand clenched in fists at her side, pleading not for her sake but her sisters, she no longer looked like the little dark haired princess who ran amuck around the castle with her fair haired sister.

She looked like a woman; a young woman but a woman none the less. She was beautiful, so much so that the captain was taken aback. Everyone knew that the princesses were lovely like their mother. It was Diana, however, whom people raved about. They spoke of her golden hair and how her beauty at sixteen was a good indicator of the fact that she would be beautiful all her life.

People didn't talk about Terra like that.

Looking at her now, Capt. Reynolds wondered how he had never noticed.

Recovering from the shock of seeing her in this new light, the captain stepped up and put both his hands on the princess's shoulders. "You need not fear for your sister. I will not tell the King what I have seen this night. So long as you promise to never lie to me again. Can you do that Princess?"

Terra heard what Capt. Reynolds had said and it took her a moment to process her sheer amount of luck. She hated to lie, it made her feel sick to her stomach, promising to never lie to the Captain again was an easy request to fulfill, especially if it meant being spared her sisters rage.

"I promise," Terra said, her voice wavering slightly. "Thank you Captain Reynolds. I truly can't thank you enough."

Pleased to see her smiling again, Capt. Reynolds pulled his handkerchief from his breast pocket and, more than over stepping his place, he reached out and dried the tears on one side of her face. Realizing just how far he had over reached he offered Terra the handkerchief so she could dry her other eye.

"Thank you," she said sweetly. She dried her eye and offered the handkerchief back to the Captain.

"You keep it," he said, "A memento from tonight." Capt. Reynolds knew he would need no help remembering this night. He felt as though the image of the princess in tears lit up by the moon and so passionate about her apology was burned into his mind. It was not something he felt he would ever forget.

Assuming the captain wanted her to keep it as a reminder to never lie to him again; Terra smiled and tucked the handkerchief into her pocket. "I can't thank you enough Captain."

"Of course you can," he said with a laugh.

"How?" She asked, genuinely wanting to repay the Captain for his kindness.

"Well, you can start by keeping that promise you made me."

"Done."

"And you can repay me by finishing our walk."

"Of . . . of course," she stammered, relieved at how simple his requests were. Capt. Reynolds offered Terra his arm again and she gladly accepted it this time. Together the two walked the edge of the forest talking over the prophecy about Diana, the increase in shadow activity which inadvertently lead to Capt. Reynolds telling her about all of the castles defenses. Not just the hundreds of guards under his command, but also the spell and warding that kept the castle and the surrounding city safe from shadow attacks.

"I would never let anything happen to you or your family," Capt. Reynolds explained as they slowly made their way back to the kitchen doors. "You believe that don't you princess?"

"I do Captain," Terra said smiling up at a man she now viewed as a friend.

"Well I must say I've rather enjoyed our walk," he said as he stepped away from the princess and moved to open the door.

"I've enjoyed most of it," Terra said honestly. Seeing a concerned look on the Captain's face she added hastily, "it was much more enjoyable once the lie was out of the way."

"Ah, well I think we can both agree that . . ." the Captain trailed off as the door stuck when he pulled it. "That's odd," he said grabbing the handle again. He pulled at the door a second and third time before he realized the door was locked.

"What's wrong?" Terra asked concerned.

"The door's locked."

"Locked? How is that possible?"

"Someone must have walked past and seen it was unbolted and locked it."

"What do we do now?" She asked fear creeping up in her mind. If this door was locked then the only other option they had was to use the front door or break a window and climb in. Neither was good option and both would raise questions that Terra couldn't answer.

A thought struck both Terra and Capt. Reynolds at the same time. While both of them had viewed their walk as innocent, there would be those who see the captain taking the young princess out in the middle of the night, with no chaperone as something other than what it was. The princess would be ruined and her family shamed.

Terra met Capt. Reynolds stare straight on. She could tell by his grim expression that he had come to the same conclusion she had. That meant that there was only one other option. Sighing, she stepped forward and took both the Captains hands.

Even in the faint light of the moon she could see the captain blush at her sudden contact. "Captain."

"Princess," he replied slightly confused.

"You and I both know we cannot go through the front door. If I'm seen out this late questions will be raised and my promise to you will mean nothing when my family hears about this. Not to mention the consequences if the two of us are discovered out here together and alone."

Capt. Reynolds nodded, taken slightly aback once again by the way her maturity shone like a light through what was left of her child like features. "I understand what happens if we're discovered princess. I know what it would mean for both of us."

"Then I need your word Captain."

"My word?"

"Yes. What I'm about to do you can tell no one about. Ever."

Confused about what would have the princess so rattled, all he could do was nod.

"All right, stand aside. I'll get the door open."

"Princess . . ." he started.

"Terra," she said, turning to face him again.

"What?"

"We're cohorts now Captain. Neither of us can ever mention to another person what went on tonight. I figure if the two of us are going to share a secret like that the least you can do is call me by my name and not my title. So, Terra please, not princess."

Smiling Capt. Reynolds said, "Terra it is. But then you must call me Eric."

"Eric," she agreed with a smile. She turned back to the door in front of them. Taking a measured step back she silently focused. She felt the aura of her magic swirling around her. Her magic was there even before she had opened the "door". Assuming her magic was out because of her training with her sister she refocused. Raising her left arm she opened her palm and asked the magical aura around her to flow through the door and pull the bolt out so she could enter.

"T . . . Terra," Eric stammered, seeing the purple and sliver threads of her magic flow from her left hand to the door.

Ignoring him, she kept her focus on the door and after a second the sound of the bolt being thrown violently could be heard. Before she could stop them the doors flew open. Eric barely had time to jump out of the way before they came flying in his direction. Thankfully the old doors didn't make much noise as they swung round on their hinges into the wall.

Terra felt her aura return to her and dropped her hand.

"Pr . . . princess," Eric stammered.

"Terra, remember?"

He nodded, looking shaken. "Terra, how did you do that? I thought you didn't possess magic?" Eric looked more than a little dumbfounded.

"I'm not officially being taught magic," Terra said, trying to skirt the truth. She started forward through the door. Without looking she could tell that he was right behind her, not willing to let her scrape by with so little an explanation.

"Then how?"

"I have your word, right Eric? Nothing about tonight ever gets told to another soul?" She asked dropping her voice so it wouldn't bound off the walls of the empty kitchen and wake someone else.

"Terra you have my word as a gentleman and as the Captain of the Guard. No soul will ever hear about what transpired here tonight."

"All right then." She took a deep breath as she moved to start closing the old wooden doors. "About six years ago my sister caught me sneaking into another one of her magic lessons with Master Bell. I had snuck into two or three before that and gotten caught once in the act. This time when Diana confronted me she told me she wanted my help."

"Your help? With what?" Eric asked helping her close the doors.

"She felt that Master Bell was being too hard on her, demanding more than she could possibly do on top of all of her other duties as a princess."

"What kind of duties does a princess have?" He asked more to himself than to Terra.

"Well for one we've been schooled on how a princess acts from the time we could walk. How to talk, when to talk, what to say, how to walk, what to wear and how to wear it and how to handle just about any formal situation we might ever find ourselves in. Then we're taught about our land, how the country is run, the old laws and the ones my father has written and changed. We're taught how the hierarchy works in the kingdom. Then we learn about our kingdoms agriculture. What grows where and how well, who grows what the best and how to handle a dispute about land between farmers.

"Then we're taught about trade, who we trade with, what we trade with them, what's fair and what's not. Then they teach us how to handle any dispute that might arise between ourselves and our neighboring kingdoms. They teach us when and on what we should stick it to the other guy and when we should take the hit. Next they'll be teaching us about the army and how it works. Who's in charge where and who should be put in charge if something happens to them."

Together Eric and Terra pulled the door closed and locked the bolt. Eric mulled over what the princess had just told him. He never realized that the princesses had to be so well schooled. He assumed being royal was one big party, all the time, at least for the princesses.

"I didn't realize you had so much to do," he admitted sheepishly.

"Not many people do," Terra said with a smile. "Anyway, Diana asked if I could start regularly sneaking into her magic lessons so at night we could practice together. She said it helped her to have someone live to practice on. I, of course, was just thrilled at the prospect of learning magic."

"So you've been secretly learning magic for the last six years?"

"Pretty much. Nobody knows, except Master Bell. He knew I was there that day six years ago. Thought he's never acknowledged me during lessons, I know he knows."

"What'll happen if you're caught?" Eric asked concerned.

She grimaced, "I don't want to think of what my mother would do if she found out."

"You'll be careful won't you?" he asked the concern still plain on his face.

"Of course," she said with a smile. "You know it stands to reason that she might not be mad about it. Mother might actually be proud of me."

He looked at her in a way that told her neither of them thought the Queen would be happy about Terra sneaking around learning things she shouldn't be.

"May I escort you to your room?" He asked, offering her his arm again.

"That would be lovely, but we should take the servant's stairs to avoid people seeing us and jumping to conclusions."

"Won't the servants see us?"

"Only if you don't know your way around," she said with a smile.

"In that case lead on Majesty," he said with a mock bow.

Laughing quietly she led him to the same stairs they had both taken to get to the kitchen. Quietly they slipped into the servant's stairs, once there Eric said, "So why do you think your Mother might be happy about you secretly learning magic?"

"Because I'm doing it to help Diana," she replied simply. "And it's not like I asked her to teach me. She came to me and asked for help. I'm doing all I can to ensure that she fulfills the prophecy."

"You know word around the castle is that your sister isn't exactly the most deserving of help," he said, choosing his words *very*

30

carefully. Everyone in the kingdom loved and praised Diana's name. She was the princess the prophecy spoke of who was going to save the world. But in the castle, where people interacted with her on a daily bases, the opinion was very different.

"I know she's hard to deal with sometimes. And there are times where she comes across kind of cold. But can you really blame her?" Terra asked. She was more than aware of the fact that her sister wasn't the most popular person in the castle. She stopped at the landing for the fifth floor. Her bedroom was all the way across the long hall. They would have to walk passed her Parents room, her sisters room and the room that housed her mother's ladies in waiting, the room that housed her sisters ladies, and Mammy's room. It was too many opportunities to be seen. Terra thought about parting company here, but she wanted Eric to understand why Diana was the way she was.

So she turned to the wall opposite of the door and felt for the small round stone that acted as a handle.

"What do you mean?" Eric asked, wondering what the princess was up to.

"Diana has an enormous weight on her shoulders. She's expected to save the entire world. Most people would buckle under that kind of pressure. And when you consider how much is expected of her, and how much has been expected of her since before she was born, it's more than most people can even fathom."

Finding the stone she was looking for, Terra turned the stone a quarter to the right and pushed. With a faint click the secret door swung open into one of many secret passageways in the castle. Without turning to see if he was following, she stepped over the small threshold and continued talking.

"It's a lot of pressure for a sixteen year old."

Eric stared blankly at the secret passageway he had never known was there. It was his responsibility to keep everyone in the castle safe and he had no idea there were passageways up this high.

31

Carefully he stepped over the threshold and pushed the small door closed. On this side he could hardly tell there was a door there at all.

"How many tunnels are there like this up here?" He asked, ignoring the last thing Terra had said.

She stopped and thought for a moment. "I'm not sure. More than I've ever stopped to count."

"Do you know your way around up here?"

"Of course," she replied, "How do you think I manage to sneak around and watch my sister's lessons? I could find my way around here in complete darkness."

Eric stepped up so he was standing next to the princess. "One day you'll have to teach me about all these passageways."

"That can probably be arranged," she said smiling.

"Alright then, lead on. And I understand how much pressure your sister is under. I can't say as I know how it feels, but I do understand it's an enormous weight to bear. But how do you explain how cold she can be?"

Slowly they made their way forward across a flat and narrow passage. Terra walked on confidently and Eric fell into step behind her.

"That's easy," Terra said, following the passage to the left at a fork. "My sister will one day face the greatest evil this world has ever known. The battle itself will be like nothing we've ever seen before. There stands a good chance that even if Diana wins, the fight will claim her life. If you knew your destiny was to save the world and you knew that the odds of you walking away were slim, would you really take time to make a lot of close relationships?"

"I would," Eric said without hesitation. "You need your friends and family to remind you what you're fighting for. They make you strong and keep you going when things get rough. Even if I knew I was going to die tomorrow in combat I wouldn't have changed a thing about tonight."

Terra felt her face color as she blushed at the Captain's words. Suddenly, she was immensely grateful for the dark of the passage.

"I don't know that I would," she admitted.

"Oh?" He asked, his voice sounding slightly deflated.

"Not because I didn't enjoy our walk or our newfound friendship. But to think that I might go off and die in battle tomorrow leaving all my friends and family to mourn the loss of me would break my heart. I would hate to think of people hurting because of me."

"Perhaps you're just too selfless," he suggested.

"I don't think it's that," Terra said, "I just don't like to hurt people. Here we are." She came to a stop in the middle of the passage.

"Where is here?" Eric asked looking around.

"Let me see your hand," she said holding her own out. Slightly unsure of what the princess was up to, he placed his hand in hers.

Without a word Terra turned to the wall on the right. She placed the back of her right hand in Eric's and laced her fingers through his. Together she trailed their fingers over the smooth stone of the wall. She seemed to be looking for something, but in the faint light of the passage it was hard to see anything.

Eric felt his heart rate spike as princess continued her search. Their hands were laced together and the way she had pulled him left him standing directly behind her. If he leaned forward a fraction of an inch he would be pressed against her. For a second, caught up in the heat of the moment, the Captain of the Guard gave serious consideration to closing the gap between them.

Then, just as swiftly as the thought had come, it disappeared. He was ten years her senior, not to mention that fact that she was only fifteen. Oh and then there was the fact that she was the princess. If he did anything, or even just thought about doing something he would be thrown out if not beheaded by the King.

Half way through tearing himself down for having such thoughts about a girl her age, Eric's fingers brushed over something round on the flat stone wall.

Before he could say anything Terra's finger found it too. "Every door in these passageways has a small round release that when pressed," She grabbed his finger and pressed it against the release button, "it opens the door."

With a small familiar sounding click the door in front of them popped open. She released his hand and stepped to the side. Determined to not look disappointed because she had let go, he followed her off to the side.

Together they pushed the door open to reveal the back of an older tapestry. Terra stepped forward and pulled it to the side. Eric poked his head around the door way to see the princess room laid out before him.

"Tada," she giggled, fanning her arms out to either side.

"That's amazing," he said, sounding more like Capt. Reynolds and less like Eric as he contemplated the ramifications of secret doors like this. "How many rooms do these tunnels lead to?"

"As far as I've found every room in the castle is somehow connected to these secret passages," Terra said, not understanding the sudden switch.

"You might have to teach me about these tunnels sooner rather than later," Capt. Reynolds remarked looking down to the end of the tunnel he was standing in. "Much sooner."

"What will you do with that information?" She asked suddenly weary. If the Captain made the existence of the tunnels common knowledge then Terra would have no way to sneak off to watch her sister learn magic.

"I'm not sure yet," he answered honestly. "But I know that as Captain of the Guard I, at least, should know the ins and outs of these secret passages."

"Only you?"

"For now at least."

Terra eyed Capt. Reynolds in a new and unfriendly light.

Sensing a change in the princess Capt. Reynolds turned to her and asked, "Is everything ok?"

"I'm not sure," she replied using his words.

"Why not?" He asked sounding more like Eric.

"I understand that to you these tunnels and passageways pose some kind of threat, but to me these passages are like my second home. They're how I get most places. When I go to watch Diana at her lessons, I use these passageways. To avoid my mother and sister when they get in foul moods, I use these passageways. If you map them out and tell everyone about them those days are over. My mother will have them monitored every minute of every day."

Capt. Reynolds sighed. "I understand your hesitation at having other people know about these tunnels, but you have to see it from my perspective. There is a hidden passageway in this castle that leads to the bedroom of every member of the royal family. It's a huge safety issue, glaring really. I would be remiss in my duties as Captain of the Guard if I let this be."

Terra could feel her anger flare up slightly. She had shared a secret with this man who had promised to keep her secrets and now was telling her that he wanted to tell everyone about her main avenue of travel. Taking a deep breath to calm herself she met his gaze.

"Captain," she said, ignoring when he tried to correct her to Eric, "you told me that you would not share with another soul what you saw this night. If you would like me to show you and only you the way around these tunnels, I would be happy to do so. But if you're asking me to show you so you can show others and break your word, I simply cannot do that."

Again the princess appeared to Eric older than her fifteen years. As much as he would have loved to argue with her, she was correct. He had given her his word that nothing he saw this night would ever be shared with another living soul. As much as it pained him to give into a child, he was nothing if not a man of his word.

"Very well Majesty," Capt. Reynolds said. She didn't bother to try and correct him. She knew he wasn't happy with her and there was very little she could do about that now. "I will keep my word and tell no one of these tunnels. So long as you promise to show me all you know of them."

"I can most certainly do that Captain. Thank you for being a man of your word, even when you don't want to be." She said the last part quietly, starting to feel guilty about the Captains obvious displeasure.

Capt. Reynolds placed his fist over his heart and bowed to the princess. "I would bid you goodnight princess, if I knew how to get out of here. Seeing as I can't be seen leaving your chambers at this hour."

"Oh! Of . . . of course, Captain," she stammered. "Keep following this passage. It doesn't fork anymore. When you get to the end look for the release like I showed you with this door."

Capt. Reynolds face colored slightly as he remembered the thoughts that had been going through his mind while she'd been searching for that release.

"I'll keep this door open until I see that you've made it safely through the other," Terra said dropping the tapestry and stepping back over the threshold. Eric had to once again make a hasty retreat to avoid having the princess run head first into him. Taking an extra step back, Capt. Reynolds placed his hand over his heart again and sank into a deep bow before the princess.

"Princess, I bid you goodnight and I thank you for one of the most interesting nights of my life." He reached out and took Terra's hand in his. Bowing over it, he lightly pressed his lips to the back of her hand before stepping back through the hidden door and walking down the rest of the tunnel to the wall Terra had told him about.

Knowing what he was looking for, Capt. Reynolds found the release and pressed it. With the same small click the door popped open. He pushed it aside and found himself standing in the middle of the eastern servant's staircase. Turning around one last time he waved to Terra before she disappeared into her room and he stepped out onto the staircase. He pushed the door closed and headed for the barracks. If he was lucky he might get a few hours of sleep before he had to be up in the morning.

Terra pushed the door closed and laid the tapestry back down. She looked down at her hand where Capt. Reynolds had kissed it. She had never taken much notice of boys before. In truth there weren't a

36

lot of boys around to take notice of. Diana always seemed to have a small flock of men and boys alike following her around and fawning over her. Terra typically didn't care enough about the prospect of men to get involved.

But tonight, when Eric had kissed her hand, she had felt something in her stir. It was like he had awoken some part of her that had been sleeping. He had awoken the woman in her.

And it was terrifying.

Diana woke and dressed early the next morning. She sat at her large ornate writing desk and waited. She had lain in bed most of the night musing over how her sister would get back in, or if she would get in at all. That's what she would have done. She would have spent the night with the captain and slipped back in during the morning rush. All the deliveries for the kitchen were made in the early hours just after dawn. There are so many people coming and going that if kept your head down no one could say for sure who was there.

It certainly wouldn't have been the first time.

Sitting at her writing table Diana picked up some random book an instructor had given her and leafed through the pages. It was a book about economic trends in the kingdom over the past ten years. Diana stopped on a page and stared blankly at the words printed there. She was more than capable of reading, but the words on the page made no sense to her.

She would be queen one day and when she was she could hire people to know this stuff for her. She had other things to worry about. She had to fight some great mythic battle and save the world. Then rule a whole kingdom. But if she was being honest, and she rarely was, she didn't really think that fighting this Shadow King sounded like a good idea.

The way the legend is told, once he's been destroyed all the shadow monsters will disappear from the earth and all the kingdoms will be at peace.

But Diana was starting to wonder if peace was really what she wanted. If all of her teachings were to be believed, then the long waging war between these shadows and the kingdom was a good thing. People were more willing to donate money to the treasury if they knew it was going to defense, there were fewer babies being born since parents were too concerned about the future to want to risk bringing children into this world. There were always enough young men willing to fight and die for the kingdom so long as the war was on and if they wanted they could charge almost anything for food and water saying that they needed more rations for the solders on the front line.

As far as Diana could tell, war was not a bad thing. To think that all of that might change once she fulfills her destiny was a thought that she was beginning to dread more and more. There were times, late at night, when Diana would lay in bed and wonder if maybe there was another way. Maybe she could find some way to fulfill her destiny without having to give so much up. More and more dark thoughts began to dance in her mind.

Shaking her head to clear away such contemplations, Diana turned her attention back to the door. Any moment now her mother would burst in with news about Terra's torrid affair with the Captain of the Guard. It would be delicious to watch her suffer. She would try to lie to protect Diana, but her mother would know almost instantly if she tried. She would wriggle and writhe under her mother's terrifying gaze.

Then Diana would step in at the last moment and save poor little sister. She would tell her mother some farce about what was really going on last night and her mother, with her complete blindness to Diana's true character, would lap up any half-baked lie she came up with. She would save Terra from total ruin and save herself in the process.

She just had to wait.

Terra rolled over and opened her eyes. The sun was streaming gently through her window. She sat up slowly and rubbed the sleep from her eyes. She wasn't sure what time it was but it must have still been early since Mammy hadn't come in to wake her for breakfast. Seizing a rare moment alone, Terra slipped off her bed and headed to her writing desk. Making sure no one was around she reached underneath and pulled out a small brown leather book.

Her secret journal.

No one in her family really ever listened to what she had to say. Not her thoughts or hopes or dreams. They didn't listen to her at all. So she started keeping a journal. It was where she kept all her most secret thoughts. She had always been careful to avoid putting it somewhere it might be found. She didn't want to think what would happen if her mother or sister happened upon it.

Waving such thoughts away Terra turned back to the book.

She took a quill from the small cup she kept them in and pulled an ink well out of her desk. Being careful not to smudge her words Terra wrote about last night. She wrote about the box her father brought in and then about her and Diana sneaking out. When it came to the part about Capt. Reynolds, she hesitated. She wasn't really sure what to say. She wrote about him coming down the stairs and offering to walk with her outside. Then she wrote about how he hadn't been fooled at all by her lie but was understanding and promised to keep her secret. She wrote about using magic at the door and showing the Captain the tunnels. But when it came to their parting, she wasn't sure how to put in words what it felt like to have a man treat her like a woman.

Blushing at the thought of it Terra closed her journal and slipped it back under the desk. She felt foolish getting so worked up over nothing. To be fair, she was becoming a young woman now. It was only natural for her to have feelings like this right?

Deciding such thoughts were best left for later, she turned to her wardrobe. Not sure why, she wanted to look more like a woman today and less like a little girl. Going through all the dresses she had, she knew nothing would suite her. Sighing she decide it was a foolish thought anyway and pulled out a pale pink dress her sister had given her a few years ago. Terra hated the way the color looked on her. It washed her face out and made her look sickly. Sometimes Diana would insist that she wore it.

A knock on the door drew her attention from her pressing wardrobe options.

"Coming," she called as she picked her dressing robe up off the chair and threw it around her shoulders.

Before she could get to the door it cracked open slightly and Mammy's face popped in. "Up already?" She asked sweetly.

"Yes," she said returning the smile. "Just looking for something to wear today."

'You don't look too happy about that," Mammy observed, her keen eyes taking everything in.

"I suppose not," Terra answered glumly. Not wanting to complain she turned back to the pink dress.

"Well what are you looking for?" Mammy asked as she wondered around the room making sure everything was clean and put away.

"Something more . . . womanly I guess?" She said, a little uncomfortable.

"Womanly?" Mammy quietly thought for a moment. It was still several weeks from Terra's birthday, but she was looking down and it always pained Mammy to see her that way.

"Hold on a moment child," she said. She walked out of the room and down the hall to her own chambers. The room was small and humble but she preferred things that way. Reaching under her bed she pulled out a large white box. There was a small card attached to the front with the words 'Happy Birthday Princess'. It was meant to be a gift for her sixteenth birthday, but at least this way Mammy could find out if it fit well or not.

She smiled at the thought of how grown her little princess would look and gathering the box, headed back to her room.

"What's that Mammy?" Terra asked, watching her walk through the door with the large box. "Do you need any help?"

"No I'm alright. Come here, I want you to open this."

Laying the box carefully on the bed Mammy stepped back and let Terra get a good look at it. With nervous fingers the princess carefully pulled the card off first. She read slowly, smiling at the time and love that had obviously been put into the card.

"Thank you Mammy," she said smiling.

"Don't thank me yet child!" She exclaimed with a laugh, "open the box and then thank me."

"Right!" Terra said with a nod. Grabbing the box by both ends she carefully lifted the lid away. Inside nestled on top of beautiful purple paper was the most amazing dress Terra had ever seen. It was deep green with velvet and fine silks. Across the bust line and down the sleeves there were accents of purple. It was cut in the latest fashions and it was cut for a woman, not a girl.

With overly cautions hands Terra pulled the dress out of the box. It had a dark green corset, accented in a lovely deep purple. The sleeves were fitted at the top but flared out with beautiful green silk toward the bottom. It had a square neck line that would make even her small growing breasts look fuller. The skirt itself was a long full silk skirt that looked like it would be light as air to wear.

"Mammy . . ." she gasped breathless. "Mammy this can't be for me?"

"Of course it is. You deserve a dress that will show the world how beautiful you are on your birthday. You're going to be a young lady now."

"Mammy my birthday isn't for weeks still."

"Well an early birthday present never hurt anyone. Come now; let's try it on before the bells sound for breakfast."

Less than ten minutes later the bells sounded as a call for breakfast. Terra stood in front of her large looking glass, hardly able to recognize herself. Mammy had put her in the dress and laced the corset tight, making her waist look slim her hips look wide. Then she had taken all her hair and pilled on her head in a loose plait. Then with careful dexterous fingers Mammy had pulled out several small ringlets to frame her face. She looked beautiful. She looked like a woman.

"You look so much like your mother," Mammy said, a tear welling up in her eyes.

"Mammy don't cry!" Terra exclaimed, turning away from the looking glass. "I'm sorry I can take the dress off."

"It's not that dear," she explained, "it's just that you're all grown up now."

Before Terra could respond the sound of her door being opened pulled her attention. Standing, open mouthed in the door way was Diana.

For a moment the sight of her sister looking like an actual adult was more than Diana could process. Terra was supposed to be in a slump on the floor crying because she'd been caught going in through the front door last night.

Instead Diana finds her standing in a new dress looking like a . . . like a woman and not at all like her little sister. That's not even mentioning the dress! It was beautiful; it was almost as beautiful as her dresses. Terra had never been allowed to have anything remotely as nice as Diana's. The princess was unsure what to be the most angry about.

"Diana!" Terra exclaimed happy to see her older sister. "Can you believe this dress?! Mammy got it for me for my birthday!" She ran over to her sister, pleased at how lightweight the dress was. She spun around once, letting the skirt lift and flow before she got to her sister.

"It's nice," Diana said offhandedly. Not willing to give her sister the satisfaction of knowing how envious she was. "Hey we need to talk about last night," she added under her breath as her sister approached.

"Oh . . . of course," Terra asked, "When . . . ?"

"I'll walk with you to breakfast. Why don't you get going now, I'll catch up in just a minute."

"Are you sure?" She asked, not sure if she was done with Mammy or not.

"You go dear," Mammy said waving her on, "I have a few more things to take care of here."

"R . . . Right," she said. She hesitated for a moment more, knowing there was some kind of tension between Mammy and Diana. But not wanting to step out of line she slipped passed her sister and down the hall.

Once Terra was gone Diana stepped inside and kicked the door closed behind her. Mammy regarded the eldest princess under half closed lids. She and Diana had never seen eye to eye. Ever since she was three and demanded she call her 'Your Royal Highness' as opposed to 'baby' or 'child'. Mammy wasn't blessed with any kind of magical abilities or psychic powers, but even she could sense that there was something wrong with the child.

There was darkness in her. It was small at first, but it's grown as she has. Mammy had grown steadily more uneasy about the Princess as time has gone by. But not wanting to stick her neck out and risk leaving Terra alone, she's kept quiet. Soon things would change. She was sure of that.

"So old woman," Diana said disrespect plain on her face. "Where did you get the money for such a fine dress? I would hate to think that you've stolen from my family and from your kingdom." Diana strolled past Mammy and leaned against Terra's smaller, plainer writing desk. She picked up a quill that was lying on its side and noted that the ink on the bottom was still wet. Terra had been writing this morning. But writing what?

"I bought that dress with the gold I've been saving for a while now. I wanted to get your sister something nice for her birthday." Mammy continued to circle Terra's room, gathering up her clothes to be sent to the laundress and checking the fireplace to make sure the young princess had enough wood for the night.

43

"Well," Diana said, tossing the quill back on the desk, "it appears we've been paying you too much old hag, if you can afford something as nice as that. Perhaps I should speak with my mother about a cut in your pay."

"Well you do what you have to do Highness, I'm sure I'll get along just fine either way." Mammy put the last of the clothes into the basket for the laundress and then started for the door. She didn't look at or acknowledge in any way the princess as she passed.

"I'll be sure to talk with my mother about your pay," Diana called after her, starting to feel her temper rise as the old woman walked passed her without so much as a bow or nod. "I'm sure she'll be happy to have the extra money in the treasury!"

Mammy had reached the door and walked out without as much as a backward glance at Diana. "I'm sure your mother knows best," she called as she pulled the door closed behind her. Diana screamed in rage at the disrespect she was being shown. She grabbed the inkwell of the table and threw it as hard as she could at the closed door.

The glass well hit the metal of the door and shattered, raining ink down on the dark wooden floor below. She screamed again and this time threw the quill, which floated through the air and stuck her in the breast, staining her lovely white dress with black ink.

Diana screamed again and stormed from the room. Knowing she would have to change again before breakfast.

Terra stood patiently waiting at the top of the stairs for her sister. This was where she and Diana always met before breakfast. She couldn't wait to walk into the grand dining hall and show everyone her new dress. She knew she would feel better with her sister at her side but she wasn't sure how much longer she could wait. Mother always got so angry when she was late. After another moment, she decided she couldn't delay any longer and started down the stairs.

"Princess?"

Terra looked up to see Capt. Reynolds standing at the bottom of the stairs. His hand was resting on the same banister she was planning to use to help her down the stairs. Her new dress was light but it was also a lot more fabric than she was used to wearing.

Capt. Reynolds had just finished checking on the new prisoner and was on his way up the main staircase to report to the King when he came around the corner and saw the princess standing on the second floor landing.

The sight of her was breathtaking.

It might have been the dress she was wearing, or the fact that she was now wearing her hair up like all the young women do. But looking at her now Capt. Reynolds had to once again remind himself that she was only fifteen.

"Captain," she said genuinely surprised to see him so soon after their parting. "It's so good to see you again. How are you this morning?" She was coming down the stairs carefully and closing the gap between them.

"I'm doing well Majesty. Yourself? Did you sleep well?" He asked once Terra stood before him.

"I did," she replied with a smile at their secret meaning. "What about you? I know the duties of a Captain of the Guard start early do they not?"

"They do," he said, his smile widening. "Sadly I found when I was returned to my chambers that sleep was harder to find than I thought."

"Oh," she blushed, elated and concerned. "However will you mange?"

"I think I'll find some way to get through."

Terra could sense a deeper meaning to what the Captain was saying, but being so inexperienced she had no idea what that deeper meaning was. Still, she couldn't help the smile that spread across her face as she stood close to Capt. Reynolds, openly talking about their secret.

"Do you like my dress?" She asked, unsure of what to say next. She picked up a handful of material in each hand and spun slowly so he could see the whole dress.

"Is it new?" he asked, trying desperately to keep his eyes on her face.

"I got it just today," she answered, pleased he'd noticed that it was new.

"It's lovely, and you are quite beautiful in it."

Terra colored from the base of her neck to the roots of her dark hair. "T . . . Thank you," she stammered.

"Captain," a voice called from the stairs above them. "I've been waiting for you."

Terra turned to see her father standing on the landing of the fifth floor. He was eying Terra suspiciously until she turned to face him.

"Father," she said, sinking into a curtsy.

"Majesty," Capt. Reynolds said placing his fist over his heart and bowing deeply.

"You may rise," King Sol said as he came to stand next to his daughter. "Tell me Terra, where ever did you get this dress? You look all grown up."

"Thank you father," she said smiling. "Mammy got it for me for my birthday and was kind enough to let me have it early. Do you like it?"

"I do," the King said, feeling a lump in his throat at the thought of his baby all grown up. It seemed not that long ago that she was toddling after him in her mother's garden, still in swaddling clothes. To see her now so grown and mature, it warmed his heart. He knew his oldest daughter Diana was the princess of the prophecy and for that she took precedence in all things. But his youngest, his little Terra, always held a special place in his heart.

"Thank you Father," she said throwing her arms around him. She knew he wasn't prone to public displays of affection, but it was just the three of them there.

King Sol gave his daughter a quick hug and then turned to address the Captain. "Reynolds," he said dropping his title as a show of familiarity. "It seems I must escort this lovely young lady to breakfast. Will you meet me in the war room in an hour?"

"Yes of course Your Majesty. I'll wait for you there. Princess," he said bowing to Terra before making his way up the stairs.

"Captain," she replied as he rushed passed.

"Shall we go dine together my daughter?" King Sol asked, offering his daughter his arm.

"We shall," she said with mock snobbery.

By the time Diana managed to get down to breakfast her family was already dining. Her mother shot her a displeased look under her lashes but didn't say anything. Diana took her seat next to the Queen and looked around for Terra. She wondered for a moment if perhaps the fool was dumb enough to actually wait for her this long. Diana has slipped down the servants stairs in order to save time. It wouldn't surprise her at all to find that simpleton still waiting for her.

"Good morning mother," she said, bowing her head slightly to the Queen. "How does this fine morning find you?"

"On time," her mother said coldly. "Unlike some other members of this family."

"I'm sorry mother," Diana said, mock sorrow in her voice, "I'd gone off to find Terra. The silly girl has disappeared and I didn't want her to be late for breakfast. Sadly I couldn't find her. I think she simply doesn't care enough about this family to make an appearance in the morning." She turned her face away so her mother would think she was feeling actual regret at not being able to find her sister. Secretly Diana smiled. Saying this would take all the heat off her and shift it to Terra.

"Your sister is seated next to your father today," Queen Elise said without looking up from her plate. "She arrived with your father looking quite lovely in a new dress. Apparently it was a birthday gift from Mammy. All the excitement of a new dress and she still managed to get here on time. Imagine that."

Diana sat forward suddenly and looked to the center table where her father sat. She had been so concerned with her mother when she first came in that she didn't even notice Terra sitting at their fathers right side eating. That seat was reserved for visiting dignitaries and other high ranking members of the kingdom. To see her sister sitting there was nothing less than a slap in the face.

"Mother you can't be serious?!" She all but shouted. "This is outrageous!"

"Lower your voice," her mother said under her breath. "People are beginning to stare."

"But mother! Terra sitting in such a place of honor! It's an insult."

"It would appear your father feels differently," The Queen said, "and he is the King so we will obey his rule."

Diana was about to say more but the look from her mother silenced her. She threw herself down into her chair and folded her arms. She refused to eat while her younger sister sat in higher honor than herself. She was the oldest! She was the princess the prophecy had foretold would come and save the world! How *dare* Terra try to place herself above her sister!

Terra looked up from the conversation she was having with her Father about the newest lessons she'd learned about the kingdoms economic boom to see her sister sitting with her arms crossed next to their mother. Smiling, she waved at Diana, thrilled to be sitting on her father's right hand side. She was sure Diana would also be thrilled at her sister's luck.

When Diana looked up it wasn't joy that was on her face. In fact the look on her sister's face chilled her to the bone. There was

48

rage and maybe even hate in her eyes. More than that, there might have been actual loathing in those sky blue eyes of hers.

Terra dropped her hand and sat back against the high backed ornate chair. Her appetite gone, she contented herself with having a nice conversation with her father and a few of the other nobles at her father's right side. She talked and laughed like a good princess should. However, unlike a good princess, she shared her opinions on the economic boom and how she thought it could be extended even after Diana completed her destiny.

Most of the nobles laughed off her suggestions, but a few seemed genuinely interested in what she had to say. When they expressed this interest to the King he beamed with pride. He had never had a son, but he had known that his daughter would be the one the prophecy spoke of. It warmed his heart to know that his youngest child was making such an effort to learn how the Kingdom was run.

As soon as Terra could sense that breakfast was winding to a close she thanked her father for the honor of sitting next to him and then excused herself. She could tell that Diana was still seething with rage and the last thing she wanted was to get caught by her after breakfast. She curtsied to her father and mother and then slipped out the doors leading to the main hall.

She wandered down the hall, unsure of where to go. If she went to any of her usual hiding places Diana would find her in less than a second. She needed to go somewhere her sister wouldn't think to look for her. Somewhere she never went.

As she continued on her way down the hall Terra was struck by a thought. She could go with her father to the war room. She didn't have much of a stomach for war or killing or blood, so she avoided the room where her father and his captains and generals met to discuss such things. She could go and tell her father that she wanted to learn more about that particular aspect of the kingdom.

That could work.

49

Diana would never think to look for her in a place she had, up until then, actively avoided.

She just had to find where the new war room was.

Her father had renovated the west wing just over a year ago and had moved his war room to the first floor. Terra had never concerned herself with seeing the new location since it didn't matter much to her. But if she stayed to the west wing she would find it.

She tried several doors in the west wing before she found one that lead to a hallway she'd never seen before. Figuring this had to be the part of the castle that was renovated, Terra stepped through the large ornate door and pulled it closed tightly behind her.

Inside the corridor was lined with a thick blood red rug that ran the distance of the hall. Along the walls intermittently placed were suits of armor. Some were polished and new, sporting the latest styles. Others were older and battle worn. Some were dented in places and a few had large long scratches running the length of them.

Between the armor and the doors were paintings and tapestries. Most depicted famous scenes from battles long ago. A few of them Terra recognized from the stories and songs she had heard since childhood. Others were unfamiliar to her. All were bloody and terrible, showing huge losses of life on either side. It made her stomach turn just look at some.

There were only a handful of doors on either side of the hall and one large set of metal doors at the end. Unsure what door would lead to the war room, Terra decided to try them all.

As she approached the first door on the right she froze.

There was something very strange going on, something that felt like a second heartbeat in her chest. Before she knew what she was doing, the unfamiliar beating her chest had pulled her to the large metal doors. There was a strange kind of keyhole in the door. It didn't look like anything she had ever seen before. Fearing that it may be locked, she reached up pulled the large handle.

For a moment the door stuck, unmoving. Then, slowly and with great effort on Terra's part, the door started to push open. It was heavy but also quite new, the hinges opened up with very little sound. She pushed against the door opening it just enough to squeeze through. Once on the other side she pushed the door closed again.

She found herself standing at the top of a flight of stone stairs. They were wide cut and new enough to still look rough. They spiraled down to an unknown location below the first floor. As far as she knew the castle didn't have a basement, at least not one this far to the west. Without much other thought, she began to descend the stairs.

"Ok Terra," she said to herself as she started down. "There's nothing creepy about this. Just a long dark stairway leading to a basement I didn't think we had." She tried to laugh at how crazy she sounded walking down stairs talking to herself. But that did little to ease the growing fear in the pit of her stomach.

As she wound round the spiral stairs she began to wonder more and more what was pulling her down. It felt like she had a second heart beating in time with her own. The further down she went the stronger she felt it. Like a rope tied to her heart, it pulled her on.

Just before she reached the bottom the stairway opened up to a large room filled with over a hundred magelight torches. Most were dark, but enough were lit that the light in the room resembled the light midday. Across the room of torches was another set of double doors. These were wooden and completely plain. The only thing that stood out about this set was the large beams being used to reinforce them.

As Terra walked closer she noticed two chairs and a small round table sitting by one of the walls. There was a rack of swords next to table with two missing from it. She glanced around but didn't see anyone. Unless there was a way out through the doors ahead of her, she didn't see another way in or out of this room beside the stairs she'd just come down.

Aside from the alarming amount of magelight torches on the wall, there was something about this room that was very unsettling. It was like the room was created for something sinister. It was as if the room itself knew that it was created for evil so that's what it emanated.

Terra stopped walking and looked back at the stairs longingly. She was standing in the middle of the room now and was starting to seriously reconsider her decision to come down here. She had wanted to get away from Diana but this might have been a bit extreme.

Still . . . there was something beyond those wooden doors that was calling to her. Not just to her, but it was calling to her heart. She had to go on, if nothing else than to satisfy her curiosity. She'd never felt anything like this before and she didn't know if she could go on not knowing what it was.

"I can do this," she said to herself. "I can do this." Mustering up all the courage she had, Terra continued on.

She reached the door and found the large bar lifted out of its cradle already. All she had to do was push the door open.

So she did.

What happened then changed her life forever.

Chapter 2

Terra pushed the door open, surprised at how easily it opened with such minimal effort on her part. What surprised her more was all the light that came pouring out of the room beyond the door. Shielding her eyes she walked in. It was so difficult to see anything that she could have been walking into a bottomless pit and she would never have known.

Inside the room now she blinked rapidly trying to force her eyes to adjust. As near as she could tell there was an assortment of torches and light balls along the walls of the room. For a moment she wondered if this was what it felt like to be on the surface of the sun.

After about a few seconds she could tell her eyes were starting to slowly adjust.

"So they send princess to do their dirty work do they?" A voice called from beyond the light.

"W . . . What? Who's there?" She called, still not able to see much.

The strange voice laughed. It was clearly a man, she could tell that. He sounded like he was in his late thirties or forties maybe, and bitter. There was anger and a bit of hate in his voice. Terra hesitated. She wasn't sure what lay beyond light, but the more she thought about it the worse it made her feel.

'*I should go*,' she thought suddenly. '*If father finds me down here he'll be furious.*'

"That's right," the voice mocked, "run home before papa finds you."

Terra stumbled back against the door, pushing it closed behind her. '*How did he know what I was thinking*?' She wondered. '*I don't think I said anything out loud. Did I*?'

"No you didn't. But you certainly think loud enough that you might as well have."

Terrified she stopped shielding her face and opened her eyes as wide as she could, hoping that would allow them to adjust quicker.

Finally she was starting to see.

She was standing in a large square shaped room that had no windows and no other doors aside from the ones behind her. Around the room there was nothing but light. Sitting directly in the middle of the room was a large glass box. It must have stood over ten feet tall and at least as wide, if not slightly wider. The glass itself looked remarkably thick. Around the edges there were runes and other spell work etched in strange patterns.

Some runes Terra knew and understood while others were foreign to her. It was the same with the spell work. She could make out bits and pieces but no one had ever taught her to read it. Diana still didn't know how to read most of it either.

Each word and rune seemed to bear the same meaning. Binding, sealing, hold, all seemed to be concentrated on keeping things in and out.

Terra felt more confused the longer she stared.

"Don't hurt your head princess; most of these runes are older than this castle," the voice said again. Standing inside the glass box was a man. Not just any man. There was something unsettling and evil about the man inside the glass cage. Just being near him felt like a terrible weight on her chest.

'Who is this man?' Terra thought feeling the fear spread through her. 'To be locked up like this, he must have done something monumentally bad.'

"Oh you have no idea," the man said with a wicked grin. He was tall, at least six and a half feet tall. His hair was jet black and seemed to actually pull in the light around it. His eyes were slanted against the light but even still Terra could tell they were a dark grey, like the slate used to build parts of the castle.

He was gorgeous. So much so that for a moment Terra almost forgot about the pressing evil weight she felt on her chest. After a moment that changed.

"Oh I see. You're the second born. Heh, that makes much more sense. I didn't figure they'd send their precious princess to face me first. Well then let's have it." The man strode to the corner closest to Terra and braced with both hands on the glass.

'Precious princess? Could he be talking about Diana? Who is this man?' Terra thought, too afraid to speak.

"Diana," he said, mulling the name around his mouth. "Di-an-a. So that's the name of the one who's set to kill me. Good to know."

"W . . . who are you?" She stammered, finding her voice at last

"Don't you know? Oh I guess you don't. What are they teaching you kids these days?"

She stared at the man, not sure what she should say or do. Part of her wanted to throw the door open and run. The other half wanted to know who this man was and what he meant when he said Diana was going to kill him.

Then like a bolt of lightning, Terra figured it out. The glass box inscribed with runes of sealing and protection, the overabundance of light, the evil presence she felt, and now what he said about fighting Diana.

"The Shadow King," she whispered.

The man smiled wickedly and bowed. "At your service my lady," he said with mock civility.

"You're . . . you're the one . . ." she stammered.

"Not great with words are you. No matter. I can see what's in your head and your heart."

It was then Terra remembered the stories her mother told her when she was little. Stories about the Shadow King and the things he could do. She was so young she never took much stock in what her mother had said. Aside from that, Diana was the one set to fight this monster, not her. No one had ever bothered to teach her about what he really could or could not do.

"So it seems you do know something about me. Let's see, yes, obviously, I can read your thoughts. Yes I'm immortal. No, I can't fly, and yes I can see straight through to your heart. I know your deepest darkest secrets and desires. I can . . ." he trailed off. His cocky smirk had vanished from his face, replaced by a look of confusion and then irritation.

Something about his sudden lack of confidence gave Terra enough courage to finally turn for the door and escape. Without so much as a second thought or a backwards glance, she ripped the door open and ran from room. She should never have come down here in the first place. She couldn't believe how stupid she'd been.

There was no way to know how much information he extracted from her head while she stood there looking stupid. For all she knew he know knew every spell and incantation she and Diana had ever practiced. Making all of their previous training useless.

Not to mention the way he'd said Diana's name! It was almost like he'd never heard it before.

Terra stumbled on her way up the stairs.

'*What if he had no idea who Diana was? What if my going down there not only told him who Diana was but what she looked like, where she sleeps and all the magic she already knows? Could I have just . . . just served up my sister to this monstrous man?!*' She collapsed at the top of the stone stairs, no longer able to keep walking. Tears were flowing freely down her face as she fell to her hands and knees.

"Diana," she whispered through her tears, "sister what have I done?"

The King of the Shadows was not a man often taken by surprise. However, when that princess had burst through the door he found himself quite surprised for the first time he could remember. It wasn't just the fact that she was the first person to walk through the door since he'd awoken in this accursed box; it was the fact that he hadn't sensed her approaching.

More bothersome still was fact that when he searched her heart and mind for darkness he found only light. All living people have at least a small amount of darkness in their hearts. When they are greedy, or when they covet what others have, and most especially when they hate others for no reason. Even the most noble of people have the tiniest bit of darkness on them.

Something about this princess unsettled him. Adding to that the fact that she wasn't even the princess from their prophecy, she was the second born, the cast off some called her. If she could surprise him, he was starting to worry about what kind of princess this Diana was.

Diana sat, arms folded, refusing to eat while her sister sat in such honor. Instead she occupied her time by openly flirting with some of the younger nobles sitting below the raised dais where her family ate. Her mother made a noise under her breath when she first caught sight of Diana's lewd behavior. But Diana ignored her as she often did.

Her mother would be angry but it wasn't her fault. It was Terra's. And Diana intended to make her pay. She decided the best way would be to corner her sister as she made her way back to her room. She would no doubt try to avoid her, but Diana knew all her hiding places. So long as she could keep her sister from getting to the passages she would have her.

Stupid Terra. Always ruining everything Diana did. She would make her suffer.

As she sat and contemplated all the ways to make Terra pay, her sister suddenly rose from the table and, curtsying to her father and mother, left the hall. Diana jumped up; ready to follow her sister and give her what was coming to her.

Queen Elise reached up, and faster than Diana could see, she grabbed her sleeve and pulled her back down. "Dearest daughter," she said smiling, "you have lessons this morning after breakfast."

"I don't care about my lessons," she grumbled under her breath.

"As true as I'm sure that is, the fact remains if you are to run this kingdom one day you will need to know how it works. So you will attend your political lesson today. You have missed too many as it is. I'm sure whatever matters you have with your sister can be seen to after lessons. And after she's come out of hiding," the Queen added under her breath.

Diana thought for a moment and then said, "Yes, your right mother, as always."

Elise smiled. "Now go and don't disappoint me."

"Yes Mother," she said, coloring her voice with fake obedience. She curtsied to her mother and father in turn and then slipped from the hall. She hadn't gone more than a few yards from the hall when she heard the footsteps behind her. Not looking back she walked on, confident she could take on any idiot foolish enough to take her on.

Diana rounded the corner leading into the grand entry way. There were people here and there, all going on about their own business. Thinking she could lose her stalker in the crowd, Diana decided the best plan of action was to walk straight through the middle of the crowded entry way.

Before she could so much as step out of the shadowed hallway a hand reached out from behind her and slapped over her mouth. Another came up and wrapped around her middle, pinning her arms to her sides, rendering her defenseless. She still needed to touch someone with her hands to affect them with her magic. Panic taking hold of her mind, Diana struggled against her captor to no avail.

She watched helplessly as she was dragged to one of the small rooms that shot off the main hall. She was through the door before anyone even took notice of her. Then the door closed and the small room was thrown into darkness.

Capt. Reynolds made his way steadily down the three flights of stairs in the main hall before he headed toward the west wing. As he passed, guards and citizens alike would sault him with a fist over the heart or a nod of the head. He paid them very little attention as he headed to prepare to meet with the King.

'I could lose my head,' he thought, 'if the King had seen the way I was looking at his daughter he would have taken my head for sure.' Capt. Reynolds sighed. He had watched the princess grow from the time she was ten. He had first enlisted with the castle guard when he was fifteen. As an orphan that was the earliest they would allow him to join.

'Terra's the same age now as I was back then,' he thought. 'Although our lives are complete opposite.'

For a fraction of a second he started to wonder what it would be like if they weren't so different. As soon as the thoughts started he shook them away. She was the princess, granted she wasn't the princes the prophecy spoke of. Still she was a princess. When she was grown her father would marry her to a noble or neighboring king. He would use Terra to forge or strengthen some alliance somewhere.

If he did anything to jeopardize that, he would be beheaded without a second thought. Not to mention what would happen to Terra if she no longer served a purpose here. He had heard from the servants and other castle staff just how she was treated behind closed

59

doors. '*Maybe that's why I seem so draw to her,*' he thought, '*maybe something about her life reminds me of mine.*'

Again, Capt. Reynolds shook these thoughts away. He was very attached to his head and he liked it right where it was. If the older princess and the Queen mistreated the youngest princess there was very little he could do about that.

In fact, he was almost certain there was *nothing* he could do about it.

'*I can be a friend,*' he thought suddenly. Sometimes just having someone around to talk to is enough to help you get through the worst times. He would have to learn to control himself better around the young princess if he wanted to help her.

When he had come around that corner and seen her standing on those stairs all thoughts of his execution and her age flew from his mind. He felt guilty just thinking about it. He knew that as far as her family and law were concerned she was still a child.

At least for the next few weeks anyway.

She would be sixteen soon. By the law of the kingdom she would be a young woman then and open to receiving calls from suitors.

Not that anyone would ever consider him a suitor.

'*Snap out of it Eric,*' He thought to himself. '*I can't meet with the King while having thoughts like these about his youngest daughter. I am the Captain of the Guard and I will act as such. Beautiful princess or no. I have a duty to this kingdom and to its king.*' That seemed to help. The more he thought about the duties he swore to uphold for king and kingdom, the less he thought about Terra that way.

He wasn't sure what it was about the princess that caught him so off guard. He'd been with women before, beautiful women. It wasn't like he had an issue with young girls. Terra was the first woman, girl, no, woman he'd ever looked at that way. He was beginning to fear the guilt of his thoughts would tear him apart.

Taking a deep breath Capt. Reynolds cleared the princess from his mind and focused on the task at hand.

The prisoner hidden at the bottom of the castle.

Somehow Terra had managed to make her way up the rest of the stairs, into the corridor and was almost to the door leading out to the first floor west wing hallway, when the sudden feeling of evil behind her drew her attention. She wasn't sure where it had come from but she could sense it as clearly as if she was looking at it head on.

Careful to keep her pace even, she continued on her way to the door. She centered herself and reached out with her mind trying to see what it was behind her. She felt something dark, evil, and slightly familiar. There was something about this evil that she had felt before.

'That man! The Shadow King in the basement, this feels like his same evil aura!' She realized with an overwhelming sense of dread what was behind her.

A shadow had somehow penetrated the barriers and protection spells placed throughout not only the castle but the surrounding town. More than that, it had found her right after she'd left the presence of their supposed King.

Not sure how it came to be behind her, Terra knew she couldn't let this creature get away and wonder the castle. There was no way to tell how many lives would be lost. If it was her fault that this creature was here, she would be sure to rectify that mistake.

Terra stopped walking suddenly and dropped down into a crouch spinning and sweeping her foot around as she spun. Physical attacks had no effect on shadows, but if you came into contact with them you would feel a freezing aura, like part of you was suddenly thrust under the midwinter ice. Sweeping like this was an effective way of judging how much distance there was between you and the monster.

Her toes hit something cold that sent shockwaves of pain through her body. Thanks to her training with Diana, she was prepared for this.

61

Still, it hurt badly.

Crouching into a ball, she rolled back, putting more distance between her and the shadow. It was a move she had practiced as part of her training many times, but this time it was much harder due to the yards of fabric she was wearing. As she sprang back up she raised her eyes for the first time.

It was horrible.

The monster stood nearly eight feet tall but less than three feet wide. It was pitch black at the top but as it trailed down to the floor it faded away so that its bottom was all but invisible. They had no arms or appendages to speak of but then again they had no real need for them. It was the eyes that made them so terrifying.

Where there heads would be there were two silvery grey slits for eyes. Typically when a shadow was hunting for prey its eyes were two thin lines of silver on its face. But once you made the mistake of looking them in the face, their eyes would widen and they would lock onto the aura of your soul. It was said, by some, that they would hunt you to the ends of the earth once they got your smell.

As Terra looked up she saw that not only were the shadows eyes open, they were bulging. They were huge, bigger than she'd ever thought they could get. Like two huge silver holes in its face. It was terrifying to see.

Caught off guard by its appearance, she froze momentarily.

Sensing her laps of focus the shadow lunged. Quicker than she would have thought possible it came at her. It made no sound as it approached but the evil coming off of it was almost visible. It was certainly more than palpable.

Terra dived to side, crashing into a suite of armor as it streaked passed. While her training made her quick, she wasn't that quick. As the shadow flew past it grazed her arm sending waves of freezing cold pain through her body.

She cried out and grabbed her left shoulder. Her sleeve was like ice under her fingers and her whole left arm could barely move.

"Damn," she whispered struggling to flex her fingers. Standing she ran part way down the hall and turned to face the shadow. She wouldn't be caught off guard again. The shadow had already turned and was coming at her again. Releasing her left arm, Terra raised her right hand and quicker than she ever had before, pooled her magic there.

"By the rights of the Creator, Shadow I . . ." she was stopped halfway through her spell when the door behind the shadow opened suddenly.

Capt. Reynolds had almost perfected the presentation he would make to the King by the time he reached the entrance to the first floor west wing hallway. His hand was on the handle when a noise from inside stopped him cold. There was the sound of running footsteps and then the crash of something or someone hitting metal.

'He's escaped!' Capt. Reynolds thought. Knowing he couldn't take the monster on alone the Captain turned to raise the alarm. He hadn't even taken a step forward when he heard the sound of Terra's voice beyond the door.

His blood ran cold at the sound and before he could think better of it, he was shoving the large door open and running inside.

"Terra!" He shouted bursting through the door. He couldn't believe what he was seeing! The princess was at the far end of the hallway, her right hand raised and her left arm was hanging limply at her side. Between the captain and the princess was a shadow.

"Eric," Terra shouted, "Shut your eyes!"

"Wh . . . What?!"

"Shut your eyes!" She could see the shadow turning to face Eric. With its eyes bulging that way Terra was afraid the captain would be unable to resist looking. Her being marked was bad enough, but she would be damned if her mistake cost him his life.

"If I shut my eyes I can't help you," he called, keeping his eyes down cast as his training had taught him.

"I need you to trust me, please Eric. Shut your eyes!"

63

"Damn it!" He shut his eyes seconds before the shadow turned to face him. As Terra had hoped its eyes became slits again as its rapid movement came to an end. It stood before Eric turning from left to right and back again. It could sense prey nearby but couldn't find him with his eyes closed.

Seeing her opportunity Terra raised her right hand again.

"By the rights of the Creator I banish you from this place of light!" Purple and silver magic exploded from her right hand flew at the shadow. It whipped around to face her as soon as she started to speak again.

Its eyes bulged as it flew toward her alarmingly fast. It was too late. She was faster than the shadow. It ran into her magic head on. Purple and sliver enveloped the creature surrounding it like an aura. As she watched the shadows eyes seemed to bulge even wider as it stared at her.

"T . . . Terra," Eric stammered, eyes fixed on the dying monster in front of him.

In an instant the shadow turned bright white and shown with a brilliance that would marvel the sun itself.

Then just as suddenly it was gone, leaving nothing where it once stood.

"I . . . I actually did it," she whispered, a faint smile on her lips. Suddenly exhausted, she felt her knees give out underneath her and she began to fall.

"Princess!" Eric shouted, rushing forward. He caught her seconds before her knees slammed into the floor. He carefully lowered her down in his arms. "Terra are you alright? Did it hurt you? How did you do that? What happened? How did that thing get in here? And why are you down here?"

Terra chuckled, "that was too many questions at once." Feeling like she might pass out, she leaned forward and rested her head on the Captains' shoulder. He was so warm and her arm was still so cold. She felt like she just needed to sleep for a while.

"Terra what in the name of the Creator are you doing down here?"

"I was hiding," she said, to weak for lies, "from Diana. I knew she was mad at breakfast and I didn't want to fight with her so I came down here to find my father and hide."

"But then how did the shadow . . ."

"I went too far," she whimpered, tears in her eyes. "I went all the way down and I . . . I saw him." She dissolved into tears at the thought of the monster under the castle and the fact she had unwittingly betrayed her family by going down there.

Eric sat back on his heels and held the crying princess. Her left arm felt like ice and her hair had completely fallen out of the plait it had been in earlier. Shushing her he gently stroked her hair. He knew he had to get her out of here before someone came to see what the commotion was. He wasn't sure what happened, but he knew he needed to be the one who questioned her.

"Terra," he said after a few moments, "I need you to tell me exactly what happened. If one shadow got in that means more shadows can get in. I need to know how this happened."

Taking a few deep breathes to calm herself, she sat back out of Eric's arms and said, "I came looking for my father. But as soon as I took a few steps from the door I felt something."

"Something like what?"

"It's hard to explain," she said thinking. "If felt almost like I had a second heart beating in my chest." She placed her hand over her heart as she remembered the strange sensation of having two heart beats. Curiously she wondered when the beating had stopped. She had been so caught up with fleeing that she hadn't noticed it stopped.

"A second heartbeat," Eric said, more to himself than to Terra. "Then what happened?"

"Well, this other heartbeat felt like it was pulling down the hall to those doors. So I followed it like an idiot. I never even thought there might be something terrible lurking down there."

65

"Don't worry about that now," Capt. Reynolds said assuming a more formal tone. "Just tell me what happened."

"I went down the stairs and found a room full of the magelight torches. Only a few were lit but it was still very bright. I walked on toward the big wooden doors and . . ."

"The guards just let you pass?" Capt. Reynolds cut in.

"There were no guards."

"No guards! Are you sure?" He asked, sounding more than a little angry.

"I'm sure. There was a table with a few chairs against the wall next to a sword rack, but there was no one else down there."

"Fools," he muttered. "Please go on."

Terra took another deep breath and then continued. "I opened the door and was instantly blinded by the light in the room. Before my eyes could adjust I heard someone in the distance talking to me. When my eyes adjusted I saw a huge glass box, covered in spells and runes. Inside the box was . . . the Shadow King."

"Terra I need you to listen to me very carefully. I need to know everything that was said between you too. The smallest detail could change everything."

She felt her eyes start to water again as she thought of everything he had gotten from her mind. Going slowly so as not to forget anything, she relayed to him everything they said. She tried her best to tell him word for word, but it felt like so much had happened since she had stood before that monster.

"Then, as I was walking toward the door, I felt an evil presence behind me. You know what happened after that."

"Terra," Eric said, "I can't say how much you may have given him or even how much he knew before he was captured. I won't lie to you, it sounds like he knows a lot more about your sister now than he did before. But please believe me when I tell you that he can never escape from that prison. It was specially crafted to keep him in and keep everything else out. He will never be a threat to you down there."

"How can you be sure?"

"You just have to trust me."

She nodded with a sigh. "What do we do now?"

"Now we find the King and tell him what happened."

Terra shuttered, a sudden premonition of terrible things to come washed over her. "Do we have to?" She asked, hoping to prevent her premonition from coming true.

"I'm afraid we must."

With a resigned sigh she nodded. "Let's go then."

Diana watched the door before her close, cursing the fools who hadn't see her in time to save her. She continued to struggle but she knew it was useless. Whoever or whatever had a hold of her wasn't letting up.

"I've been waiting for you princess," a voiced hissed in her ear. "I thought you'd never leave that damn hall."

Diana stopped struggling. She knew this voice. She had heard it before. With an enormous sigh of relief Diana parted her lips under the hand and licked them provocatively. The man behind her moaned quietly in her ear and then released his hold on the princess.

"If it isn't Richard Howe," Diana said in a sultry voice. She pressed herself against the man before stepping away to face him.

"For a moment I wasn't sure you knew it was me," Richard said, his voice deep with passion.

"I thought you liked it when I struggled." Diana leaned against the man as she ran her fingers up and down the length of him.

"Oh I do," he said grabbing her by the shoulders and forcing her down on the pile of robes at their feet. "Let me show you just how much."

"Don't you dare rip this dress, it's new," she warned as she felt his greedy hands fumble with her corset.

"I haven't ripped one yet," Richard said his voice thick with lust.

"See that you don't."

67

Terra stood silently at Capt. Reynolds side as he explained to the King what he found when he arrived at west wing. He then explained about the fight with the shadow and questioning Terra after it was all over. King Sol stood gravely as he listened to the Captain. His greatest fear in bringing that monster to the castle was that something like this might happen.

Her father stood at the center of a large round table with generals at either side. Terra knew all their names and which had provinces and where. The table before them was a large ornately gilded round table. There was no top but only a small border on which her father now rested his hands. Instead inside the table itself there was an exceptionally detailed model of the kingdom. Everything from the forest that border the castle grounds to the small village of Westmore that sat at their southernmost border. The rivers in the forest had even been added. Each structure that sat on the model could be easily removed should something terrible befall its real life counterpart.

Directly behind her father sat a smaller, but no less ornate throne flocked on either side by large less ornate chairs for the generals and captains. The rest of the room was taken up by a large wooden table in one corner covered in maps and scrolls. Large weapon racks sat along most of the walls with a few large glass cases for special battle worn weapons.

The rest of the wall space was occupied by charts and maps detailing trade routes and peace agreements with neighboring kingdoms. It was a very large room, standing there next to Capt. Reynolds made Terra feel exceptionally small.

When Capt. Reynolds came to the part about Terra using magic the King turned a disbelieving eye to his youngest daughter who, as far as he knew, had no magical abilities to speak of. When the captain continued talking the King held his hand up to silence him.

"Terra," he said, "tell me child is this true? Did you see the Shadow King and speak with him?"

68

"Yes father," she answered, her eyes downcast.

"And from your mind he pulled thoughts about your sister?"

"Yes father."

"How long after that before you realized there was a shadow trailing you?"

"I paused at the top of the stairs for nearly ten minutes after I ran from the prison. It was only moments after I passed through the doors that I felt it behind me."

"And you defeated this shadow?"

"Yes father."

"On your own?"

"Yes father."

"Using magic?"

Terra hesitated. "Yes father."

"Tell me child what happened when the monster was defeated? How did it die?"

Struck by the odd nature of the question, she hesitated again.

Capt. Reynolds spoke up when he saw Terra's hesitation. "It was enveloped in the princess's magic for less than a moment before it turned white and shone like the sun. We had to cover our eyes to avoid being dazed. When the light faded and we could look again, the creature was gone. No trace of it remained."

"Are you sure Captain?" the King asked. "There's no way you're mistaken about what you saw?"

"No Majesty."

"This is most troubling news indeed," King Sol said as he mulled over what their next course of action would be.

Terra glanced nervously around at all the faces in the room. There seemed to be some issue with the retelling of how the monster was defeated. She was almost certain this situation would end poorly for her. She just wasn't sure how yet.

"Majesty," Capt. Reynolds said.

"Yes Captain?"

"Perhaps, if there is doubt, we could always have her recast the spell so that you may all see it firsthand."

"I'm afraid that unless you have a shadow in your pocket that won't work," Master Bell said, stepping up to stand next to the King. He nodded to the captain and bowed to Terra.

"Why wouldn't it work Master Wizard?" Capt. Reynolds asked.

"The princess can cast her spell again but all we would see is color of her magic. Without an actual shadow for her to purify, we won't be able to see anything."

"P . . . purify?" She asked confused. "I thought that spell banished the shadow back to its own realm?"

"Normally," Master Bell explained, "that's exactly what would have happened. However, if what you say is true and the shadow was enveloped in a blinding white light, than that shadow was purified, not banished."

"I've never heard of a shadow being purified before," Capt. Reynolds said. He looked to the King who, aside from being the King, was well versed in all the lore that concerned shadows.

For a moment King Sol was silent, mentally going through all he knew of the shadows and their king. He thought he might have heard something similar to this once many years ago. "I seem to recall an incident similar to this in my studies. However it has been many years since I read about it. I'm afraid I don't recall much."

"I believe I know the incident you mean Majesty," the oldest of the Kings Generals said, stepping forward.

"General Swain," the King said, "please tell us what you know."

Walking up to stand next to Master Bell, the old general saluted the King and bowed to the princess. "It was many years ago now," he started, speaking slowly. "I heard the tale when I was a boy working on my father's farm out near the Western Woods. A man came to the door asking if we could give him shelter for the night. He told us his traveling companions had been attacked by a rouge group of shadows.

"As he told it he and a number of other men had set out into the woods to gather firewood for their village. Though my father expected they had actually been poaching in the Kings woods. They had wandered deeper than they normally do and gotten lost. After searching for the way home for several hours it got dark and they set up camp for the night hoping to make a fresh start in the morning.

"Sometime during the night a group of shadows came upon them. The first man they took stood no chance. He woke up feeling the freezing pain of the shadows and died moments later. In the space of a few moments they had taken all but the man who stood at our hearth.

"Hearing his friend's die the man took off running through the woods. He couldn't say for how long or far he ran but in time he came upon a small lake in the center of a clearing. At the edge of the water stood a beautiful woman clad all in white. As he approached she turned and faced him. He couldn't recall much other than she was beautiful and that her eyes were a brilliant green. Like the emeralds of the crown."

Terra looked up at the man, her own eyes shining green.

General Swain smiled at Terra knowingly. "Before the man could say anything to the woman she ran from the edge of the water and met the shadows head on. Without a word she raised her hand and the shadows erupted into pure white light. Shocked and exhausted the man went to the woman and thanked her for saving his life and destroying the monsters.

"She told him that the shadow hadn't been destroyed but purified and sent home."

"If there was a way to do such a thing, wouldn't we have heard of it by now?" Capt. Reynolds asked.

"Not necessarily," Master Bell countered. "It is possible to purify a shadow instead of just sending it away. But the ability do so is so rare that most people don't even know the gift exists. I myself have never heard of a confirmed case of it."

71

"So a shadow can be purified by a rare gift," King Sol said as he processed this new information. "Master Wizard tell me, does this gift matter? If we can kill the shadow without purifying it, what difference does it make so long as the outcome is the same?"

"A wise question your Highness," Master Bell remarked with a nod. "A shadow does not exist in the same plane of existence as we do. Put simply, they are from a different dimension than we are. Because they cannot fully exist on our plane, physically we cannot hurt them. However, every time we kill a shadow all we are really doing is sending them from this world back to their own. They are not truly dead, nor are they really alive. Banishing them sends them away the same way waving your hand sends away a fly away, for a moment."

"But in time the fly returns," King Sol said, picking up what the wizard was saying.

"So to, do the shadows," Master Bell said, nodding at the King. "All we can do is swat them away for a time. Unfortunately there is no way to tell for how long they disappear. For all we know we could banish one here only to have it reappear on the other side of the world or in the next room. It is regrettable, but what we know about these creatures is limited."

"If we purify them," Terra asked timidly, "do they come back?"

Master Bell turned to the princess and smiled. He had always admired her wit and abilities. As far as he was concerned one of greatest disappointments in his life was being unable to train a gift like hers. More times than he could recall he had gone before the Queen and asked for permission to train both princesses. Each time her answer was the same.

No. It was more important that Diana get trained and ready for the fight than Terra get trained because the wizard wished it so.

"No princess. Once purified, the shadows can never return."

"How do you know?" A Lord from the north asked. "If our knowledge is so limited, how do we know if they don't come back?"

"Every shadow has its own unique aura, just like we all do. Though each bears the same evil as their master, they are all different.

Years ago some of the Masters came together and through careful comparison and many arguments, they discovered that most of them had fought the same shadow at one time or another. After that they began sending out all under their power who had the gift and skill to detect an individual's aura to fight these shadow and return to tell them of the auras they felt.

"Soon it became clear to everyone; we were not killing these creatures at all."

There was a sudden outburst of talking and shouting from around the table. Some people believed what the Master Wizard said was impossible. They shouted about how such a thing couldn't be true or surely they would have heard about it by now. Others cried out in fear. Saying that the Wizards information was a sure sign that they would never be truly rid of the monster and they would all perish.

Men shouted and yelled back and forth over the round table while the King walked back to his throne and sat, deep in thought. Even Capt. Reynolds was caught up in the argument. Slowly Terra backed away from the table. She kept her head down and the men circled around to the spot she left open. Once her back was to the door she curtsied to her father and slipped out.

Stepping lightly into the hall she pulled the door closed and rested her head against it. She could still hear the men arguing on the other side. Even this argument was her fault. She had given away Creator knows how many of her sisters secrets to the enemy, gotten into a fight with a shadow, forced Eric to take her to her father and out her about her magic which would undoubtedly get back to her mother and mean the end of lessons with Diana and a sever scolding if not a beating.

She had somehow managed to destroy her entire life, all before noon. Somehow she knew that must have been a record.

To depressed to even cry anymore, Terra made her way slowly down the hall. She would go and face her mother and sisters wrath. There was no use hiding anymore. She had tried to hide earlier and look what happened.

Terra made her way slowly to her room. She smiled and nodded when people acknowledge her. In the back of her mind she noted how more people than usual were taking notice of her. Typically she was out shined by Diana who was her nearly constant companion.

Terra wondered if she'd ever be let out of her room again.

Her mother would want the passageways and tunnels mapped once she knew about them and that would limit where Terra could go and when. She supposed she should become accustomed to her room. It's probably where she would spend most of the rest of her life.

Diana painstakingly adjusted her dress and hair. She couldn't have people knowing what she did in her free time. Richard was already dressed cracking the door open.

"There's a lot more people out here now," he said, cursing under his breath. "We'll have to head out separately."

"You can wait here," Diana said dismissively. "I have to get to some boring lesson or my mother will have my head."

Used to the princess's mistreatment of him, Richard only smiled. "How long do you want me to wait?"

"I don't know, maybe an hour."

"An hour?!"

"Yes," Diana sapped, poking her head out. "Wait an hour and then come out."

"I can't be gone that long! My father is already searching for me by now."

Not feeling up to arguing with or threatening Richard, Diana opted for a third option. She turned from the door and pouted her lips. "I'll make you a deal," she pressed herself against the length of him, "if you wait and hour like a good boy, I'll let you into my bed tonight."

Richard was already having a hard time thinking. Diana was a beautiful woman with a tight firm body that drew the blood from his brain faster than he'd care to admit. When she pressed herself against him this way and he could feel every supple curve of her body against his, he was powerless.

Never before had she offered to lay with him in her bed. She always had some excuse or another. He had never pressed the issue because he greatly enjoyed their time together. She could excite him in ways the whores never could. Just the thought of taking the princess in her own bed was more than he could bear.

"I would wait in here all day for a chance to have you in your bed," he whispered, his voice deepening with lust.

"Good," Diana said, pleased as she always was when she got her way. "Do you still have that ridiculous little writing scroll on you?"

"Of course," Richard replied, reaching into one of the pockets inside his traveling cloak. "You know my father insists I take this with me everywhere."

"Let me see it." Diana took the small scroll and unrolled it. "Do you remember the time I had you meet me in that passage by the kitchen?"

"Yes."

"This is a map that will lead you from that door to the door to my room. Be sure you go far enough down the hall or else you'll end up in my parent's chambers and I will deny any knowledge of you."

"Understood," he said taking the map from the princess. He studied it carefully before rolling it up and returning it to his pocket.

"When should I come to your room?" He asked, lifting a lock of hair from her neck. He kissed down her neck to her shoulder.

"Once they put out the fires in the kitchen come to my room. I'll be waiting." She walked away from him and out the door as though they were having a perfectly civil conversation and not arranging another intimate encounter.

Richard turned and punched the pile of coats that they had just made love on with all his strength. He hated how she treated him. Like he was less than the other foolish boys she had her way with. He was the son of a Lord, and she would treat him as such if it killed him.

Diana made a b-line for her room, knowing that the dim light of the closet wasn't enough for her to put herself back together. She never went anywhere without looking her best. Being a princess and the savior of mankind was great, but being the most attractive woman in the kingdom got her out of more bad situations and into more enticing ones than anything else.

She would have to look quite inviting to avoid her mother finding out how late she was to her lesson. Catching a faint whiff of herself she realized she smelled of old coats and sweat.

'*This will never do,*' she thought, '*I'll have to summon that old hag to run me a bath.*'

Smiling at the thought of how much it would pain the old woman to have to bathe her Diana hurried on to her room.

Terra closed her door and threw the bolt. At least she wouldn't be surprised by someone coming in unannounced. Kicking off her new slippers, she walked to her bed and threw herself onto it. Noon or not, she didn't feel much like being awake anymore today. She rolled onto her back and stared at the faded purple canopy of her bed.

'*I can't believe how stupid I am,*' she thought, '*I gave away everything to that monster!*' Feeling more useless than she ever had before, she lay on her bed and wished to sleep forever. '*Everything Diana's worked so hard for, everything we've practiced, every hour we've spent at our lessons. Even all the physical training father insisted on. All of it. For not. Because of me!*'

Terra felt herself start to cry again, but somehow she couldn't bring herself to care. What did it matter if she cried now? It would probably be best to get the tears out now before her mother got a hold of her.

'*Mother,*' she thought, '*will you still love me when you know what I've done? Will you still be able to look at me when you know all that I've betrayed this day?*' Not that it mattered. Terra doubted she would ever be able to look at herself in the glass again.

76

'Father. The way you looked at me when Eric told you what I'd done, like I was no longer your little girl. When he told you about my magic you weren't proud or happy to have a second gifted child were you? No. You were disappointed in me. Sneaking around the castle at all hours of the night like some kitchen maid. Lying to you and mother about what I can do. Will you ever forgive me?'

Terra thought of the way her father had looked at her when Master Bell had told him that she had purified the shadow and not killed it. It was like he didn't know her, like she was something foreign, and unpleasant. He would never forgive her. She knew that.

"Oh Diana what have I done?" Terra sobbed out loud. She rolled onto her stomach and clutched a pillow to her face to stifle her cries. "How could I have been so foolish?! How could I let him use me like an idiot?! You trusted me to keep you secrets and to help protect you from that monster and I failed you! I failed you! Sister I'm sorry!" She was shouting into the pillow now as she sobbed uncontrollably.

For a moment she wished she could just disappear and never be seen or heard from again. She could do no more damage that way. She could simply fade away into nothing. It wouldn't even be that hard for her. She was so often in the shadows people probably wouldn't even notice her absence.

The Shadow Princess.

That was what many of the people called her. Very few people knew what she looked like or even anything about her. Being a princess didn't seem to matter much when Diana was around. She soaked up all the light and left none for Terra. She was left with the shadow and the dark. It seemed like she could fade away and no one would ever be the wiser.

Knowing such luck was impossible she shut her eyes against the light streaming in through her window. Her mother would be there soon enough. She might as well rest while she can. Her late night excursions with Eric had robbed her of most of her sleep the previous night. It wasn't long after she closed her eyes that sleep took her over and she finally stopped crying.

Fresh from her bath and in a clean dress Diana felt like a well groomed cat as she slipped into the passage behind her large tapestry depicting her in the battle she was destined for. It didn't really look like her at all in truth. Someone had done it years before after they heard the description of the golden princess.

'At least they got the hair right,' Diana mused as she looked at the woman made of woven threads. Her hair was long and golden. But in her opinion, Diana was much better looking than the woman on her wall. She understood how they could make such a mistake. Diana was more beautiful than any other woman in the kingdom, living or dead. How could these fools know such beauty would be born into the world?

With one last glance in her looking glass, Diana slipped through the hidden door and into the secret passage. Deciding the best path to take would be to head down to the second floor and use the door near the main stairs to get to her lesson, she set out.

She hadn't gone more than a few feet before she could feel someone behind her.

'Richard,' she thought, mildly irritated. 'You were supposed to wait until near midnight before coming up here.'

With a sigh Diana stopped and turned, ready to give Richard a sound lashing for not following her instruction to the letter.

It wasn't Richard.

Not even close.

Diana let out a blood curdling scream that bounced off the stone walls around her.

She tried to scurry back and away, but a loose stone tripped her.

As she fell backward the world around her grew dark. Just before all the light was stolen away from the world her thoughts turned to her family. If she died here, would they find her before her body became ugly and gnarled?

Capt. Reynolds bowed to the King as he made his exit from the war room. Sometime during the fighting and debating Terra had slipped from the room and no one had notice. They had finally come to a course of action regarding what had transpired that day between her, the Shadow King and the shadow.

They had turned to her to see if she agreed only to find her gone.

He felt foolish for not noticing her absence before. She had been attacked only hours ago in the middle of the castle. Somewhere that was arguably the safest place in the whole kingdom. He never should have let her out of his sight. If anything happened to her because of his over sight he would never forgive himself.

When they had discovered her gone it was the Master Wizard who had suggest that he, as the Captain of the Guard, go and find her and bring her back to the war room so they could make preparations. Once he found Terra he was instructed to go to the school room and collect Princess Diana as well. They would need both princesses for what was in mind.

Stepping out of the west wing, Capt. Reynolds was surprised to find the sun was setting. Most of the day had been wasted arguing back and forth over what was truth and what was not. Or what could be done and what was impossible. It worried him greatly to think that Terra had been gone for nearly five hours and he hadn't noticed.

Running up the stairs he passed a few maids and housekeepers even a laundress, none had seen the princess in several hours. With a growing sense of panic Capt. Reynolds turned and decided to check the school room where the princesses had their lessons. He knew that by now the princesses should be practicing the physical training the King made them do.

Frankly the Captain couldn't agree more with King's choice to ensure the princesses knew how to protect themselves. He had made a lot of changes since becoming the Captain of the Guard, but even still there were several high ranking men whom he wouldn't trust with a potato knife, let alone a sword or bow.

Teaching the princesses how to defend themselves is probably what saved Terra this morning. Knowing how to react to a threat and keep yourself safe is essential information. In times like these you can't be too prepared.

"Captain!" A voice in front of him called. It was one of the princess's instructors, although the captain couldn't be sure which one.

"Instructor," The Captain said coming to an abrupt halt. "What can I do for you?"

"It's the princess!" He cried in a panic.

"What about the princess?" He demanded.

"Something terrible has happened!" The man was practically falling all over himself as cried at the Captain.

Seizing the man by the shoulders the Captain shook him once and yelled, "What happened to Princess Terra?!"

"T . . . Terra," the man said stammering, "This has nothing to do with her. This about Princess Diana! She never showed up for any of her lessons today!"

Capt. Reynolds dropped the man to the floor and began walking away. For a moment his heart had dropped at the thought of something terrible befalling Terra. To find out that Princess Diana had simply skipped her lessons again. He felt like he could cry out in joy and kill that man in frustration.

"But captain you don't understand," the man called after him. "I've been searching for her since midday. She's nowhere to be found!"

"Why didn't you say so fool?!" He shouted turning back to the man.

"I tried to tell you, you dropped me on the floor," the man said whimpering.

Enraged Eric Reynolds, Captain of the Kings Guard, lifted the man by his collar and pinned him to the wall of the hall. "Tell me, and tell me now, everywhere you looked and when you looked there."

It took that fool nearly twenty minutes to accurately recount where and when he had searched. Then it had taken him an additional thirty to sound the alarm and get the men organized into search parties. Night had fallen by the time they started searching in earnest. Worse than that, the Queen had come and spoken to the men before they set out.

He had thought she would appeal to them as a mother. Beg them to leave no stone unturned in their search for her daughters. Instead she stood before the men cold and emotionless. She told them to remember that Diana was the priority. Once she was found safely they could turn their attention to locating Terra.

It had taken all he had in him not to react to the Queen's words. That she could stand there so cold and place the life of one child over the other. It seemed unbelievable. At least they were finally getting the search underway. While the rest of the castle searched for Diana, he would search for Terra. He would start in her room.

It wasn't quite as late as Richard had expected, but as he made his way into the kitchen, the fires were out. Smiling at his good fortune he made his way to the secret door Diana had showed him some months ago. It took him a moment but once he found it he was on his way at a run. Just the thought of being in her bed made his blood hot.

It didn't take long for him to follow the map she'd given him. He was at the fifth floor in the passageway she had indicated. Once there he discovered a problem. It was so dark in the passage that it was nearly impossible to see the outline of the doors. Unsure of how to proceed, Richard decided to make his way while trailing his hand along the wall. If he could keep it at the level of the release buttons then he could count each door he passed.

Finding the first button he made his way down.

One.

Two.

Three, the royal chambers. Richard tiptoed passed this door, terrified at being caught on his way to princess's chambers.

In his attempt to walk quietly, his foot caught on a rock and he stumbled. Catching himself as quick as he could, he continued on his way.

Four, finally. He was starting to worry he might have missed the door when he tripped. He'd walked for quite a while before finding the fourth door. Pushing the catch he stepped through the door and brushed the tapestry aside.

"Diana?" He whispered into the darkness. "The fires in the kitchen are out and here I am. Where are you?"

A small noise from what Richard assumed was the bed, drew his attention. It was night but the moon was bright enough for him to make out shapes. There was definitely a bed over there and he could see someone moving on it.

'Could it be?' He thought. 'Is she really going let me play this fantasy?' Richard had always been a man of particular taste. He was the son of a great Lord and commanded a good deal of power and respect. But for him it wasn't enough. He wanted more power. When he and the princess had first started fooling around she would ask him what his desires were, what fantasies did he have?

Afraid that telling her would scare her away he started small. As the months progressed he started opening up more and more to her, telling her his darkest fantasies. She seemed to enjoy hearing about them as much as she enjoyed acting them out.

Lately he'd been pressing for a particular fantasy. He wanted to take her in her bed while she "slept", then once he entered her she would awaken and struggle against him as though he was taking her by force.

A room covered in darkness, the princess sleeping on her bed. It seemed she had finally decided to grant his request. His body quivered at the thought. He ached to be inside her already.

He kicked off his shoes and undressed completely. Then, tiptoeing, made his way to the bed. He climbed on and at first he laid next to the princess, careful not to touch her. He laid close enough that he could feel the warmth coming off her skin. Even the smell of her was intoxicating. Being this close and not allowing himself to touch her was a way of flexing his own will power.

When he'd taken all he could stand, he made his move. He jumped up, grabbing and spreading her knees he placed himself in between her thighs. She was warm and soft and he wanted her now.

A noise drew his attention to her face. It was too dark to see but she was clearly awake now. Before she could speak he threw his hand over her mouth like he had earlier. He leaned down so his face was close to her. She was starting to shake as she attempted to speak through his hand. All of which made him harder. She cried out against his hand when his hardness jabbed her in the thigh.

"Don't worry princess," he whispered against her ear. "I won't be gentle." Taking advantage of being so close to her face, Richard licked her ear and then started kissing down her neck. Stopping at the top of her left shoulder, he bit down. She cried out again and really started to struggle.

Her hands came up to push him away. In a quick movement he had both her wrists in his hand. He pinned them against her belly and shook with desire as she struggled to be free.

Richard couldn't believe his luck. She was fighting him like her life depended on it and he was eating it up. It was all too much for him. He had wanted to spend time biting her making her hurt before he made her feel good but he couldn't take it any longer. He was going in.

Capt. Reynolds tried Terra's door only to find it locked. Feeling his heart lift at the first sign of luck he'd had all day, he decided to try the secret door she'd shown him last night. Racing down the hall to the main staircase, Capt. Reynolds felt like he wasn't moving fast enough.

He was through the secret door and making his way up the passageway in a matter of moments. Something felt wrong. He couldn't put his finger on it but his heart was racing. He needed to get to Terra now. When he got to her door his heart dropped.

Her door was open.

Without hesitation he burst through the secret door and flew through the tapestry. Her room was pitch black, making it impossible to see what was going on.

The sound of laughter and muffled crying drew his attention to left. His eyes were adjusting quickly and he could make out general shapes. There was someone on the bed, no two someone's. And they were . . . they were . . .

"T . . . Terra?"

Terra was asleep. It wasn't a sound or happy sleep. It was sleep that left her tossing and turning. Filled with strange dreams, it was a sleep she dearly wished she could wake from. In her dreams everyone was walking away from her. Her mother, her father, Diana and even Eric had their backs to her and were walking away. She called to them and tried to run but she was stuck in place. Something was holding her back. She struggled but she couldn't get away.

"Wait!" She called, "please don't leave me! Come back!"

Still unable to move she looked down. Her legs were trapped in shadows. An inky black mass was tangling up her legs. Keeping her rooted to the spot. She thrashed and struggled trying to get away. Nothing seemed to work. No matter what she did she couldn't budge.

She looked up again; they were almost out of sight.

As she opened her mouth to call to them again pain shot through her knees as they were forced apart and she fell to the floor.

Her eyes shot open. The room was dark but she could still make out the shape of a man kneeling over her. He had a hold of her knees and he was forcing her legs apart. She opened her mouth to cry out in pain but before she could his hand clapped down over her lips preventing Terra from making any sound at all.

Then, to her absolute horror the man leaned forward and whispered, "Don't worry princess, I won't be gentle."

84

Then he starting kissing her neck and bit her on her left shoulder. Still sensitive from the fight with the shadow the bite seemed to burn her skin. Terra cried out again and began to thrash desperately trying to escape. She could feel something hard jammed in her thigh and it was starting to scare the hell out of her.

As the man steadily made his way down her neck to her shoulder and then the top of her exposed breast, Terra's mind began to grow fuzzy. She knew what was going to happen. She knew what this man wanted from her. She didn't know who he was or how he had gotten in, but she knew exactly what he was there for.

Without her knowing it, her hands came up and tried to protect her, but he easily thwarted her week attempts at defense.

Her vision was starting to go dark as the man straightened above her. She knew what was coming and she knew there was nothing she could do stop him. Part of her mind wondered if this was some kind of punishment sent by the Creator. Perhaps this was what she deserved for her betrayal of her family.

There was a small voice in the back of her mind that demanded she do something. Fight, move struggle, anything. It demanded she take action.

Her vision was almost completely blurred. Soon she wouldn't be able to see at all. Maybe though, that was for the best. She didn't need to see what was coming next.

A sudden new presence in the room pulled Terra out of her haze. She wasn't sure who else was here, but without a doubt there was someone else in the room.

"T . . . Terra," a familiar voice whispered from somewhere far away. But who was this voice, why was it so familiar?

Like a bolt of lightning Terra knew it was Eric. It was so dark in the room she couldn't see to confirm it was him. Still, she was sure she could feel him now. She could sense his aura somewhere near the foot of the bed. As far as she could tell he wasn't moving.

Confused for a moment she racked her mind trying to understand why he wasn't helping her. Couldn't he see the man on top of her? Didn't he see what he was going to do? What made him hesitate?

'*It's too dark,*' Terra thought, '*It's too dark and he can't tell what's really going on. Light! I need light!*' Suddenly she was engulfed by purple and silver flames. It was like her aura had caught fire and was burning around her. She was on fire.

Richard pulled back. He had had his fun and was ready go on. He would have greatly enjoyed spending a little more time playing at their game, but he knew he couldn't delay too long in a royal bed chamber. He reached down and began to fumble with her dress.

She continued to struggle under him and yell, but the blood was pumping in his ears so hard he couldn't hear her even if he moved his hand.

Suddenly he was surrounded by fire, strange purple and silver fire. Her entire body seemed to be made of it. It jumped suddenly from her to him. Being completely naked there was nothing to protect him, nothing to shield him from the intense heat of the flames that snaked up his body.

'*Diana,*' he thought, '*why?!*'

Capt. Reynolds wanted to run from the room. He had completely misjudged Terra and now he was face to face with his foolishness. She was with a man in her room. That was why the door was locked and no one had seen her all day. She'd been locked up here with him.

A blinding purple light coming from the bed cleared all thought from his mind as he stared at Terra, on fire. Not just any fire but strange purple and silver fire seemed to engulf her entire person. It was as if she was made of the fire and it was a part of her.

With the room suddenly cast in light Capt. Reynolds could see the man holding his hand over Terra's face, he could see the fear and horror in her eyes at what was happening. He had been wrong. She wasn't locked in the embrace of a lover; she was trapped in the arms of a rapist.

Eric's vision went red. All thoughts of arresting this man and bringing him to justice flew from his mind, replaced by a red seething rage. He wanted, no, he needed to hurt this man to break him. He wanted to wrap his hands around his neck and squeeze until the life ran out of him.

Before he had time to think he was running across the room toward the bed. He charged the man, with a massive shove the Captain pushed him from the bed and sent the man tumbling to the floor. Eric got to his feet, on the bed, and leered down at the man. Once he was no longer in contact with Terra, the flames on his body vanished and he lay on the floor, naked and burnt.

"Eric!" Terra cried out from the bed.

Ignoring the princess he jumped from the bed and pulled his sword from its scabbard. He raised his sword over the man who cowered in a ball at the sight of the enraged Captain of the Guard. He looked up and it seemed to Eric he was trying to say something. His lips were moving but there was no sound coming out. It was as if Eric had gone deaf.

Not caring what trick this animal was up too, Eric raised his sword to finish him off.

Terra watched as Eric jumped from the bed after the man who had been attacking her. Taking deep breaths the princess tried to calm herself, hoping that once she was calm the flames would subside. Try as she might she couldn't get the flames to go out.

Assuming you could call them flames. It was more like her aura had taken on the likeness of fire. She was in no danger and her bed didn't seem to be caching either. Even Eric when he had stood on the bed didn't seem to be burnt. It was only her attacker that took any damage.

Turning she saw Eric illuminated in the strange purple light raising his sword over the man. His usually gentle aura was tainted with rage. He was going to kill that man if she didn't stop him. There was no way to know who the man was or why he came to her room if he was dead. Terra needed answers and she couldn't condone the taking of a life. Even if it may be deserved. She had to stop him.

Knowing words wouldn't reach him while he was filled with rage she rolled off the bed and ran for him, she just had to touch him, the heat from her aura would clear away the rage that clouded his mind. She knew she just had to get there.

"Eric wait! Don't kill him!"

With deadly precision the Captain of the Guard brought his weapon down, severing head from body. Blood shot out from the newly exposed arteries drenching the captain in hot red blood that matched his rageful aura.

Terra screamed as Eric beheaded the man on floor. She looked up as blood came flying at her, the fire of her aura flared burning up the blood before it ever got close.

Most of it anyway.

A small drop, no bigger than the top of a thimble, flew past her aura and landed on her cheek. Disbelievingly she reached up and touched the blood on her face. Pulling her hand back she looked at the now bloody tip of her finger.

"Eric," she said, falling to her knees. When she hit the floor the smell of blood hit her like a toxic wave of smoke rising up to choke her. Her aura went out suddenly and she turned to the side and vomited until her stomach was empty. Exhausted and nauseas she collapsed on the floor.

Eric stood, his sword still stuck in the dead man's shoulder. A sound from behind drew his attention. Turing he saw the fire around Terra brighten and then fade completely as she fell to the floor. He tried to help her but it felt like his muscles were made of stone. The princess turned and threw up before falling backwards into the growing puddle of blood and passing out.

When he could finally move, Eric dropped his sword and fell to his knees next to the princess. He laid his hand carefully on her cheek. Her skin was hot but she was breathing. With a sigh of relief he carefully lifted her out of the pool of blood. As he had feared her entire left side was completely soaked. From the top of her face down to her bare feet, Terra was covered in blood.

A million questions raced through his mind. Who was that man? How did he know about the secret door in Terra's room? Why? Why would he attack Terra? She was one of the kindest souls he'd ever known. He couldn't fathom why anyone would want to hurt such a girl.

Regardless, the princess had been attacked. He had stopped the attacker and now he would have to find the King and report what had happened to his youngest daughter. He wasn't sure how he would explain to the King, and especially the Queen, why he checked Terra's room. Should he tell them the door was locked or leave that out. He had promised the princess not to tell anyone about the tunnels but after all that had happened tonight; he was beginning to think that was a promise he would have to break.

How would he explain his knowledge not just of the tunnels but of the door to Terra's room? He could just leave out the fact that the door was locked. But to him that felt dangerously like lying to his King. Something he was not alright with doing. How could he tell the King about the passage without telling him about last night?

Things were starting to get very complicated for the young Captain of the Guard.

Knowing that standing around wasn't going to help anything; he lifted the princess in his arms and kicked the door open.

The journey from the Princesses room to the throne room felt as though it took a lifetime to complete. Capt. Reynolds held the limp princess in his arms as he carefully crossed the castle. He couldn't imagine what they must have looked like to the people they passed in the corridors and hallways.

Both of them were covered in blood, the princess especially since she had passed out in it. He was sure there were leaving a trail of blood across the castle, but that mattered very little to him. He had saved the princess from certain shame and possible death at the hands of that unknown monster. Whatever repercussions came from that he would bear it with a light heart, knowing he had ultimately done his duty.

"C . . . Captain?" A voice behind him called.

Not halting he glanced over his shoulder to see one of his men standing behind him. He wasn't certain of the man's name. He was newer if Capt. Reynolds recalled correctly. John something maybe.

Seeing that the captain wasn't stopping, the man ran to catch up to him. "Sir," he said saluting as he came to walk alongside him. "Sir what happened? Is the princess alright? Do you require any help sir?" The man reached up to help with the weight of the unconscious princess.

A fraction of an inch before he touched her the Captain said, "Don't touch her. Run ahead and tell the King and Queen we're coming. Fetch the Master Wizard and insure they send for healers. When you're done with that, take a handful of men and post outside Princess Terra's room. We're going to need answers."

"Yes sir!" the man shouted saluting again. He took off running across the main hall toward the throne room. At least they would be expected now.

By the time they reached the large ornate doors that lead to the throne room, word had reached nearly every ear around that the Captain of the Guard was coming with the princess in hand, covered in blood. Doors flew open as they approached and people rushed out to help them. A few people tried to take the princess from Capt. Reynolds but he refused every offer of help and crossed into the throne room.

Both the King and Queen paced nervously at the head of the room. Neither, it seemed, could handle sitting in their thrones. Master Bell was standing off to the right talking with a small group of people who nodded and looked around as he spoke. A small stretcher had been brought in from the medical wing and was sitting on one of the large ornate tables usually used to hold the gifts of subjects who come to visit the royal family. Mammy was even there. Standing next to the stretcher she cried quietly as she wrung her hands on her apron nervously.

As they entered every face rose from their various tasks to take in the sight of the Princess and the Captain. For a moment no one moved, everyone too shocked by the sight of them to think. It was Mammy who rushed forward first. Tears streaming down her face at the sight of Terra. She ran forward and, careful not to touch either the Captain or the Princess, led them to the table where he could lay Terra down.

Eric stopped in front of the stretcher. He needed to lay the princess down so the healers could ascertain if she was just passed out or something worse. When he went to pull her away from his chest, he found he couldn't move his arms. He could no more release her than he could wriggle his fingers. His arms were completely locked.

"Captain," Mammy said, tears streaking her ageing face. "You can give her to me. We'll take care of her now."

"I . . . I can't," he said. "I can't let her go. My arms are locked."

"Not locked," the Master Wizard said as he came over. "It's the princess. She's been traumatized and her aura has latched onto yours for strength."

"She can do that passed out?" Mammy asked disbelievingly.

"It would appear so," Master Bell replied. "Give me just a moment and I'll free your arms up." The wizard reached out to place a hand on both Terra and Eric's shoulders. Before he could touch them, however, his hands were zapped and forced back.

"Eh?!" Master Bell said in shock and pain.

91

"What's going on?!" The King demanded as he approached. "What happened here Captain?! Explain yourself!"

"Just a moment your Majesty," Master Bell said circling the two. "Captain," he said quietly behind the young man. "You must let her go."

"I can't," Eric whispered, hanging his head in shame.

"You have to. Your aura is clinging to hers as tightly as hers is to yours. You must release her so we can help her."

He didn't understand what the wizard meant but he knew Terra needed to help. Sighing to himself he held her tight for a moment and whispered, "I promise I won't be far." Then with a sound similar to static, Eric laid the princess on the stretcher.

Once she was out of his arms he felt like collapsing himself.

"Stay with us now Captain," Master Bell said grabbing the young man under the arm. "You're all right now." Where the Wizards hand touched his arm, Eric felt a kind of warmth spread through his body. He felt strong enough to stand and face the King and Queen again. He knew it was some kind of magic, and he was grateful to the Master Wizard for his help.

Healer, Mammy, and Master Bell turned to Terra and began to work.

"My poor baby," the King muttered as he watched them. "Tell me Captain, what has happened this night."

Capt. Reynolds turned to the King, still unsure of what to say. "Majesty," he said bowing with his fist over his heart. "The Princess was attacked in her room. When I entered the room was dark and there was a man naked and top of her, preparing to take the princess by force. I forced the man from the bed and ensured he would never threaten the Princess again." The Captain felt sick to his stomach. He knew he was omitting large sections of the story he told the King. He hated to do it but right now he need the concern to be on Terra and not on what was going on between them. As soon as he could he would explain everything to King Sol.

"Meaning what?" The King asked.

"Beheaded, sir."

King Sol took a deep breath and nodded. "Captain Reynolds, please accept my deepest and most humble thanks for the service you have done my family this night. Thanks to your actions my daughter is safe. I thank you sir."

Before Eric could graciously accept the King's thanks, the Queen circled back around in her pacing and said, "How did you get into her room?"

"Majesty?" Capt. Reynolds asked, feigning confusion to buy time.

"If there was a man in my daughter's room attempting to rape her, as you say. Why didn't he react when you came through the door? From her the bed the door is clearly visible, not to mention the light that would have come in from the hall when the door opened."

"I . . .," Capt. Reynolds started.

"My King," Master Bell called, "The Princess is waking." Both King Sol and Captain Reynolds were at the princess's side before her eyes had even opened.

"Terra, baby," the King said, slipping his hand under her neck and helping her get up into a sitting position.

"P . . . papa?" She asked her eyes still closed.

When Terra was very small her mother often left her with Mammy or another nurse. Being such an active and curious child, she would often chase after her mother. Sadly the Queen would always have other things to do. Many times the King would be coming or going and see the princess crying chasing her mother. Hating to see her cry, he would scoop her up and rock her in his arms. He would tell her he loved her and that papa was there for her.

Papa was her special name for him. It always warmed his heart when she would call him that.

"Papa is here," he soothed. He brushed the hair away from her face and her eyes fluttered open.

"Papa!" Terra cried out when she was him. "Oh Papa." She threw her arms around the king's neck.

"There, there my little princess, Papa is here."

After a moment Terra pulled away. She was still covered in blood and she would feel terrible if she got any on her father.

She looked down at herself. Her new dress was caked with dried blood all down the left side. Even her hand was covered in blood. Reaching up Terra could feel blood on her face and in her hair. Her stomach turned over and she felt like she might be sick again.

"Princess," Capt. Reynolds said stepping forward. He could see her face go pale under the blood and knew she was going to be sick. Without thinking he stepped past the King and put a hand on her shoulder. He helped her turn and throw up over the side. He held her shoulders until she was done and then helped her sit up straight again.

"Captain?" The King grumbled with something similar to anger with a dash of defense in his voice.

Freezing, Capt. Reynolds suddenly realized what he had done. He had stepped up past the King to place his hands on the princess like it was his right to do so. He was still standing there, holding the princess while the King probably stood behind him plotting his execution.

"Majesty, if I may," Master Bell interjected.

"If you may what?" He asked, sounding angrier by the second.

"It would appear that the Princess and the Captain have bonded," The Wizard said, as thought it was the simplest thing in the world.

"Bonded!?" The King demanded.

Capt. Reynolds and Terra both turned to face the Master Wizard, like much of the room they were confused about what Master Bell was saying. Although most everyone else was more interested to see what was going to happen between Reynolds and the King.

"Yes, bonded. Princess Terra has been through a terrible ordeal this evening. Through everything she seemed to have expelled all her energy. When that happened her aura reached out to someone she could trust, someone she knew could protect her. That someone was Captain Reynolds."

Terra looked to Eric and he looked to her. For a moment their eyes locked and an unspoken feeling of gratitude passed between them.

"I don't understand," Capt. Reynolds asked, turning away from Terra. "I don't know much about magic."

"It means that tonight you may have saved the princess's life twice. When her aura reached out to yours not only did yours accept it, but it grabbed hold of hers too. You shared energy and your souls connected. The two of you are now bonded."

"For how long?" The Queen asked, finally showing interest in her younger daughter. "How long will they be bonded this way?"

"That's hard to say," Master Bell said, folding his arms into his long sleeves. "It could be hours it could be forever. Only time will tell."

"How will we know?" Terra asked. "How will we know when the bond is broken?"

"It's hard to describe. For most people it's similar to the feeling of static shock. Others say it feels more like being hit by a bolt of lightning. But you'll know. No matter the sensation, you'll know when it breaks."

"And until then," the King demanded, "what happens between the two of them until it breaks?"

"With a connection like this the Captain will always know where the princess is and whether she's in danger or not. If she feels fear or anger he'll feel it and vice versa. In truth Majesty, for the time being Captain Reynolds would make and excellent personal guard for the princess. At least until we ascertain who attacked young Terra tonight and why."

"Thank you Master Wizard," the King said looking pensive. "I'll take that under advisement."

Terra looked back to Capt. Reynolds. He was looking down at her with concerned eyes. Giving her shoulder and hand one last squeeze, he released her and stepped back out of respect and a little bit out of fear for the King.

Like an arrow through her heart Terra suddenly felt an incredibly evil presence. Jumping off the table she turned and fell into step beside Master Bell. Both faced the door with arms raised and auras up. Before anyone could react to Bell and Terra, the huge, and exceptionally heavy, double doors slammed closed with an earsplitting boom.

Chapter 3

Seconds after the doors closed a small hoard of shadows shot up out of the floor forming a seething black wall of evil blocking the only visible exit. People started screaming and running around. Terra and Bell stood their ground. Without having to look up, she sensed when Eric was at her side. In seconds the other soldiers in the room had flanked their positions and put the king and queen behind them.

"Terra," King Sol called.

"Majesty," Capt. Reynolds called, "stay behind the soldiers and keep your eyes closed."

King Sol, too shocked to argue, did as his Captain of the Guard asked and pulled his wife behind him and closed his eyes.

There were at least twenty to twenty-five shadows blocking the door. Each of them had their eyes closed. Not slits or bulging. Closed. It made it difficult to tell where the eyes were at all. Terra scanned each shadow waiting for movement, looking for any sign of which might attack first. When nothing happened and none of them moved, she took a deep breath and sent her aura out, trying to sense the intent of the monsters before her.

Surprised to find it still surrounding her, and not behind the door as it should have been. She made a note to ask Bell as soon as things calmed down.

As soon as her aura ventured from her body the shadows seemed to zero in her. Every set of silver eyes bulged as their heads turned to face her. It felt like their eyes were boring into her soul. She could feel it then, the same evil aura as the man downstairs. They had been sent by him.

"Hello again Princess," A voice rang out. Terra kept her eyes focused on the shadows but she could see most everyone else looking to find the source of the sound.

"Who is that," Eric asked, glancing at her out of the corner of his eye.

"It's him," Terra said, her voice shaking slightly, "It's the Shadow King. I'd know that voice anywhere."

"Indeed. It is me."

A shadow in middle of the group seemed to shimmer and in a moment the Shadow King stood before them. He was mostly transparent and at times the image of him seemed to waver.

He looked just like he did the first time Terra saw him in his cell. He was standing with his hands on his hips smirking evilly as he scanned the room. When his eyes came to Terra he held them there. He seemed fixated on her. Maybe it was her imagination, but he seemed to *only* be staring at her.

"Well, well, well. What have we here? Looks like the whole royal family all in one place. Makes delivering a message so much easier."

"How are you doing this monster?!" The King called moving forward. He stepped up next Master Bell but was careful not to put himself farther forward than the wizard. "You're locked away beneath our feet. How can you appear here?"

"Your Majesty," the Shadow King said, bowing mockingly to the King. "You are correct. I am still locked safe and sound underground, just as you said. But the funny thing about taking a powerful being and locking them away in a box is that with as much power as I have, there's going to being some lingering wisps for a while.

"Lingering wisps like this?" The King demanded.

"What do you want monster!?" Capt. Reynolds demanded sensing the rising fear not just in the room in general but more specifically in Terra.

"I want to make a deal of course."

"A deal," the Queen laughed. "What deal would we possibly make with the likes of you?"

Looking slightly annoyed at the Queens demeaning tone, he said, "Well I just thought you'd want your eldest daughter back."

"What did you say?" Queen Elise demanded.

"Your eldest, goes by the name Diana, tall, golden hair, eyes blue like the sky, real spitfire. That eldest. Surely you've notice she's missing by now. Ah so you have. Oh my, you've had quite an

98

interesting evening haven't you Terra?" He purposely dropped her title and flashed her an overly intimate smile. Terra shuddered and looked away. Not sure she'd be able to keep from getting sick again.

"I'm assuming the owner of the blood you're wearing is dead now? He was killed by our young captain here and in front of your own eyes. How terrible for you. What was his crime I wonder?

"Attempted rape?" He laughed and slapped his thigh, "An actual rapist running rampant in the castle? What kind of place are you running around here Sol? Do you have any security at all?"

"So you can indeed read minds it would seem," Master Bell observed.

"Indeed I can Master Wizard, although your nut's a little tougher to crack." The King of the Shadows spoke to Master Bell, but his eyes never left Terra.

"Where is my daughter you bastard?!" Queen Elise yelled, tears streaming from her face.

"Oh she's safe and sound. If you want her back I suggest you come pay me a little visit in person. Oh and make sure you bring the princess and the Wizard. You may have need of them."

Before another word could be spoken The King of the Shadows wavered before their eyes and disappeared. Seconds later his wall of shadows followed his example and they were gone. Silence followed in their wake as everyone in the room tried to process what just happened. It was Bell who spoke up first.

"King Sol," he said, "we must go."

"You can't be serious," the Queen shouted, outraged. "Why would we do anything that . . . that creature said?"

"If he is telling the truth and he has your daughter, we may be running out of time." Bell replied calmly

"Time for what?" Terra asked.

"Time to save Diana."

As rapidly as it could be done, the King, Queen, Terra, Bell, Reynolds, and a small army of the Kings personal guard were hurrying

99

to the basement door. Everyone was under strict orders to only allow the King or Master Bell to speak to the prisoner. Reynolds would stay outside the last set of doors with Terra and the Guards. They would be called in if needed.

When they got to the last set of doors the King turned to his daughter before heading in.

"Stay out here and be safe," he said. "We'll get you sister back if indeed this monster has her."

"Papa," Terra whispered, "are you sure this is wise? That . . . monster is evil. He's the most evil thing I've ever felt."

Smiling at his daughter the King placed his hand on her shoulder. "We'll be fine. Soon will have you both safe and sound and we can get you into a bath."

"Alright," she nodded, still unsure. "But please be careful."

"We will. Captain Reynolds," King Sol called, turning from his daughter. "I am leaving Terra in your care. I can't say I understand what has transpired between the two of you, but I will find out. For now I expect you to use that bond you have to keep her safe."

"I will my King," Capt. Reynolds replied.

With that the King led the small party of three into the inner prison. Terra sank into one of the wooden chairs up against the wall and put her head in her hands. For a moment she thought she might be sick. As she bent and sat her dress creased and blood flaked off. Knowing it wasn't the time to be ill she decided to instead send up a silent prayer to the creator to keep her sister safe.

She knew that the monster in the next room would most likely make outrageous demands of the King and Queen which they would have to deny. Terra worried that their denial of those demands would end up being the death of her sister. She assumed they would be in there most of the night arguing. So she leaned her head back against the cool wall and prepared to settle in for a while.

It was no more than ten seconds later that the door opened again and Master Bell stepped out. "Princess, Captain we need you, please hurry."

100

Terra shot out of the chair and was running past Bell before Capt. Reynolds could even process the request. Once in the room she stopped short. Her father was standing near the glass prison holding her mother who had dissolved into manic sobs. The Shadow King was leaning against the wall of his cell staring at the King and Queen with his evil smirk on his face. The floor seemed to be covered in a thick black smoke that swirled around the ankles of all who stood in the prison.

Next to the cell there was another, smaller, wall of shadows. This time there was a transparent image of Diana.

She was lying on the floor not moving. Only the slow, steady rise and fall of her chest gave any sign that she was alive. There was a small gash on her forehead and a scratch or two on her arm. For the most part she seemed unharmed.

As Terra stood and watched, the image of Diana wavered and nearly disappeared twice. Each time it happened she felt an over whelming sense of dread. She couldn't tell where her sister was and if this image of her was current or somehow manipulated to make them think she wasn't dead.

Terra could feel her knees suddenly go weak at the thought of her sister being dead. It seemed like she couldn't get enough air.

A hand at her elbow helped her stay standing upright. A sudden rush of strength and energy flowed into her from the contact at her elbow. Without needing to look up she knew it was Eric. He had felt her sudden weakness and come rushing to her side. She couldn't put into words how grateful she was for his support.

"Terra," he whispered to her as he helped make her way to her parents, "you can do this. Your family needs you and I'm here for you, whatever you need. Just breathe."

Terra straightened up and looped her arm through the Captains. She felt stronger just having him nearby, but by her mother's reaction, she might need more of his strength then she yet knew. She would be strong for her sister and her parents. It was the least she could do. After all, this was all her fault.

As if he suddenly realized she was there, the Shadow King's eyes focused on the princess and the Captain. "So we're all here then. Good. Let's begin."

"Just give me my daughter," the Queen sobbed from her husband's arms.

"Oh I will, in time. But first I want something's from you."

"No matter what you say I will not release you from this prison," King Sol said firmly. It might have only been Terra, but she felt she could hear her father's voice waver.

"Oh don't worry about that," he said touching the walls of his cell, "I'm perfectly fine where I am. My demands for you aren't about freedom."

For a moment Terra could feel the evil in the room weaken and the image of Diana nearly disappeared. Alarmed, she shot a look to Mater Bell who was on her other side.

Meeting her eye, the wizard nodded ever so slightly. He too felt the evil weaken.

When she looked back to the cell, the Shadow King was staring at her again. His smirk was still there but something seemed off. He didn't seem as confident as he had a moment ago. Not to mention the evil that was suffocating seconds ago now was barely more than a whisper. Even the strange darkness swirling on the floor had nearly dissipated. Something was happening. She just couldn't put her finger on what.

"I get it," she realized quietly, staring back at the monster. "You're power is weakening. The seals and runes are starting to work."

An ugly grimace spread across his once cool and collected face. "Well, well, little shadow. Look at how sharp you are," he hissed bitterly. "I'm afraid young Terra here is correct. The longer I'm in this box the more my power weakens. Soon I'll be unable to call the shadows to bring your darling ray of sunshine home."

"What!?" The Queen demanded as her head flew up out of her husband's embrace. "What do you mean you can't bring her home!?"

"Elise," King Sol said under his breath. "Calm yourself. I'll handle this." Turning back to face the cell he said, "Tell me your demands monster."

"Firstly, this slop you call food is unacceptable. I am a king in more than one right and I will be treated as such. Prisoner or not, I will be treated as my station dictates."

"Your food can be changed. Is that all?" King Sol demanded.

"Oh no," he said smiling. "These meals will be hand delivered by your darling daughters, every meal every day. If I'm to eat in this hole in the ground, I'll require some . . . shall we say *delightful* company."

"No," the Queen shouted, "not my Diana. I won't have you tainting her with your evil. You can't have her."

"I agree with the Queen," Master Bell added, "exposing the princesses to this kind of man three times a day would be more than enough to taint them. Or worse."

"Well that's too bad then," The Shadow King said. He turned to look at the shadows projecting Diana's image. In the blink of an eye she was gone. One by one the shadows followed.

"NO!" The Queen cried out, "Please not her! What about Terra?! We'll give you Terra every day if you want. Just don't take my daughter!" Elise broke down into sobs and the rest of her words became lost and garbled.

Terra felt her mother's words slice through her like a knife and stab her in her heart. She had always known her mother loved Diana more. It was obvious in everything she did and said. Terra understood. Diana was going to save the world from this monster and she needed every advantage she could get. Including most of their mothers love.

To hear her mother so carelessly and callously throw her at this man for the sake of her sister made her feel so small and so unwanted. She thought for a moment she might actually fade away to nothing the same as her sister's image had. Perhaps that would even be best.

Capt. Reynolds wrapped his arm around Terra's shoulders and laced the fingers of his other hand through hers. He knew that he was overstepping his boundaries with the young princess by miles, but he could feel the heart in her chest break at her mother's words. She needed him and he was happy to do all he could for her. Maybe it was the bond they were sharing, maybe it was something else, but Eric Reynolds was not going to allow this girl to suffer if he could help it.

King Sol glanced to his young daughter and could tell by look on her face just how much her mother had just hurt her. As he watched, Capt. Reynolds grabbed her hand and held her. He wasn't sure he was happy about how familiar the Captain seemed with his daughter, but at that moment he was glad she wasn't suffering alone.

"I suppose one Princess is better than none," The Shadow King muttered contemplating. "I accept your counter offer."

"Majesty I must object," Master Bell blurted. "Terra is young and this man radiates evil the same way the sun radiates light. Exposing her to that three times every day would most certainly corrupt the strongest of us, let alone a young girl. If it doesn't corrupt her it will surely kill her."

The man in the box sneered at the wizard. "Now, now wizard, there's no reason to but in when you're not wanted." A twitch of his eye sent a huge wave of something dark at Bell.

The Master Wizard fell to his knees. He began cough and struggle to breath.

"Master Bell!" Terra shouted. She knelt down next to him and went to place her hands on him to try and help. For just a second there was a small shock and a bit of resistance, then it disappeared and her hands fell lightly onto his shoulders. "Are you alright? What can I do?"

"Princess," Bell coughed, sounding better. "Truly amazing."

"What is?" She asked confused.

"That you could resist an evil so strong and purify it. Amazing."

104

"I didn't do anything Master Bell. I just wanted to make sure you were ok."

"I know princess," Bell reassured her, "Thank you for your kindness."

Terra blushed, unsure what to say.

"As touching as all this is, are we making a deal or not?" The Shadow King said, sounding bored.

"I'm afraid I must agree with the Master Wizard. I would not expose any of my daughters so carelessly," King Sol countered.

"Even if it means losing your precious princess forever?"

"No, Henry we can't lose her," Elise begged, pleading with the King. "Not Diana. What about one meal?! Would one meal a day suffice?"

There was an uncomfortable silence all around as everyone considered the Queen's words. As people looked around considering, no one looked at Terra. Even the Master Wizard couldn't look at her. Everyone knew Diana was essential for the survival of not just the kingdom but the world. Would exposing one princess to save another really be so horrible? Could Terra really say no when her sister's life was on the line?

No.

She couldn't put herself above her Diana.

No matter the cost.

She stood silently and faced the monster on the other side of the glass. She met his gaze head on and didn't blink. She knew what she had to do. In a way she was grateful that no one in the room had jumped up and agreed for her. Even though a few of them could have. They were allowing her to make this decision on her own.

She had made it.

Terra would endure this. She had to.

This was her punishment.

This is what she deserved for all the mistakes she'd made today. She stood there, still covered in blood, and faced her future. Until Diana was ready to fight this monster and kill him, Terra would sit here in this dark hole and break bread with him. Even if it meant that every day, little by little, he corrupted her soul. At least Diana would be safe and the world would go on.

"Well, it seems little shadow here has made her own decision," the Shadow King said, the wicked smile on his face spreading from ear to ear. "Why don't you tell them princess?"

Unwavered by his smirking sense of victory, Terra held her head high and her gaze. "I'll do it. I'll do what he asks if it means we get Diana back."

All three men outside the box spoke at once.

King Sol said, "Terra I understand you want help save your sister but I can't ask you to make that kind of sacrifice. But if you're willing . . ."

Master Bell said, "Princess I can't in good conscience let you do this. The risk to your person is too great to be allowed no matter the cost."

Capt. Reynolds said, "NO! Terra you can't!"

Ignoring them all, she kept her eyes locked on the man in the glass box and he kept his eyes on her.

"What meal?" She wasn't shouting, but the room fell silent when she spoke all the same. "I'll need to know when to be down here every day, so what meal will we be sharing?"

"Let's say dinner? Last meal of the day, certainly the most important," he decided smiling. "I choose dinner."

Before anyone could raise an argument Terra said, "Very well. We can start tonight assuming my sister is returned immediately."

"Very well indeed. You'll find your darling princess returned to her room. Safe and sound, no harm done," his smile was wicked and clearly displayed his feelings of victory. "Oh and just so we're clear, the princess and I dine alone or no deal."

Again Terra spoke before anyone else could, "as you wish." She turned to everyone else in the room. "We should go and make sure that Diana is well. She'll need us to be there when she wakes and

I'd like to not be down here anymore. I'll have to be back soon enough."

Everyone moved to her, even Queen Elise. The King put his hand on her shoulder, silently conveying his thanks and his pride at her sacrifice. Queen Elise wrapped her arms around her youngest daughter for the first time Terra could remember. "Thank you," she whispered quietly before quickly letting her go.

Master Bell stepped up to her next. His eyes were full of concern and possibly pride. He pulled her into a hug and whispered in her ear, "Before dinner meet me in the school room. I have something that may help you." Terra nodded slightly before releasing Master Bell.

Taking a deep breath she readied herself for what Eric would say. He walked up to the princess, saluted her as her position dictated he should and walked away.

Not a word.

Hanging her head she sighed. She could feel through her bond with him that he was angry and hurt and possibly betrayed by her choice to dine with this monster every night.

Terra accepted his anger. As she knew she would have to accept many thing before the battle between her sister and this monster was finished. Not sure how she knew it, she was sure that this was only the beginning of the change this man would bring to her life.

"Oh Princess," The Shadow King called as she turned to leave.

"Yes," she replied turning back. To depressed to say much.

"You and that Captain, you've bonded haven't you?"

"Yes."

"How?"

"Don't you already know? Can't you look into my mind and see what's happened? Why bother asking me questions you already know the answer too?" She snapped at him. Normally she wasn't usually so rude, but she hated this man and she felt too drained to be polite to anyone.

"Funny thing, bonded the way you are makes that whole reading your mind thing a little harder. That's why I ask."

Terra stared at this man for a moment. He was being honest with her and not the least bit cocky or arrogant. Not caring enough to figure out why she simply said, "Well, at least there's that." She turned and started walking away.

"Oh and Princess, one more thing."

"Yes?" She asked, not turning to face him.

"You might want to clean yourself up first, you're a bit of a mess."

Feeling her last reserves of strength abandon her. Terra put her hand against the door and whispered, "Very well." She walked through the door and pushed it closed. Everyone had gone from the adjoining room already. Seizing a quick moment of privacy, she sank down to the floor just outside, put her head in her hands and cried.

She wasn't sure how long she sat crying outside the door. She knew at one point she made a note of how private it was down here. There was only the monster in the next room. Even he couldn't bother her since her bond to Eric kept him out of her head. Part of her was glad he was unable to see what she thought, while on the other hand she didn't know if being bonded to the captain of the guard was a good thing.

An image of Eric with his sword raised over head flashed in her mind. He was so full of rage and hate and he never even knew his name. Terra didn't feel sorry for the man who had attacked her. He was a dark man with a twisted aura. What bothered her was how frightening Eric had become. He had resonated hate. It was hard for her to admit, but in that moment, she was more afraid of him than the man he was supposed to be saving her from.

As a child Terra had seen the young captain rise through the ranks and at all of the royal functions she would see him and when he made captain there was a big ceremony where he was introduced to the royal family as the new Captain of the Guard. So she had known him for a while. In all that time she'd never seen anything from him like this. She wasn't sure she could carry on the kind of friendship she had originally thought they could.

After a time the sound of footsteps coming down the stone stairs drew Terra's attention. Looking up she saw Mammy rushing down the stairs flanked by two guards she didn't recognize. Mammy's eyes were filled with tears as she rushed towards her.

"Princess?" She asked, "oh little princess are you alright? What happened?"

"So much, Mammy," Terra said getting to her feet. "It feels like lifetimes have passed since this morning. And . . . I'm afraid the dress you got me is . . . ruined." She wanted to cry again. She wanted to throw herself in Mammy's arms and weep her problems away. There were no more tears. It seemed she had cried them out.

"My dear," Mammy soothed, trying to brush some of the dried blood from the princess's face. "I would rather the dress be in tatters than you be hurt."

Terra nodded and let Mammy start to lead her away from the door and toward the stairs. "He was certainly right. You do need some help, and a bath," Mammy said idly. "But don't you worry we are gonna get you all cleaned up."

"Who told you what Mammy?" Terra asked.

"Captain Reynolds," she replied. "He came into the throne room and said you would be down here and that you would need help. He said that the blood makes you sick so you'll need help bathing. I laughed at him and asked him if he knew who he was talking to. I've known about your weakness to blood from the first time you scraped your knee as a child."

"Eric told you I needed help?" She asked too tired to use his title.

Mammy didn't miss a beat. "Eric told me you were in bad shape and needed help. He said it had to be me because I would know what you need."

"He did?"

"He did."

Diana woke on her bed. For a moment she wasn't sure what had happened, but the room was dark and the last thing she could remember it was only afternoon. She was going somewhere . . . Terra! She was going to find Terra and give her a piece of her mind. She'd gone into the passageways and then . . . and then . . . and then what? What the hell had happened to her?

'*The shadow*,' she thought suddenly.

She had been in the passage outside her room when she felt something behind her. Thinking it was Richard come early, she turned.

It was not Richard.

It was a shadow.

Somehow one had gotten in and it had come after her.

'*It must have known who I was*,' she thought. '*But if it knew who I was, why didn't it kill me? Why am I here?*'

Diana got off the bed and walked to the window. She pulled the curtains back and looked around outside. There were people everywhere. Groups of soldiers were running around in organized lines combing through the streets. There was even common people running around with lanterns and torches. It felt like everyone was in a frenzy.

Diana laughed. She could tell they were looking for her.

Fools.

Let them go crazy looking. She was going to find Terra and lay into her before anyone could think to look in her room. Treading carefully she made her way to the passage and closed the secret door tight behind her. If anyone went looking for her they would find her room empty. Let them keeping looking for her everywhere. She enjoyed thinking about everyone thinking about her.

Heading down the passage Diana could see that Terra's door was open. She must have just gone back to her room and forgotten to close the door. It was a perfect opportunity for her to get in unheard and strike some fear into her sister's heart.

Diana leapt through the door and passed the tapestry that acted as a cover for the secret entrance to her sister's room. The room was empty and only a single candle burned on her writing table. At once she was overcome by the smell of blood and death. There was a pile of clothes on the floor in front of her. Diana kicked them with the toe of her shoe. They seemed oddly familiar, but she couldn't place them.

Scanning the rest of the floor she found the source of the smell. She walked up alongside the bed and found the body of a man, naked and burned on the floor with his head removed. Surrounding the body was a puddle of blood so large she wondered for a moment if perhaps two people had been injured here. She walked all the way up and nudged the head on the floor. It rolled around and Diana found herself face to face with Richard.

"You idiot," Diana scoffed. "You went too far down! How could you possible miss-count the doors? And at this hour?! You're lucky it wasn't my hands that found you."

She kicked his head across the room and continued looking around. There were two spots where there was no blood, where the blood must have hit something or someone. On the floor next to the body was a pile of vomit. Diana knew it must have been Terra. She was so weak. She could barely handle a bloody nose. This much blood must have almost killed her.

She smiled at the thought.

She deserved at least this. Traipsing about in her trashy new dress and flaunting how much their father loved her and then daring to sit at a place of higher honor then her. It was a shame she didn't have to go through more.

Diana had to go through so much. People were always demanding things of her. Asking her to save the world and kill all of these shadow monsters. People didn't understand how hard it is to be the first born in a royal family *and* the savior of mankind. So many demands, so many people constantly on her about the things she did. People just don't understand.

111

It was all Diana could hope for that Terra might have gotten hurt. Then she would understand how much it hurt her to see her sisters placed above her. She was first born and the princess from the prophecy. All she wanted was to be treated with the level of respect her position afforded her.

Deciding there was very little to do here. Diana walked back across the room, kicking Richards head again as she went. She was sure someone would wise up and come looking in her room.

She paused at the hidden door and turned back to the pile of clothes on the floor near her. She knelt down and rifled through them until she found what she was looking for. The small scroll Lord Howe insisted his son carry with him. If it was discovered in the clothes then Richard would be identified and that would raise too many questions.

Questions Diana couldn't have coming back to her. She pulled the scroll and, after thinking better of it, she laid her hand on the clothing and lit it on fire. Once the flames had engulfed the material she tossed the scroll on the blaze.

Satisfied the clothing and scroll was beyond recognition, Diana put the fire out and left.

Eric stood on the side of the castle next to the kitchen doors. It was the same place he had seen Terra in tears, looking like a woman for the first time. He had been so overcome when he'd seen her. From the time he enlisted he had always known who the princess was. It was only since last night that he had gotten to know her on a personal level. Sure in a sense everyone who worked at the castle knew about the princesses and their general attitude and behaviors. But nothing personal.

Last night he had stood right where he was standing now and seen this young girl in a new light. More than that, there was something about that light that had drawn him in. Much the same way he was drawn to fireflies as a child, he was drawn to her now.

He knew it was wrong. He knew she was young and royal and special, while he was none of those things. In his heart he knew he would never act on those feelings. Not now anyway. When she was older and able to make her own decisions things could be different. He might be a general by then. Possibly even a landowner. Maybe then . . .

No.

He would be lucky if by then there was anything left of the princess he was drawn too. Tonight she had made the choice to dine with the enemy. Not just tonight, but every night until her sister could finally put an end to his evil. However, according to the Master Wizard, by then the evil that he resonates might have completely corrupted Terra. Leaving nothing left. It might even be possible that when the final battle goes down they're on opposite sides.

Eric decided then. No matter what he felt or thought he felt for Terra, he would never let himself be with her the way he had been today. He would respect her as the princess and keep a respectable distance from her. That was only thing he could think to do. Certainly the only way he would keep from going insane at the thought of that monster getting his hooks into her.

No matter what it cost, or what he had to do, he would no longer allow himself to be around her.

"Captain," a solider said coming up and saluting Eric. "The King is looking for you."

He nodded and followed the man back into the castle.

All the kitchen staff had returned and was busy preparing a late dinner for the castle. Eric looked at the food and felt his stomach turn when he realized that Terra would be sharing that meal with the so called King of Shadows.

Shaking off such thoughts, he followed the solider as he wound his way up the stairs to the Kings chamber. Saluting him one more time the solider informed Eric that the King was waiting in his presence chamber for him.

Returning the salute, Eric thanked the man and went in.

King Sol stood in front of his large fireplace, leaning heavily on the mantel, staring at the flames. He had a glass of something brown in his hand and fresh decanter of the same liquid sitting on a polished silver tray nearby. His shoulders were slumped and by the way his head hung the young captain could tell the King was nearing exhaustion.

"Your Majesty," Eric said, saluting the King. "You summoned me?"

"I did Captain. Please, close the door."

Eric pushed the heavy door closed and turned back to the King. He had turned to face Eric and the captain could see the dark circles under his eyes. It was clearly taking all the strength he had to stand before him now.

"Today has been one of the most trying days in all my years," King Sol said being frank. "However, my father always taught me that it is through struggle and hard times that you see who is truly faithful and who simply wears the mask."

Eric nodded, keeping silent.

"Today, at every turn, you were there for my Terra, for my little princess. Even when I, as her father and her King, could not be. Captain I don't need to tell you how dear my youngest daughter is to me."

"No Majesty."

"Then you understand why the deal that was struck tonight pains me in a way only a father could truly understand."

"I understand that this decision has hurt many people. But no I do not understand the pain of a father as I am not one."

"You will be one day," the King said, "It's the most wonderful and terrifying experience a man can ever have. That aside, Terra is going into a very dangerous place, and there is very little I can do to help her."

"I know Majesty. It is an untenable situation."

"That it is Captain. But this is why I have called you here. As I told Master Bell earlier, I do not pretend to know what kind of magic has passed between you and Terra. Certainly I do not understand the nature of your bond with her."

Eric lowered his gaze. His bond with the princess was confusing for everyone involved.

"But it seems to me that a well-trained guard who can instinctively feel when my daughter is in danger might be the best thing for her. It isn't much, but it is all I can do." He met Eric's gaze and the tears the King was holding were threatening to break loose. "So Captain Eric Nathan Reynolds, I, your King, grant you the honor of becoming my daughter Terra's personal guard. Will you accept this duty?"

Eric felt his heart soar while simultaneously sink. He needed to stay away from Terra, not be around her every minute of every day. On the other hand, if he was with her every day he could use his bond with her to keep her pure and chase away the darkness and shadows that monster would certainly set in her mind.

"Take a moment to decide if you need it," King Sol offered, seeing the perplexed look on Eric's face.

He nodded his thanks to the King, even though he knew the King was not a man to be kept waiting.

Being a personal guard for a royal family member was at least two ranks above his current standing, he realized. Still, this wasn't about ranks or money or power. Eric had promised himself he would stay away. Things got overly complicated when the princess was around.

"Tell me Captain, have you made a decision?"

"I have sir."

Terra had been taken to Mammy's room to be bathed and redressed in something fitting. It had taken nearly an hour for her to really feel like all the blood was off her hands. Even now she was sure she kept seeing spots from the corner of her eye. The dress they had brought in was one of Diana's old ones. It was a lovely Lilac color with dark blue trim. It was a beautiful dress that mammy had altered to fit her.

Between the long bath and the freshly altered dress, Terra knew she should have been happier. However, the knowledge that this lovely dress would only be seen by the Shadow King made her sadder than she could say. Not to mention that Eric had taken off and said nothing to her. She doubted a pretty cut dress would make much difference now.

Still, she had agreed to the terms of her punishment and must adhere to them no matter what. News had come as soon as they had found Diana. In her room just as he said she would be, safe and unharmed. She had told the people who had found her that she remembered nothing from her time with the shadows. Only that she had been terrified the entire time.

With one last glance at her appearance in the looking glass, she headed to the door.

"Terra," Mammy implored, "You don't have to do this. You could just stay."

"No Mammy. As much as it pains me, he held up his end of the bargain, so I must hold up mine. As a princess I must hold the honor of my word above everything else. Besides, if I don't do this, he could take Diana again."

"You said yourself his power outside the box has waned. For all we know he can't touch her." Mammy was pleading now and it hurt Terra's heart to hear the pain in her voice.

"He has before, Mammy and I can't take that risk. I must go." Before she could say anything else, Terra opened the door, stepped into the hall, and pulled the door closed behind her. Leaning against the old wood, she took one last deep breath and started down the hall. She would head down through to the kitchen and then down to the prison.

As she approached her parents room, Terra could hear talking and the sounds of footsteps. She hesitated for a moment, she wasn't sure who was coming out, but she knew she wasn't in the mood to talk. Her father would congratulate her on her bravery; tell her that she was doing her kingdom a great service. Her mother might hug her again and that would be more than she could bear. Diana . . . she didn't really want to see her sister at all.

Standing where she was, there was nowhere to run. As the door started to open, Terra just kept walking. Hoping whoever it was would understand her need to be alone and leave her be.

Eric walked out, right in front of her. She had to stop short to not walk right into him.

They both froze.

Neither would look the other in the eye and neither could think to speak.

Terra looked around, desperately trying to think of something to say. Part of her wanted to throw herself in his arms and ask him to forgive her. She wasn't sure what she did wrong but she didn't want him to be mad. She needed his friendship, now more than ever. On the other hand, he had stormed past her without so much as a goodbye or anything. She could tell thorough the bond that he was mad at her. She didn't do anything wrong. She did the only thing she could think to do.

Then on yet another hand there was the fact that she and Eric had only really known each other for less than twenty-four hours! Felling like this at all seemed ridiculous to her.

Yet she still stood there, feeling like she might die if Eric was still mad at her.

Eric bowed to the King and left. He wasn't even through the door when he nearly ran into Terra.

She had recently bathed and her hair was still slightly damp, though wound up onto her head again. She was in a different dress now, something purple that made her eyes shine.

She was beautiful.

But sad.

She looked so incredibly sad.

He could feel it, through their bond. Feel how sad she was, how hopeless and forlorn things seemed. Eric had been so busy being

117

angry with her and mad about her choices and, if he was being honest, the fact that she didn't' seem to care about what he thought or what her choices made him feel. He hadn't taken time to stop being mad and see what she was feeling.

He was almost overcome by her despair. So much so, he couldn't even speak.

Terra fidgeted nervously as she and Eric continued to stand in silence. Knowing that her duties required her to be elsewhere, she decided she had to go.

"Captain," she said quiet and awkwardly.

"Pr . . . princess," he stammered as she started forward.

"Yes?"

Eric hesitated, "I'm not a Captain anymore."

Terra's heart dropped, "Tell me father didn't discharge you because of me?! Because of our bond!?" She felt frantic. She couldn't possibly handle destroying one more person's life tonight. Her heart would stop and she would die.

"No," he said, a smile playing at the corner of his mouth. "He didn't discharge me. I've been promoted."

"Oh," Terra said not sure if that was better. She knew that after Captain of the Guard you became the Guard Major and then a Lieutenant or maybe then it was a Royal Guard. Meaning he would be by her father's side every hour of every day. He would be higher in rank, but she would hardly see him.

Maybe that was for the best though.

"I'm now a Royal Guard." She nodded, it was as she expected. "I'm now *your* Royal Guard."

"I'm sure you'll do a wonderful job protecting my father," she whispered, suddenly finding tears in her eyes. She hung her head and started to move quickly passed him. "I'm happy for you," she lied starting to run.

"Terra?" Eric asked, not understanding anything she had just done or said. He pushed the King's door closed and ran after the princess.

She couldn't take it. She just wanted to get this day over with. Before she could go too far, Eric caught up with her. He ran in front of her, stopped and grabbed her by the shoulders. Before she could react, he had pulled her against him and was holding her. Not the way a friend hugged friend, more like the way one lover held another.

Eric held Terra against his chest and wrapped his arms around her. He put a hand behind her head and just held her. She needed him. He could feel it. She needed someone to hold her and tell her it was all going to be ok. Someone who was going to be on her side and support her, in so many ways she was still a child. Only fifteen and already so much was expected of her. She was becoming a beautiful young woman and she couldn't even see it.

"I said I am *your Royal Guard*," Eric said, putting specific emphasis on the last three words. "Not your mothers guard, not your father's guard, and not your sisters guard. I am your personal guard. My whole job, my whole existence now, is only to protect you."

Terra buried her face in his chest and cried. She tried to say something but between his uniform and her sobs, Eric couldn't understand her. So he just held her close.

"I know I was mad before. But the last twenty-four hours have been to most exciting, difficult, gut-wrenching, and heart lifting I have ever had. I'm sorry I overreacted."

She nodded.

"I'm your guard now. So no matter what, I'll be here for you." He squeezed her tightly one more time. He put his hands on her shoulders and gently pushed her back until she was an arm's length away. "So right now we're going to go down the kitchen, we're going to go get the food for that damn monster, I'm going to walk you down and wait outside the door and when you're done, I'll be waiting to walk you back."

Terra only nodded, not trusting her voice to convey her gratitude.

Taking the Princess by the arm, he led her down to the kitchen.

Eric knew when he took the position he was going back on everything he had promised himself before. He had wanted to stay away; he had wanted nothing more to do with this crazy complicated situation. Unfortunately it seems the Creator had other plans for him. He will be more careful now, though. He will keep distance and he will be professional.

Terra stood at the wooden doors collecting herself. She and Eric had exchanged apologies all the way down to the prison. They even talked briefly about their bond and what they think it means. Eric noted that he would be the best Royal Guard any royal had ever had. He would know in less than a second when something happens to her. Terra noted that it might make things awkward for him and his personal life.

Neither really felt like talking after that.

With one more glance to Eric for support, she pushed against the door, slipped in, and kicked it closed behind her. She walked slowly toward the wooden table that had been placed in there for her and set down the heavy polished silver tray. Eric had carried it most of the way for her and she was very grateful. Fine silver trays like this were heavy enough without an entire dinner for two on them.

Standing next to the table was Master Bell. He had been in the prison overseeing all the preparations that were being made for Terra. He stood tall but she could tell that the darkness swirling around in the room was starting to wear on him. He looked tired and older somehow. Like the dark was enough to age the man.

"Master Bell," she said nodding to the wizard. "Tell me how this works."

"Oh yes, do tell," the Shadow King sneered leaning against the glass with his arms folded. "I'm starving."

"If I had it my way monster, you would starve," Bell replied calmly. "Now Terra this cell is one clearly made of magic."

"You're kidding?" the Shadow King jeered.

"I understand," Terra said ignoring him.

"No magic can enter or exit so long as the glass is unbroken. He *especially* cannot pass through the glass. However, in keeping with your father's wishes, this cell is a humane one."

"How do you mean?"

"There is a way to get food in and out to him without putting anyone in unnecessary risk and without giving him a thrice daily opportunity to escape."

"Alright," she said, "I understand. Tell me what I must do."

"It's very simple," Bell explained. "This cell and all its magic can be set to recognize the aura of one person and one person only. That person would have unrestricted access to the prisoner. They can pass objects in and out of these glass walls at will. But nothing living can ever pass these walls."

"Especially not him, right?" Terra asked, worried that something so evil couldn't really be alive.

"No, not him," Bell confirmed. "The only way he's ever getting out of there is if the glass is completely destroyed. And that is physically impossible."

"Ok then," she sighed feeling relieved.

"All you have to do princess is come in, set your food on the table out here and place the tray with the rest of the food on the table in the corner of his cell. That's it."

"That's not it," the man in the cell chimed in. "Don't leave out the best part Wizard. Tell her how not only does she have to serve me dinner, but she's also practically my maid now too!"

"Maid?" Terra asked confused.

"Oh yes princess, my maid. Tell her wizard!" Despite being imprisoned, the man in the cell seemed to be greatly enjoying himself.

"I'm afraid he isn't mistaken. Once the cell is keyed to your aura, you and only you can add or subtract anything from his cell. Meaning that . . ."

"I understand what it means," she cut in quietly, drawing on her last reserves of strength. "It means that I will be in charge of everything that happens in here. When he is fed, it will be me bringing the food. When his sheets or clothes are to be laundered, it will be me who retrieves them."

"I'm afraid so princess," Bell said sounding genuinely displeased about the situation. "Originally we were going to key it to the aura's of at least three people. Your father, myself, and your sister Diana."

"Why can't you do that now?" She asked.

"Because they messed it up!" The Shadow King all but shouting with enthusiasm. "In their rush to complete this damndable box and throw me in it, they only left a small enough gap for one person. No . . . wait," He said, his demeanor changing instantly. He stalked to the other end of his cell near to wear Bell and Terra stood. He stared intently at Bell for a moment before making a noise under his breath and walking back over to sit on his bed.

"Hurry this up already will you? I'm starving!"

"Master Bell?" Terra asked confused. "What was that about?"

"We may never know child," Bell said. "My time here is growing short so I must show you what you are to do before I go. Here on this pane of glass there is a gap in the runes that bind his magic. I expect this is how he was able to maintain his hold on magic outside for so long."

"How do we fix that then?" She asked.

"We don't, you do. I know you've never been taught to read runes, but these ones here," he indicated to a group of runes that ran up to the gap, "they deal with the limit of magic going to and from the box. Your name goes in the space between the lines. So it will read that only you and your magic can pass to and from the magical barrier."

122

"How do I do that? I don't know how to read or write runes."

A scoffing noise came from inside the box.

"Send out your aura child. When it sees the gap it'll know what to do," Master Bell instructed.

Nodding, she closed her eyes. She felt the magic around her, swirling around her body. At this distance she could also fell the cool breeze that was Master Bell's magic. Taking a breath, she opened the "door" only to once again find it already open. So she sent her magic out again. It brushed past the Master Wizard who took a deep breath as it flowed around him. Then her magic hit the glass box before her like a wave crashing against the rocks on the beach. It flowed up and over the whole of the box until it was completely surrounded by her aura.

"This can't be right?" Came a stunned voice from inside the cell.

Terra ignored him.

In her mind she could see the entire box. Every rune and every etching were clear as day in her mind. While she couldn't read the markings, she did understand their meaning. At last her magic found the empty place in the line of the spell. Without needing to be told, her power set to work.

In moments her name was carved elegantly in runes across the side of the glass.

"You never cease to amaze," Bell commented as Terra opened her eyes. "It would have taken me a better part of an hour to do what you did."

She smiled. "Master . . ." Terra cried out suddenly in pain. Just like before it felt like there were two hearts beating in her chest. She clutched her hands to her chest and sank to her knees.

"Terra!" Master Bell shouted.

Behind her, somewhere, she heard the sound of the door flying open and footsteps running in. Before she was on the ground Eric's arms were around her. He lowered her gently and started shouting at the Master Wizard.

"What the hell is going on Bell!?" Eric shouted. "What's happening to her?!"

"I don't know," Bell stammered, sounding as though he was losing his legendary cool. "This is not supposed to happen. She was to write her name and be done. Nothing more should have happened!"

Terra's head was spinning; she couldn't make the pain stop. Her eyes rolled over the prison and stopped. Lying on the floor, clutching his own chest, was the Shadow King. He had fallen off the bed and was holding his chest the same way Terra was clutching hers. In a moment their eyes met and an unspoken understanding passed between them.

They both felt the same pain.

For a moment there was a voice in her head, a voice that was not hers.

'*You feel it too,*' the voice said.

'*I do,*' she responded.

Then, just as soon as the pain came, it was gone. She could suddenly breathe again. She sat up out of Eric's arms and looked around.

"I'm ok," she said, starting to stand.

"Careful," he cautioned helping her to her feet. "What just happened?"

"I'm not sure," she said, shooting a glance in the cell. The Shadow King was sitting on his bed same as he was before.

'*Did I just imagine that?*' She wondered.

Ever so slightly the so called King shook his head. Before Terra could express some kind of gratitude for his answer, he shot her a disgusted look and scoffing he turned away.

"You must be exhausted," Bell said concerned. "It's been a very trying day for you and writing your name there must have taken the last of your strength."

She only nodded. She didn't want to lie to Bell or Eric, but she couldn't explain to them what had just happened, especially when she didn't know herself.

"Then let's get this over with," Eric said. He led the wobbling princess over to the table and helped her sort through the food. Once the tray ready to be handed off Eric looked at Bell and both nodded.

"If you need me I'll be just outside," Eric said, placing a hand on her shoulder.

"I know," she said smiling, feeling grateful for his concern. "I should be along in a while."

With one last menacing stare at the man in the box, Eric went with Bell out of the room, pulling the door closed behind them.

Wasting no time, Terra rounded on the so called king.

"What was that?" She demanded.

He walked to the glass and sat down on the floor as close to Terra as he could get. "I don't know."

"How do you not know?" She asked. "Wasn't that something you did?"

"No."

"I don't understand then."

"Terra, while you think can I have my food?" He dropped her title again, not evening bothering to ask if she was alright with that level of familiarity.

She eyed the man suspiciously. Seconds before he had been treating her and every other person in the room like they weren't fit to be around him. He even had the gall to call her his maid! Now suddenly he was sitting on the floor and asking nicely for food? Even the darkness of the floor had dissipated.

His sudden turn around made Terra nervous and more than a little suspicious.

"Of course," she said finally. She lifted the tray and walked to the prison. Not sure what to do she moved the tray to the glass. As if there was nothing there, the tray passed through the wall and into the prison.

125

"Impressive Terra, for a princess," he said smirking. He took his tray and pulled it the rest of the way through. Setting it at his feet he began to eat as though he hadn't eaten in years. Mildly disgusted, she walked to the table and began to eat her dinner too.

After a few moments of silently staring at her food as though it might save her, Terra looked up to find the man looking at her. "How's your dinner Terra?" He asked, amused.

Annoyed at his constant and deliberate dropping of her title, she asked, "Since we are going to be dinning together every day for the foreseeable future, may I ask you a question?"

"Of course," he replied intrigued.

"Since you insist on being so familiar and not addressing me with my title as I am do; what am I to call you?"

"What do you mean?" He asked, still smiling.

"I'm assuming you'll want to have conversations while we eat, yes?"

"As lovely as you are to look at, I was hoping for conversation."

"So, since you insist on calling me Terra, what am I to call you? Or would you prefer I call you Shadow King? Or maybe *The* King of the Shadows. It's a little long winded is all."

"Did you know that I was taken from my home as baby?" He said suddenly.

"I . . . well I've heard similar stories. But I can't say I knew that, no."

"I was," he said, "I was only a few days old when the shadows took me from my crib. My mother had had a very difficult delivery and was unable to get out of bed. So my father decided to wait for her to recover and then they would name me together. But I was gone before they had that chance."

Terra sat silent and stunned a piece of bread halfway to her mouth. She had heard stories about when and how the shadows had found him and taken him. Other stories told that he had sought the shadows out, knowing that he belonged with them. To hear that he had been robbed from his cradle while his mother still lay in her delivery bed. It hurt her heart to hear something so sad.

She looked up him, feeling her eyes water. "I'm sorry, I didn't know . . ."

"Don't feel sorry for me." He said simply but firmly. "I don't need or want your pity."

Terra nodded. "If . . . if you don't have a name what do I call you?"

"I'll tell you what," he said, setting the bone of his chicken on the tray. "Since you have been so gracious though this whole thing, and since I don't think you're going to drop the subject anytime soon, you may select a name for me. Any name you chose. And it will be my name, at least between us."

"Any name?" She asked.

"Any name." Pushing the tray aside he stood from the floor and sat in one of the chairs at his table.

She leaned back in her chair and thought. There were a lot of possibilities for a name for a man like this. He wasn't a good man and at first Terra considered naming him something that spoke to that. Then it dawned on her that he was denied the right of being named when he was still a baby, still pure and innocent. She should name him something that spoke to the man and not his nature.

She looked at him for a long time, completely forgetting about the dinner she was supposed to be eating. He was leaning back in his chair, hands behind his head and feet stretched out and before him. He kept his eyes closed and his face turned away from her. Knowing what she knew now, about who and what he was, Terra was still struck by how good looking he was.

He seemed slightly taller now than he had the first time she'd seen him. His face was well cut with a noble brown and strong chin. His dark hair was long, down past his shoulders. Those very broad shoulders looked very well defined, even under his loose shirt. As she watched he turned his head and looked at her.

"Grey," she said.

"Grey? Like the color?"

"Like your eyes," she said. "Your eyes are as grey as the stone our walls are made from. They are by far your most striking feature."

He stood from his chair and walked to the glass. He eyed her suspiciously, not sure how to respond to what she said. "You choose the name Grey then? Not something else?"

"I choose Grey," she confirmed.

"Not monster, or evil or something else to that effect?"

"You gave me the option to choose and I chose Grey. That is what I would like to call you, unless of course you've changed your mind?" Terra could tell what she had said had struck a nerve. She wasn't exactly sure what she had said that set him off, but she was enjoying her small moment of victory.

"Of course I haven't changed my mind. If that is the name you choose, than that's what you'll call me. My name is Grey. Or Lord Grey if you're feeling formal," he added, flashing her his wicked smile.

"Well then, Grey, I'm afraid my dinner has grown cold and I have grown weary. I will take my leave." She stood and walked to the glass. "May I have the tray please?"

Grey stalked away from the glass and flopped down on his bed. "Get it yourself," he said rolling to face the other wall.

Shocked at his sudden childish behavior, Terra threw her hands up in frustration and stalked out of the prison, much the same way Grey had stalked to his bed. She pulled the door open, stepped through and pulled it closed so hard it slammed, sending loud, angry echoes through the prison and the adjoining room.

Eric jumped at the silence of the small room was suddenly shattered by the sound of a slamming door. Recovering, he quickly rushed over from the rut he was cutting in the floor. "What happened? Are you ok? Why do you feel so angry?"

"This is going to be so much harder than I thought," Terra said. Too tired and frustrated to explain. "I really want to go to sleep . . . I can't go to sleep."

Eric was about to ask why when he remembered that her room was still covered in the blood of the man who tried to rape her. He now knew that there was no way she could stand blood at all. Her room would most likely kill her.

"What do I do?" She asked him.

"I'm not sure," he said honestly. "Could you stay with Mammy tonight?"

"I don't know. I guess I could ask."

Mammy was, of course, more than willing to share her bed with Terra and was happy that she wouldn't be spending a night like tonight alone. Eric had wanted to set up another bed in Mammy's room for himself, stating that it was his job to protect her so he should be nearby. Mammy gave him and a stern look and a told him that only improper ladies sleep in a room with a man and she would die before she let the princess be an improper young lady.

Terra had smiled at the sight of the two of them arguing back and forth about her. Mammy so stern and loving, like a mother and Eric over protective like a good soldier. She felt loved. Loved and exhausted. It was time for sleep. She laid her head down and before she knew it she was asleep.

"She's sleeping," Eric said without turning away from Mammy.

Mammy looked over and her face softened. Eric could see the love she had for that child. She was more like her mother than her mother. He was happy that Terra had someone like this in her life. He didn't know what she would face in the next few months, possibly years, but he knew she would need a good deal of help to get through it.

"Alright Mammy," he said, "You win. I won't try to sleep in here. But I do need to be close. It's my job to protect her."

"It's not just *your* job," Mammy said, placing a hand on the young man's shoulder.

"I know."

"Well there's a storage room that connects to this one. It used to be a room for the Kings personal servant, but that was back before the remodel. Now it holds all of the girls' old furniture. There won't be much space but it would be a place to sleep and it would be just a room away from Terra in case she needs you."

"I'll take it," he said nodding.

Mammy wasn't wrong. It was dark dusty and cramped. He pushed a few beds together and was able to make a mostly comfortable place to sleep. After the day he had, he was almost certain he could have slept on rock and still been fine. He laid his head down, closed his eyes, and slept like a man who'd been awake for days.

Grey turned over on his bed, mulling his new name around in his head. He had given the princess and opportunity to choose a name for him, any name. It could have been cruel or worse. He half expected that it would be. Instead she had named him for his eyes. He had never had a proper name. More than that, the entire time the princess was with him, he had scanned her heart over and over again. He could find no darkness. Not even a hint of it.

It wasn't possible.

It wasn't human.

More than that, it annoyed him. There was clearly something wrong with this princess. While he wasn't sure what that something was, he was sure he would find out. Then he would use that oddity to weaken and corrupt her.

Everything was coming together precisely as he had planned. True he had to settle for the shadow princess instead of the one foretold of. Maybe that would prove to be the best. After all he was the Shadow King and she was the Shadow Princes.

Grey stretched out and prepared to sleep. He was starting to think that this Terra would be the key to everything.

Chapter 4

Terra was dreaming, that much she could tell right off. Something about the way the walls seemed to shift around her told her she was asleep.

She was standing in a room that was completely dark except for the pool of moonlight that was spilling in from a window. In the center of the room there was a large ornately carved crib, a crib fit for a king. There was nothing else around that Terra could see, just the crib and the window.

Crying from the crib pulled her attention.

She walked slowly forward, not sure what she would find inside. As she got closer the crying got louder. Terra looked over the edge of the crib and sighed.

Inside was a tiny newborn baby with jet black hair and slate grey eyes. Once the infant saw her he cried louder and louder until Terra reached in and scooped the baby out. She held him in her hands and rocked him slowly back and forth until his crying subsided.

As she continued to rock him she closed her eyes, lulled by the simple rhythm of the movement. When she opened her eyes again she

131

wasn't holding a baby anymore. Now she was slowly dancing with a man. His face was turned away so Terra couldn't see him, but he held her like she expected a lover would. Felling comfort in his arms she closed her eyes again.

This time when she opened them it was Diana in her arms. Only this Diana looked wrong somehow. She seemed dark and tainted. Her face was contorted in an evil glare and even her body radiated hate.

Terra tried to scream and get away, but Diana held her tight, pulling her into an embrace. Closer and closer she laughed. Just before Terra lost sight of everything she heard Diana whisper something. Try as she might she couldn't hear it and before she knew she was completely swallowed up.

Terra's eyes shot open and she sat up in bed like a bolt. She wasn't sure how long she'd been out but it was still dark outside. Mammy slept soundly on the bed beside her, not even seeming to have noticed the princess's sudden waking. A few feet away she heard the sound of a door being opened. Felling Eric before he was there, she was unafraid.

Eric emerged from the dark of the next room, his sword sheathed but still at his side.

"I'm sorry," she said as he approached. "I didn't mean to wake you. It was just a bad dream."

"I know," he said, laying the sword off to the side. He knelt on the ground next Terra and took both her hands in his. "I want you to know that I care about you, "he said brushing stray hair from her face. "I can't stop actually. Terra I think I love you!"

Before she could react or say anything, he leaned forward and kissed her. Wrapping his arms around her, he held her close and kissed her again and again.

Terra's heart was beating in her chest so fast she thought it might burst. She knew she had feelings for Eric but she wasn't sure

132

what they were or how to react to them. All she knew was he was holding her and kissing her and she was kissing him back.

For a moment they melted into each other's arms. When she could finally put enough words together in my mind as to why she needed to stop him, she pulled back to talk to Eric and find out what was going on and did he mean what he said? How did he know he felt that way? What were they going to do if she felt the same? What were they going to do if Mammy woke up?

She realized then that she did love him. She could feel it in her heart; the way it fluttered so fast it was like there was two hearts in her chest. There was something about the way he held her and the way their hearts seemed to beat like one that told her how much she cared. "I think I love you too," she whispered pulling away.

"I'm so glad."

Terra froze. It was not Eric in front of her. It wasn't her Royal Guard whose arms she was in and whose lips she had been kissing.

It was Grey. Kneeling on floor in front of Mammy's bed, arms wrapped around her, eyes shining brightly at her declaration of love; it was Grey.

"Don't worry princess," he said, his face rippling slightly, "I'll protect you for as long as you love me." Suddenly he was a much younger looking man. Before he had seemed in his thirties or early forties, but now, now he looked no older than Eric. His face was softer and his eyes looked less like stone.

His face changed again and he was as she knew him now. Evil. He started to laugh like he was crazy. Throwing his head back and cackling like a madman. Suddenly he wasn't Grey anymore but a shadow. Not just any shadow, but the shadow that had come at her in the west wing with its eyes bulging. It had its arms around her and was pulling her in.

Her skin burned where it touched her and she cried out in pain. She tried to struggle against it but it was too strong and too close. It was going to take her and she was going to die.

She was going to die.

"Terra WAKE UP!" A voice shouted.

She opened her eyes and saw a dark shape standing over her and screamed.

"Terra stop!" The voice shouted, throwing a hand over her mouth. As soon as he touched her she knew it was Eric. Something in their bond made her instinctually recognize his aura on contact. She stopped screaming and lay still so Eric would know she was alright.

"What is it, what's happening?!" Mammy shouted, finally rousing. "Eric Reynolds what do you think you're doing?! I don't care whose guard you are you take your hands off her!" Mammy was out of bed and coming around to shoo Eric away.

He looked down at Terra, she could feel him try to reach through the bond to see if she was ok. Fumbling was more like it, but then Eric had very little experience with magic. She met his gaze and nodded. She was alright. It was then that she discovered he'd come running in wearing just a pair of pants. His chest was completely naked. It was a very nice chest. Terra had never realized just how nice until now. His captain's uniform was fitted but not tight, and the sash he wore across his chest to denote his rank masked most of his definition.

Eric caught her gaze and flushed red making Terra flush an even brighter shade of red.

He stood back and raised his hand, not wanting to give Mammy any more reason to distrust him.

"What in the name of the creator is going on here?" She demanded of the two of them. Terra sat up and swung her legs over the side of bed. She tried to stand but wobbled badly on her feet. Eric reached out to steady her immediately. He put his arms around her shoulders and scanned her face to make sure she was well.

"It was just a dream," Terra explained, head still spinning. "It was just a nightmare."

"Eric Reynolds don't you hold her like that!" Mammy snapped, "She's not properly dressed! Princess you should know better, you're in your dressing gown."

Terra's face flushed red, again. She hadn't thought about the fact that she was in just a thin cotton shift. She had underwear on underneath of course, but that was all. There was only a thin layer of cotton separating their skin. It was suddenly very hot in Mammy's little room.

Mammy herself, wasted no time stepping up between the two of them and helping Terra sit back down on the bed. It didn't help much. She was now overly aware of Eric standing close by, shirtless. She was starting to think she would never get her face back to normal.

Eric let Mammy take Terra and set her on the bed. He didn't think he could move at that point. When he had felt her distress he hadn't thought about the fact that she was sleeping and wouldn't be dressed. He just knew she needed him and he had to be there.

Standing there now, it was all he could do to not openly stare at Terra. She was usually wrapped in yards of fabric like all proper young ladies. When she had come down the stars in that green dress yesterday he had nearly fallen over. It was the first time he'd ever seen her in something figure fitting and something that was cut low enough to reveal her . . . her . . .

Eric glanced over at her again, the shift was loose to be sure, but it must have been made for her when she was younger and not as full chested.

Flushing red from the base of his neck to the roots of his hair, Eric looked away. He was starting to feel things for the young princess that he really shouldn't be feeling about a fifteen year old. Especially one that was now in his charge.

"Well if you ladies are all right I'll return to my room," he said all but running to the door.

"Eric," she said, not looking up from the floor.

"Yes T . . . Princess?" He said correcting himself.

"Thank you."

"You're very welcome." He stepped through the door and pushed it closed. He collapsed on his make shift bed and held the pillow over his mouth. He screamed into it at his unimaginable idiocy. He was acting more like an awkward teenager than a man. It wasn't like he'd never been with a woman. He was nearing his twenty sixth birthday, he'd been with several women already.

It was something about Terra. Maybe it was her innocence and awkwardness that made him feel this way. He really wasn't sure how things worked with this bond of theirs. He knew if he was quiet he could feel what she was feeling. While he slept, he kept getting these flashes and images from Terra. He was sure he was seeing her dreams. He had seen the Shadow King holding her in his dream and seen when he changed to a shadow. As soon as he was able to wake he was in the room waking Terra.

It just timed out that as he woke her she started to scream.

From the other room Eric could hear Mammy talking to Terra.

"I'm sorry Mammy," the young Princess said. "The nightmare had me scared and Eric felt it through the bond. He was just trying to help."

"I know dear," Mammy said, climbing on to the other side of the bed. "But I would be remiss in my duties if I didn't do everything I could to take care of you. Even if it means I have to yell at your Royal Guard." She reached out and placed at hand on her shoulder.

Pain seared through Terra's body.

She screamed and fell forward into her own lap.

The sound of a door being kicked open signaled Eric's arrival.

He was shouting something and Mammy was saying something else. To Terra's ears it all sounded very far away. She bit down on the inside of her cheek, trying to keep from crying as a hot red pain ripped around her shoulders.

"What happened?" He demanded again.

Mammy turned to Eric, pale as a sheet, "I have no idea. I just touched her."

He walked to Terra, careful not to touch her, he knelt down and tilted his head so he could see her. Her face was buried in her knees. Her eyes were shut tight and it looked like she was biting down on her shift.

"Terra I need you to tell me what's wrong. I can't help you if I don't know what's wrong," Eric pleaded trying to keep his panic in check. Taking the chance, he set his hand on her knee.

Through the bond Terra could feel the pain Eric was feeling along with hers. In the back of her mind she was impressed that he could bear so much pain without showing it. When his skin touched hers, however, the hot pain returned, burning away any other thoughts in her mind.

"What happened?" Mammy asked alarmed.

"I don't know," Eric said, nursing his hand. "I touched her and she burned me."

"Are you alright?" Mammy asked.

"Yea, I'm fine, but it's not me that I'm worried about. Mammy, I know it's a lot to ask, but will you please try and touch her. I need to know if it's just me."

"Of course," Mammy said. "Terra, baby, I'm gonna touch you now ok?"

"Please, don't," she pleaded, her voice muffled through her knees and shift. "It hurts so much."

Eric nodded to Mammy to go ahead. She reached out and, with just the tip of her finger, touched Terra on the arm.

She pulled her finger back immediately, cursing under her breath. "Like touching a hot coal," She confirmed with Eric.

Terra had asked them not to touch her and still they had. Her whole body burned. She could feel herself starting to get light headed.

The pain and confusion was more than she could bear. She forced her eyes closed and prayed to anyone who was listening to take the pain away.

'Let it go,' a voice in her head whispered. 'You have to stop holding on to the pain. Let it go.'

'Let what go?' Terra thought frantically.

'The pain, let it go. Let the darkness in. The darkness will make it better.'

'Darkness? What darkness?' It was then Terra could feel it. Just beyond Mammy's window, a sudden feeling of evil. It wasn't close enough to see, but it wasn't so far away that it couldn't be there in a moment.

'Just let it in. The darkness will take away all the pain. No more suffering. Just let it in.'

'No!' She screamed in her head. 'I would rather die than allow that monster to touch me!'

'Too bad,' the voice said, starting to fade. 'It would have been so much easier that way.'

Suddenly the pain was too much to bear. Everything around her went quiet and dark. Her vision started to double and then the world around her faded away.

Diana laid in bed waiting.

It was getting later and later. Soon the castle would be asleep and she could sneak out. Ever since she'd gotten back her father had insisted on their being two guards outside her room at all times. She wasn't to go anywhere without the two of them in tow. Her plans for tonight would be nearly impossible if she didn't do this just right.

She pulled her door open ever so slightly and peeked outside. Both guards were standing at attention. Neither moved nor even blinked it seemed. Diana pushed the door closed and cursed at her bad luck. She had wanted to avoid taking the tunnels. There was no way to get where she wanted to go from the tunnels. It would actually take her further away from her ultimate destination.

Not that Diana would admit it to herself, but she didn't want to go back in the tunnels where she was attacked. Her trip to Terra's room was hard enough as it was. To have to go through the tunnels this late, alone, it wasn't something she really thought she could do.

Diana decided the only way to get out was to trick the guards.

She glanced at herself in the looking glass. She pulled a few strands of hair away from her face and lifted each breast so that they almost fell out of her bodice. She would be more than enough to distract both guards.

She opened her door again, this time all the way.

"Princess," both guards said, falling to a knee saluting her.

"Thank you," she said, signaling them to rise, "I hope you won't find this rude but I'm so hungry."

Both the guards' eyes went wide. Diana was stunning in her tight dress with her extremely low cut bodice. "Hungry princess?" The older one asked.

"Yes," she said starting to whine. "This whole day has been so long. I think I just wasn't feeling well enough to eat. But now . . ."

This time the younger one stepped forward, eyes going up and down the sight of her. "Princess it would be my honor to bring you something to eat."

Diana smiled, she had them. "I'm afraid I'm just so picky I wouldn't know what I wanted unless I could see what was in the kitchen."

Before the younger of the two could speak the older stepped forward. "I would be honored to escort her Majesty to the kitchen."

"Would you?" She asked, bouncing around a little for effect.

He bowed, "It would be my greatest honor."

Diana looked to the younger guard. "Could I ask you to stay and guard my room? I don't think I could sleep tonight if I knew my room wasn't being watched. I'd toss and turn all night thinking that somehow another shadow got in." She trembled slightly, knowing they couldn't resist the thought of a princess in distress.

Looking slightly upset about being left behind, the guard nodded. "I will wait for you here then, majesty."

"No, not here," Diana said. She reached out and grabbed the guard's hand. "What's your name?" She asked, stopping midstride.

"Jack," he stammered, eyes fixed on her hand.

"Ok Jack, in here." She pulled him into the room and dragged him toward the bed. Turing she pushed him onto the bed and "fell" on top of him.

"Oh I'm so sorry," she said, pretending to struggle to get up. "I'm so clumsy today." She struggled a little more, making sure she was rubbing all the right parts against Jack the guard. When she could feel that he was good and hard she carefully got back up.

"I'm so sorry. I need you to wait right here, where I sleep every night. This is where I want you . . . to wait. Can you do that for me?" She put a hand on each of his knees and pushed herself up slowly.

Even in the dark she could see how hard he was. He wasn't going anywhere.

"Yes princess," he said breathlessly, "I can wait here."

"Thank you so much," she said. "I feel better already."

Diana left Jack the guard on the bed and went to face her next challenge. This guard was older than Jack. Meaning he would be harder to sway to her side. So, just to be safe, she walked out and closed the door.

"Jack has kindly agreed to wait here," Diana said. She reached out and placed a hand on his shoulder. Letting lose her aura she sent her magic through her arm and into the man. She pulled every ounce of energy he had, which considering the hour wasn't much. Looking horrified the guard crumpled to the floor.

He wasn't dead, just passed out. He would sleep for a while. Smirking, she walked away.

Diana stood in front of two huge wooden doors, another guard passed out at her feet. It wasn't personal; she just needed to deal with some things and deal with them alone. She stepped over the man and pushed the door open and walked inside.

Sleeping on a small bed at the back of a giant glass cell was the monster whose very existence consumed her every waking moment. The supposed Shadow King, a monster so terrifying her entire life was put on hold. So absolutely horrifying as he slept on his bed, wrapped up in his blanket like a boy no older than ten. Diana couldn't even find the words for her disappointment.

"Why so sad, Princess?" The man called from the box. "Not what you were expecting?" He sat up and got out of bed. "Oh yes, I can read your mind just like you've heard." He walked to the edge of the cell and leaned against the glass.

"If you can read my mind than you know why I'm here," Diana sneered.

"Oh I do," he confirmed. "But I'm afraid you'll be disappointed."

"Oh, how so?"

"Well for one, you can stop calling me monster, I have a name."

"Do you?" Diana scoffed. "I've never heard it."

"It's brand new, got it just today in fact. From your darling little sister Terra."

Diana's blood boiled at Terra's name. She had a score to settle with that little rat. It caused her great pain to know that she had escaped what was coming to her for a whole day and had somehow managed to get an audience with this monster before her.

"Oh, did I strike a nerve? Not our sister's biggest fan are we?"

"Shut up," Diana barked, "stay the hell out of my head!"

"Well look at that Princess," Grey said. "Look at how dark your heart is. You know you're almost making this too easy."

"My heart is not dark," she said laughing. "Don't you know who I am? I am Princess Diana, of the kingdom of Sol. I am the princess the prophecy has foretold would come. I am the savior of the

141

world." She felt herself swell with pride at all her titles. That should show this fool.

"Sure you are." Grey said, turning to go back to bed.

"Where do you think you're going?!" Diana demanded. "I'm not done with you!"

"But I am done with you princess," Grey called over his shoulder, lying back down.

Diana was infuriated. Her temper completely boiled over and her vision went red. She stalked over to glass box and raised a fist to beat against it. She didn't care at all who the hell this man was supposed to be. All that mattered to her was that this arrogant bastard had dared to turn his back on her. He had dared to treat her like less than she was.

As soon as her fist made contact with the glass there was a sound like static or lightning.

Diana was thrown from the glass prison. She flew back nearly ten feet and skidded all the way back to the door. She laid there for a moment, dazed.

Grey sat up on his bed and laughed.

"How *dare* you laugh at me," she growled, sitting up. "What the hell did you do to me?"

"*I* didn't do anything," Grey said mockingly. "It's this box. Look at the runes, no one gets in this thing and no one gets out. So all your thoughts of murdering me while I'm weakened and telling everyone I managed to escape in the night because Terra weakened my cell, those thoughts you can kiss goodbye." Grey was gloating. He could see every dark thought and evil intention in her heart and mind.

If he was being honest he was a bit surprised to see all that was in this young girl's heart. Hate for her sister, so intense it rivaled anything he had ever seen in a human. Then the way she viewed anyone who wasn't her! Not for the first time, Grey was a little alarmed about their impending battle.

Diana glowered at the man in the box. Wishing she could get her hands on him. She scanned the box for some crack or a weakness.

142

Anything she could exploit to get in and get her hands on that monster. As she looked over the cell she noticed something that made her smile.

"If no one gets in or out, then explain to me how you ended up with my mother's polished silver tray? Number one of a set of four, if I'm not mistaken. Given to my parents as a celebration gift to commemorate my birth."

Grey's cocky smile disappeared. "Did I say no one?" He asked, "I meant no one but your sister."

Diana couldn't see. Her vision had gone completely red at the thought of one more thing that Terra had that she didn't. It felt like her skin was on fire. Like she *was* fire.

"How," was all she could manage.

"The box is specially tuned to your sister's magic. Only she can manipulate the barrier and pass. Terra, and *only* Terra, has the power to reach me." Grey walked forward and leaned his back against the glass, turning away from Diana. He could feel how angry his turning away made her.

Without knowing what she was doing, Diana walked forward and held up both her hands. Without touching the barrier, she sent out her magic. She had never been good at releasing her magic away from her, but right then it didn't feel like she was in charge of her actions.

Where her magic hit the barrier, sparks flew. Somehow the magic pushed through the barrier and made contact with the glass, the glass Grey was now leaning against.

Crying out in pain, he fell forward on his hands and knees. The part of his back that had been touching the glass was now on fire. It was an odd black and gold fire that burned on his skin for a few seconds and then disappeared, leaving angry dark patches on his flesh.

Diana looked down at this supposed monster, now writhing on the floor in pain.

She laughed.

She threw her head back and laughed.

143

For nearly a minute Diana stood and watched this man suffer, laughing so hard she could hardly breathe. Tears ran down her face as she finally managed to stop.

"I have to say I certainly feel better now. Thank you, whatever you name is now," Diana said. She turned to walk away. She was in such a good mood that she didn't even think about the fact that Jack was sitting on her bed, still waiting for her return.

"Princess," he said, "I've waited, as you asked." He stood and saluted her again.

"Good boy Jack," Diana said, closing her door. "How about I give you a reward?"

Grey lay on the floor, unable to move as Diana disappeared from the room. His shoulders felt like they were on fire and his whole body ached. He was trying not to move as he contemplated all the ways he would make that bitch of a princess pay, when he felt a strange sensation. It was like before, the second heart in his chest.

He could sense it then.

Terra.

Somewhere she was suffering just like he was. Hurt as he was he couldn't pass up an opportunity. He had shadows still around the castle, with just a thought he could sense one move up to be near the princess. Close but not too close.

Then through the strange link between them he reached out.

It was like talking to someone at the other end of a dark tunnel.

He tempted her with darkness, told her that she could be free of pain if she just said yes. All she had to do was agree and the shadow would sink into the dark crevice in her heart and she would be his. He would slowly widen that crack. Little by little he would corrupt her. Blacken her heart and turn her against her friends and family. He would use the so called "Shadow Princess" to kill her sister. Then nothing would stand in his way. He would rule this world without opposition.

He just had to make the crack.

'*I would rather die than allow that monster to touch me!*' Terra thought, nearly shouting in her mind.

'*Too bad it would have been so much easier that way.*' Grey thought, not the least bit disappointed that she'd chosen the long route.

Then there was a blinding light coming from the other end of his connection to Terra. It was a nearly pure white light, except it seemed to be tinted purple and it felt like the Princess was standing there with him.

To Grey, it seemed like the light materialized into the shape of the princess. She stood before him, a being of purple and white light. She knelt down and placed her hands on his shoulders. In a moment the pain that had kept him pinned to the floor was gone.

He shot up and spun around.

She was gone.

Carefully he peeled his burnt shirt off and looked at his reflection in the glass. He had two burn marks wrapping around his shoulders. They almost looked like black wings burned onto his back. He rotated one shoulder, only to feel it pinch tightly and sting. He wasn't sure what Diana had done to him but he was damn sure she was going to pay for this.

Eric paced nervously back and forth in front of Mammy's door. After Terra had passed out he had run to get the master wizard. It was early; dawn hadn't even started to brighten the sky. Still, the master wizard was up and it seemed that he was waiting for Eric to knock on his door.

"Master Bell, it's Terra, we need you!" It was all he had to say. In the next instant they were running down the hall at top speed. When they returned to Mammy's room Bell went in and told Eric to wait outside. Something about the bond and his energy messing with things, he wasn't sure. It was hard to hear and comprehend anything they said.

When Terra screamed last time, right before she blacked out, he had felt the pain she felt. After that, nothing. It was like the bond was gone. Ever since he had scooped her up off the floor of her room and carried her across the castle he could feel her. He knew where she was what she was feeling, everything. Even after she'd fallen asleep he could still feel her. Now there was nothing, he was alone in his own head.

His worst fear was that she was dead.

It made the most sense in his mind.

Something had happened to her, maybe while she slept, maybe when she was dealing with the prisoner under the castle, he didn't know. He just knew that all of a sudden she was gone. Like she had died.

So he paced.

Waiting for someone to come and tell him what had happened.

After what felt like an eternity, Bell opened the door.

"Come, Eric. We need you."

Nodding he followed Bell in.

Terra was lying flat on her back, her arms folded over her stomach, raven black hair brushed out to the side. Mammy was on her right, running her fingers through the princess's hair. She was mumbling something Eric couldn't hear and there were tears silently running down her face.

It looked like she was dead.

"Please no," he whispered.

"She's not dead," Bell said reading Eric's expression. "But she's closer to it than I would like."

"What happened to her?" He asked.

"She's expended all her energy somehow," Bell explained. "Her body has gone into a hyper-recovery mode. Basically her body has shut down all non-essential functions until it can recover enough energy for her to awaken."

"So what can I do?" Eric asked.

146

"You can give her energy."

"How?" He turned to face Bell, more than eager to help.

"Your bond," Bell answered simply. "Even though I'm sure you can't feel it right now, you are still bonded to the princess. That makes you uniquely qualified to help her."

"Tell me how."

Bell grabbed a hold of Terra and carefully lifted her up off the bed. Then he instructed Eric to lie on the bed with his back propped up against the headboard. Then, with only a minimal argument from Mammy, he laid Terra in between Eric's legs so that her back was lying on his chest. He then told Eric to wrap his arms around the princess and hold he like he had before. After he had done so Bell walked around the bed making sure everything was right.

"All right Eric," he said. "I'm going to help you out just a little, but I need you to understand one very important thing."

"What's that," he asked as he worried about how cold Terra's skin felt.

"You must not give her all of your energy."

"Why not?" Eric had fully intended to give her all he had if it would help.

"If you give her all of your energy you'll die."

"Die? Won't I just go into a hyper whatever mode?"

"No. The princess was able to manage that due to the impressive amount of magic she controls. You would not be able to do what she has done."

"Oh," Eric said, still contemplating giving her everything.

"Now, lean your head back and close your eyes," Bell told him. Placing a finger in the center of Eric's forehead, Bell released a small wave of energy, knocking the young man unconscious. Carefully he felt around in the young man's mind until he found his "door". Using a minimal amount of his own magic he managed to open Eric's door and release his magic. He guided this small stream of green and dark blue magic on to Terra.

"Now we wait," Bell said looking to Mammy.

Terra's eyes opened slowly. She blinked heavily as she tried to clear the fog of sleep away. For a moment she was still, trying to remember what had happened the night before and why she felt so weary waking up. She moved to roll over and a sharp stinging across her back brought the night back into frightening clarity.

Careful of her shoulders, Terra pushed herself up in bed. She was in Mammy's room, as she had been last night. Mammy was gone, no doubt tending to her morning chores. She looked to the door across the room. It was standing open and Eric was nowhere to be found.

Slowly she swung her legs over the side of the bed and wobbled to the dressing table. She picked up her faded blue robe and wrapped herself up.

There was something in the back of her mind that plagued her. There was something she couldn't remember, something very important. She went over last night in her head. She had that crazy dream about Eric and then Grey. She woke up Eric came in . . . shirtless no less . . . and they had a very awkward moment. Then . . . then what?

Pain.

She had that searing, burning pain all over. Mostly it had been her shoulders that burned. She assumed that was why they hurt this morning.

After the pain there was nothing. No memories or dreams. Just a blank, until now.

Terra had a strange feeling that there was something huge missing from her memory. Something happened last night and she couldn't remember, but she needed to.

She sighed miserably and went to go through the dresses Mammy had pulled out of her room for her. There were a few dresses she had never seen before. She wondered if Mammy had gotten them or if they were ordered up after last night. Either way Terra found a lovely pale silver dress to wear. She was sure it had at one point been

Diana's. She could see now where it had been let out in the bust and along the bottom seam.

It was a beautiful dress and Terra felt this was the dress for today.

Careful of her shoulders, she dressed herself quickly.

As she was pulling the dress up something in the looking glass caught her eye. Stretched out across her shoulders were two pink-ish white scars. They looked old, like she had had them for years, even though she knew she hadn't. Either she had healed herself or healers had attended her while she was sleeping.

Neither was a particularly comforting thought.

Looking at her back again she couldn't help but notice that the scars seemed to stretch out across her back like white wings. If it hadn't been for the insane pain they had caused, they would be a little interesting.

Sighing, she pulled up her dress and continued to get ready.

As she did up the buttons and adjusted everything, her mind began to wonder again. Trying to figure out what happened last night and why she couldn't remember.

A knock at the door drew Terra out of her train of thought.

"Come in," she called as the door was opening.

"Princess?" It was Mammy.

"Mammy!?" Terra said shocked. She looked terrible. Her face was pale and drawn. There were worry lines all over her face and bags under her eyes. "What happened?"

"Just a long night dear," Mammy said, her face brightening at the sight of the princess up and around.

"Was it me? Did I snore? Or was I a bed hog? You can tell me Mammy."

"No nothing like that," she said smiling, "Just a long, long day and longer night."

"I'll agree to that," Terra said. "Hopefully today is better."

"Let's hope," Mammy said.

Terra smiled as she thought about what she would do with the day. Then the realization that she had to take breakfast to Grey, the idiotic child monster, down in the prison under the castle. Just like she would have to take him his lunch and his dinner. Well dinner she would have to actually eat with him. Today and tomorrow and every day until Diana fulfilled her destiny.

Her outlook on the day much changed, Terra sat down at Mammy's dressing table and contemplated how to get all of her hair on her head. It was a lot of hair and she really wasn't very good at making it do things. Regardless, Terra picked up her brush and started working it through her tangled raven colored mess.

"What are you doing dear?" Mammy asked.

"I'm getting ready," she replied, "I have to take breakfast down to that monster under the castle."

"Terra, it's nearly one in the afternoon," Mammy said carefully.

"One!" She exclaimed. "Oh no Mammy I'm so late! I have lessons with the new martial arts expert father brought it and then I need to check in with my economy professor. Not to mention by now that man is in a way about his lack of food." She sighed, "I'm so late."

"My dear most of that has been canceled due to yesterday," she said kindly. She went to put a hand on the girls shoulder and stopped. She knew the pain it might cause her.

Terra saw Mammy's face in the looking glass. She knew about the pain in her shoulders and was looking pretty grim about it. This thing that she couldn't remember, the huge nagging she felt in the back of her mind, whatever that thing was, Mammy knew. Judging by her face, it was bad.

She set down the brush she was holding and turned to Mammy. Her face was still drawn in concern as she looked the princess over. Mammy was looking at her the same way a person watches a tea cup teetering on the edge of a counter.

"Mammy, tell me what's wrong."

"It's nothing dear," she said trying to force a smile. "Just a long night is all."

"Mammy I have known you all my life. You've never lied to me. Not once. So why are you lying to me now?"

Her face seemed to fall; it became filled with worry and concerned. "Oh Terra," she said, tears in her eyes, "He told us not to say anything to you. Said the guilt of it would tear you apart."

"He who Mammy?" She asked, feeling the icy fingers of dread on her heart.

Mammy shook her head, she was sobbing so hard now she couldn't get the words out.

Terra, feeling inexplicable panic, reached out with her bond. She needed to feel Eric and know that he was safe. She needed to feel him out on rounds or training with the other guards or even eating lunch. She just needed to feel him.

She couldn't.

He was gone.

She couldn't feel him at all.

"Mammy what's happened?!" Terra demanded frantic. "Where's Eric?!"

At the sound of his name Mammy completely dissolved into tears.

Terra turned to the door and ran, hair down, barefoot, she ran out the door and down the hall. She could hear Mammy calling after her but she didn't care. Her heart was beating so loudly in her ears that she couldn't really comprehend the sounds Mammy was making.

Not sure where she was going she ran down the hall. Angry at herself for not noticing that the bond was gone, she ran. Tears in her eyes because she thought he was dead. It was the only thought that made any sense in her head.

She was so upset and so distracted that she didn't even see Diana until she nearly barreled into her.

"Terra!" Diana exclaimed, caught off guard by the sight of her sister running full tilt down the hall. "What the hell are you doing?"

"I'm sorry sister I don't have time to explain," She uttered frantically. She moved to sidestep her sister and keep running, but Diana stepped in front of her. She moved again and again her sister copied the move.

"Diana I need to go, move!" She yelled.

"Oh no little sister," Diana said, loving every moment of her sisters suffering. "We have things we need to discuss." She reached out and grabbed a hold of Terra's arm.

Enraged that Diana would try to stop her when she so clearly needed to get going, Terra slipped her hand from her sister's grip and flipped it around on her. She grabbed her arms and pushed her against the closest wall.

"Diana you need to MOVE," she screamed, "You are my sister and I love you but I swear to the Creator that if you do not get out of my way I will hurt you until you do. Not a lot because you're my sister and I love you but enough so that you fall down and move."

Not realizing she was doing it, Terra sent out a wave of magic that pinned her sister to the wall. Once she was sure her sister was done trying to stop her she ran again. She was nearly to the great hall when someone else stepped up to block her.

"Terra," a familiar voice said. "What's going on?"

Unable to stop, she ran straight in to Bell. He held onto her as she tried to break away and keep running. She struggled for a moment but she was frantic and couldn't see well through tears that had sprung up from somewhere.

"Please Master Bell," Terra pleaded. "I have to find him."

"Find who?"

"Eric I have to find him, something's wrong. I can't feel him through the bond. I can't . . ." she completely dissolved into manic sobs.

"Come this way," Bell said, leading the princess out of the hallway. He had his arm around her shoulder and he spoke lowly and quietly as he hurried her along down another hallway. Terra could tell he was trying to calm her down, but she couldn't understand a thing he was saying to her. It just sounded like water crashing against the rocks.

After a time, and she couldn't say how long exactly, they arrived at a door. At Bell's urging she went through door into a dark room. There was a heavy smell of incense in the air and it was nearly impossible to see. Terra walked forward slowly, not sure where she was or what was going on.

It struck her then that Eric must really be dead. That's why the room was so dark. It was a viewing room. She was going to walk forward and find Eric's body. He would be lying on a bed, ready for a grave. She stopped. She couldn't walk forward anymore. She couldn't see him lying dead because of her.

She still had no idea what was going on with her and Eric.

She knew that they had been thrown into an odd situation that resulted in them being bonded to each other and him being promoted to her Royal Guard. Still, there was more than that. It had truly felt like maybe, in time when she was older, there might really be something between them. Her dream last night had showed her that she cared a great deal for him. Terra felt so stupid now. She had never known any boy or man for that matter, long enough to care for him.

With Eric it seemed like things were moving at lightning speed. It was only two nights ago that she had her first real conversation with him. She had felt so grown that night. Walking in the cool evening air with a man and having a real grownup conversation. Even though there were a few points where things got a little rough, and they fought a little. Still the whole night seemed like a dream.

She thought about it all night and all the next morning as she got ready. Then Mammy gave her that dress and she must have looked nice. Eric's jaw had nearly hit the floor when he'd seen her coming. She felt beautiful for the first time that day.

Eric made her feel beautiful. He made her feel like a woman not a girl. No one had ever treated her that way. She wasn't the shadow princess to him.

To think that all of that could be over, that she would never see his smiling face again, or hear him laugh at her or see the face he made when he got embarrassed. Just the thought was more than she could handle.

"Terra," a weak voice in the distance called.

Her head shot up, flinging tears out of her eyes.

"Eric?!" She shouted, voice cracking.

"Terra, you're awake. Oh sweet creator, I can't tell you how happy I am."

Terra squinted her eyes, trying to see in the dark room. She could just barely make out the bed and maybe a shape on it. She rushed forward wishing there were more lights on so she could see or at least a few less drapes on the windows.

A candle next to the bed sputtered to life seemingly on its own.

There was Eric, lying in bed looking up at Terra. His skin was pale and waxen and he had black bags under his eyes. He looked sick and exhausted. But there was a smile on his lips and a sparkle in his eyes. He was so happy to see her that he didn't even seem to notice, or care how unwell he was. For a moment it seemed like she could actually hear her heart break. That he would be able to smile at her and be happy she was there, when it was she who had put him there.

"Eric I'm so sorry," she said. She rushed forward and threw herself onto the bed so that she was still standing but the top half of her rested on top of Eric. "This is all my fault! You haven't even known me for three days and already you've been hurt so many times. I'm so sorry!" She sobbed into Eric's chest.

Reaching up he stroked the Princess's long dark hair. It was down today and it was getting so long it seemed. This poor sweet girl was so worried about him. It made him smile and despite himself, he chuckled.

Feeling the shaking in Eric's chest Terra sat up to make sure he wasn't hurt worse by her foolishly throwing herself on him. He wasn't hurt, oh no. He was laughing, or as close to laughing as he could manage considering the fact that he was almost completely exhausted.

Smiling at the absolutely shocked look on Terra's face, Eric reached up and put a hand on the side of her completely shocked face.

Eric smiled at the way Terra's face went from shock to completely unsure in less than a second. He reached up with his other hand and cupped her face in his hands. She was beautiful. Not just beautiful, but smart and funny and tougher than most other people he knew. When he thought he had lost her, when he thought she had died, he realized that in this short space of time, Terra had found some way into his heart.

It was ludicrous, he knew that. To think that in the span of a few days she went from being the shadow princess to being part of his heart. He cared about her a good deal, probably more than he really wanted to admit to himself. He knew she was a princess and only fifteen, and he was a royal guard and twenty five. But here and now, in this room, he was just Eric and she was just Terra. He grabbed her wrist suddenly and pulled her toward him. She landed mostly on top of him with her face inches from his.

"Terra," he whispered searching her eyes, "I thought you died. For a moment I thought you had actually ceased to exist. Now I don't know if it's the bond, or if it's something else. But I know that I care about you, more than I should care about you. I know that ever since that night with the fireflies, something about you stuck in mind and in my heart.

"I don't know what's going to happen but I know that I needed to tell you. Just in case something else happens and I never get the chance.

"Oh and I needed to do this too." Leaning forward Eric closed the gap between them and kissed her.

Terra froze.
She'd never been kissed before.
It was amazing.
Eric's lips met hers and she froze. Her whole body seemed to suddenly be on fire. Without knowing what she was doing, Terra jumped back suddenly. Away from the kiss, away from Eric and even off the bed.

"Eric I can't . . ." she stammered. "I'm sorry but I can't."

"Terra," he faltered, unable to keep the hurt from his voice. "I'm sorry I shouldn't have done that. I overstepped. I crossed the line and it was a mistake. Please forgive me."

"Forgive you," she repeated. She could have laughed if it wasn't so devastating. "You don't have to apologize to me. I should apologize to you." Tara sat down and grabbed both of Eric's hands. "Look at what's happened to you in the last few days. Look at how many times in the last three days something bad has happened. Eric you almost died. All of that was because of me, because of your proximity to me.

"If this happens, if we give in to these feelings and get closer, I'm afraid you might actually end up dead. We simply cannot feel this way."

Eric took a deep breath. He was still so worn from everything that it was hard to keep up with everything that was going on. "Terra, I care about you. You telling me that you don't want me to because it could be bad for my health isn't going to stop that. Trust me I tried to stop it. You're only fifteen. I'm ten years your senior, not to mention your Royal Guard. I tried to stop myself from looking at you this way, but it doesn't work."

"Eric," she pleaded miserably, "you have to stop. I can't have your death on my conscience."

156

"No," he replied smiling. "I can't stop. Honestly, I don't think I want to."

Terra sighed. She was hoping he would understand. She wanted him to get that he was in danger if he cared about her. Why couldn't he see that? She was trying to protect him! She cared about him, like he cared about her. But she wouldn't allow herself if it meant she was putting him in danger. She would have to expose herself to the darkness in Grey's heart every day. It was more than possible that one day she might try to hurt him, or herself.

"Terra," Eric said, "I won't stop. You understand that don't you? I can't. I don't know how and I'm not sure I would want to anyway." He put his hand on her face again. This time when he pulled her face closer she knew what was coming.

"Don't ask me to do the impossible."

He kissed her again. Terra didn't pull away and she didn't freeze either.

This time she kissed him back.

He wrapped his arms around her and pulled her against him. Terra let him.

When he pulled back, joy and something a little darker, sparkled in his eyes.

"You can't tell me that you didn't feel anything," Eric said, sounding breathless.

"I can't," she uttered miserably, silent tears streaming down her face. "That's the problem."

Without warning Terra jumped up again and ran from the room. She was out the door and down the hall before Eric could even think to react. She ran down the main hall and around corner after corner. She didn't know where she was running she just knew that she had to get away from him. She couldn't take this feeling in her heart. It was more than she could handle right then.

"Princess?"

Terra skidded to a stop and looked up. There was a young kitchen maid in front of her looking more than a little alarmed. Somehow she had run all the way down to the kitchen and not realized it.

"Jenny," she said.

"Princess," Jenny replied, bowing. "Have you come to take lunch to the prisoner?"

"Prisoner?"

"Yes ma'am. The prisoner you have to serve food to," Jenny said in a whisper.

"Oh right. Yes that's why I'm here. Where is the tray?"

"Right here princess," she said, she stepped back and indicated to a tray sitting on one of the kitchen tables. "Will you be taking it now?" Jenny asked eyeing Terra's bare feet and her loose hair.

"Yes. Like this, right now." Terra snatched up the tray and headed for the basement. She passed by a number of people, all who stared openly at her and her odd appearance. Terra hardly took note. She moved through the common areas and down into the basement as fast as she could.

Diana stood pined to the wall.

She had never seen Terra so angry. She had certainly never felt Terra's magic so intense before. Her little sister wasn't exactly quick to anger. In her lifetime Diana couldn't say for sure if she'd ever seen her sister the way she had been just then. She had certainly never dared to attack Diana before. Just thinking about it made her vision go red.

She tried again to get off the wall.

Still stuck.

Diana was furious.

Aside from the fact that it was humiliating being stuck to the wall like some kind of idiot, the nerve of Terra treating Diana like this.

She was already going to get a beating like she wouldn't ever forget. Now to add this on top of all of that?! Diana was going to have to get really creative. She wanted her sister to know just how much she had messed up. She wanted Terra to cringe at the thought of ever overstepping her bounds again.

Like the snapping of fingers, Diana was released.

She pushed herself off the wall. She was too mad to go to lunch. She didn't want to see anybody and risk murdering the next idiot who was foolish enough to cross her. Deciding she needed to think of how best to handle Terra, Diana returned to her room and to her spell books. She had always thought the dusty volumes Bell made her study were outdated and not worth her time.

As she picked up the book that dealt with curses and hexes she started thinking she might have been mistaken.

Terra approached the large wooden doors at the bottom of the spiral staircase. As she made her way across the floor the two guards who had been posted outside the room jumped up to attention. One of them nearly knocked over the table they had been playing cards on.

"Princess," they said simultaneously, giving her a formal salute and bowing.

"Is everything alright?" One asked, looking over her strange appearance.

"Yes everything is fine. I just want to get this over with as soon as I can." Terra added seeing unconvinced faces of the two guards.

"We understand, highness," the other guard said shooting his partner a shut-the-hell-up face. "We understand you've had a hard few days. Let us get the door for you." They stepped aside and each one grabbed a door and pulled them slightly apart. Terra nodded to both guards and slipped through.

As soon as she was through the door she could feel Grey's eyes on her. Ignoring his very probing stare, she walked to the table and set down the tray. There was no food on it for her right now so she didn't have to sort anything.

"Princess, is it just me or do you feel somehow less . . . bonded? Is it safe to assume than that our dear Captain Reynolds has perished? Or is it too early in the afternoon for good news?" Grey asked, probing at Terra's exposed mind.

"I hate to disappoint," she said, "But *Guard* Reynolds is fine. He's just weak and so the bond is weak. Can you please pass me the tray from last night? I'm afraid if I don't return it to the kitchen, the chef will have me drawn and quartered and then severed for dinner."

"Oh no," Grey said, "There's something more going on than that. Look at you, hair down, barefoot, eyes red from crying no doubt. You, Terra, are a mess."

"And you, Grey, are nothing short of a cad."

"A cad? Seriously, that's the best you have?" Grey laughed, grabbing the trey from his table and walking to the wall. He tried to push the tray through but it hit the glass and glanced off. "Convenient." He muttered.

"How do I get it out?" She asked aloud.

"How should I know? This isn't my pretty glass box, you tell me."

Ignoring him, Terra walked to the box and placed her left hand on the glass. It was smooth and cool under her hand. It seemed to almost hum with power. Taking a deep breath, she pushed against the wall harder. Then, like it was as solid as water, the glass gave way and her hand pushed through.

Alarmed, Terra yanked her hand back.

"I guess it really is keyed to you," Grey said under his breath.

"I guess so," she muttered. "Well now that we know how that works, hold up the tray and I'll pull it through."

Curious, Grey did as she asked.

Again Terra put her hand to the glass and pushed through it. Her hand came through the other side and grasped the tray. Grey released it and she pulled it through. There was no sign on the glass that anything had passed through, and both Terra's hand and the tray were fine.

"Amazing," she marveled, the faintest smile playing on her lips. It was the closest she'd come to smiling since Mammy came in the room this afternoon.

"Yes, truly remarkable," Grey quipped sarcastically, "now can we get on with the food. I didn't get breakfast today ya know."

"Of course," she said, her smile vanishing. She set down the polished silver tray and picked up the one with Grey's food on it. She passed the tray through the glass and handed it off to him. He sat at the table and started to devour the food.

Terra walked back to the other table and looked at the polished silver tray. Her reflection stared back up at her. Grey was right. She looked terrible. Her eyes were puffy and red and her skin seemed unusually pale. Her black hair was down and a mess from running all around the castle as though she was a crazy person. She reached up and pulled her hair over her shoulder. She ran her fingers through it until it looked alright and started to braid it.

A strange sound drew her attention back to Grey. For a moment she was afraid he might be chocking. *'Please don't be dying,'* Terra thought frantically as she turned. *'I don't know if I can get in there to help.'*

Grey was still sitting but his face was different now. He was seemed to have stopped halfway through chewing the chicken that had been served for lunch. As soon as she turned to face him he changed back to his usual cocky self. He kept eating but now his eyes were intently focused on Terra.

"What's wrong?" She asked sensing something was off.

"Nothing," he said through a mouth full of food.

"Something's wrong," Terra said studying his face. "You didn't look right a second ago."

"Look this isn't dinner. You can take you pretty tray and leave. I don't want to have to look at you anymore right now." Grey was bitter and angry, so much so that Terra was actually shocked.

161

Shocked and hurt.

Which she knew was stupid.

This man was a monster. Not just a monster, but a murderer. Countless lives had been lost because of this despicable man. He was darkness incarnate. That's what everyone always told her. Shadows killed so many people. One had almost killed her and another had taken her sister.

This man was the enemy.

There was nothing good inside him anymore.

Maybe there never was in the first place and that was why the shadows took him so young.

Terra knew all of that. But there was part of her that refused to believe that a person could be all bad or be all consumed by darkness. She could sense the darkness in him. It was like looking down a dark well. It was pitch black and she couldn't see the end.

Still, she refused to believe there wasn't even a spark of light in him.

All people had light in them. She had to believe that.

So, standing there, listening to the words he had said, Terra felt her eyes start to water, she felt like an idiot. She grabbed the tray and turned away. Not bothering to look back she walked slowly out the door.

Grey watched Terra go. It was all he could do not to laugh at how pathetic she looked head down, shoulders slumped. This princess was nothing short of an idiot. She stood there and thought on and on about how he was a good man inside and he couldn't be all bad.

Ridiculous.

He was nothing but darkness. He never had been and never would be anything other than the darkest shadow the world would ever see. If Terra was so sure he could be saved, than corrupting her and turning her against her friends and family might be easier than he thought.

Done with his food, Grey stood and started to pace the length of his glass cell.

Without her bond to Reynolds, the little shadow had been much more vulnerable. Like the first time she had come wondering down into the basement, with just a bit of work he was able to get into her mind and see her thoughts.

Reynolds featured predominantly. He wasn't able to see all of it, but he could tell that Reynolds had made a move and she had shut him down. He could also see the feelings she had for him. There was something about the situation that tickled him. She cared for him and him for her but she wouldn't make the move to protect him.

It seemed that the best way to get to Terra might be through Reynolds. Which would take care of two of his problems for the price of one. Reynolds was the one had led the group of men that had fought and caught him. Then he went and got himself bonded to the princess that he needed to use to get to Diana. At every turn that simpleton seemed to spring up to complicate his plans.

After another moment or two of careful thinking, Grey decided. He would use Eric to make the crack in Terra's heart. Once the crack was there, he would pour his darkness into it and widen it. Little by little every day he would darken her obnoxiously bright heart and corrupt her. Then she would be his little shadow and he could use her to get to Diana.

All he had to do was get to Reynolds.

That shouldn't be too hard.

His only real problem was that, for whatever reason, Terra now bore the same scars he did. Except that hers were white and his were black. He had been so caught off guard his breath had actually caught in his throat. He knew that she was in pain last night; he had felt her feel something. He wasn't sure how much she felt or even if had known where the pain came from.

In truth, he was more surprised that she felt anything at all.

Typically you had to be bonded to feel the pain of another. Well, bonded or hexed. As far he knew he wasn't either. Still, somehow she had felt his pain so much that she was scared the same as him.

The pain and the scaring aside, he was sure Terra had appeared before him. Not physically of course, more like her aura took from and appeared to him. He'd never heard of something like it happening before, at least not without the person knowing they were doing it.

She appeared before him, all silvery white and purple. Her very being seemed to radiate light and purity. It was the first time he had experienced such a radiating purity. If he hadn't been so distracted by the pain he was pretty sure her light might have actually burned him.

Despite the fact that she was his enemy and the fact that he was planning to brutally murder her entire family, she chose to take away his pain.

Then, just now, she had walked in dressed in silver. She looked so much like she had the night before. He actually stared, openly in fact. It was a very good thing she had been ignoring him when she came in. If she had seen his face then she would never have left. He knew so little about what had happened last night and the last thing he needed was the so called shadow princess demanding answers of him that he didn't have.

Worse than that, if she had seen his face and he had refused to tell her she could go back on her word and stop coming down. That was something he could not allow to happen. She was instrumental to all that he had planned.

The more he thought about it the more he realized that the sooner he started to corrupt that girl, the better off he would be.

Chapter 5

Eric sat in bed.

He was still too weak to be up for too long, even though it had been weeks since he helped Terra and since that devastating night when he had been fool enough to cross a line with her.

His body had taken a lot longer to heal than he had thought.

His mind was sharp as ever though.

This meant he could sit there and go over every agonizing detail of his conversation with Terra that ended with her flying from the room in tears. At the time it felt like the right thing to do. He needed to tell her how he felt. When he thought she was dead it was the worst feeling he had ever experienced. He didn't know what the future held for them. He knew he was her guard, and that he would do anything to protect her.

Having that monster in the basement wasn't helping much.

He had to tell Terra how he felt.

Then when she was sitting there, looking so beautiful, crying for him. He felt this rush of emotion and he had kissed her.

Everything seemed to go downhill from there.

Beating his head against the headboard Eric cursed his own foolishness.

She barely knew him.

He barely knew her.

He didn't know what he was thinking, or even if he had been thinking.

It must be that damn bond! Ever since they had bonded with each other their emotions had gone from one crazy extreme to another. It wasn't possible to feel about someone the way he thought he felt about her. It had to be the bond. Well the bond and the fact that she was beautiful. She also struck him as very brave. There was also a lot to be said of her kindness and . . .

He shook his head frustrated.

165

He had trained a lot of men in his time and he had a pretty good sense about people. It's part of the reason he had been promoted through the ranks so fast. As he would train people he would get this sense of who was cut out for it and who wasn't. Every so often he would also get a sense about people who wanted the power of the military for something else.

Eric wondered suddenly if that was part of the reason he felt so flustered and off kilter. He could always tell about people. Except when it came to Terra.

Where she was concerned nothing made sense.

Three days.

That's how long he'd known her on a personal level. Just three days and already he felt like he couldn't live without her. This bond may be good for keeping her safe, but it was hell on his emotions. With it weak the way it was now, he thought it might be best to take a moment and really think about how he felt about the princess.

The weeks of his recovery had been spent in bed going back and forth over every single interaction he and Terra had. After going over every minute, every second of their time together, he felt more and more certain that it was the bond that had forced him to act that night.

"How are you feeling?" Bell asked, entering the room.

"Oh . . . fine," Eric said, surprised he hadn't heard the man approaching. Today he was meeting with the Master Wizard to discuss his returning to work and to Terra.

He'd hardly seen her in the three weeks he'd been out. The first week he'd seen her twice and then once more the second week. Never alone.

She always had Mammy in tow.

Terra would walk in and stand a few feet from the bed. She would ask how things were going and how we was feeling. Eric would answer but all the while he would stare at her. Willing her to understand his need to be alone with her through their bond. It was no good of course. Their bond was weak because he was weak.

166

Last week though, he'd gotten lucky.

Terra and Mammy had brought him a bottle of mead to strengthen him while he healed, (a gift from Jenny and her mother in the kitchen.) Mammy had reminded her as they were walking out the door. She had turned and set in on the table next to his bed. Just before she could turn and walk away, the door had closed and it was just the two of them.

Eric reached out and grabbed her arm. "Wait," he said quietly eyeing the door.

"Eric . . ." she started.

"Please," he said again, annoyed by the hint of desperation in his voice. "I *have* to talk to you."

"Mammy's waiting," she said leaning toward the door.

"Terra you have to understand how sorry I am. I never should have done what I did. It wasn't right to put that on you and I'm sorry. But please, don't avoid me."

Terra stopped pulling on him, trying to get free. Instead she seemed to slump where she stood. Her head hung down and she sighed.

"I can't see you right now," she whispered.

"Why?"

She sighed again. "I can't put you in harm's way like this. Not again."

"I'm your guard," he said simply. "Putting myself in harm's way for you is my job. But more than that, I care about you and I don't want to see you get hurt. If that means I have to put myself in situations like this than so be it."

Terra turned suddenly to face him. "Tell me you'll stop," she demanded, eye's wide and brimming with tears. "Tell me you'll stop going down this road, a road you know we can't go down. Stop now, promise me, and I'll be here to see you every day until you're well enough to resume work."

He opened his mouth to speak and then thought better of the comment he was going to make. Initially he wanted to lie to her, say

167

whatever she wanted to hear so she would come back tomorrow and not be mad at him anymore. Then he realized that caring about her meant that he should be honest with her. He cared and there was nothing wrong with that. He wanted her to know he cared.

Finally he said, "No."

"No?" She asked confused.

"I told you before. I care about you and I won't stop. I can't stop."

Quicker than he could react, Terra pulled her arm out of Eric's grasp and walked out of the room without so much as a backward glance at the bed.

After that Terra hadn't been back.

Not that he blamed her.

"You don't seem fine," Bell said, his sharp eyes taking in Eric's thoughtful expression. Eric came out of the haze of the past few weeks to see Bell looking down at him like a man who already knew what plagued the young guard.

"Can I be frank with you Master Wizard?" Eric asked, feeling grateful for someone to talk to. Someone without the power to take his head off.

"Of course Guard Reynolds, you may speak with me about anything."

"Well," Eric said taking a deep breath, "I think this bond thing I have with the princess is starting to mess with my head. I'm having a really hard time getting a read on people the way I used to. Not to mention the emotional turmoil it seems to be causing. I've never been so loose lipped about my emotions before. Especially when I don't understand how and why the emotions I'm feeling are there in the first place."

"So we're talking about you and the princess," Bell said smiling. "Tell me, what kind of emotions are you feeling? And how strong are they when you feel them?"

"I feel like I've never felt before," Eric said, struggling to explain. "I've never looked at a woman and cared about her the way I feel like I care about Terra. She's in my mind every minute of every day. When's she's close to me I feel like I can't see straight. When she's in trouble or when someone threatens her, my vision goes red. I don't know what's going on with me anymore."

Bell smiled knowingly at the man. "Well I'm afraid there is very little I can do in this situation."

"Whatever you can do to help would be greatly appreciated Master Wizard."

"Firstly let me tell you this, the bond only amplifies the emotions of the people caught in it. So if you're feeling thoughts of love and caring, it's because they existed before the bond. The same can be said with thoughts of fear and hatred. All are amplified by the bond."

"So I already cared for Terra, but the bond made that stronger," Eric pondered, more to himself than to Bell.

"Yes. So not all of what you feel can be blamed on the bond. Secondly, while your bond is weak I can help you assess what is bond and what is you. It is however a fairly difficult task to do. You would have to delve into your own heart and see what secrets lie there."

"Will it help me to differentiate between real emotions and the bond in the future?"

"Yes."

"Then sign me up."

"Very well," Bell said. "Lie back on the bed and close your eyes. I want you to be completely comfortable. Very good. Now relax." Bell placed a finger on each temple and sent out a small wave of energy. He found the spot where the bond resonated very easily.

It was, as he assumed, surrounded by emotion. Some of it made sense, while some of it was well beyond what it should be. Bell could easily see what Eric felt for Terra without the bond, and what the bond amplified. He did care for her quite a bit. More than he

169

probably realized and it seemed that's what the bond was playing off of. Bell just needed to rein that in.

Try as he might, Bell couldn't manage to manipulate the bond. It had never been a problem before. He'd helped many people with troublesome bonds in the past. He had never encountered a bond so stubborn. After another couple of tries Bell decided he would leave a little magic here and let it set for a while. See if maybe that would help.

Bell checked to make sure Eric was sleeping soundly before he pulled away. He walked quietly out the door and closed it behind him. Eric would need some time to work through the issues the bond was causing.

Terra slammed the door to the prison closed. Frustrated beyond words she didn't even notice when the guard jumped at the sound. Grey had been especially nasty this afternoon when she'd brought him lunch. He had seen something of Eric in her head and had let into her about him, not stopping until she had reached the door and slammed it closed.

She was so sick of the back and forth with him. She felt like she was losing her mind.

Terra had gone to the kitchen, returned the tray and had wandered until she found herself outside her parent's door. She thought about walking past and hiding in Mammy's room. Until she realized Mammy would question why she was so upset and what was wrong with her and then before she knew it she would be crying and spilling her guts to Mammy. Who would, in all seriousness, chase after Grey with a broom threating to beat him into next week if he ever upset her again.

Then things with Grey would get worse and Terra was almost certain that if things got any worse than they were now she would scream and run as far and as fast as she could.

She really wanted to go to her room and hide.

Except her room was still . . .

She couldn't go to her room.

So she thought that she would see if her father was around and if he knew when she could go back to her room. It had been more than long enough now. She needed to get her privacy back. She loved Mammy, more than she could say. Having her around every minute of every day was more than she could really stand.

She knocked on the door and heard a group of voices quiet down. Footsteps approached and the door was open by her father's page.

"Hello Markus," Terra said.

"Princess," he replied saluting.

"Is my father available to talk?" Terra asked.

"Of course I am," King Sol said from somewhere behind the door.

Markus bowed again and swept back, opening the door as he went.

"Good Afternoon Father," Terra said formally, dipping into a deep curtsy. "Does the day find you well?"

"Indeed it does," King Sol said, putting a hand on her shoulder. "How does it find you my dear little princess? Are your scars healing?"

Terra reached back and swept the few loose curls Mammy had left down off her shoulders so her father could take in the sight of her wing like scars as he so often did when she was around. She watched as his face fell again. It hurt him to see his youngest daughter hurt so badly.

"You seem to be healing," he remarked quietly.

"I am father."

"What of your young guard? Is he still out of commission?"

"Yes, He should be back up and around soon."

"It's been weeks hasn't it?" The King asked. "Was he truly injured so gravely?"

"Yes. After the attack I was badly hurt, and more than that, I was near death due a lack of energy. Guard Reynolds stepped in and

171

put his own life on the line to protect me. It nearly killed him to save my life the way he did."

"Quite a hero that young man," a man from behind King Sol offered.

"Indeed," the King said. "Tonight we will honor him with a grand dinner. And to follow up we'll have a ceremony right after to announce his promotion and to reward him for his outstanding service to me and to the kingdom."

"Thank you father," Terra said, so happy for Eric she could almost burst.

"Was there anything else my dear?" King Sol asked.

"Yes father," she hesitated. "I hate to be a bother but I was wondering what we were going to do about my . . . my room."

"Oh yes," he said, "I've given that much thought to that over the last few weeks. It seems to me that now that you and your sister are older and perhaps in need of rooms that aren't quite so small, and also in light of recent events, I have decided to move all of our sleeping chambers."

"To where?" She asked.

"The old west wing," King Sol announced. "Ever since the remodel it has sat useless and idle. I've already started the renovations. They will be ready in less than a week."

"I suppose that's good," Terra said. "But is it safe there?"

"Don't worry my dear," King Sol said. "It is deeper in the castle, where the walls are thicker and harder to penetrate. It will be much safer for all of us. Just you wait and see my little princess. Now run along. We have many things still to discuss here."

Terra leaned over and saw three of fathers closest advisors circled around a small table. There was another man who was pacing back in forth in front of the fireplace. It took her a moment but she eventually recognized him as Lord Howe. He had a son name Richard that was always chasing after Diana. She couldn't remember what he looked like but it seemed Diana liked him. Or at least she tolerated him.

She couldn't help but wonder what was wrong. Everybody seemed to be carefully tiptoeing around him. Something terrible must be going on somewhere. Not wanting to delay her father any longer, she said quickly, "Where shall I stay until then?"

"You'll have to speak to Mammy dear, she's making the arrangements. Now I'm afraid I must go."

"Of course father, thank you," Terra said curtsying again. She stepped backwards, careful not to show her back to her father until he showed his to her. Then she walked out into the hall again. She had very much wanted to be alone, but there didn't seem to be any hope of that, so with a defeated sigh, she walked to Mammy's room.

Eric opened his eyes.

He was still lying in the Master Wizards room. There was still a faint bit of light coming from the windows. It was dusk and that meant that he had been in bed all day. Carefully he sat up. He could feel his bond with Terra, still going strong. Although now there seemed to be something different about it, something changed.

It was still just as strong as it was before, but now when he thought about Terra, he didn't get that same strange feeling in his chest. He didn't feel like his heart was fluttering around inside him like a caged bird. He still felt her; she was just up the hall, most likely in Mammy's room. She was feeling some kind of dread. Being that it was close to dinner time he understood that. She was in no immediate danger. She was safe and that pleased him.

It didn't make him feel so happy he thought he might cry. Not like it had before. Before it felt like everything hinged on her. How he felt, what he did. All came down to her. Now he was glad she was safe, as she was his charge, but nothing more.

Whatever the Master Wizard had done, had worked. He felt like himself for the first time in weeks. He would have to thank Bell wholeheartedly the next time he saw him.

Eric stood, glad to see that his weakness had passed, and started to dress. He would need to meet with the King and discuss what happened that night with the princess. Then he would have to hand in his Captain's uniform and get fitted for a Royal Guards uniform. He would have to find out from Terra what colors her magic was. She wasn't old enough to have a crest of her own, for letters and legal business. So his uniform would have to be colored in the colors of her magic. As a Royal Guard his uniform would have to be matched to the person he protected.

If he recalled correctly it was purple and sliver maybe?

He would have to ask.

Aside from that he would have to put in a recommendation for the next captain of the guard. He would need some time to think about that. Greggor maybe, or possibly Jones, although Smith was a hell of a fighter and scrappy when he need to be.

Dressed, Eric pulled on his boots, still deep in thought over who would make the best Captain of the Guard. He would have to be trustworthy and loyal. Not to mention that Eric would have to have no doubts about the person at all.

Standing, he crossed the room, filled with more books that he had ever seen, and opened the door.

"Well it's about time," A man at the door remarked.

"Jones?" Eric said, startled to see the man hovering in the hall outside. "What are you doing up here?"

"I came to find you of course. The King sent me. Wants to make sure you aren't late to your own dinner." Jones stood about half a head shorter than Eric with dirty blonde hair and hazel eyes. He was older than Eric by nearly four years, but looked much younger. Eric often called him the kid guard.

"My dinner?" Eric asked. He exited the room and pulled the door closed. He and Jones started walking down the corridor toward the main hall. "What do you mean my dinner?"

"Do you really not know?" Jones asked disbelieving. "Everyone has heard about how you saved the princess from the rapist, and then later that night how you nearly died saving the princess again. All anyone can talk about is how you saved the princess and bonded with her through magic and got promoted. It's been a rumor goldmine for the people of the town."

"Wow," he said, "I didn't realize people had heard about all of that."

"It is literally all anyone can talk about." Jones laughed as the made their way from the main hall to the grand dining hall.

"So then this dinner?"

"It's to honor your service to the King and the country and announce your promotion."

"I wish someone would have told me about all this," Eric said, not enjoying the thought of being praised openly in front of so many people. It always made him feel a bit like a dog.

"Well regardless," Jones said, "the tailor has almost completed your new uniforms; he just needs to know what the princess's colors are so they can be finished for dinner."

"Well than, lead on my friend," Eric said. "Let's get this over with."

Mammy had finally finished fixing Terra's hair. It was so thick it seemed to have a mind of its own. After much manipulation, she finally had it in pile on her head looking beautiful. She had made sure to dress Terra up for tonight. It was a promotion ceremony, for her very own royal guard. It was important to look the part of the lovely young princess.

Terra had suggested wearing something simple so she didn't outshine Eric, who the ceremony was really about, but Mammy would have none of that. She had chosen for Terra a deep violet gown with green trim. In a lot of ways it was similar to the dress Mammy had bought her. Only this gown featured sheer capped sleeves as opposed to the long flowing ones she had so enjoyed.

Terra sat in front of the looking glass staring at her reflection. Mammy had used some strange pencils and powders and made her look much older than fifteen. It was beautiful to be sure, but to Terra it seemed heavy. Especially when she remembered that she was only going to be at the ceremony for five minutes before she would have to leave and take dinner to Grey.

A knock at the door announced her father's arrival. With a final glance at the looking glass, Terra stood, grabbed the silk shawl and wrapped it around her nearly bare shoulders. It was a beautiful dress, and the low shoulders would have been beautiful, if it hadn't been for the scars she now bore.

Fading from the pink they had been when she woke up to a slightly off colored white. Terra was becoming more and more accustomed to them now. It had taken nearly three weeks for her to not be startled by the sight of them in the mirror.

She rushed to the door and opened it. Her father stood, dressed in a fine new coat, flanked on either side by her sister and mother. Both looked stunning in their matching red dresses. Terra truly did pale in comparison. Still, she smiled at her father and curtsied. As her family passed she took her place in the back. Together they walked to the grand dining hall.

Terra had stood and watched for less than five minutes before the striking of the clock told her she must go. King Sol was still busy explaining all the changes that were being made and all that had transpired the weeks before. He hadn't even had a chance to bring Eric up to the dais where they King's table sat.

With a nod from her father, Terra stood quickly exited back to the kitchen. Jenny had the tray ready and waiting for her. Thanking the maid for being so prompt, she grabbed the tray and headed the long way round to the west wing.

When she got the bottom of the stairs she found only one guard waiting there. It was a man named Lewis, she thought. Tom Lewis if she remembered correctly. He had been in the service for a while now. Every time promotions came up there was always some reason why he was passed over. A good number of the maids in the castle talked of cover ups. But Terra didn't have much of an ear for gossip.

"Good evening princess," he said, eyeing her, "my don't you look lovely tonight." He formally saluted her and bowed. As his head went down so did his eyes. He raked in every inch of her. Not in a good way either.

"Good evening, Lewis isn't it?" Terra asked. Over the past couple of weeks they had changed the guards at the door several times, trying to find a suitable person for the night watch.

Somehow they'd decided on this man.

"I'm flattered you remember my name," he said. He was a good looking man, tall and strong, with a well chiseled face and strong brown eyes. His hair was golden like Diana's. A fair number of women flirted and fawned over him. All Terra could really see when she looked at him was his wandering eyes.

"Well, if you would be so kind as to get the door," she asked awkwardly. "I have to take dinner to the prisoner."

"Of course Princess," he said. He pulled the door open just a crack and stood so near to the opening that Terra had to squeeze past him to get in. It was uncomfortable the way he seemed to watch her. She had never before been so glad to be in the prison.

"If you could hear the things that man is thinking about you princess, your hair would curl. Oh wait it has," Grey joked mockingly.

Terra, still not exactly happy with Grey after the way he had treated her earlier, tried to smile and brush it off. Sadly it came across as more of a grimace. She sat the tray down and started to separate the food.

"Oh, not still mad about earlier are we?" Grey asked sarcastically. "Can't take a little fun being poked at you, eh princess? Or do you not like hearing about your guard that way?"

"Enough," she exclaimed, slamming the tray down on the table and spinning to face the cell. "Enough! No more of this!"

"No more of what?" He asked, still looking wholly entertained.

"No more of this you treating me like I'm your own personal whipping boy!" Terra shouted. "You demanded that we treat you as your station dictated, so here I am, serving you dinner. But now I have some demands." The last three weeks dinning down here and been a nightmare. Some days he was kind and treated her like a dear friend, other days he was every bit the monster she knew him to be.

"Demands," he asked, enjoying the sight of Terra losing her temper. "What kind of demands could you have?"

"For one, if you want to be treated respectfully, so do I. I am a princess of this realm and I will be treated as such by you at the least. For another, not picking on me like we're in a school yard somewhere. If you cannot be nice then I will simply stop coming. Word or no, I will not be treated this way."

Once she had started, there was no stopping the words from coming out of her mouth. She wanted to turn and run for having been so bold with so monstrous a man. Deciding there was nothing for it, she raised her chin and stared him down.

"Well, well princess. Look who finally found a voice."

"Are you going to take me seriously or not?" She demanded.

"Very well Terra, I will be civil, or as close as I come to civil. Understand this though; I am not a civil man. So don't expect much." Grey's voice took on a strange and, if she wasn't mistaken, evil quality. Even the room around her seemed to grow darker as he leaned on the glass. He was a great deal taller than she was. She'd never noticed before since he was always stalking around the back of the box whenever she was near the front.

Now she could see he was taller than Eric, maybe even taller than her father who stood at an impressive 6'2. As she stared at him it seemed like all the light was being sucked out of the room. She couldn't place it, but she felt something in the air. Not darkness exactly, but something very close.

It occurred to her then that one of the ways they kept Grey in the box was by the constant amount of light in the room. If the room was suddenly plunged into the darkness she wasn't sure what would happen, but she knew it wouldn't be good.

Terra spun around quickly. Most of the magelight torches were still on as far as she could tell. As she spun a torch to her left sputtered and went out. Confirming what she had been afraid of.

Grey was trying to put the lights out.

She looked up at him as he was staring down at her, his eyes twinkling with something dark. He was doing this somehow, he was taking away the light. Not sure what else to do, Terra rounded on him. She grabbed the chair from the table, dragged it over to the cell, and stepped up onto it. Now she and Grey were at eye level. She placed both hands on the glass and leaned in until her forehead was nearly touching glass too.

"Enough," she said using her magic to power her voice. "You've had your fun, now stop."

A light started to emit from Terra. It originated somewhere near her heart and very quickly enveloped her and then the entire room completely. Lastly the light hit Grey. He grunted angrily for a moment before he finally backed off the glass.

Once he had taken a step, the room returned to normal. No more impending darkness, no more torches going out and no more strange light emanating from Terra. Same prison it had always been. The only thing slightly out of the ordinary was that Terra was still standing on a chair. She looked around the room one last time, letting her eyes linger on Grey who was standing away from the wall of his cell not looking at her. With a final glance around, she decided it was finally safe to climb down. Not taking the extra fabric of the dress into account, she stepped on her hem and tripped.

She went careening to the ground. There was just enough time to bring her arms up to protect her face before she hit.

Seconds before she met the ground, Terra felt two arms encircle her and she was pulled back and away from the floor. She was suddenly being held by somebody, protected. She had closed her eyes when she realized she was falling and found now that she couldn't open them.

179

Someone was holding her. She felt two arms around her and her face was resting on someone's chest. She just couldn't open her eyes to see who.

It had to be Eric. He must have felt her fear when the room went dark and rushed down to see what was wrong. He had come running in when she fell and that's why she didn't hear him. She reached out with the bond and found that Eric was still quite far away. He was in the dining hall. He hadn't even come to see what's wrong yet.

Terra reached up to force her eyes open. Then, as if moving suddenly broke some spell, her eyes flew open. She was kneeling on the ground, alone. She looked around frantically; the only other person in the room was Grey. He was up against the glass next to her on his knees, looking at the princess as though he hated the very sight of her.

"What . . . what happened?" She asked, confused.

There was the briefest flash of something in his eyes, possibly concern but maybe not. It was gone before Terra could be sure what she had seen. He stood suddenly and stalked back to his table. "You fell out of your chair," he said forcing his voice to sound mocking. "It was quite hilarious."

"But I didn't fall, did I?" She asked more to herself than to Grey. "I tripped on the dress but I didn't hit the ground. It felt like someone grabbed me." Slowly her brain tried to force the pieces together.

"That's impossible," Grey said. "I'm the only other person here and I'm stuck in this glass cage. Now if you're done trying to fly, perhaps we can eat?"

"Of course," Terra said, feeling foolish. There wasn't anyone here; she must have imagined the whole thing. Or maybe her magic had saved her? It wasn't like her magic hadn't stepped in before to save her without her knowing.

"Anyway," she said, eager to not have to think about her magic out of control. "Care to explain what that was earlier?"

180

"I'm not sure I know what you're talking about," he said walking back up to the glass.

Terra stood slowly, making sure nothing was hurt in her quasi-fall, grabbed the tray off the table and started passing it though the cell. "You know exactly what I mean. Before, when the room went dark and I got up on the chair to yell at you. That was you and I know it."

"Maybe it was," he offered, taking his tray and sitting down. "Or maybe it was you. Seems to me that of the two of us, you have hardest time controlling your magic."

"Grey," she explained, trying not to look annoyed at the fact that he was, once again, pilfering around in her mind. "I realize that being fifteen somehow means I must know next to nothing. But, *please* do not be so foolish as to think that I cannot tell your particular type of darkness when I feel it."

"You can do that?" He asked, suddenly keenly interested.

"Of course," she said, a little annoyed that he was still treating her like a child. "Your aura, even though it's dark, is unique to you and you alone. Just like my aura and magic are unique to me," Terra spoke slowly, like she was explaining to a child. Partly because she wanted to prove that despite her lack of schooling on the subject, she wasn't a complete idiot. "Everybody's magic is different. I haven't been formally trained, but I'm not an idiot either."

Grey paused for a moment and then said, "Terra, I'm not trying to belittle your intelligence, I am simply pointing out to you that most people cannot differentiate between two magical auras without a good deal of training."

"What?" she said laughing, "That's ridiculous, I've always been able to do that." The princess waited for a moment, sure that there was some kind of joke coming. Knowing Grey, it would be a joke at her expense.

Grey was silent as he stared intently down at his dinner. He had never before heard of anyone who could do the things this girl claimed to do. It seemed to him that the more he got to know these two princesses, the less and less confident he felt about moving forward. He would have to move his plans along rapidly if he wanted to get to Terra. As she grew stronger it would become increasingly harder to crack her. Since she was instrumental to his plans, things would have to be expedited.

"Well I guess that means you're quite the talented little shadow," he replied finally, still not looking up.

"Not even ten minutes have passed and you're already getting snarky," Terra said smiling. She wasn't precisely sure why Grey was reacting the way he was to her ability, but she was certainly enjoying the effect it had. It was a rare for the Princess to be able to get under the prisoners skin so effectively. When these fleeting moments came, she was sure to enjoy them to their fullest.

"I'm not snarky," he countered before he could stop himself. "I don't snark."

"If you say so," she commented off-handedly.

Grey was not the kind of man to be condescended to by fifteen year old, stuck up, uneducated, overly sheltered princess. He was the King of the Shadows! He had legions of monsters and damned creatures at his every beck and call since before he could remember. He would be damned if some girl managed to get his goat so easily.

"So how are things with your young guard?" He asked sweetly.

Just as he had hoped, Terra froze. Her mind raced with thought and memories from the past weeks. All of them centered on her guard and the awkward encounters they'd had since the night Terra was scarred. Instantly any smugness and self-appreciation vanished. Her mood fell faster than she did off the chair moments ago.

Terra looked down at her shoes as she shifted uncomfortably under Grey's knowing gaze. She had been so happy a few seconds ago, having bothered him so easily. Now, with her thoughts turned back to Eric and the growing fear she had about their next meeting, all her happiness vanished.

Things with him didn't appear to be getting any better. Every time she had spoken with him since the accident he had been adamant on not stopping how he felt or even trying to deny his feelings as she was constantly struggling to do.

As Terra's mind drifted through thoughts of Eric and their future, a strange thought wondered into her mind.

"You just said that to make me sad," she observed quietly, looking up at Grey.

As she had surmised, he was sitting back in his chair, a cocky smirk spread across his face as he watched the thoughts play miserably through her mind.

"I did no such thing," Grey said. "I'm simply concerned about your wellbeing."

Terra scoffed. "I don't think you have the capacity to be concerned about anyone but yourself," she whispered hurt.

He shrugged.

"Another stipulation then," she stated, gathering her few remaining scraps of dignity.

"More rules?" He asked with a sigh. "What'll be now?"

"Our conversations," she replied simply. "What you see in my mind is not there for your viewing pleasure. Especially things between myself and my guard."

With an overly dramatic sigh, Grey pushed himself out of his chair and waltzed over to the wall of his cell. "What are we supposed to have our civil conversations about then?!"

She smiled for a moment, pleased to see him so upset about a lack of conversation topics. Checking herself, Terra cleared her mind of such thoughts before he could see them and lash out again.

"Well we could have civil conversations about normal things like how the kingdoms are faring, the weather, books, or magic," she answered. "Oh! We could talk about you and what you do when you're not out terrorizing the world!"

Grey stared at her in a way that made her want to burst out laughing.

"What a lovely conversation that would be!" She exclaimed, not letting his clear displeasure bother her. "What *does* the Shadow King do in his down time?"

"You're hilarious," Grey sniped sarcastically.

"I wasn't trying to be funny," Terra admitted, still laughing at the mental image of Grey in a great chair sipping wine from a fine goblet in front of the fire with a pipe in the other hand. "I'm honestly curious. So little is known about you personally."

"I like it that way," Grey said. "I'm a private fellow."

"Well, what if I promised that nothing we said here left here? If everything you said to me and I said to you stayed in this room?"

"Meaning what, exactly?" He asked, his eyes sparkling with curiosity and something else Terra couldn't name.

"Meaning that I promise not to tell another soul what we talk about here. I understand that the way the world perceives you is important to you. So you can tell me all about yourself and I won't tell anyone else. That's my promise. No matter what you say. It stays here."

"You do understand that I'm your enemy right?" He asked. "I'm set to face your sister in a battle to the death? Foretold by the last of the great sages and the deciding factor as to whether or not darkness with overtake the light?"

"I know," Terra answered seriously. "I know what the prophesy outlines. I could recite the whole thing for you if you wanted. Or well, the general meaning of the thing anyway. You don't have to remind me of the fate that awaits my sister and this world.

"All I'm suggesting is that until that day dawns, I don't see the harm in us being civil and discussing things privately. You are a prisoner here, that is true, but you are also a guest in my father's keeping. As a princess I have been taught to be gracious and civil to all guests of my household. No matter the reason for their stay."

"Well aren't we a perfect little princess," Grey mocked. "Now tell me the truth."

184

"Ah, yes," muttered to herself. "I forgot you can read my mind." She smiled sheepishly at being caught.

"Not just minds," he said, "I can see into your heart too."

"Then you tell me," she asked, feeling bold. "What do you see?"

Grey smiled wickedly. He could see so many things in the princess's head. Her heart, however, remained quite difficult to read. Knowing that she was instrumental to his plans, he decided to see for himself if she could in fact be trusted.

He scanned through her unguarded mind. As far as he could tell, she seemed to be genuine in her promise to keep his secrets. Other than that, she was overly curious. With her green eyes and dark hair she much resembled a black cat stalking around the castle, meddling where it wasn't wanted. He theorized she had to be at least half cat.

"My, my so curious aren't we?" He asked.

Terra balked at the subject. Her mother was constantly telling her that curiosity didn't suite a princess. It wasn't for a woman to ask questions so frequently. She should be silent and still.

"Don't listen to that," Grey said, seeing the memories flash through Terra's mind. "You shouldn't let people make you small that way."

"She's not making me small."

"No, I suppose you do that all on your own."

Terra didn't really want to talk about herself. So she forced a smile and started to eat quietly. She didn't like discussing herself or her relationship with her mother, or her sister for that matter.

"Well I suppose so long as you can keep a secret, I can answer a few questions about me. So long as you agree to answer my questions as well," he decided after a few moments of silence.

"You can read my mind," she asked confused. "What kind of questions could you possibly want to ask?"

"I can mostly read your mind," Grey answered, finishing with his dinner. "Your bond with Reynolds makes it harder to see what's going on in there. And, as much as it pains me to admit it, when it comes to you it's a bit harder to see much aside from what you're currently thinking."

"So you can't read my mind as easily?" Terra asked.

"Something like that," Grey said irritably. "So do you agree?"

"I do."

Something flashed in Grey's eyes then. Happiness maybe, or possibly victory. "Very well then ladies first," he said smiling wickedly.

Terra smiled hesitantly, something in his face gave her pause. Just as she was ready to ask her first question a sensation from her bond drew her attention.

"It would seem our dear Mr. Reynolds is coming," Grey remarked.

"Yes, he is," she said offhandedly. There was something so strange about the bond. It was still Eric on the other end, but now there was a different feeling around him. Not bad of course, just different. For a moment Terra wondered if her rejection of him was why the bond felt so different now. Maybe her telling him to stop caring actually made him stop caring.

If so, that was a good thing, right?

She wanted Eric to stop caring. It wasn't safe for him to feel for her that way. Not just because of the whole princess thing, but because she could hurt him if she wasn't careful. There was no way to tell if the darkness that surrounded Grey would corrupt her or not. She couldn't take the risk.

"Heh, you really are too much," Grey said as the door behind Terra opened.

Eric walked in wearing a fine new Royal Guard uniform. It was beautifully done in dark silver, almost grey, with purple trim. He now wore a dark blue sash across his chest denoting that he guarded the royal family. Pinned to that new sash was a sun cast in solid gold with a pentacle inside. Each of the star's points bore a different jewel; the different gems denoted whom the medal had been issued from. At the top point there was a sun stone, a rare and hard to come by gem in the kingdom. It was used primarily for the King and his decorations. Very few medals like this had ever been made, let alone handed out to anyone less than a lord.

Eric puffed his chest out when he caught sight of Terra staring. He strode in the room like a big colorful bird, chest out, head held high. He walked to the table where she stood and formally saluted her. He hoped that things would be different now he was on his feet and that it had been a week since their last encounter.

"Good evening Princess," he said.

Terra heard it then and everything fell into place. He was colder, more distant. It wasn't that he was trying to be respectful and not care for her; it was that he simply didn't care about her at all anymore. She was more than shocked to look up at him and realize that everything he had felt for her, all the things he had said to her all of that was just gone.

"Eric," she asked, "are you alright? You seem . . . different."

"I'm better than alright," Eric said. "I feel clear again. Oh and I wanted to talk to you about what happened before and the other day when we get a chance." He looked up at the monster in the box, sitting back in his chair and staring intently at the two of them. His overly wicked smile broadened when he saw Eric looking at him.

"Oh don't mind me," he said throwing up his hands. "I'm just here for the food."

Terra stood and brushed the food from her dress. "Eric what you have to say to me you can say here. I don't have a room right now so I don't have any privacy. I'm the only person Grey sees so he's not going to be telling anyone and I don't really like having a personal discussion . . ."

"Grey?" he interjected.

She walked over until she was standing just a few feet away from him. "Yea, uh, that's his name." She spoke softly, she knew Grey could hear no matter what she said, but she didn't want to announce what they were talking about. Not to mention she could feel something shift in Eric at the mention of his name.

187

"Since when do monsters have names?" He spat as he glared at the man in the cell.

"Since your little princess there gave it to me, or didn't she tell you? She gave me a name so we could have pleasant conversations, like people."

"You really named him?" Eric asked, sounding disgusted.

"I didn't know what to call him," she explained, honestly. "I have to be down here every night for dinner. And I didn't want to have to keep referring to him as the Shadow King or King of the Shadows. I asked for his real name he said he had none so I gave him one."

Eric stepped back, away from Terra, as she tried to step forward. He looked at her with something similar to abject disgust. "I don't know what I was thinking before," he muttered. "You are not the person I thought you were. Everything I said before, the kiss all of it. Forget it.

"I don't know who I thought you were, but I was wrong."

He stopped and for a moment it seemed like he wanted to say something more. Deciding it wasn't worth it he shook his head and said, "I'm sorry princess; I'll wait to escort you outside. You and your *friend* can finish your conversation."

Terra felt every word he said like a slap to the face. He was leaving and she had to stop him. She had to explain to him what was going on and make him see that it wasn't that bad.

She reached out to grab Eric's hand to stop him. He pulled his hand away like she had burned him. He looked down at her and shook his head. Without another word he turned on his heel and strode out of the room, slamming the door behind him.

Terra stood frozen, her arm still outstretched.

Eric had been cold, not just that, he had been cruel.

She fought back tears as she made her way slowly back around to the table. She sat down and stared blankly off passed Grey and his box, at the wall across from her. Her eyes glazed over and she slumped down in the chair.

Grey stared at her curiously for a while, before he finally stood and walked to the glass. "Hey can you pass me that last roll," he asked, taking a chance on an assumption. If he was right he had found the way to break her.

"Of course," she replied meekly. Her mind was racing with thought after thought about what Eric had said and assumptions she was making about herself based on those words. Her body got up and started moving without her thinking about it.

She picked up the roll and walked to the glass wall. Without a thought she pressed her hand against the wall and pushed. Her hand, roll and all, slipped through the wall and into the cell. Grey walked up and stopped short of grabbing the roll.

"You did promise to keep everything that we do and say secret, right" he asked.

"Yes," she answered. "It's not like I have any friends to talk to about it now."

"Good," Grey said. He grabbed Terra's wrist and pulled her though the glass. Still stuck in her own thoughts, the princess didn't have time to react. Grey held on to her wrist until she was completely through the glass. Then he used her loss of balance and momentum to spin her on her heels and pull her in close. He wrapped his arms around her and hugged her.

"I swear to your creator if you *ever* tell anyone I did this I will decimate you," he grumbled into the top of Terra's hair. "But I had the unfortunate luck of looking in your heart when that charming young man made his exit."

Terra, who had been too shocked to move or even speak until then said, "I . . . I don't understand. Grey what are you doing?" She tried to push against him but he held on tight.

"I am offering you a onetime only chance to use my shoulder to cry on. I can see in your head that you've got no one else to talk to and your heart wants to cry. So one time only, white flags up. Let it all out."

"Grey," she whispered, pushing back so she could look up and see him. "How did you know I would come all the way through?"

"Lucky guess. Now hurry up before someone comes in here and we have a lot more explaining to do."

Terra was so unsure what to do. Eric had just treated her like she was some kind of monster. What he said and the way he reacted to her trying to touch him made her feel like maybe she was. Eric was supposed to be her friend. He was the one person she was supposed to be able to talk to about anything and he had just treated her like something less than dirt. In fact, now that she thought about it, Eric had actually treated her worse than her mother.

Then there was Grey, her enemy whom she was forced to dine with every night. He had seen what Eric's words had done to her and acted to comfort her. Even though the two of them were on opposite sides of the coming war, he pulled her in and held her like he was her oldest and dearest friend. Giving her an opportunity to cry like she so desperately wanted to.

Regardless of her overwhelming need to cry to someone about what happened, Terra didn't know that she could trust his word. Using her contact with him she sent her magic out to try and sense what his intentions were.

"I'm going to try and not take offense to that," Grey said feeling her magic wash over him. He was surprised at how warm her magic felt. It was like he was suddenly wrapped in warm blanket next to a fire. Comfortable, warm and completely at ease.

"Can you blame me?" She asked.

"I suppose not. Satisfied yet?"

She nodded. As far as she could tell he was being completely honest about his offer of a momentary truce. She rested her head on Greys chest and he held her, although somewhat awkwardly while her tears ran silently down her face. She was careful not to make any sound; the situation was awkward enough without her blubbering like a baby on her enemies shoulder. As strange as it sounded in her head, it was actually kind of nice to have someone to lean on.

Grey shifted slightly and put his back against the glass. Terra, too caught up in her own thoughts again, leaned back with him. He slid down the wall until he was sitting on the floor, carefully taking Terra down with him.

"What's going on?" She asked.

"Just got tired of standing is all," he replied, looking out the glass to his left. He kept his whole head turned away from her. When she didn't look away he glanced at her out of the corner of his eye. She was half kneeling half lying next to him leaning against his chest. If she shifted just a little to her right she would be in his lap.

Needless to say, she was very close. Grey didn't get close to people. He never had. Proximity seemed to make quite a difference.

Terra returned to resting her head on his chest and slowly waited for her tears to stop flowing. She was oddly comfortable in the box. She could still see everything, but the walls protected her from anyone getting in. More than that, inside the box the bond seemed to be weaker. She could no longer feel the disgust Eric felt toward her.

After a while she could feel Eric's frustration mounting. He wanted to get going and he wanted her to hurry so he could take her back to Mammy's room and be done. She might have been reading into it too much, but she was in a mood. He didn't wait too long. Maybe five minutes later he was getting further away and heading up the stairs.

He had left without her.

"Don't think about that," Grey whispered, seeing the thoughts in her mind. He was still looking off to the side but he kept his arms around her. "Don't think like that either. I'm only being nice so you'll stop crying."

"Oh," she said. "Well in that case I'm feeling better now."

"Are you sure?" He asked, finally turning to face her.

She was *really* close, maybe half a foot away or less. Her green eyes were huge and sparkling with tears she hadn't finished crying.

Grey stood suddenly, not sure what else to do in that situation. He brushed off his dark black pants and carefully checked to make sure Terra wasn't angry that he jerked away so suddenly.

When she stood to face him she was smiling.

"Thank you Grey."

"You don't have to thank me," he said. "I told you, it's a onetime only thing and if you ever tell anyone I'll destroy you."

Terra laughed and said, "I'm so glad you told me not to tell anyone, I was going to go and shout from the rooftops that I was having a bad day so I crawled into this glass prison and cuddled up with the monster that stalks children's nightmares. You know, for laughs."

"Look whose snarky now," he commented.

"I'm not snarky. I'm grateful. You said it yourself," she explained, "We're enemies. But despite all that, you saw that I was hurting and needed someone, so you volunteered. Even though you're trapped in this cell, you showed me kindness and compassion. Not traits one would attribute to a monster or a creature comprised entirely of darkness."

"Just stop right there," he countered. "I told you who and what I am upfront. Don't get those kinds of ideas now."

"It's too late for that now," she teased walking to the wall Grey was leaning against. "I see who you really are." She put her hand on the glass, ready to walk through when a thought struck her. She turned to Grey, he was leaning against the glass in such a way that he was only slightly taller than she was. Before he could see her thought and stop her, Terra leaned over and kissed him lightly on the cheek and ran through the glass.

Grey, caught completely off guard, slipped from the glass and fell over. He jumped up and spun to face the princess who was standing on the other side of the glass, smiling ear to ear.

"Are you insane?" He demanded, hand on his cheek looking like he might lose his mind at any moment. "You can't just go around kissing people you don't know!"

"But I do know you. I named you," she said, in serious way that gave the Shadow King pause. "You know Grey you may be the only friend I have right now."

There! Grey could feel it. A crack. Not a very large crack, but a crack none the less. He could feel it in the room, he could sense the break. He just needed to slowly pour darkness into it until it got wider. If all it took was for him to be nice, he could do that. He could be the nicest idiot the world had ever seen.

He would still need Reynolds though. He could corrupt him easy and use him to drive Terra closer and closer to him. There would be very little anyone could do to stop him now. He just had to sit back and wait for the perfect time to make his move.

Terra could feel something in the air shift, something change. She wasn't sure what it was but it seemed to her that there was something different about Grey. Not just the way he was standing there, but the way he was looking at her and even the smile on his face was different. Not wanting to think of what might have changed when he could so easily read her mind; she decided it was time to go.

"Well, thank you again and don't worry I won't tell anyone. But I think I should be getting to bed. It's been a day." She tried to pull random thoughts in her head to make a kind of fog around the thoughts that were important.

Grey stared at her. She had a lot of really random things going on in her mind, some made sense, and some were as odd as cats at the river begging for fish. She was covering something, and whatever it was he couldn't get to it. Deciding to test his theory he smiled at her and nodded.

"It has been a long day. With everything that's been going on you need rest." He looked around awkwardly for a moment and then said, "Will you be able to stay long at breakfast tomorrow?"

He was right, Terra was caught completely off guard by the way he was staring at her. She blushed up to her eyes and glanced around awkwardly. "Um I don't know if I can. I missed breakfast yesterday because of this stupid fight with Diana and I know my mother probably doesn't like having to make excesses for me. But I'll see what I can do. Oh can I get your tray before I forget?"

"Of course," Grey said. "Here." He held the tray up to the glass. He had a thought that would prove his theory once and for all.

Terra put her hand to the glass again and pushed through. Before she grabbed the tray, Grey pulled it back and took her wrist. He bowed to her and kissed the back of her hand. Her heart skipped a beat and all the thoughts in her head stopped. All she could think about was his lips on her skin. She was still just a child. Despite all of her talk and he demands, she was a child who wasn't able to recognize genuine emotion.

As he hoped, he could feel that crack again. It didn't widen but it did seem to weaken. He couldn't tell if it was her heart, or very soul that was cracking, either way, it was all he needed to get in.

He straightened up, careful not to let go of Terra, and handed her the tray.

"W . . . what was that for?" She stammered.

Grey could have laughed. Women were so easy to manipulate. "Just returning the favor," he replied tapping his cheek. He handed the tray to Terra, it took everything in him not to laugh at her face. She was red up to the dark roots of her hair.

Her face was so red in fact that her freckles disappeared. She had fallen for his more than obvious fake chivalry.

Getting her on his side would be so much easier than he had thought.

Terra walked slowly up the steps to Mammy's room. She was so tired she was actually afraid that if she stopped moving she would fall asleep standing up. It was late by the time she had gotten out of the basement. Lewis had stopped her on the way out and was

194

pestering her continuously about why her face was red and what had happened between her and Reynolds? He had stormed out so mad. Was it a lover's quarrel? Were they lovers?

It had her so flustered that she had simply turned and walked away. She had too much on her mind to sit and deal with this man's questions. So she walked away. As much as it pained her to admit, she was princess and she could do that without being questioned.

After that she made her way to the kitchen and dropped the tray off where she was supposed to. Then she was finally able to make her way up the long staircase to Mammy's room. She was so tired that it felt to her like she had been walking though the castle all day. She wanted sleep.

She got to Mammy's door and looked around. Eric was nowhere in sight.

Terra hadn't really expected him to be, but it was still disheartening to think that he wasn't even going to wait to make sure she got to her room ok. When she had asked him not to care about her she had wanted him to not love her. She had still wanted him to be her friend. She needed someone to talk to, someone who would listen to all that was wrong and tell her it was ok. Even if they didn't know it was going to be ok.

She needed a friend.

Maybe she should have sat down and explained to Eric better what she meant. Maybe if she had told him not to love her but to still be her friend things would be different.

She knew she could reach out through the bond and find out where he was and what he was thinking. It would be easy but if she found him somewhere else *with* someone else, she would be devastated. Frankly, she'd had enough devastation for a while.

She pushed the door open to find Mammy asleep on the bed and her shift laid out for her. Terra smiled, Mammy was so kind to her. She really was like a mother to the young princess. Terra undressed quietly and then pulled her shift over her head and braided her hair. Careful not to wake Mammy, she climbed into bed and pulled the covers up. Comfortably situated, she sat up and blew out the candle on the nightstand.

For a moment the room was completely black. Then her eyes adjusted and the light from the moon cut through the darkness. It made her think about Grey. He had always seemed so cold and angry, and that was ok. He was the enemy and he was supposed to be that way. Honestly she was surprised he was as decent as he was. She was prepared to have to face an evil enemy every day until the end.

An image of him bending to kiss her hand flashed in her mind.

Tonight was so strange. He was so different. He had been kind to her when she needed kindness the most. He had held her for a long while as she cried through her problems. She knew it made her weak to have to cry like that, but something about Grey made her feel stronger. Maybe it was just that he was her enemy and he was kind to her. Or maybe it was because the way he looked at her when he was kissing her hand.

Either way, Terra was starting to think that maybe Grey wasn't all bad. Maybe somewhere in all that darkness there was still a little light, fighting to keep going? Perhaps if she tried hard enough she could find that light and make it brighter. If she could do that, if she could chase the darkness away from Grey's heart, then maybe he could be saved and maybe there would be no need for a fight between Diana and Grey.

Maybe she could save them both.

Chapter 6

"Terra you lazy girl wake up!" Mammy yelled as she pushed the princess off the bed. Still completely asleep, she was rolled right off the bed and landed on the cold stone floor with a thud.

"Ow!" Terra howled sitting up. "Mammy what was that for?"

"You weren't waking up. I had to do what I had to do," Mammy said, making the now vacant bed. "What time did you get in last night?"

Terra balked, she didn't want to talk about her and Grey again. Over the past two weeks her dinners with Grey had been growing longer and longer every night. He was opening up and they would talk for hours after they had finished eating. Eric had stopped bothering to come with her at all. For the first few days he had come out of obligation, but after a rather large and angry fight he stopped coming all together. As far as Terra was concerned that was for the best. He was a jerk and it hurt her every time she had to be around him.

"It wasn't that late," she lied, not actually sure what time she'd actually gotten in. Mammy looked at her; she didn't believe her for a minute.

"Anyway, you didn't have to be so mean," she said sulkily.

"You needed to wake up! Sixteen and already so lazy," Mammy said, tisking under her breath.

"That's today isn't it?" She asked looking up at Mammy over her bed.

"It is," Mammy said smiling so wide Terra was certain her cheeks must be hurting. "Oh Terra," she said, tears starting to run down her cheeks.

"Mammy what's wrong?" She asked, standing up.

"I'm just so happy for you. Sixteen and a real lady now. You'll have your debutant ball tonight and be presented to the whole kingdom as a woman." Mammy wiped away her tears. "You've grown up so fast. Now look at you, so beautiful and so kind. I would be the most blessed woman in all the kingdoms to call you my child."

Terra walked to Mammy, feeling her eyes watering too. "Mammy I would be the one who would be blessed to have you as my mother." She threw her arms around her beloved care taker and held her tightly. She loved Mammy so much. She had wished many times that Mammy was her mother. She would be loved then. Even now she wished it.

"Now, now," Mammy insisted pulling away and wiping the tears from Terra's eyes. "None of this today, today is a day for celebration. Now dry your eyes. Your new room is ready and we're going to head up there and supervise where all of your things are placed. Then we have to get you ready for your ball."

Terra hesitated for a moment. If they were going to move things in her room she would have to grab her journal and hide it somewhere before anybody found it. She would have to get away from Mammy for at least a few moments.

After another moment of mental debate, Terra had it.

"Don't forget I have to take breakfast and lunch down to the prison," she added.

"I hate that you're like a maid for that monster," Mammy grumbled angrily.

"I know," Terra said. "But I had to save Diana."

Mammy grumbled something under her breath that Terra couldn't understand. She didn't need to though; she knew very well Mammy's feelings about her sister.

"She would do the same for me Mammy," she insisted. "I'm going to put on the wrap and head down to the kitchen before anyone else gets up."

"Not that thin wispy thing," Mammy objected, "I don't care what people are wearing in the Moon Kingdom. It's not proper for lady to be out in so little fabric."

"I know Mammy," she said, "But we don't have time to get me all laced up in a corset. So hand me the wrap so I can get going. You said yourself there's a lot to get done today."

Mammy muttered something under her breath, but did as Terra asked. She pulled the wrap from the small wardrobe they had set up for the princess in her room and handed it to her. It was a thin pale green material that had "excellent flow value" as Terra has said the first time she wore it. All you had to do was slip your arms in, wrap it around and tie it. It was like a robe but long and beautiful. Terra liked how simple and easy it was to put on.

She tied it on and slipped into the beautiful green slip shoes that had come with it. "Alright, I'm going to get going so we can get up to the room. I'll be back soon," she said, turning for the door.

"Not just yet!" Mammy yelled, "You're a young lady now and you have to at least look like it. Sit and let me put your hair up."

"Oh right!" She giggled. She ran over and jumped in the seat in front of Mammy's vanity. Mammy with skilled deft hands had her hair up in a beautiful plait on her head in a matter of moments.

Mammy sighed at the princess with her hair up. She turned to gather up the princess's shift off the floor and walked to the laundry basket. Seeing a chance to make her move, Terra got up as quickly and quietly as she could and snatched the journal from underneath Mammy's writing desk. She moved it behind her back as Mammy turned back to face her.

"Alright," she said satisfied. "Get going before someone sees you." She shooed her out the door and watched as she ran down the hall. It was hard to her to believe that sixteen years ago the Queen had handed her off to Mammy like pup she no longer wanted. She sighed and turned to start packing Terra's things.

Diana cracked her door open and watched as her sister ran past in one of the wraps the Moon Kingdom had given them. She never should have given Terra one. She looked good in it, too good. Diana was supposed to be the one that shone. Now more and more, people were talking about how beautiful Terra was becoming and how she would grow into a great beauty.

They'll be singing a different tune after tonight.

For weeks Diana had been planning how to best exact revenge on her sister. So many things ran through her mind that she had to spend an entire week just shifting through them all. Then it hit her one night. She was sneaking through the tunnels to see Jack; who had turned out to be a good deal more fun than she had originally thought. She was about to pop out from behind a large painting of her father and mother at their wedding when she'd heard shouting.

It was Terra and her guard.

They were going on and on about her spending too much time with someone or something called Grey. Guard whatever-his-name-is looked disgusted and Terra looked like she would cry. They yelled for the better part of five minutes until he shouted something about not being able to stand the sight of her and stormed off.

Her sister promptly collapsed to the floor in tears.

Diana knew then how to get back at her sister.

She just needed to raise enough dark magic to do it.

With tonight being the night of the new moon, Diana would have enough dark magic to cast this curse multiple times if she wanted to.

She just had to wait for her parents to leave their room and she would make her move.

Terra would never see it coming.

"Jenny?" Terra called over the noise of the kitchen staff, busy making breakfast for the whole castle. "Jenny is the tray ready? I need to get down there quickly, it's a busy day."

A few people walked up and saluted her, wishing her a happy birthday and giving her blessings for the next year. A few of the young men in the kitchen took notice of the slim fitting dress she was wearing. One nearly lit his shirt of fire.

"I'm here princess," Jenny said appearing in the thick of all the people carrying the tray for Grey. "Sorry we just got it done. Be careful with the bread it's really hot. Oh and happy birthday princess." Jenny curtsied to Terra once the tray was handed off.

"Thank you Jenny," she replied ready to run off. "Oh are you coming tonight?"

"Tonight?" Jenny asked confused.

"Yea, to my ball thingy?"

Jenny looked around like she was waiting for someone to jump out and say gotcha! When she realized Terra was serious she said, "No princess, we weren't invited."

"What?" She asked laughing. "That's ridiculous, of course you're invited."

An older woman stepped up to Jenny's shoulder. It was her mother Tamera. "You are very kind to invite her," she said, "but I'm afraid the Queen wouldn't take kindly to kitchen staff being at a ball."

"Well it's my party," Terra said simply. "I should be able to invite whoever I want. So I say you're all invited. If my mother the Queen is angry than she can talk with me about it. You know where and when it is. I have to get going. See you all tonight!" She called running off, her need to hurry making her bold.

She was down the stairs and at the wooden doors faster than she thought was possible whilst carrying a tray full of hot food. As she came down the stairs she was surprised, and a little disappointed, to see Lewis still standing guard. His shift usually ended in the morning. It meant that nearly every night she had to face him as she went through the door.

He would stare at her every night as she came down the stairs. He didn't even try to hide the fact that he was leering at her. He would watch the way she walked down the hall and his eye would linger on the parts of her that she considered extremely private.

Over the last few weeks Terra had really begun to enjoy her time with Grey. They talked over everything and he was very helpful when it came to her serious concerns about her upcoming ball. She would stay for hours and talk to him. For the first time in nearly all her life, she felt like she had a friend.

"Princess," Lewis said openly leering again. "I don't know what you're wearing, but I like it."

"I will take that as a complement, thank you Lewis. Will you get the door please?" He looked like he was going to say something else. Still he reached over and opened the door letting her pass. Terra quickly shot through the door and passed him before he could say anything further. Without looking back she kicked the door closed and sighed.

"Terra," Grey said sounding somewhat breathless.

She smiled privately at the sound of him saying her name like that.

"Really?" He said smiling to. "Just the way I say your name makes you smile?"

"You promised not to read my mind the second I walked through the door," Terra said, stopping halfway to the table.

"Did I say that?" He asked playfully. "It seems I can't recall that conversation."

"Well in that case I don't know if I can recall what I'm supposed to do with all this breakfast. Hmm maybe I should take it out and see if Lewis is hungry."

"You go do that, in that dress," he laughed, "I'll wait here and then when you want help to hide his body, come find me."

"How do you know I would kill him?" She asked, continuing her walk to the table. "Maybe I'll just give him a stern talking to."

Grey shot her an are-you-serious look.

202

"A *very* stern talking to?" Terra set the tray down on the table, she looked around quickly and pulled her journal out from underneath the tray.

"What's that?" Grey asked curiously.

"Nothing," she said securing it under the table.

"I didn't know you kept a journal," he laughed as he read her thoughts. "Does it say anything about me?" He asked, keeping his tone light.

"Maybe," she said with a smile.

"Does it say anything about Lewis and his lewd thoughts?" Grey asked sensing Terra's heart spike at the thought of him in her journal.

She laughed, happy for the subject change and leaned against the glass wall. "The thoughts you think I'd kill him for?"

Grey matched her position and leaned his head down so he was closer to her eyelevel. "I *know* you would kill him because I know what he thinks about you. I can see what's in his head every time you walk by."

"And what does he think exactly?"

"Terra, if I told you what he thought about you it would curl your raven hair. Now I do believe there's something important going on today isn't there?" He asked, tapping his chin.

"Oh, you know there is!" Terra laughed. "I forgot today is the day you told me you were going on that crazy strict diet. Can't rain fire and damnation down on the world with a potbelly. I'll take this away for you." She grabbed the tray off the table.

"Happy birthday Terra," Grey said sincerely.

"Thank you," she replied smiling, "here." She put the tray up to the glass and pushed it through slowly. It was hard to balance the tray on just one end.

Grey grabbed the tray and pulled it though. He reached out with his free hand and caught Terra's hand before she could pull it back. He gave her a small tug. "Come here."

"Grey," she mumbled, "I have to get going. Mammy will only wait for me for so long. Then she track me down like one of father's hounds." When he didn't let go she added, "What?"

"Come in here so I can wish you a proper happy birthday," Grey said pulling on her hand again. He leaned over and set the tray down on the table and grabbed her hand with both of his.

"You have two minutes," she sighed, stepping through the glass. As she came through the cell wall Grey pulled her into a hug. It wasn't the first time he hugged her. In truth it was closer to the fifth or sixth time. She and Grey talked about everything, sometimes Terra would get really upset and he would offer to hold her until she finished crying. She didn't always take him up of the offer, more often than not she did.

"Happy birthday my little shadow," he said into the top of her head.

Terra blushed. He often called her little shadow, it was one of his names for her. He had never before called her *his* little shadow.

"Th . . . Thank you," she stammered.

"Can I ask you something?" He inquired, not pulling away.

"Of course."

"Who gets the first dance?"

She laughed, "My father." At a coming out ball like this the girls' first dance was always with her father or grandfather. Whomever a princess danced with after that was the person the family favored to wed the princess. Grey was essentially asking who her mother wanted her to marry.

"You know what I mean," he said giving her a squeeze.

Her heart fluttered and her whole mind started to race with thoughts about him and her dancing. She was a fool. Sooner or later he was going to completely exploit her, use her against her own sister. For now, he was going to play this part and widen the crack he had made.

"I don't know," she answered truthfully, starting to pull away. Mammy was going to be wondering where she was.

Grey pulled her back and in a quick movement he had her hand in his and a hand on her waist. He started slowly dancing with her.

"Grey," she asked confused, "what are you doing?"

"Well," he said as they spun slowly together, "I am a King in my right, so I thought I would get the first dance in."

"Stealing the first dance with the daughter of the King who's holding you as a prisoner? Sounds like a bad idea to me." She said laughing.

Grey laughed with her as they spun in circles around his cell.

After a few minutes they were both laughing too hard to keep dancing. They stood, in each other's arms, laughing about the way they danced. Terra wished she could stay. It was so much easier to be around Grey than to be around her family. Her mother was all over her about the party. Her colors, the music she wanted played, will she be able to dance in the new heeled shoes she had to wear, and finally could she behave herself during the dances she had lined up for her?

It was exhausting.

She really didn't even want to have a dance.

Sadly, she would have to go through with it.

"I should get going," she said finally.

"I know," Grey said. He kissed the top of her head. "Will you be by for lunch?"

"I should be," she said, blushing. "But I should get going. I don't't' want Mammy to come looking for me down here. This would be hard to explain."

"That is very true," Grey said. As she stared to back away he suddenly felt overcome with something or some kind of feeling he'd never experienced before. Everything suddenly seemed to be moving in slow motion. Terra was looking up at him smiling as she backed away to leave, her face looked almost like it was glowing. Before he knew what he was doing he had grabbed a hold of her again. He put one hand behind her neck and other wrapped around her waist.

He pulled her close and turned her head up to face his. His lips were less than inch from Terra's when he realized what he was doing. Her hands were on his chest and she was breathing rapidly, for that matter so was he. Her eyes were huge and they were frantically searching his for some kind of answer to what was happening.

She didn't stop him though.

"G . . . Grey?" She gasped.

"Terra," he whispered, still breathless. He leaned and put his forehead against hers. He wanted to throw her away from him. She was clouding up his mind and making him feel strange things and do things he didn't even know he was doing.

Part of him wanted to pull her in the rest of the way and finish what he started.

"Grey," she asked. "I don't understand?"

"I don't . . . I don't know," was all he could say. He couldn't kiss her. That was moving forward to fast. He knew at some point it would get there, but not yet. He had only been working on corrupting her for a month. He knew if he rushed things he would mess everything up.

Still, he couldn't let her go.

Terra wasn't sure what was going on. All of a sudden Grey had grabbed her like he was going to kiss her. Then, at the last second, he froze. Now he had his forehead pressed against hers and looked so sad. She realized what was going on and it made her feel sad too.

She reached up and put her hands on either side of Grey's face. They had gotten so close the last month and while Terra will admit that Grey was a very attractive man, she wouldn't allow herself to think about him that way. She would not have feelings for a man who was responsible for so much death.

She turned his head so he was looking at her. "It's ok," she uttered. "I get that you're trying to be nice I guess, but you don't have

to force yourself to do something that clearly you do not want to do."
Her voice was starting to crack and she had tears in hers eyes.

"Terra?!" He shouted alarmed that she thought he was
hesitating because he was forcing himself to be near her. He searched
her mind. She was so sad. She thought he was forcing himself to be
close to her as kindness for her birthday. She wasn't exactly wrong. He
did have to force himself to touch her in a way that wasn't homicidal.
Still, he hadn't banked on her looking and feeling this way.

It was like the part of Grey that was trying fight against
whatever Terra was doing to him, just cracked and fell away. He pulled
her in the rest of the way and kissed her. He knew even as he was
doing it that it was a bad idea, but he was so caught up in everything
he didn't care.

As soon as his lips touched hers there was this feeling that
surged through him. Like his whole body was suddenly hit by a bolt of
lightning. He couldn't have broken away from her if he had wanted to.
He could tell by the way Terra's breath caught in her throat that she as
feeling something too.

"Terra!" Grey yelled! "What's wrong with you? Are you ok?"

"What?" She asked slightly disoriented. She shook her head
and everything in front of her tuned to smoke and vanished. She was
standing with Grey in his cell and he still had a hold of her hand. It was
like they were still dancing. Terra jumped back out of his arms and
spun around. "What happened?"

"What do you mean what happened?" He asked a little
offended that she had jumped back like he had bit her. "We were
dancing and all of a sudden you just stopped. You froze. I tried talking
to you, I even shook you and nothing happened. I tried to look in your
mind but it was blank.

"It was like you were gone and your body was still standing
here."

Terra shook her head again. Nothing was making sense. They
danced he kissed her she had seen it, hell she had felt it! There was no

way she made that up in her head. She wouldn't. She wouldn't let herself feel about him. She wouldn't even think about it.

So why was this happening now? Why could she still feel his lips on hers? She needed to go. She needed to go right now.

"I'm sorry Grey I have to go." She turned on her heel and ran. Straight out of the box and through the doors, she didn't even stop when Lewis said something to her she was sure was inappropriate. All the way up the stairs and through the west wing hall, she didn't stop until she was sure she was out of Grey's range.

She didn't know what had happened, but she knew she needed answers. She needed to find Master Bell. He would know what was going on with her.

Grey watched Terra run from the room like it was on fire. He had been slowly pouring darkness into her as they danced. He had been trying to decide how best to make his next move when she had suddenly stopped moving.

He had actually been afraid that something was wrong with her.

Fear was not an emotion he felt, ever.

Grey paced nervously back and forth in his cell. He wasn't sure if he was more alarmed about what happened to Terra, or the fact that he was alarmed at all.

Diana stared intently out the door, eyeing the master jeweler as he approached her parent's room. He was carrying a small black box in his hands and he had the look of a very proud man. It was Terra's signet ring. She was turning sixteen. Diana could care less about her sister's birthday or her ball. All she cared about was getting her hands on that ring.

For almost a month Diana had planned for tonight. She had cast all the proper runes and pulled all the dark magic she could get her hands on. Everything else was ready; she just needed to get that ring to finish it all off.

208

Diana waited until the jeweler started to make his way back down the hall. As nonchalantly as she could, she wandered into her parent's room. Her father was now holding the box with Terra's ring and her mother was shouting at the men who were moving her large oak dressing table.

"Diana my dear, what can I do for you?" Her father asked. She gave her father a halfhearted curtsy and barely nodded at her mother.

"Hello Father, Mother," she said. "I was wondering how the move was going?"

"Fine," her father said. "I'm actually on my way to see about that right now. Elise will you be alright here?"

"I'm going to follow these incompetent morons," Queen Elise replied, "I don't trust them not to damage something."

"Oh well I see you're both so busy," Diana said, searching her mind for an excuse to take the ring.

"Diana," King Sol said looking as though he'd just been struck by a marvelous idea, "how would you like to present your sister with her signet ring tonight at the ball?"

Diana could have laughed at her luck. "I would love to," she exclaimed, her voice full of fake excitement.

Queen Elise looked over at her eldest daughter and eyed her and her overly enthusiastic behavior suspiciously. Diana met her gaze head on and her mother turned away.

"Good," King Sol said happily. He handed her the small black box and clapped her on her shoulder.

The princess waited until both her parents had left the room before she snuck off to Terra's old chambers. Her sister had been avoiding it ever since Richard had attacked her. Since she was the youngest and that least important member of the castle, as far as Diana was concerned, her room would be handled last. So it was the perfect place for her to set up a small alter to work her hex.

It had worked out quite well for Diana, especially considering that Richard had been too badly burned to properly identify. Had the guards been able to ascertain who he was questions might have been raised. While Diana was always very careful about not being seen meeting up with any of her young . . . suitors . . . all it took was one person knowing the truth to cause irreprehensible harm to her and her reputation.

Shaking off such unpleasant thoughts, Diana turned back to the work at hand.

She opened the box and pulled out the small silver ring intended for her sister. It had her variation of their family crest cast in fine silver at the top. There was the bright sun on the outside with the pentacle in the center. Three of the five points were amethyst and two were moonstones. For Terra, on the inside of the pentacle there was a crescent moon that sat at the bottom pointing up. She claimed she had done it to honor her mother's family in the moon kingdom. Diana didn't really care why she did it. All she cared about was that her mother had it cast in silver and not gold. More than enough to show anyone that Terra was the so called shadow princess.

Diana flipped the box closed and laughed as she placed the ring in center of a small dish filled with blood. Not hers of course, the spell she was using on Terra's ring only required the use of blood, not necessarily the blood of the caster.

Carefully she made her way around the room lighting the thirteen black candles that circled the room. Then back around the room lighting the seven white candles that made a circle inside the black ones. Finally she approached the table in the center and lit the five red candles that encircled her make-shift alter. Fire magic was something Diana did excel at.

With all the candles lit Diana turned back to the ring. She opened the small black book of curses and hexes and turned to the page she needed. After having to prepare for so long, Diana was sure she could have recited the curse by heart. Still, she didn't want to take any chances so she pressed the pages down to keep it open and started to recite the lines.

She paused halfway through. She had reached the part that required her to summon the dark magic. At first it was hard to call on any dark magic. She hated the way it felt when she started. It was hard to breath at first, and the dark magic took all the light in the room away. She was frightened until the power started to surge through her.

It was like nothing she had ever felt before.

There was so much power swirling all around.

Dark or not, she loved it.

It wasn't even half the power she needed to curse Terra's ring. Every night she pulled more and more dark magic, careful not to pull too much and alert anyone who might be able to sense such dark things. It had taken the better part of three weeks to get everything she needed together and since the ring wasn't ready yet, Diana just kept pulling dark magic, night after night.

She pulled all the magic she had left hovering around the room and, using herself as channel, funneled it into the ring. Darkness whirled around her as she started to call out the last of the curse. There was moment where Diana was afraid things weren't working like they were supposed to. She finished the curse but the dark magic just kept coming.

It swirled around her like a dark black tornado. It obscured all the light in the room and made her feel like she was trapped in a dark cell somewhere.

For the smallest moment of time Diana was afraid she had made a terrible mistake dabbling in such dark magic.

Finally, it stopped.

Diana looked down at her alter. Terra's ring started to glow with a black light. Slowly it absorbed all the blood in the dish and flashed red three times. Her curse was complete and the ring was hexed. She threw her head back and laughed. She would finally show her sister once and for all that no one puts themselves ahead of her.

She grabbed a small pair of tongs and picked the ring up. As careful as she could she put the ring back in the box. She had to make sure she didn't touch it or the curse would rebound on her. She snapped the box closed and set about cleaning up her alter before the movers set in on Terra's room.

Terra knocked on Bell's door. She had managed to calm herself on the walk to his room, although her heart felt like it might fly out of her chest. Finally she could hear the sounds of someone approaching. Bell opened the door.

"Master Bell I have to talk to you," she said walking past him through the door, and into his room. "I hate to barge in on you but this is an emergency." She walked a safe distance away from the door and turned to face him. Not saying anything he pushed the door closed and walked over to her.

"Happy birthday Princess," He said bowing to her. "Now tell me what has you so worried that you're at my door before breakfast."

"Ok, I need to ask you a question but to do that I need to tell you about something that happened," she explained, "but I can't tell you everything and I need you to be ok with that."

Bell smiled calmly, "Princess tell me everything that you can and I will help to the best of my abilities."

"Thank you Master Bell," she sighed. "So I was visiting a . . . friend."

"A male friend?"

"Yes," she admitted blushing, "and he was wishing me a happy birthday and we were joking about the ball tonight and um, he started dancing with me, just as a joke. Then . . . well I was going to leave and I thought . . . I thought." Terra stopped. Images flashed through her mind of her and Grey holding each other, kissing each other. For a moment she couldn't speak.

"Terra just tell me what you can, don't feel like you have to tell me anything you don't' want to. Do the best you can," he prompted. He took the princess by the elbow and led her to a small dark blue couch. He sat down and pulled her to sit next to him.

"Ok," Terra said, taking a deep breath. "I thought he kissed me. I swear to you it was like he pulled me close and kissed me. I could feel his lips on mine and his hand on my neck. But more than that it was like I was in his head. I could hear his thoughts and feel what he felt. It was like nothing I've ever experienced before.

"Then the next thing I knew everything in front of me disappeared. It was like smoke, there one minute gone the next. Then I was standing there, nothing had happened. According to him we were dancing one minute and I was gone the next. He couldn't get me to move or speak or anything."

"Master Bell what happened to me?"

Bell was quiet as he considered what she had said. "Princess may I ask, this man, did you want him to kiss you?"

"No," she exclaimed with a defeated sigh.

"Well then I believe you had a premonition."

"A premonition? How? Master Bell I've never had any kind of precognitive abilities before." Terra couldn't believe that it was as simple as a premonition.

"To be fair Princess," he commented, "You've never officially been my student and so you've never been fully tried and tested. We don't really know what you are or aren't capable of. At least for now."

"What do you mean by now?"

"Tonight I think you'll understand fully what I mean. Until then, I hear that Mammy is looking for you."

"Master Bell."

"Don't worry Princess. All that happened was your magic warned of what was going to happen if you continued to keep dancing. There's nothing to be alarmed about. Now go. Mammy is not a woman to be kept waiting."

Terra nodded, not sure she really understood what Bell had said. Still, if he said things would be fine than she trusted him. She nodded her thanks and excused herself. If Mammy really was combing the halls for her than it must be time to start moving her room.

She headed up to Mammy's room assuming that would be the best place to start looking.

Eric paced the floor in his room. Ever since he had become a royal guard he no longer stayed in the barracks. He had been given a room very near to Terra's new room. Not that he was enjoying the proximity to her. He could barely look at her lately. Ever since they had that huge blow out in the hall, he'd been avoiding her completely. He would follow behind her and make sure she got down to the prison ok and he would wait in the hall until he felt her coming up the stairs. Then he would go and hide in the passage off the stairs until she was safe in her room.

He couldn't look at her.

Every time he did he could hear that monsters voice in his head talking about how she had named him! He didn't understand how she could do such and intimate thing. It made him sick to his stomach to think about it even now.

He would still do his duty by her. Even if it meant he did it in shadow.

Tonight, however, was a completely different situation all together.

He would have to be by her side all night to make sure none of the guests tried anything funny while they were dancing. He would have to literally be over her shoulder the entire evening.

At least until she went to take dinner to that monster.

Eric took a deep breath.

It was going to be a very long night.

Terra stood in front of her new door. She was finally all moved into her new room. She wasn't sure how to feel about this new room of hers. It was over double the size of her last room, and it was certainly more private. Her only problem was that the old west wing had a turret at the end. It was old and sturdy and stood so tall you could see over the castle walls. It was Terra's favorite place to play when she was little.

That was her new room.

214

If you took the grand staircase all the way up to the fifth floor and then then up the old staircase to the seventh floor there was a door at the top that opened up to the turret. There was a room there at the bottom of the spiral staircase, for Eric, and a door that lead to the bottom half of the stair case. Those stairs lead to the very bottom floor of the castle where the rest of her family's rooms were. Another set of stairs to the right of Eric's door spiraled up to her room.

Terra originally felt bad that her family was so far removed from her. After careful thought though, she was glad for the privacy. She had a way to get to and from her room without having to pass by Diana's. That alone was something to be grateful for. With the exception of Eric, she was alone in her own little corner of the castle.

Deciding it was best to be grateful for such and nice room, Terra pushed the door open and headed inside.

Her room was lovely.

Mammy had said that as part of her birthday present, her father had commissioned new furniture for her new room. Her bed was huge! She was pretty sure she could sleep comfortably in any position. It had a lovely purple and green canopy and a thick purple and sliver quilt. She had a new writing desk against one wall and several large bookcases up against another. She now had a beautiful couch and matching chair near the bed and finally a much larger wardrobe and dressing table.

For Terra, the best part was huge bay window. It had padded seat so you could sit and look out the huge window for hours. She loved every bit of it. It was the most beautiful thing she had ever seen and to think that it was all hers! She couldn't believe how lucky she was.

"Good you're here!" Mammy said coming up behind her. She was huffing up the stairs carrying a dress and some heeled slippers.

"Mammy," she smiled pushing the door open all the way and standing back. "Do you need help?"

"No dear," Mammy said. "I just need to get you cleaned up and ready for the ball."

It took literally all day to get both the room and the princess in order.

At least it gave Terra an excuse to avoid lunch with Grey.

Mammy had her in a traditional white dress with a tight laced corset and full skirt. Instead of having long sleeves this dress had sheer white cap sleeves that hung off her shoulders. It was beautiful. Add to that the way Mammy wound her hair up on her head and pulled down little ringlets of curls around her face. Terra looked like a woman now.

She caught sight of Mammy in the mirror behind her. Her eyes were glassy with tears but she was beaming with pride.

"Mammy I swear if you cry I'll cry," she warned, "then all the work you just put in with the funny pencils and creams will be for not."

"I know," Mammy said drying her eyes, "it just makes me so proud to see you all dressed up like this. Now, will Guard Reynolds be escorting you tonight?"

Terra made a face and looked away.

"I'm sorry dear," Mammy said seeing the princess's face, "I don't know what you two are fighting about but I'm sure everything will work out ok. Once you two cool down everything will go back to normal."

"Well whether that's true or not, I think I will be escorting myself tonight," she sighed, forcing a smile.

"Don't be ridiculous," Eric called from the open doorway.

Terra spun quickly to see him standing quietly outside her door. She hated that her heart leapt at the sight of him, even more so she hated that Eric could sense that through the bond and it made him grimace. Terra's heart felt like it might break every time he looked at her like that. Her shoulders drooped and she looked away.

"Good evening princess," he intoned formally saluting her with his fist over his heart. "I've come to escort you to your ball."

"Of course," she replied glumly, not looking up. "Thank you Guard Reynolds."

Mammy stepped up behind her and wrapped a sheer and sparkling shawl around her shoulders. It was made of the same material as the skirt of her dress and the small cap sleeves. She took one last look at herself in the looking glass; she looked beautiful but so very, very sad.

"Thank you Mammy," she mumbled quietly.

"Don't think of it dear," Mammy said. She kissed Terra on the cheek and pushed her gently toward Eric. "Have fun and Eric you look after her."

"I will," he replied standing aside so Terra could walk through the door.

She stepped past him and kept walking. She didn't want to wait for him. She just wanted to go alone and not have to deal with all the crazy that seemed to surround them. She hadn't even reached the first step before Eric was silently at her side.

She thought of hundreds of different things she could say to start a conversation with him. Every time she looked up to say something his face made her pause. So she hung her head and said nothing on the trip down to the ballroom. The very long trip down to the ballroom.

Outside the double doors to the ballroom, King Sol stood waiting for them. His eyes lit up when he saw her coming down the hall in her dress. The princess couldn't help but smile at her father and rush forward throwing her arms around him. He laughed at how young she still was and wrapped his arms around her.

"My dear little princess," he said cupping her face in his hand. "Can it really be you've grown so much?"

Terra smiled; she loved when her father called her his little princess. She always felt so loved when it was just the two of them together.

"I don't know that I'm any older Papa," she replied, "I feel the same as always."

"Well you look more like a young lady today, beautiful and strong. Are you ready?" King Sol nodded toward the double doors of the ballroom. His page, Markus, was standing exchanging pleasantries

217

with Eric, but when the King turned he walked to the door and grabbed the handle. He watched the King waiting for the sign to open.

"I think so," she answered. "Wait Papa, where's Mother and Diana?"

"Oh they're already inside," he answered offhandedly.

"Oh," she muttered, her heart sinking, "I thought that we were supposed to be the first one's in tonight? Since you're the King and it's my ball. I thought that's what we did with Diana."

"Oh that," the King said uncomfortably. "Well your mother and sister just wanted to make sure everything was perfect for you."

"Well that's very kind of them," she stated, knowing her father was lying. "I'm ready Papa."

King Sol smiled and nodded toward the door. Markus cracked it, stuck his head in and whispered something. King Sol took Terra's hand in his arm and turned to the door. She could hear the trumpets sounding on the other side. Her heart felt like it was beating a mile a minute. She had to keep reminding herself to breathe.

She glanced back at Eric before the door opened, he was fiddling with something on his uniform, he didn't look up, even though Terra knew he knew she was looking. With a defeated sigh she turned and faced forward just as the doors were opening.

There were people lining either side of the doorway packed together and craning their necks to get a look at Terra and the King. Toward the back she could just make out Jenny and a handful of other kitchen staff waving wildly at her. She smiled at them as her father started forward looking noble as he lead her down a carpeted entry way toward a small stage set at the end of the ballroom. Queen Elise and Diana were standing at one end of the stage not paying any attention to Terra or her father.

Her mother and sister stood in near identical gowns. Both were deep red color and both had an even deeper neckline. The only difference Terra could see was that her mother's gown had long sweeping sleeves and her sisters and sheer red cap sleeves. As Diana and Elise turned to converse about something in quite whispers, Terra

218

saw that her sisters dress had a number a rubies laid into the fabric while her mother's was plain.

Only the best for Diana.

Slowly, they made their way down the long carpet toward the stage, waving and saying their hellos. Terra didn't recognize most of the people crowded around them, she could tell some of them were from other kingdoms and some were from other places around their own kingdom. Still she smiled and waved as they walked.

When, finally, they made it to the stage, King Sol stepped up and pulled his daughter up too. He walked to the edge of center stage and held up both hands to hush the crowd. He glanced around, smiling benevolently as a King does. When the crowd went silent he motioned for Terra to join him.

"My friends and kinsmen," King Sol called his voice booming through the ball room. "Allow me to thank you for being here tonight as we present my youngest daughter to the world. So without too much fuss, please allow me to introduce Terra Elisabeth Princess of the Kingdom of Sol!"

Terra wasn't sure what she was expecting, but the quiet applause and ripple of approval wasn't what she had in mind. Still she smiled graciously and waved at everyone. She was really trying to look the part of the gracious princess on her birthday. It was exhausting. Terra's arm was starting to hurt from waving so much.

King Sol lifted both his hands again to quiet everyone down. "Now, may I present the eldest princess of Sol, Diana Regina. Our princess of prophesy!"

The entire ball room erupted in applause. People were cheering and shouting as Diana walked from the side of the stage to stand next to her sister. She curtsied deeply to her father who offered her his hand to help her up. She smiled magnanimously at every one, dazzling them with her natural beauty and charm. Terra wanted to walk to the back of the stage and hide from all the people who had clearly forgotten about her.

King Sol turned and put a hand on Terra's shoulder and then walked to the back of the stage to stand with the Queen.

Diana faced all the guests and said, "I'm so honored you could all be here tonight just to see my little sister. As is tradition in our kingdom, I will now present my dear little Terra with her signet ring." Diana produced a small black box from a hidden pocket in her deep red dress.

Terra hadn't noticed before, but Diana was wearing the exact same dress as she was. Only hers was in a deep red and encrusted with rubies that accented her pale skin and made her hair look golden. Terra couldn't believe her sister would do something like that. Diana completely outshone her in every way tonight. Feeling exceptionally low, she turned to look at her sister.

"This ring is a sign that dear Terra is now a woman. She will use it to seal letters, mark important documents and show the world that she is a member of this royal family. It also signals that Terra is now of age to receive suitors for marriage. Of course that's only after I get married. "Diana smiled and flirted with the crowd, generally making Terra feel sick. After a few moments of shameless ego stroking, Diana opened the box and presented the ring to her sister.

Hesitating for only a moment, she reached forward and pulled the ring from the soft black velvet it was nestled in.

A sudden pain her chest made it hard for her to focus. She slipped the ring on her finger and focused all her will on keeping the smile on her face. Something felt wrong, really wrong. It seemed dark and frightening and Terra was sure that soon she wouldn't be able to hide that something was wrong.

She could feel the air around her get sucked away and turn stagnant. Her vision began to swim and she was certain she would die. Her hand felt wrong, dark somehow. And that dark feeling was creeping up her arm toward her heart.

Suddenly she felt it, the second heartbeat in her chest. It was the same as it was the first time she felt it. It beat in her chest a few times and then suddenly everything was fine. She no longer felt unwell or like she might faint. She was fine.

She looked down at her finger.

Her ring was beautiful.

Silver too!

She had always hated gold. It was too loud and seemed to demand too much attention. Silver suited her better. Not to mention silver was one of the colors of her Magic. She had wanted it in silver but was afraid of what her mother might say if she asked.

"We have one more announcement to make this evening," Queen Elise said as she walked up to center stage. "It has come to our attention that our youngest child, Terra, may in fact be blessed with some magical abilities."

Terra turned wide eyed to face her mother. She had always told people that Terra had no magical power. She told her from the time she was little that her getting trained would just take away from Diana's training and if she did that Diana could die during her epically prophesied battle. So naturally Terra did what her mother expected of her and didn't fight about being trained.

What her mother was saying now made no sense to her.

"Both the King and I are elated to think that both our daughters might be so blessed by the creator. Starting tomorrow morning, Terra will begin training with the Master Wizard." Elise turned and smiled at her daughter. Her face was tight and Terra could tell she wasn't happy about what she had just said.

Not wanting to incur anymore of her mother's wrath, she curtsied deeply and said, "Thank you Mother."

Elise turned to head back to her husband's side but stopped next to Terra. She stood shoulder to shoulder with her daughter facing the back wall. "Do not mistake this for something that it is not. This was your father's idea as a means to say thank you for saving your sister. That is all."

By the time she had gotten back up her mother and Diana had moved back to the back of the stage and her father was approaching her and waving to the musicians to start up.

At the sound of music, everyone surrounding the stage moved off and assumed their dancing positions. King Sol took Terra by the hand and led her to the dance floor. She had been practicing this dance for a long time, but still she was so nervous.

"Don't worry," her father said, "I know you'll do fine."

"I'm so nervous Papa," she muttered under her breath.

"Now, now chin up and keep smiling. You're my daughter and I know you can do anything. Now, just as we practiced."

King Sol led his daughter around the dance floor as the music played on. She stumbled a few times and stepped on his feet a number of times. Not that anyone watching them would have known. King Sol danced with his baby and enjoyed every minute, knowing it would be the last time he danced a first dance with his daughter. She was a young woman now.

Diana stood near to her mother and waited.

Any minute now the ring would start working and her father would look down at her sister in complete disgust. Then everyone around would start to feel it and they too would look at Terra and realize she was nothing. Diana secretly hoped it would get violent. A good fight was just what she needed to brighten her night.

Still they danced.

Not just danced, but apparently they were both quite witty as they started to laugh.

Diana didn't understand the ring should have started working by now. If she had read the curse correctly it should have stated working the second she touched it. Maybe it was all of her obsessive goodness that kept the ring from working right away. Still by now there was no reason why the thing shouldn't be doing its job.

Diana was really starting to get mad.

A thought struck her then.

Could it have been possible that Terra had somehow purified the dark magic?

No, it wasn't possible.

There was simply too much dark magic for something like that to have happened.

Still, it was the only thing that made sense.

Infuriated, Diana slipped to the back of the room and out through one of the many secret passages in the ball room. She wasn't sure what happened but she intended to find out.

Eric stood silently off to the side of the stage. He wasn't sure he'd be able to stay awake all night at this rate. He looked back up to the stage. Diana was saying something about getting married, Eric wasn't all that interested.

Terra pulled out her ring and instantly Eric could tell something was wrong. There was a strange pain in his hand and for a moment he couldn't see or breathe. He was sure he was dying. Which meant Terra was dying.

Then, just like that, the pain was gone. He was fine for a moment, until a searing pain in his head halted him again. It was like his mind was on fire. Everything was starting to spin. He leaned back against the wall to help steady himself, hoping it would pass soon.

He looked up at Terra, terrified she was dying, and everything faded away. There was no more pain, no more fire, and no more dizziness. He was fine. He stared at Terra and suddenly there was a rushing of air around him. It lifted the sash from his chest and ruffled his long brown hair.

Terra, he could feel it, he could feel his emotions for her come back in a rush. A moment ago he was convinced he hated her, hated the way she was kind to their enemy, but more than all of that, he had hated her for being bonded to him.

He didn't hate her.

To the contrary, he cared a good deal for her. She was beautiful and funny and her compassion was something he truly admired about her. It was easy to hate an enemy, to loath everything they did or said. It was an incredibly difficult thing to show kindness and compassion for one such as the Shadow King. That kindness and compassion were things he loved about her.

Then he remembered all things he had said to her in the past month.

He had called her such awful names and said terrible things to her and about her. He had abandoned his duties as her friend and as her Royal Guard. He thought he might be physically ill as he thought about how he had treated her.

It was the spell from Bell.

He had wanted to separate his real emotions from the bond emotions. Not because he didn't want to care about her, but because he thought he loved her. He wanted to be sure that was how he felt before he told her. Somehow things had gone wrong and now if she didn't hate the very sight of him she should.

He had to tell her.

He looked up and realized she was already dancing with her father. He didn't know the song they were dancing to well, but he knew enough to know it was almost over. If he could sneak in and grab her before the next dance, he might have the opportunity to explain before the dancing started again. It wasn't much but he had to try.

Terra smiled as she danced with her father. It was easier to handle things if she just pretended it was the two of them, dancing alone like at practice. Sadly their song was ending. Soon she would have to go face her mother and find out who the Queen had planned for her to dance with. At least after tonight she would know who her mother wanted her to marry. That was something she supposed.

"I'm afraid our dance is almost done," King Sol said sadly. "I had hoped it would last a little longer."

"Me too Papa," she said. "Will you stay? Then maybe we can dance together again?"

King Sol looked down at his daughter with sadness in his eyes. "I'm afraid not my little princess. I have to look over some reports concerning Lord Howe's missing son."

"I understand," she said. "Have they still not found Richard?"

"I'm afraid not. It's been near two months with no word. We're starting to assume the worst."

"I'm so sorry Papa. I can't imagine how hard that must be for him. Is there anything I can do to help? I would gladly do anything to help find the young man. I know the Howe's are very dear friends."

King Sol smiled kindly at his daughter. Her need to help others gave him such pride. "I will tell Lord Howe of your concern and if there is anything you can do I will let you know."

"Thank you Papa," Terra said as the music faded out.

As was tradition, both the Princess and the King bowed to each other and then parted. Applauding the band, she began to make her way to her mother to find her next dance partner.

A hand on her wrist stopped her.

She turned to see Eric holding her with something strange behind his eyes. She wasn't sure what it was but she really didn't have time be insulted right then.

"Let me go Eric, I don't know what I've done now but can you be cruel to me later? I don't want to keep my mother waiting."

"Terra," he pleaded with difficulty. "I need to talk to you, please, right now before the next dance starts."

She glanced at Eric and then back at her mother. She was staring at her and she wasn't happy. There was a man standing next to Queen Elise and he was staring at her awkwardly. She needed to get up there before she enraged her mother and she decided to take back her promise about Terra getting trained.

"Eric whatever it is, it can wait. I don't have time for you to belittle me right now. I must go." She turned away from him and tried to keep walking. Eric, still holding her wrist, walked with her.

"Terra please I really need to talk to you. It can't wait it has to be *now*," he whispered at her as they walked across the dance floor.

225

Seeing the princess with a man in tow, the musicians started up again. Everyone around them assumed their dancing positions. Terra looked around frantic. She was still half a room away from her mother and there were now hundreds of people in her way. She looked to her mother who was shaking her head in shame.

Queen Elise looked at her daughter and mouthed the word 'dance'. When Terra didn't understand that, she mouthed it again and made small dancing gestures with her fingers. She looked at her pleadingly. She would have given anything to not have to dance with Eric. Unfortunately the music was starting and there was no other choice.

"Do you know this dance?" She demanded, rounding on Eric.

"What," he asked, caught off guard.

"This dance starting and I haven't got time to make my way to the other end of the room before the dancing starts. And I'm pretty sure if I try to walk through the dancing people, my mother will murder me. Now tell me, do you know this dance?"

"Yes of course," Eric replied, he was trained as a gentleman as well as a soldier.

"I'm sorry then," Terra sighed, resigning herself. "We'll have to dance this one together."

Queen Elise smiled as she watched her youngest daughter take the arms of her guard. She had intended her first dance to be with her half-wit second cousin, but this was much better. Her cousin, half-wit though he may be, was still royalty. He was only a few heartbeats from the throne of the Moon Kingdom. That Terra would take her first dance as a woman with a commoner was truly fitting.

Eric took Terra by the hand and placed his hand on her waist. He pulled her in as the dance required and felt his heart leap at her closeness. It had been so long since he had been able to enjoy his proximity to her. For a moment he just smiled and started to dance.

He reached out through the bond as he used to do, to see if she was as happy as he, only to be reminded that she was still thinking he hated her. Taking a deep breath for courage he spoke.

"Terra, I'm sorry I messed up your first dance, but I really need to talk to you."

"Why," she asked forlornly, "Haven't you said enough already?"

"Terra please," he said desperately. "I'm so sorry. I never meant to hurt you or to say those things to you . . ."

"Then why?!" She demanded, tears in her eyes. "Why would you say such things to me? What did I do to so incite your hate?"

"Oh Terra," Eric whispered, his heart breaking at the sound of pain in her voice. Pain that he had caused her. "I asked Bell to help me sort through my emotions."

"What is that supposed to mean?"

"After what happened in Bell's room last month, I didn't know what emotions were mine and what were caused by the bond. So I asked the wizard to help me sort through them."

"Why?"

"Terra," he explained, as he spun her around the dance floor. "I thought I loved you. When I kissed you that day I wanted to hold you and kiss you and tell you that I loved you."

"I see," she acknowledged. "That was a problem so you asked Bell to make it go away."

"No," Eric exclaimed, almost shouting. Glancing around making sure no one had heard him, he continued. "It wasn't a problem. Terra if I was going to hold you and tell you that I loved you, I wanted to know for sure that it was what I felt and not what our bond was making me feel."

She was silent.

She danced around the room with Eric as she pondered what he had said. She had wanted for so long to make up with him and to make things the way they were before. What he was saying made sense. Although part of her wondered if maybe it all made sense because she wanted it to. She wanted to makeup with Eric and so much. Was it possible that she was making sense out of nothing?

"Terra, please say something," Eric begged as the song started to wind down. "I know you can't forgive me just yet, but please tell me you at least believe me."

"I want to," she confessed. "Eric I want to believe you so much. I want to believe and to let everything go back to the way it was. I hate fighting with you, I hate fighting in general."

"But . . ." Eric said, sensing the princess wasn't done yet.

"But I don't know if can take you at your word right now." She admitted as the second song started to end.

"Then don't. Use our bond. Reach out and feel that I'm being honest with you," He urged, knowing his time was almost up.

Terra nodded and closed her eyes; she knew the dances so well now that she didn't need to see to dance. She reached out through her bond and felt Eric at the other end. She was hit with an overwhelming sense of remorse. There was guilt and remorse battling for top emotion in his heart. He was so sorry for all he had said and done. Terra could feel that now. He was being honest, about everything. What had happened with Bell, and about how he felt about everything.

There was only one thing that wasn't the same as far as Terra could tell.

When she had last reached out through the bond to see how Eric was feeling about her, he had been close to loving her. He cared for her a great deal then.

Now, however, it seemed that only a fraction of what he had originally felt was there. He cared for her very much, but only as a friend now or maybe a bit more. Bell had, it seemed, not just separated his emotions for her, he had destroyed them. Terra wasn't sure why some of it had come back and some hadn't, but she was grateful to know that at least she would have her friend back.

"Eric," she whispered quietly. "I'm glad that you're ok and I do believe what you've told me."

228

"But . . ." he prompted again.

"But what you said and how you treated me hurt in a way I can't really explain. I know now that you weren't yourself."

"Bell . . ." Eric started.

"I know," Terra cut in, not letting him finish. "I can't tell you how happy it makes me to know that you aren't that man and that you didn't mean those terrible things."

"I see," Eric said reaching out through the bond. "You're still hurt."

She nodded, not trusting her voice.

"Is it that you can't trust me? Or are you just too hurt to try?"

"It's not that," she tried to explain. "Part of it is that the words hurt and even though you don't mean them, they still hurt. Then . . ." She stopped, unsure of how to go on.

Eric reached out again to see what Terra wasn't saying. Their song was ending and he knew he couldn't get away with sealing a second dance. It only took a second to find the problem she was still having. It was one of the most prominent thoughts in her mind.

"My emotions aren't all back," he said simply.

Terra nodded.

"Does that make you afraid?"

She opened her mouth, a lie ready on her lips. Thinking better of it she said, "a little, yes."

As the last notes played Eric pulled her close and whispered in her ear, "I know things aren't exactly the same, but don't mistake the lack of emotion for a lack of caring. I do care for you more than I can say. I promise you I will make this up to you."

The song ended then and the two stepped back from each other and bowed.

Terra glanced at Eric, unsure of what to say to him now. So she smiled tightly and headed toward her mother. When she got to the stage she was shocked to find her mother smiling down at her as thought something was funny.

"I'm so sorry Mother," she said hurriedly.

229

"Don't be child," she said still smiling. "Did you enjoy your dance with your guard?"

"Yes," Terra lied badly.

"Good then. Here's your dance card, hurry along now and try not to step on any toes."

For Terra, the next few hours seemed to drag on.

She danced with noble after noble and Lord after Lord. She stepped on toes, capes and at one point she actually managed to topple a man over. Still they came to dance and she was forced to endure what she considered to be the worst punishment she had ever faced.

Finally the trumpets sounded the call to dinner and the time to stop dancing. Terra bowed to her last partner, a very handsy middle aged man who was some kind of baron in her mother's kingdom. He watched her bow and then watched her come back up, his eyes never leaving the low bust line of her dress.

Eric stepped in before the man could say much and explained to the man that the Princess was needed at her father's side for dinner. He smiled and said he understood and then bowed to the princess, before walking away.

Dinner looked like a lovely feast, made in her honor with all her favorite foods. For the first time in weeks she wished she could stay and eat with her family. She knew that wasn't possible. She had duty to do to her kingdom and to her friend.

So she sat with her father for a moment and then explained that the excitement of the day was getting to her and she would have to retire. She urged everyone to stay and enjoy the night and then curtsied and thanked them graciously for attending her ball. The whole hall stood and formally saluted her with their fists over their hearts.

Terra exited through the main doors and then doubled back around the hall to the kitchen. Jenny was waiting as always with the tray of food for Grey. She was ready to grab the tray and go when a noise from Jenny stopped her.

"What's wrong?" She asked when she saw the girl's odd expression.

"Your shoulders majesty," Jenny exclaimed, "when did you get such scars?"

"Oh," she uttered. She had completely forgotten about the scars that now adorned her shoulders. She and Mammy had come to call them her wings. She hadn't thought about the fact that they would show in this dress. She grabbed her wrap and pulled up tight under her chin and picked up the tray up again.

"It's just an old scar," Terra said, half lying. "I'm not really sure how I got it."

"I'm sorry Majesty," Jenny said, "I didn't mean to pry."

"It's ok. Don't worry about it Jenny. I'll see you in the morning."

"Princess, don't you look . . . womanly tonight," Lewis said as she made her way down the stairs. It was a very difficult thing to do in heels, a long skirt, and with a plate of food for two.

"Lewis," Terra said irritably. "Would you be so kind as to get the door please? This tray is heavy and the food hot."

"Of course Princess. Another long night tonight?"

Terra ignored him and walked through the door kicking it closed again.

"Terra!" Grey said a little surprised.

"I know I'm late but it is my birthday so you should just pretend I'm on time ok?" She asked light and jokingly as she set the tray on the table and started to divide the food.

"Terra," he called irritably.

"Yes Grey?"

"Are you really going to stand there and talk about being late when you still haven't explained to me what happened earlier? Why you ran out of here like the room was on fire?"

231

"Grey I don't know what to tell you." Terra wasn't sure what she could and couldn't say. She knew she didn't want him to know what she had seen earlier. Still, she knew him well enough now to know that he wasn't going to let up until he got answers.

So, being very careful about what she thought, Terra thought about Bell and the prophecy thing without actually thinking about the prophecy. She let her mind wander over the conversation she had with Bell and the things he had told her about the possibility of her having visions.

"What's this?" Grey said, displeased. "Your bond is so much stronger tonight. What happened?"

Before she could help it, Terra was thinking about everything she and Eric had talked about that night. Every detail was still fresh in her mind so it didn't take much to call it forward. She could tell by the way Grey became quiet that he was seeing it to. She thought about how things were still different now even though they were better. She knew that most of what he felt for her was gone.

"I see," he said. "So you and the young Mr. Reynolds have made up then." He was trying to sound like he didn't care but Terra wasn't convinced. He seemed to care at least a little about the fact they were friends again.

"We sort of made up," she said honestly. "Apparently there was some kind of a mix up with a spell Master Bell did. He knows now that we're friends and he cares about me in that capacity. Nothing like before."

"I can see that," he stated. "Isn't that what you wanted?"

"It is," answered quietly, loading Greys food on to his tray.

"So what's wrong then?"

She sighed. "Can't you see?"

"Sadly no. Your bond with Reynolds is stronger now and it makes it hard enough just to get into you head. Your heart is masked to me."

"Oh." She thought for a moment. Realizing that coming right out with it would be best she said, "Can I be honest with you Grey?"

232

"Of course, I would hope you are always honest with me. We agreed to that before yes?"

"Yes, but there are things I don't tell you. This is one of those things."

Grey walked to the corner near where Terra was standing. "You can tell me anything. It's not like I'm going to tell someone else."

"I know that," she explained as she put the tray to glass. "The simple fact is I don't know what my continued exposure to you will do to me in the end."

Grey froze halfway through pulling the tray through the glass. "What, uh, what do you mean?"

"I mean that you excrete darkness. It's almost always floating around the floor when I'm in here. I don't know if that's a conscience or an unconscious thing, all I know is that you do. For all I know you could be sitting in there purposely trying to corrupt me with your darkness."

Grey opened his mouth to say something but Terra put a hand up to silence him. "Grey, if you're not, then you're and idiot. I know you well enough, now, to know you are no idiot. My point is that I could wake up tomorrow and have a darkened heart. If and when that happens I become a threat and a liability to everyone I love and everyone who loves me.

"The only way I can keep things from getting any worse is to limit the people who are exposed to me. That means that I don't let anyone else get close enough for me to hurt. It's not an ideal situation but it is what it is."

"So why don't you just fight the darkness I'm attempting to pour into you?" Grey asked. He was a little alarmed that Terra had an idea of what was going on. He knew that eventually someone would catch on but not now. Without turning away from her, he set the tray of food onto his table.

"I am and I will continue to do so for as long as I can. But I'm not strong enough to fight forever. I'll admit that at first I thought I

233

could purify your darkness, like I purified that shadow you sent after me the day I met you."

"You did what?"

"I purified the shadow."

"How the *hell* did you do that?" He demanded.

"I don't really know. I was trying to banish it but instead I guess it got purified. Master Bell seems to think it's something I was just born able to do. It doesn't happen often I guess, so we don't really know much about it."

Grey was silent. He wasn't sure what to do with this information. A gift to purify darkness in such a way was rare. So rare he hadn't encountered it in his lifetime. If Terra could do that, then it might take a fair sight longer to corrupt her than he thought.

"Anyway," she continued, "At least I won't have to wonder for much longer. My mother announced tonight that I will start to receive training with Master Bell, real formal training." Terra was so excited she was grinning again.

"So how does this explain your sudden departure earlier?"

"Oh I had this possible premonition," she muttered awkwardly. She filled her mind with random thought trying to keep Grey away from what she had seen. Unfortunately, Grey was on to her tricks and wouldn't be thrown off.

"What was your possible premonition about?"

"Uh . . . stuff," she said trying to keep her mind off her premonition.

"Come on Terra, we're being honest here. Don't throw up all these walls."

She sighed. "You can't judge me for this." She started to think about the premonition. How they had been dancing and then stopped. She thought about how he had grabbed her and pulled her toward him.

"Terra," he sighed. "I can't see anything. It's all blurred, whatever you saw has more to do with your heat than your head. Your bond with Reynolds is too strong for me to see. Can you just tell me?"

234

Terra looked at him, eyes wide, face red and shook her head. There was no way she could actually use words to describe what she had seen. There was no way to know how Grey would react to her thinking about them close that way. He could think it was funny, he could think it was an invitation or he could think it was outrageous and fly into blind rage.

"I can't say it, it's too complicated."

Grey looked at her for a moment. Whatever she had seen must have been pretty bad if she couldn't tell him. Deciding it was worth it to find out, he didn't let it go.

"Then come here," he said extending his hand to the glass.

"What?" She asked. She had been in there with him once already today and that hadn't ended well. Still, she knew him quite well now. If she didn't tell him he would hold onto it and never let up. It would be easier to just tell him.

"The only way to get through the bond is physical contact," he explained offhandedly. It wasn't that big of a deal to him. He was dancing with her not twelve hours ago. For the past month she'd been going in and out of his cell with no problem. Her hesitation now made him all the more curious.

"Right of course." She stepped up to the glass and slowly pushed her way through. Grey grabbed her hand as soon as it was through. He pulled her the rest of the way in and grabbed her other hand.

"Now just focus on the premonition, I'll do the rest."

Terra nodded and closed her eyes. She didn't want to be looking at Grey when he saw what she had seen. She kept one heel up against the glass in case she had to make a quick exit. She thought back to the premonition again, bringing all the images back in a rush. She focused and made the memory play out in order.

Grey mumbled something about things not working before he moved and put his arms around her. It was much harder to keep focused while he was holding her so much like he had held her in the vision. She kept playing the premonition over and over again in her

235

mind. Waiting for some reaction from Grey to tell her he'd seen it. He kept moving around, shifting this way and that.

Finally he said something about not enough skin and he pulled away. She kept her eyes shut tight and tried not to think about what he meant by skin. She just kept the vision playing over and over again in her mind. Every second, every agonizing detail she recalled.

Her eyes shot open at the sound of fabric being pulled at. She looked around to see Grey taking off his dark black shirt and tossing it aside.

"What are you doing?" She demanded, alarmed.

"Calm down," he teased, enjoying the way his being shirtless made her blush a bright red. "I need skin to skin contact and while your dress," he eyed her dress and its low bust line, "provides more than enough of that, my shirt does not."

Unable to speak, she just nodded. Doing all he could not to laugh at her face, Grey wrapped his arms around her again.

For a moment he stopped focusing on what was in Terra's mind. All he could think about was how warm and soft her skin felt against his. He found himself staring down at her, unable to look away. Something about the way she felt against him and the way she felt in his arms.

Ignoring his own strange train of thoughts, he focused again.

"Oh," Terra mumbled awkwardly as Grey pressed his skin against hers. She kept her eyes closed and tried not to think about anything but the premonition. Grey was very fit and really nice to look at without a shirt on. There was a small voice in the back of her mind that urged her to run away. She was having visions warning her about them getting too close and somehow she knew standing in a cell, alone with him while he got naked wasn't going to help.

"Now, keep your eyes closed and try again," he instructed. He put a hand on the back of her neck and rested her head on his chest. Terra's heart rate spiked as she thought about the premonition. This time she could tell it was working because Grey stopped moving and became very still.

She really had to work to keep her mind on the premonition now. Grey was naked from the waste up and holding her tight against him. With her corset and low cut bodice good deal of her skin was pressed against him. Taking deep breaths she focused.

As the images played through her mind she knew Grey was seeing them in his. Once she had played through it she opened her eyes and tried to see him, tried to gage his reaction. She couldn't really see his face but he was stiff around her and she was starting to worry.

"You have interesting thoughts in your head," he muttered unmoving.

"Interesting?"

"I'm not sure what else to say," he answered honestly. He let go of her and walked back to his bed. He really wasn't sure what to make of what he saw in her head. Most of it was fuzzy and all had to do with the night she was having and possibly a dream that featured him and that damn sister of hers. There was nothing of prophecy here. He would never admit to it out loud but seconds before she had spaced out he had something of a premonition himself.

He had thought about pulling her in and holding her until he felt the darkness take her heart. He had stopped seconds before she had because the thought of doing such a thing had hurt him.

He hadn't wanted to hurt her.

He hadn't wanted to hurt her so badly that he actually hurt himself just by thinking it.

Terra felt her breath catch in her throat.

On Grey's back were scars, scars just like hers.

Only his were a blackish grey where hers had gone white.

Did he know he had these? He knew about hers, he'd seen them a few times.

Now that she thought about it, he had gone awfully pale when he'd seen them for the first time. He'd gotten rude too. She had left early that night because of it.

Never in the past month had he said anything about having scars like hers.

"Grey," she stammered. "You're . . . scarred."

Grey turned and saw the look on Terra's face. He hadn't thought about his scars when he had taken his shirt off. He just wanted to know what future she had seen. He had so many plans for her. He couldn't risk her seeing something about them and destroying everything he was working for. He needed to know what she had seen sooner rather than later.

Those damn scars had completely slipped his mind. Now Terra was staring at him and he could see all the trust he'd worked so hard to build with her start slipping away. He needed something to tell her and he needed it now.

"Scarred?" He asked, buying for time.

"You don't know?" Terra asked, her distrust slipping into concern.

"Know what?" He asked irritably. He saw his way out, it was simple denial. She had provided him with his excuse and he just had to sell it to her.

Terra turned around and leaned against the glass. She had forgotten her shawl on the table so her scars were more than obvious. "You see my scars? The ones shaped like wings I told you about a while ago?"

"Yes, what of it?"

"You have the same scars on your back. Only yours are black where mine are white. Do you really not know they're there?"

"I have scars?" Grey asked, going with complete denial. He turned and stared at his reflection. He could still see his scars across his shoulders. They were exactly the same as Terra 's. Somehow that

238

night when Diana came in and threatened and burned him, she had burned Terra too.

Grey still didn't understand how that was possible. He wasn't tied to her, they weren't bonded. There was no way she should be burned. He had thought and thought and thought about it, but it still didn't make sense. There must be something he wasn't seeing, some small detail that eluded him.

Quietly she stepped up behind him and touched the marked flesh of his back. His shoulders when up and for a moment she was sure he would pull away. When he didn't move she brought her other hand up and traced the outline of his scars with her fingers.

"I can't believe you didn't know," Terra whispered, somewhat suspiciously.

"It's not like I have a looking glass or anything," Grey remarked, still acting like he was seeing his scars for the first time. Although it was a little hard to focus on the lie while she was touching him the way she was. Something about the way she touched his scars sent little shocks through his body. Not bad shocks. They were more . . . intense than that.

"I remember pain," he said, seeing that Terra wasn't buying what he was saying. He turned to face her, looking confused.

"It was soon after I got here, I felt this pain on my shoulders. It knocked me off my bed. I just assumed it was something the box was rigged to do. Or that maybe I was dying cut off my power in here."

"It was me," she gasped, "I had a nightmare that night and woke up in terrible pain. I don't understand, how is it possible that a nightmare I had could affect you? Unless . . . unless I reached." Something close to a realization dawned on her.

"Reached?"

"Yes, it's something Diana learned about a long time ago. When you're hurt or alone and need help, sometimes you can reach.

When you do that it's kind of like a bonding only it lasts less than a minute.

"You use your magic to reach out to someone you love or trust greatly. That part's important; if there isn't a connection you can't be reached."

"So what, you called out for help?" Grey asked, not liking the way this whole "reach" thing was sounding.

"Well sometimes yes, sometimes you pull energy, other times strength or courage, and sometimes, in a strong reach you can share the brunt of the pain one of you is feeling. It's a way to help someone you care about with or without a bond."

As Terra continued to speak, she got quieter and quieter. Could it really be possible that she was able to reach out to Grey when she didn't even know him? Master Bell had made it sound like something that can't really be done by just anyone whenever or for whatever reason.

Perhaps she had misunderstood? It was mostly second hand information from Diana she was working off here.

She needed to talk to Master Bell.

Tonight if she could.

He was probably still up at the feast. As much as she didn't want to, Terra was going to have to cut things with Grey short tonight.

"Terra what you're saying can't be possible," Grey countered. He knew the truth that it wasn't Terra who had reached, assuming that's what really happened anyway. *He* had reached out to her when Diana had attacked him. Could he really have reached out to someone he didn't know?

If it was a question of power, he was sure he had enough for that. If what Terra said was to be believed though, he would either have to be head over heels in love with her or trust her with his life. Neither of these things was the case so how could it be?

It couldn't.

That was the point. There was no way she was right.

None.

There was another explanation, he was sure of it.

"I could be wrong," she offered. "I think I should talk to Master Bell about this." She was halfway through the glass before Grey had processed what she had said and managed to formulate a reply.

"Is that wise?" He called after her.

"I know Master Bell, and I know he won't press me for more information than I can give him. I know you don't know him, but trust me in this. I haven't lied to you yet."

Terra was out the door before he could say anything else.

Everyone was still eating and dancing in the grand dining hall when Diana slipped in. She had been gone a while now. Seething in her new room, trying to figure out how things had gone wrong with Terra's ring. She had gone back over the spell and as far as she could tell everything was done right.

When the hexed object was ready it would flash red. It had done that. So why hadn't things worked out?

Could it have been Terra?

Could she have somehow purified the ring?

No.

She wasn't nearly powerful enough to do that.

At least as far as Diana knew.

A terrifying thought went through her mind. What if Terra was truly that powerful? Not even *she* could have purified it. She poured so much darkness into that thing it should have turned the kingdom against her. Was it really possible her sister could be that strong and none of them know?

Diana decided then that she would have to keep a much closer eye on her sister. If she was going to get trained by Bell now, then she might very well pose a problem to the plans Diana was still hatching in her mind.

241

Terra found Bell sitting near her father and a few other nobles discussing ways to safe guard trade routes. She walked up, curtsied graciously to her father and nodded to the nobles. She looked to Bell; she knew he could tell she needed him. It was just a matter of making the proper excuses and getting away from her father's ears.

Terra said goodnight to her father and started to walk slowly away. She wasn't even to the door before Bell was at her side.

"What's the matter princess?"

"Not here," she explained leading him away and out into one of the smaller corridors. "Master Bell something very strange has happened and I don't know what to do or who else to turn to."

"Tell me what's happened," he said, his face calm.

"Do you recall the night I almost died, and then Eric almost died trying to save me?"

"Yes, it was the night you got your scars." His eyes twinkled in a way that made the young princess wonder if perhaps he already knew why she was there.

"Tonight I was down having dinner in the prison when the Shadow King removed his shirt and I saw that he has the exact same scars as I do. Not similar, not alike, the same."

Bell was silent as he considered what Terra had said. "Why did he take his shirt off?"

"Laundry," she lied, hating the sick feeling in her stomach as the thought of lying to Master Bell.

"Does he know where he got them or how?"

"He didn't seem to know he had them."

"Didn't seem to know, or didn't know?"

"What's the difference?"

"You said he didn't seem like he knew. Does that mean he didn't know, or he led you to believe he didn't know?"

Terra was quiet for a moment as she considered what Bell had said. Grey had acted like he didn't know they were there. Still every time she thought about it, it seemed like he wasn't really being honest. If she considered that he might be lying about the scars then that meant he could be lying about everything. They had promised to be honest with one another since they were stuck in a situation where the other was the only person they talked to.

If he was lying then it threw a lot of things into question. Most importantly it made her wonder if he was actually her friend or it was all just about trying to corrupt her.

No, she couldn't think like that.

She had to have faith in him so long as he proved to be worthy of it.

"He didn't know," she answered finally.

"If you're sure princess. . ."

"I am. I saw his face when he looked in the glass, he didn't know."

"Either way, what matters is that somehow you and he seem to share a connection."

"Like a bond?" Terra asked terrified.

"No a bond wouldn't do what this did. This is something else altogether."

"So like a bond but . . . stronger?" Her voice shook as she considered what that would mean. She was already bonded to Eric and that was hard enough to deal with. If she was bonded or even something similar to Grey, of all people, she couldn't imagine how much harder it would make life.

Still, if she was somehow connected to him, maybe that would make saving him all the easier. If she could figure out what the connection was and how to use it, she could save him. If the bond could burn it could heal to, right? She would use anything she could to help him and in turn, help Diana.

"Stronger would be putting it mildly," Bell explained. "Even the strongest bond can't cause simultaneous damage like this. I'm sorry princess but I'm afraid there isn't much more I can tell you,"

"It's alright," she replied. "I know more now than I did before I came to you."

"Princess, if I may," he asked, pointing to her scars. Terra nodded and turned so her back was to him. He reached out and carefully touched her scars. He had heard her and Mammy call them her wings and for good reason. They did appear to be two white wings spreading out from her spine down and along her shoulders. They were jagged and looked like burn marks more than scars.

As he touched them he noticed a strange power seemed to emanate from them. It wasn't Terra's power he felt, it was a males but he couldn't be sure who's. It seemed tinged with darkness, though not much. For a moment Bell wondered if it was possible that it was the Shadow Kings energy he felt.

He dismissed the idea immediately.

That monster was locked away in a box where no one could get to him and he could not get to anyone. To think that somehow he could have bonded with Terra was nothing short of impossible. Terra herself was more than gifted enough to have deflected any kind of advance he could make at her. She was the singularly most gifted child he had ever seen.

Bell didn't like it. He was a Master Wizard, advisor to the King, and a bearer of silver magic. Any of these things in their own right more than qualified him to be able to solve this puzzle. There should be very few things that confuse him.

"Is it bad?" She asked.

"No, just puzzling is all."

"Oh,"

"I'm sorry I can't be more help," he said sitting back. "I can however tell you that these scars didn't come from you."

"What?" She asked, turning to face Bell.

"Your scars give off a particular kind of energy that is not yours. It seems to be the energy of whom ever gave you the scars you now bear."

"So, can I ask, is there a chance this was an extreme case of reaching?" She knew it was long shot at this point, but at least then she would know one way or the other if it was possible.

"A reach? Between you and the prisoner? I don't see how that could be possible at all," Bell contemplated. Even as he was saying it the gears in his mind started to turn. If it was that he had somehow reached to her, as unlikely as that was, it made Bell wonder about a number of things.

Firstly, if he could reach to her through the prison than there was serious doubts in his mind about it holding up to his darkness long term. Secondly, if he could somehow reach to her then he was somehow connected to her in ways none of them had considered. A connection like that was a frightening thing. A bond beyond measure would be needed to affect a person this way. Thirdly, if Terra was scarred like this than that meant she had felt him reach and had reached back to him. Similar to how she and Guard Reynolds had bonded to each other during a time of great stress. A person could reach but if the person on the other end didn't reach back than a connection couldn't be made.

"I know it sounds crazy, and I know I don't know much about magic, but it seemed like all the pieces fit for a reach," she explained to Bell when he was silent.

"You may not be far off," Bell conceded. "Princess, with your permission, I'd like to examine you and the prisoner in the same room."

"Why would you need my permission for that?"

"You are the jail keeper in this instance," Bell explained. "You've already been down there several times today and I don't want force you down there again."

"It's not me I'm worried about," she tried to explain. "Grey isn't the most social of people and he wasn't exactly happy about me coming to talk to you right now."

"Grey?"

"Yes," Terra said, not believing she had let his name slip again. "I call him Grey because his title was too long. He has no real name and he allowed me to name him. So I call him Grey."

"A fitting name," he replied with a nod.

Terra could have cried she was so relived at Bell's reaction. She had been horrified thinking that his reaction would be similar to Eric's. Granted Eric's reaction had a lot to do with Bell trying to separate his feelings from the bond. Still, she had been terrified when Bell turned to her.

"Well I guess we could go and see how he feels about some more company tonight," She offered. "I would like to know what's going on with all this."

"Agreed," Bell said, mentally preparing himself for the darkness that lay ahead.

Grey sat quietly in the middle of his cell, searching within himself for this supposed connection to Terra. As much as it troubled him, her explanation of reaching seemed to be the only thing that made sense to him. What troubled him even more was the need of deep connection between the two people reaching. He had never met the princess before the day she walked into his room all doe eyed and lost. He knew then the decision to use her to get to her sister had been the right one.

So far it had been pretty easy going. He makes a promise to be civil, she opens up to him a little more. He lets her name him, suddenly she's ready to be his friend. He spends a few nights holding her while she cries away her teenage problems, now their best friends. He'd spent the last month slowly warming her up to him, figuring out how best to get her trust.

With each passing day she trusted him more. As her trust in him grew, he was able to pour more and more darkness into the crack he'd made in her heart or soul. His only real problem was that now she knew about his scars and was dragging the Master Wizard into things. It wouldn't take Bell long to realize that the scars didn't originate from Terra. Then he would either have to lie miraculously or come clean about the whole thing.

Each option had pros and cons.

Mostly he didn't think Terra would believe that her sister was capable of such a thing. He's seen how she views Diana, like she was some kind of goddess. She would never believe that darling older sister had come down into the prison, unseen, threatened him and then somehow managed to get past the barrier and burn him.

In many ways it still didn't make sense to him.

So that left him with lying. Getting Terra to believe a lie was easy, she would have believed anything he said to her at this point. Bell, however, would not be so easily swayed. Whatever he told them would have to be as close to the truth as he could manage.

Terra had said something earlier about how she was having a dream. She thought she was dreaming when she was burned, or at least thought the pain came from the dream. Maybe he could use that. He could say he dreamt of Diana hurting him. He was set to face her in a battle to the death at some point after she turned twenty one or so. His having a nightmare about her hurting him, that would be believable.

Or at least more believable than the truth.

Pleased to at least have something to say to Terra and Bell when they arrived, Grey got to his feet and walked to his very small chest of drawers. He pulled out a clean black shirt that had been given to him when he was captured. Most of the clothes he had been given were white, eventually, like all things light, they darkened after being exposed to him.

Terra would do the same.

Soon enough.

Grey could suddenly sense the princess's heart nearby. Her heart, despite his constant searching, was pure. Not a spot of darkness on it. Something he had thought was impossible. As far as he knew every human had some darkness in them. She was an anomaly, in more than one way. It was one thing about her he was tired of.

It was nearly a minute later that Grey could sense Terra and Bell's minds coming closer. Terra's mind was still foggy thanks to her making up with Reynolds. He hadn't anticipated that and it set his plan back nearly six months. He would still be able to use him to corrupt her; it would just take much longer this way. Her heart he could sense but not see into, also thanks to Reynolds and the obnoxious bond. Bell, however, his heart was usually easy to see in to, as long as he was close

At the moment, however, he could scarcely tell that it was Bell coming toward the door. Once he met a person he could tell when they got close. Bell should have been an easy read. He must be protecting his mind somehow.

Either way, it was nearly impossible to protect your heart from his power.

As he went through some final preparations for his story the large wooden doors in front of him opened. Terra slipped in and pushed the door closed again. She smiled sheepishly at him, she knew he knew Bell was outside.

"Hey," she called. She stepped forward her leg bent suddenly to the left and she was on the floor.

"Terra!" Grey shouted as he ran up to the glass.

"I'm ok," she growled, sounding angry. "It's these damn shoes! I don't know how ladies get anything done in them!" She swept her legs in front of her and undid the buckles on her heeled shoes. She pulled them both off and threw them across the room, nearly knocking a magelight torch off the wall. She made a face as the torch wobbled and then stilled.

"Oops," she giggling.

Despite himself, Grey laughed a little too. "That may be the most un-lady like thing I have ever seen."

"Well you just wait," she laughed standing up. She glanced behind her and made sure the door was still closed. Then she reached up her skirt and started pulling on something.

"Terra what in the name of creation are you doing?!" He shouted.

Smiling she continued to pull until she was yanking white stockings off her feet. She balled them up and was about to throw them when she suddenly thought better of it. With her luck they would probably catch on fire and burn the entire castle down.

"There," she exclaimed happily, "That is so much better!"

"You're right," he smiled. "That was *much* more un-lady like."

"Well I maybe a young woman today, but that doesn't mean I have to like the clothes." Terra tossed the stockings over by the table and walked over to the glass where Grey was still standing. "So on a more appropriate subject, Master Bell is outside and he would like to examine both our scars and see if he can draw a better conclusion about what's going on."

"So you what, want? Permission to bring him in here?"

"I don't want to bring him in if you aren't going to be civil," Terra replied.

"I am the model of civility," he countered in mock offense.

"Sure you are," she muttered. She turned and ran barefoot through the room to the door and pulled it open. She made a small gesture with her hand and the Master Wizard stepped through.

"Ah Master Bell," he crowed "Come to visit the prisoner in his lowly cell?"

"Good evening, Grey is it now?" Bell asked.

"Ah so young Terra has told you she named me?"

"She has." Bell answered simply. "More importantly, she's told me that you and she seem to bear the same scars."

"Maybe."

"Grey," she whispered, shooting him a look.

"What?" He asked, looking right back at her.

"Civil, remember," she said, half under her breath.

"That was civil," he claimed, copying her tone.

"*How* was that civil?"

"I didn't insult him did I? No. Hell I even answered his question!"

"You didn't really answer his question!"

249

"I said maybe! How is that not an answer?"

She opened her mouth to say something but Bell suddenly stepped in between the princess and the prisoner. "Alright children lets calm down now."

"I'm sorry Master Bell," Terra apologized, instantly sorry she had let herself argue with Grey like a child in front of her soon-to-be teacher. "He does have scars, I've seen them."

"You're no fun at all," he uttered, scowling at Terra. "But she is right. She and I do have the same scars, with one difference. My scars are black where hers are white."

"May I see your scars?" Bell asked neutrally.

"Not even going to buy me dinner first?" Grey mocked. Terra shot him a warning look. He rolled his eyes and added, "Fine!" He pulled his shirt off and turned so the wizard could see his back.

Bell stepped up to the glass and, careful not to touch it, he examined Grey's scars. "Terra can you face the glass so I can see your scars next to each other?" She nodded and stepped up to the glass. She leaned against the wall and tried to stand still so Bell could examine them.

"So this isn't awkward," Grey whispered.

"Sshh," she hissed. "I'm trying to be still."

"Good luck with that," he muttered.

"Could you at least pretend to be nice for like five seconds?!" Terra whispered through the glass.

"This is me being nice," he shot at her.

The princess made noise under her breath but didn't say anything. She could feel Bell put his hands on her back so she held still. He made a few sounds and seemed to be mumbling under his breath. He hit a spot near her spine that sent a shock wave of pain through her body.

She cried out, at the same moment Grey cringed and cursed the wizard's existence under his breath.

Bell pulled his hands back and made a noise that both the princess and prisoner knew wasn't good.

250

"Master Bell?" She asked turning around. "Is everything ok? What was that?"

"I'm afraid it's as I feared," he replied, keeping his voice level.

"And what exactly are we talking about here?" Grey asked, pulling his shirt back on.

"You two were burned due to reaching."

Terra and Grey started talking at the same time. Bell raised a hand to silence their onslaught of questions. Grey made a face about being silenced like a child, but didn't say anything.

"I'm afraid the news gets worse. Not only were you two victims of reaching, but it was Grey who reached, not the Princess."

Terra looked up at Grey.

He didn't look right.

She was shocked, completely and utterly caught off guard. She knew what Master Bell had said before they had come down to the prison, but still. To hear it confirmed was something completely different. Grey on the other hand, his shock seemed forced somehow. His mouth was right in the way it hung open, but not his eyes. His eyes didn't' match the rest of his face.

"I don't understand," she questioned. So many thoughts were racing through her head she couldn't make sense of most it. "How could he have reached to me?"

"I don't know," Bell stated. "Grey would you like to share some insight as how this is possible. Seeing as it was you who reached in the first place."

"How should I know?!" He demanded stalking away from the glass. He walked to his bed and threw himself down. "I'm the one trapped in a box, how am I supposed to know what the hell is going on?"

Terra looked to Bell who looked back at her and shrugged. He wasn't sure what to do now. Honestly he was surprised Grey had allowed him to look at his scars in the first place. He wasn't expecting a conversation with him. To be truthful, he wasn't sure if the monster

251

knew how to talk at all. The first night they had brought him in he looked more like a feral animal than a man. With glowing eyes and teeth that more resembled fangs, he was a terrifying sight to behold.

Deciding there was nothing left to do; Bell folded his arms and turned to Terra. "I'm afraid there isn't much more that I can do here. Without his cooperation I can't ascertain what happened or how to stop it from happening again."

"Master Bell, may I ask you a question?" She realized the only way she was going to get Grey to cooperate was if she walked into that cell and dragged him back to the glass. As her teacher, Master Bell was required to report back to her parents about everything and anything she does that is of note.

Being able to walk into an impenetrable glass prison would be of note.

"Of course," he replied.

"As my teacher, do you have to tell my parents about everything I do? Or just what I do in class?"

"Everything," Bell explained, understanding Terra's direction. "Thankfully I don't become your teacher until tomorrow morning."

She looked at Bell to see if he was just stating fact or if he in fact was willing to keep something from her parents. "So anything that happens tonight?"

"Is strictly the business of two friends and . . . him." He gestured to Grey.

"Thank you Master Bell." She faced the glass and put her hand on it. "Oh and don't be frightened. I know what I'm doing," she said over her shoulder. "Last chance to come willingly Grey!"

"Don't threaten me with a good time princess," he shouted back at her.

With a stressed laugh, Terra pushed her hand through the glass and then stepped through to the other side. She heard Bell draw in a sharp breath. It was too late to turn back and explain now. She strode across the cell, her bare feet making strange echoing sounds on the glass floor, and stopped at Grey's bed, folded her arms across her chest and glared at him.

"What are you doing you idiot?" Grey demanded opening his eyes to see Terra standing in the cell. He was sure that if people found out she could come and go through the glass walls as she pleased, there would be a sudden stop to their dinners together. Not that he had to see her, but it was certainly better than being stuck with no one to talk to. Not to mention she was essential to his plans for Diana and the entire world for that matter.

He needed their dinners to continue.

"I'm not an idiot," she objected defensively, "I'm doing what I have to do to get some answers. If you would just come to the glass and act civil for a few minutes then I wouldn't have to be standing here. Now are you going to get up or am I going to have to drag you?"

"I would love to see you try princess," Grey challenged, his words heavy with a hidden meaning Terra didn't quite understand. She did, however, understand the challenge.

"Fine then, you were warned." She grabbed his arm with every intention of using her aura to help drag him across the floor to the wall. When she grabbed him, he cried out in pain and jerked away from her.

Terra jumped back, looking horrified. She had no intention of hurting him, she hadn't even had a chance to summon up her aura yet. There was no way she hurt him with her magic. Still, she felt appalled at the thought that maybe some how she had harmed him.

"Grey," she said quietly, backing up. "I'm so sorry, I don't understand what happened."

"You burned me," he shouted angrily.

"No I didn't I . . . I just touched your arm. I swear I wasn't trying to hurt you."

Grey pushed the sleeve of his shirt up.

His arm was fine and unmarked.

253

She carefully scanned the length of his arm, trying to find the spot where she had hurt him. Instead she found no indication that there was anything wrong with his arm at all. No burn, no blister, not even a red mark.

"I don't see a burn," she stated.

"What's going on in there," Bell called from outside the box.

"Hold on Master Bell," she called over her shoulder.

Grey looked at his arm disbelievingly. "Huh," he muttered.

"There's no burn there you big baby," she teased, grabbing him by the hand this time. "Now come on, don't make me use my magic just to drag you across the floor."

Still confused and staring at his arm, Grey got to his feet and let the princess drag him across the room to the cell wall where Bell was standing and staring at the two of them.

"Alright I'm here," he complained, shrugging her hand off.

"Now stay here or I swear I'll pin you to the ground," she joked, laughing.

"Can you even do that?" He teased, joking along with the princess.

"I don't know," she answered honestly.

"I can teach her how," Bell chimed in, a strange look on his face as he watched the princess and the prisoner.

"There!" She crowed, all but sticking her tongue out like a child.

"Whatever," he laughed, pushing Terra as she headed to the glass.

She was about to step through the wall when Bell put his hand up and she halted.

"How long have you been able to do this?" He asked.

Terra looked to Grey and then back to Bell. "I think I've always been able to do it, but we didn't know I could until . . . um," she struggled to remember exactly when she had first walked through the glass.

"It was the night you told Reynolds you named me," Grey offered. His voice was dripping with disdain when he said Eric's name.

"That's right," she confirmed, her face falling a little. "It was the night Eric was named my royal guard. And the night you . . . left the magic in his head." Terra's voice got considerably quieter as she continued to talk.

"Yea, brilliant move that," Grey muttered angrily.

Terra reached out and lightly put her hand on Grey's arm. It was hard enough thinking about that night and how Eric had made her feel and the things he had said to her. Even now after they had made up it still stung to think about it. To toss a fight between Bell and Grey on top of those feelings and she might start to cry again.

Bell watched as the smallest gesture from Terra calmed what had looked like an oncoming storm from the supposed King of Shadows. He had heard what happened when Eric and his men had cornered the monster on the edge of the woods near the castle town. Nearly all of the men had been lost trying to capture him. He had unleashed a storm of darkness unlike anything they had ever seen. It wasn't until he had made the mistake of trying to take Eric on, sword to sword, that he had finally been beaten and captured.

To see Terra, who was not just young, but untrained and inexperienced; calm that same monster with just a touch. It was nothing short of amazing. An idea started to form in Bells mind. It wasn't much, but it was certainly something. There was no doubt in his mind now. Somehow Terra was connected to this monster and through that connection she was calming him.

He hadn't noticed before, but it was much easier to breath in the prison now. There was less darkness in the room. Not much less, but enough that Bell could take notice. It must have been due to Terra. She was having an effect on the prisoner.

"I think I've seen enough," he stated. He knew that the crystal he had in his pocket would only keep Grey out of his mind for so long.

He needed to get away and process what he'd just seen and work out the idea he was starting to take shape.

"So you know what happened?" Terra asked.

"Yes. Grey when you were injured were you up against the glass?"

"Yes," he answered suspiciously. "I'd fallen asleep in bed sitting against the glass. I had a nightmare about Diana trying to kill me; I woke suddenly to burning pain across my shoulders."

"As I thought," Bell confirmed. "Because your cell is attuned to Terra's magic, when you experienced that pain, you naturally reached out. When you did this your aura came into contact with Terra's magic swirling around your cell. That's why you reached to her."

"But I reached back didn't I?" She asked.

"You did," Bell said, "But I'm afraid I don't have the answer to that. I will take my leave and ponder on these things so I can provide you with an answer." Bell formally saluted Terra with a fist to his heart and a bow. "Good evening Princess. Grey." He turned and started for the door.

Grey looked at Terra and nodded to the door. He didn't need to speak; she knew he was concerned that Bell's hasty exit meant he was going to inform someone about something he had seen or heard tonight.

With nod, she ran through the glass and caught up with Bell. "Master Bell," she stated tentatively.

He stopped and put a hand on her shoulder. "Do not worry Princess," he said smiling. "I've no intention of sharing what I've seen tonight. I just need to think and this room isn't exactly conducive to private thought."

"I suppose that's true," she agreed. She threw her arms around Bell and whispered, "thank you." Smiling, he returned the embrace and headed out of the room. She watched the door for a moment, still nervous that Bell might burst back in having changed his mind about keeping their secret.

"What did he say?" Grey called from his cell.

With one last look at the door, she headed back to the cell. "He said he has no intention of telling anyone what he saw tonight."

"Do you trust him?" He asked as she sat in the chair at her table.

"You can read minds," she queried. "You tell me. Was he being honest?"

Grey made a face.

"What is it?" She asked, fearing the worst.

"Nothing," he said, trying to brush it off.

"It's clearly something," she observed, eyeing him suspiciously. "Tell me what's wrong."

"I couldn't read his mind," he muttered quietly.

"Couldn't at all?" Terra asked disbelievingly.

"I could sense it, but I couldn't see into it. Like looking at a book on a shelf where all the words are in a different language, I know what it is but I can't read it."

"How could he have done that?"

"Magic of course," Grey stated, tossing himself down into his chair. "So you tell me, can we trust him?"

Terra was suddenly overcome by this strange dark feeling of foreboding. Her brain was trying to remember something that she couldn't. She couldn't put finger on why, but she felt very afraid of those words. It seemed like he had said those words to her before, or maybe he would say those words to her soon? She couldn't be sure but she didn't like the way she felt.

"Terra is everything ok?" He asked, suddenly on his feet.

"I think so, what's wrong?" She asked startled by his sudden movements.

"Reynolds is on his way down here, very quickly. So tell me again, is everything alright?"

"Yea I had a weird feeling when you asked me about Master Bell but that's it."

Grey cursed under his breath. "You don't suppose Bell ran in to Reynolds and decided to have a little conversation do you?" His voice was bitter and she didn't need to ask why.

"I don't think Master Bell would do that. I trust him." She met Grey's gaze head on and didn't flinch at the cold grey eyes that stared back.

For a moment he held her gaze. Then sensing Reynolds was close to the door, nodded and said, "Alright but we can't trust Reynolds. He'll go straight to the King."

Terra grimaced. "There's a problem there," she said quickly, feeling through the bond that Eric was very close.

"What kind of problem?!" He demanded in a whisper.

"I sort of promised Eric the night they brought you here that wouldn't ever lie to him so long as he never lied to me. I won't bring it up but if he does I can't lie." It came out in a rush that left Grey staring at her, mouth open, dumbfounded.

"Yes, yes you can lie to him you have to." His voice was a whisper but she could still feel the power behind it.

"I can't!" She pleaded in a horse whisper. "I gave him my word!"

Grey stared not sure how to keep her from blowing his plans. "Terra I don't have to tell you what would happen if someone else found out what you can do. You would never be allowed down here again and then you would be breaking your word to *me*."

"If I lie to him then not only am I breaking my word, which is my bond as a princess, but I would be invalidating every other promise I have or will ever make. How could you trust me to keep my word to you if I break my word to someone I've bonded with?!"

Grey didn't have a chance to respond as Eric came bursting through the wooden doors at the other end of the room. He face was frantic and his eyes darted all over the room. He took in Grey in his cell, Terra practically at his side save for the glass wall between them. His eyes took in the food on the table that neither of them had really eaten, and finally Terra's shoes and stockings on the floor.

"What in the name of the creator is going on here?!" He demanded.

"Nothing," Grey replied coldly. "Just having a conversation, you just missed the Master Wizard himself."

"Terra?" Eric asked walking over. "What's going on? People are saying you came running out of here like you were being chased by the devil himself. Then they say you grabbed Bell by the hand and pulled him down here with you!"

She took a calming breath and tried to send calm to Eric through their bond. She could see him take a deep breath and his shoulders come down a little. Whenever he got angry, his shoulders would come up and his neck would disappear. His shoulders coming down meant that he was feeling her calm and calming down too.

"Everything is ok," she explained. "There was an interesting development and I needed to speak to Master Bell about what was going on. That's all."

"What kind of a development?" He had covered the distance between them in a few quick steps. He reached up and put a hand on Terra's shoulder defensively. He pulled her close and glared at Grey as though everything that was wrong was somehow his fault.

Grey shot Terra a warning look. She gave him a what-else-can-I-do-face to which he made a face and walked away from the glass. She turned to Eric; she had to explain what was going on without telling him too much. She didn't want to lie to him either. She had to find some middle ground.

"Grey has scars like I do," she blurted, deciding that was the best place to start. "I saw them earlier. He had no idea he even had the scars. So I went and got Master Bell and brought him down here so he could see and tell us what it meant."

Eric shook his head, confused. "What does it mean?"

"Grey had a nightmare about Diana trying to kill him," Terra started.

"Can't imagine why," Eric muttered under his breath.

She ignored him and kept talking. "When he had the nightmare it burned him somehow, just like I thought my dream had burned me. When that happened he was up against the glass, the glass that is surrounded by my magic."

"Alright, I follow you so far," Eric said, still eyeing Grey like he might leap out of his prison at any moment and attack them.

"Because he was hurting and in shock, he reached."

"Wait isn't reaching like a bonding thing?"

"Similar to it, yes."

"So he bonded with you?" He asked something similar to disgust in his voice.

"Only for a moment," she explained. "And only because he's surrounded by my magic. So his aura hit that and me at the same time. He was asleep and didn't realize he was scarred until just tonight. I brought Bell in to make sure it wasn't anything like we were bonded."

"And?" Eric demanded, "Are you?"

"No," Grey and Terra said together.

"No," Terra said again. "It was a onetime thing. It was just strong and I was worried."

"But you're ok now?" He asked. His rage had seemed to dissipate. He reached out to put a hand on her face but stopped short. He looked confused. It seemed as though he wanted to touch her but didn't know why. After a moment he pulled his hand back.

Terra swallowed and tried to hide the pain she felt at his not wanting to touch her. She knew he was different still and that the things he had once felt for her were gone now. Still, it hurt to watch him reach to her and then stop. She glanced around the room blinking rapidly, trying to keep the hurt away. Carefully she blocked off part of their bond.

She didn't need Eric to feel guilty and confused.

"I'm fine," she replied, stepping away from him. She walked over to pick up her shoes, glad for an excuse to get away. She had learned how to keep emotions from going through the bond to him, it was how she had survived the last month.

So she kept her hurt inside and picked up her shoes. She stood and looked around blinking again. She could feel tears threating to escape. As she glanced around the room her eyes came to rest on Grey. He was leaning against the glass closest to her with a strange new look on his face.

It was pity.

He actually pitied her.

Terra met his gaze and ever so slightly shook her head. She didn't want pity, especially not from him. She was trying to save him, trying to drive the darkness out of his heart and purify him so that he and Diana wouldn't have to fight. She was dedicated to spending however long it took to make him better. She couldn't handle him looking at her like that, she was trying really hard not to cry and this wasn't helping.

She turned away from Grey and walked back to the table where Eric was standing glowering at him.

Grey however, didn't seem to be taking any notice as he followed Terra while she walked.

"Does he always do that?" Eric asked, jerking his chin at the prison.

"Do what?" She asked, already tired of Eric and Greys hatred of each other.

"He follows you everywhere you walk and his eyes are always on you." Eric was still looking at Grey, hadn't taken his eyes off of him actually.

"Well she's the best looking thing in here," Grey jeered. "Just because you don't see her doesn't mean I don't."

"What's that supposed to mean?" Eric demanded, puffing out his chest as his shoulders came up again.

"I think you know damn well what it means," Grey hissed, clearly agitated also.

Terra could sense a change in the air. It was the same kind of change she had felt when Grey had tried to steal all the light from the room. He was getting angry and still seemed to have some kind of power outside his box. If things kept going at this rate she and Eric would be in a great deal of trouble.

Eric looked at Grey like he was some beaten down dog, something not deserving of his respect. Thinking like that will get him, and possibly Terra, killed. Knowing she couldn't let things continue the way they were going, she decided to intercede.

"Eric," she urged, putting a hand on his shoulders. "I think perhaps it's time for bed."

"What!" He shouted. He wasn't trying to yell at her, he was getting extremely amped up the longer he was in the room.

"Bedtime, right now," Terra repeated.

Eric finally turned to look at her. His face was angry, his brows were drawn down and he looked ready for a fight. When he looked at her he realized that there was something wrong. Her eyes were dark and glassy like she'd been crying and her mouth was turned down in the corners. She was upset, maybe even sad.

All the anger went out of him like the air out of a balloon. His shoulders dropped and he nodded at her. "You're right, it's very late. I'm sorry," he said as he looked around the room awkwardly. "I'll go and talk to Lewis while you . . . clean up in here."

He turned and walked away quickly leaving Grey and Terra alone in the room again.

"Good riddance," Grey grumbled as he walked back to the glass wall closest to Terra. "You know I seriously hate that guy?"

"I know that," she sighed, exasperated. "I get that you two hate each other but it would be great if you guys could think before you go all crazy with the hate in here."

"He's the one who burst in here looking for a fight," Grey snapped defensively.

"He came bursting in here because he thought I was in trouble. He was worried about me."

"And didn't he do a stand up job?!" Grey shouted bitterly. "I've never seen you look so hurt. Bastard."

Terra was ready to fire back a quip or retort when it died on her lips. Grey wasn't just angry at Eric for no reason, he was mad because Eric had hurt her. Not intentionally of course, but he had hurt her and Grey had seen that. Now he was mad at Eric for it.

"Oh my creator," Terra muttered under her breath in awe. She knew she had been right about him. She knew that deep down inside him there was still something good. She smiled at Grey and felt like she could almost laugh at how happy she was.

She was right, she *could* save him.

"What are you smiling at?" He asked eying her suspiciously.

"You care," she stated, still smiling.

"Care about what?" He demanded looking a little concerned now.

"Me. You care about me."

"Don't be absurd," he laughed walking away. "I care about very little, certainly not a little shadow princess like you."

Terra ignored his words. "You care about me. So much so that you're mad at Eric for hurting me. Not because of the history you two have or the fact that he burst in here. You're mad because what he did hurt me. Because you care."

Grey was nearly across the cell when he stopped cold. Terra's words rang true and that, for him, was a terrifying thing. He hadn't bothered to think about why he was mad at Reynolds. He was always mad at Reynolds. Reynolds was an idiot, and the ass who had captured him, not to mention he treated Terra like . . .

He stopped.

She was right. He was mad because of the way he'd treated Terra. He actually cared about her. He hadn't meant for anything like this to happen. He was supposed to fake caring about her so he could corrupt her. If he was lashing out at Reynolds because the way he was treating the princess, that wasn't fake. That was real and it was bad.

Worse than bad it was terrifying.

He didn't care about people. He never had and as far as he was concerned, he never would. If he was beginning to actually care it might throw a wrench in his plans for everything. Not to mention having feelings for someone meant that Terra was right. There might actually be some good in him.

Just the thought made his stomach turn.

If some tiny part of him had somehow been purified then it was only a matter of time before the darkness got to it and made it right. Maybe his getting close to Terra so quickly had caused this. He hadn't anticipated the level of her power; maybe this is what he got for underestimating his opponent.

It was a mistake, and not one he would make again.

Terra watched as Grey froze suddenly, midstride. She could tell she'd hit a nerve. It proved that she was right. He cared about her enough to be upset that someone mistreated her. Feeling much more awake and just a little flattered, she turned for the door.

She walked across the room and turned back, Grey was still standing frozen. Terra smiled and shook her head. She pulled the door open and quietly pulled it closed again. Best to leave Grey to figure out what's going on by himself, he could be a while after all.

Terra walked with Eric up to her door and said goodnight. As nice as it was not to be fighting with him, things were still awkward. She understood why of course, but that didn't make it easier to deal with. He said goodnight and bowed.

Then he just walked away.

Terra had wanted to talk to him about everything that had happened, but one look at his face told her to leave it for the night. Apparently he also needed to process some things. Maybe men just couldn't process things as fast as women could. Either way she wasn't getting anything from him tonight. So she headed into her room and closed the door, more than ready for sleep.

Morning dawned cold and grey over the top of the castle. King Sol stood waiting with his closest advisors for the Master Wizard to arrive. The King had been awoken early by his page telling him the Master Wizard had been by and given him a note for his eyes only. He had broken the seal and found a brief letter asking the King to assemble only his closest and most trusted advisors and to meet him on the roof just before dawn.

Here he stood, waiting in the cold. Fall was reaching its midpoint and it seemed the warmth was slowly being drawn out of the world. It would be a cold, hard winter. King Sol made a mental note to start making winter preparations early this year.

"You're Majesty," Bell greeted as he appeared from one of the trap doors that led to the roof. "Thank you for meeting me here so early. I wanted to talk to you before any of the staff gets up and starts their daily routines."

"And what, Master Wizard, is so important?" Lord Howe asked.

"My lord it is as we hoped," he started, only addressing the King. "It would appear that Terra is the key to the Shadow Kings undoing."

There were murmurs and whispers among the few advisors around the King. Bell waited patiently while Sol considered his words. After a few moments he raised his hand the men around him silenced immediately.

"What proof do you have?" He asked.

"Last night I went to see the monster in his cell along with Princess Terra. It would seem the scars that stretch across the princess's shoulders originated from the prisoner."

"How is that possible?" King Sol demanded, suddenly livid. "You assured me that box was impregnable. How is it he is able to have an effect on my daughter this way?"

"I'm afraid I haven't worked it all out just yet, but from what I can tell the scars are the byproduct of a reach."

"A reach," the King said considering. "A reach means there's a bond. A bond would be a good thing for us."

"Exactly," Bell smiled. "More than that, as I was examining both the Princess and the prisoner, several times Terra would calm him with just a word or a look."

Everyone began to talk at once except for the King who remained silent as he pondered what Bell had said. If this so called King of the Shadows could be weakened or made to care for his youngest daughter than that might just be the upper hand they've been searching for. Diana was young still and she had much training to complete. It was going to be several years at least before she's ready to face that monster.

If Terra could be used to weaken him, then they would have to use Terra.

"Was there anything else?" King Sol asked. "Any other bit of information we may be able to use?"

Bell looked to his King. After only a seconds hesitation he replied, "No sir, nothing else that I've seen would be of any use to us."

"Very well then," the King said. "Keep us informed on any other developments and we will hold a council soon to discuss what we do with this information. Thank you Master Wizard."

Bell bowed, fist to his heart as the King and his small gathering of Lords walked past him and headed down the stairs. Bell waited for a while, watching the sun come up over the mountains in the distance. He had chosen not to tell the King about Terra's ability to come and go through the prison walls as she pleased. Not because he had promised her, but because he felt it was necessary to keep some things secret.

Chapter 7

A knock at the door woke Terra. She sat up slowly and stretched. It couldn't possibly be morning already. She was still so sleepy. Another, more impatient knock got her up and out of bed. She shambled over to her dressing chair and grabbed her robe. Throwing it on, she hurried to the door and pulled it open. Eric was standing outside with Mammy.

"What time is it?" She asked yawning.

Mammy tisked at her under her breath and swept into the room. The princess hadn't noticed at first the small army of men and women standing behind her guard and caretaker, but they swept into the room carrying an assortment of things with them.

"What is all this?" She asked, standing against the wall as more people poured in. "What is all this for?"

"Honestly I think you'd forget your head if it wasn't properly screwed onto your shoulders. Did you forget that you're sixteen now?" Mammy asked as she helped a few women set things up.

"I didn't forget," Terra replied sulkily. "I'm just not awake enough to be thinking straight right now."

"That's a terrible excuse," Eric said laughing. "You could just say you forgot, she'll be less cranky that way."

"Thanks for the advice," she muttered shooting Eric a sarcastic glance. "So really what's going on?"

"Dress fittings dear," Mammy replied. "You're a young woman now and your father wants you to look the part. So you're getting fitted for new dresses." She was clearly excited about the prospect of Terra getting new clothes. She seemed to bounce along from one person to another, happily making sure they were doing as they should and seeing if they needed any help.

"Wow she is really excited about this isn't she?" Terra asked under her breath.

"You have no idea," Eric whispered. "I've been at this for over an hour now."

"You have my sympathies for that," she laughed. "Anyway you should get going. If I'm going to be poked and pinned I want as few witnesses to my humiliation as possible."

Eric laughed and nudged Terra with his elbow. "You know when you put it that way I want to stay."

"Yeah, as funny as it would be for you, Mammy would end your life."

Eric grimaced, "Well there is that."

"Yeah, so I'll see you at breakfast then?" She asked smiling.

"Yeah, see you then." He jokingly pushed Terra in the shoulder and left.

"Are you ready dear?" Mammy asked. She had set up a miniature boutique in the room. There was a large three piece looking glass, a platform to step up on and yards of fabric in every color. Alongside Mammy stood half a dozen women of varying ages holding an assortment of needles, threads and measuring tapes. They looked ready to work.

"Let's get this over with then," she muttered.

Two hours later Terra was headed down the stairs in a dress Mammy had taken out of the stack of old dresses being sent out. She and another woman had worked for a while making it suitable for a young lady to wear. Terra wished they asked her opinion before they chose the dress to work on.

Mammy had selected the pale pink dress that had belonged to Diana for less than a day. She had given it to Terra after deciding that the pink color would look good on no one. She wasn't wrong. Pink seemed to do strange things with the color of her face. Sometimes it made her look flushed other times it washed her out completely.

She knew Mammy was just choosing the nicest dress of the lot for Terra, so she smiled and told Mammy how much she appreciated her hard work. It had a lovely cut to it now and Mammy had put so much effort into making it appropriate for a young woman that it was quite pretty. Despite its color. At the very least, she still had her dark green cloak and that helped to balance the color of the dress and the way she looked in it.

Terra walked down the spiral stair case, careful to keep the fabric up so she could walk while balancing the tray with Grey's breakfast. It was much harder getting anything done in a full length skirt she was learning. Now she had to grab a handful of the skirt just to move at any speed faster than a saunter. Not to mention stairs had become the enemy. She had tripped and fallen due to this skirt twice already and she'd only been out of her room for fifteen minutes.

"Good morning Princess," the guard at the door said as he put his fist to his heart and bowed.

"Good morning John," she replied brightly.

"Let me help you," He said pushing the door open for her.

"Thank you." She liked John. He was a good man and a fine guard. Eric had told her that he was young but one of the best. That was why he had been assigned to guard the prisoner despite his youth. Terra liked him because he was kind and always offered to help.

Once through the door John nodded to her and pulled it closed again.

"Where did you go last night?" Grey demanded angrily before she had even turned from the door.

"I went to bed, it was late," she replied walking to the prison cell.

"Funny," he sneered sarcastically. "Is there a reason you just walked out and didn't so much as say goodbye?"

"Oh," she stammered with mock concern, "I'm sorry. I didn't mean to hurt your feelings."

Grey's eyes got huge as he stammered for a reply. "I didn't . . . you didn't . . . feelings aren't hurt!"

"I only caught some of that," she laughed as she pushed the tray through the glass.

He grabbed the tray and all but ripped it out of Terra's hands. "You didn't hurt my feelings!" He finally managed to yell.

"Oh but you have feelings be hurt then?"

"What! No! I don't have feeling like that. Nothing got hurt because there's nothing to hurt!"

"If you say so," she called turning to head back out. She had her first magic lesson and she didn't want to be late.

"Wait! Where are you going now?" He called after her.

"Lessons. Today is my first real lesson with Master Bell."

"We're not done talking about this!" He shouted as Terra pulled the door open.

"I'll see you later," she called pulling the door closed behind her.

"Is everything alright highness?" John asked, hearing Grey shouting through the door. "Should I send for Guard Reynolds?"

"No," she replied kindly. "He's going to be in a foul mood for a while, just ignore him if you can."

"I will do my best," he said as Grey continued to shout.

It took Terra less than ten minutes to hastily eat her breakfast and head off to meet Master Bell in the school room. She gathered up her skirt in her hands and ran the whole way there, too excited to walk. She stopped just outside the door and took a few deep breathes to calm herself down and pull herself together. Satisfied she no longer looked like she had run all the way down here, she knocked on the door.

"Come in," Bell called from inside.

Smiling, she pushed the door open and stepped in. Instantly the door behind her slammed shut with a kind of finality that told Terra it wasn't going to be opening again. The room itself was thrown into darkness as the door sealed them in.

"Master Bell?" She called out. "Where are you? What's going on?"

"Princess," he called, his voice sounding strained and far away. "Run Princess."

Terra's heart started racing. Master Bell was in trouble, she could feel it. She had to find him and help him. But the room was so dark she couldn't see anything. She could stumble forward but if she fell and got hurt both she and Bell would be in so much more trouble. She needed light and she needed it now.

"Light," she whispered. When she had been attacked last month she had needed light then too. She had simply thought it and her magic answered. She closed her eyes and tried to focus on how she had called her magic in such a way.

A cry of pain across the room pulled Terra's focus.

She started forward but ran straight into a table, slamming her knee into the solid wood and sending waves of pain through her leg. She cried out and held her knee while it throbbed.

"Princess you must get to safety," Bell called. His voice was fading fast. Whatever was going on sounded like it was killing him. She had to save him before it was too late.

"Hold on Master Bell," Terra promised, "I'm coming."

A strange and familiar feeling behind her made Terra suddenly turn. Behind her she could see the sliver eyes of a shadow, small and slitted, they hadn't seen her yet. Fully grasping what was going on, she knew she had to get Bell out now. Putting her hands together Terra sent up a small prayer for strength and help and once again tried to call the light.

"Light!" She shouted. Her magic's response was instantaneous. As soon as the words left her lips the purple and silver fire sprang up around her, throwing light and shadow across the room. Now she could see the near dozen shadows wondering the room.

Mouth agape, Terra desperately scanned for the Master Wizard.

There! In the corner by one of the magical cabinets the Master Wizard stood slumped against the wall. He was gasping for breath and there was a near solid wall of Shadows closing in on him. He was exhausted. Bell glanced up for a second and his eyes locked on Terra.

He was finished and he knew it.

"NO!" Terra yelled. She ran forward, not caring about the Shadows that had turned their attention to her, or the assortment furniture that was in her way. She had to save Bell. There was no time left to worry about simple things like chairs and desks. She had to move.

As Terra ran, shadow and furniture alike, seemed to fly from her path. Still it didn't seem to matter; she wasn't moving fast enough to get to Bell in time. At this rate he would be dead before she got there. She needed to do something else, anything else to buy time.

But what could she do? She didn't have any kind of proper training. She knew only what her sister had taught her.

Bell cried out in pain as a shadow got close enough and brushed his arm. He screamed and went down to a knee. They were moving faster now, closing in on him to finish the kill. She was out of time, she had to act now.

Her body started to move before she knew what she was doing. She jumped up on a table that was nearby and started to pull all

272

her magic into the very center of being. Her heart raced and seemed to ready to fly out of her chest. Still she pulled all her magic in until it was all contained within her.

"Leave him ALONE!" Pure white magic shot out of her in a giant circle. It spread through the room covering everything in a pale white light for less than the length of a heartbeat. Every shadow it touched dissolved into beautiful and blinding white light before disappearing.

In less than a second the entire room had been cleared and washed in a radiant white light. Then, as though nothing had happened, the room went back to being a simple classroom. No darkness, no shadows, nothing out of the ordinary, except that Terra was standing on a desk and Master Bell was still on the floor.

"Master Bell!" She shouted flying off the table and over to the wizard.

He was shaking but still alive. Carefully she kneelt down beside him and put a hand on his shoulder. He was freezing cold and shivering violently.

"Master Bell," Terra asked worried. "Master Bell are you ok? Are you hurt? What can I do?"

He opened his mouth to say something but his teeth chattered so hard any words he got out were impossible to understand. Out of options and worried that if he stayed this way to long he would die, Terra wrapped her arms around the wizard and thought of heat, fire and light.

Her magic obeyed without hesitation this time. She was once again surrounded by the warmth of her purple fire. She held Bell while the warmth spread from her to him. After a minute or so he stopped shaking and after another two or three he was breathing normally. Terra, too afraid to open her eyes, kept them shut and held on to Bell, silently willing him to be ok.

"Princess," Bell whispered, his voice weak but not shaking anymore.

"Master Bell?" She asked, still not opening her eyes or letting go. "Are you alright?"

"I'm fine. You should stop now, you'll waste all your energy and be exhausted," the more he spoke the stronger his voice sounded.

"Energy?" She asked, confused.

"Yes," Bell laughed weakly. He stood slowly and let Terra's arms fall away. As they fell the fire around her went out. "The amount of energy you just expelled should be more than enough to leave you exhausted." He looked down at the princess who was standing staring at him like she was afraid he might keel over at any moment.

"I feel fine," she stated. "I didn't realize I was expending anything." Terra looked around feeling rather foolish now. "Is that bad?"

"Quite the contrary," Bell explained smiling down at her. "It simply means you're stronger than I thought." He started forward, made a strange noise and nearly sank back down again. Terra threw his arm over her shoulders and wrapped an arm around his waist.

"You're still hurt," she said, leading him to a nearby chair. He collapsed gratefully into the red padded chair he kept at the back of the room.

"I'm alright," he said, "just a little winded I think."

"Master Bell," she asked, kneeling in front of him. "What happened? How did those shadows get in here? Why was there so many of them?" She was horrified she already knew the answer. It wouldn't be the first time Grey sent shadows after her. If he had been mad enough about her just walking away this morning, who knows what he might be capable of.

Terra hoped she was wrong. She and Grey were really getting along and she had been considering him a friend for a while. After last night with the realization that he cared, Terra was sure she was on the right track to heal him. She just had to be patient and in time she could purify the darkness in his heart. She knew she was having an effect on him.

Or so she thought.

If Grey was behind this, an unwarranted attack on a member of her father's inner council, then maybe she was wrong. Maybe he was too far gone to be saved and she was just fooling herself into thinking he could be anything other than a monster. After all, he wouldn't be the King of the Shadows if someone as unremarkable, as she was, could save him.

Still, part of her was unwilling to accept that. Unwilling to think that there was no good left in him. If he could care about her being hurt, then he couldn't be all bad.

"I'm afraid," Master Bell started, pulling Terra out of her train of thought, "that I am the one responsible for the shadows finding their way in here."

"What?" She asked, shocked and confused. "How is that possible? Why would you do such a thing? You nearly died!"

Bell raised his hand and Terra's next question died on her lips. "I was trying to summon one shadow to test you when you arrived for class today. I set things up as a sort of impromptu test of your abilities. I simply wanted to ascertain where you were at, power wise, so I knew where to start with you lessons. Unfortunately, my test got away from me and had you not come in when you had, my mistake would have claimed my life."

Terra stared blankly at him.

"Princess," Bell said when she remained silent. "I am sorry to test you this way. It's the only way to get an accurate reading on your power levels. I beg you, don't be angry with me."

"I'm not angry," she replied quietly. "I'm relieved."

"Relieved?" Bell asked confused.

"Yes," she whispered letting out a breath she didn't realize she's been holding. "I thought for moment that . . . but no, it's ok."

"I see," Bell said, eyeing Terra. "You thought this was Grey's doing."

It wasn't a question, but still she nodded. "Yes."

"And now you're relieved to find it was me all along?"

"Yes."

"Princess, if I may speak frankly?"

"Please."

"I have to say that I'm concerned with the bond that is forming between you and the prisoner. I know that you must deal with him every day, as is your agreement, but I still worry that you may be becoming too attached to him."

Terra considered a moment before she answered. "I know that he and I have become friends rather quickly. However, if I can be honest," Bell nodded, "I think I can help him."

"Help him how?"

Terra looked at Bell for a moment, really looked at him. She tried to gauge how much she could trust him. He knew she could pass through the prison walls and as far as she could tell, he'd told no one. Maybe Bell could be the person she could trust with her secret. If she was wrong, however, that would mean the end of all her attempts to heal him.

"Terra," Bell said, taking her hand, "you can trust me with anything. I will not tell your secrets to anyone else."

"What about the fact that you're my teacher now. You have obligations to my father."

"Seeing as how the first lesson hasn't started yet, I do believe my obligations are only to myself still."

"Very well," she sighed. She needed to trust someone with this information. She would need help as things progressed and Master Bell seemed the most suitable person she knew. "I believe that I can heal Grey." When Bell didn't say anything she continued. "I think that somewhere inside him there is still goodness and light."

"What proof do you have of this?" He asked in as neutral a voice as he could manage.

"When you put the magic in Eric's head and he forgot that he cared about me, he was very cruel to me. Especially after he found out I named Grey.

"When he first insulted me and left me standing in the prison, I was devastated. Eric had been close to telling me he loved me days

276

before hand and now he was treating me as thought I was garbage. I couldn't really think. Grey called me over and pulled me through the glass."

"That was the first time you passed through?"

"Yes. Grey pulled me through and he told me that he was giving me a 'one time only, white flags raised,' chance to let it all out."

"Meaning what?" He asked his brow arched in concern.

"Meaning he was giving me an opportunity to cry. He told me he had been looking through my heart when Eric had said what he said. He told me that he had felt the pain I had felt at Eric's words."

"He held you as you cried."

"He did. For quite a while I sat with my head on his shoulder and cried. It was an unexpected act of kindness. Something I didn't expect to see from him."

Bell considered the princess's words for a moment. "Is this the only such incident?"

"No," she replied sheepishly. "He's been kind like that several times."

"May I ask, the man you danced with yesterday, the one you had the premonition about, was that Grey?"

Terra blushed up to the roots of her hair. "Yes. It was him. Master Bell am I crazy?" She demanded suddenly. "I know he's the enemy and I know he's a very bad man, but is it crazy to think that I could help him? Or to think of him as my friend?"

"Well tell me this," Bell said. "Why do you want to help him?"

"Why?" She asked confused. "I don't understand."

"Why do you want to help him?" Bell didn't sound calm anymore. In fact he was starting to sound a little angry. "Do you want to help him to prove to people that you're better than your sister?"

"What?! No! That's ridiculous!"

"Do you want to help him to show everyone that you're the better sister? The better princess? Do you want to show your parents that you're the princess they should have favored all these years!?"

277

"No! Stop! Master Bell it's not like that!" She shouted over his incessant questions.

"Do you want to help him to prove once and for all whose the most gifted in the kingdom?!" Bell shouted. His questions were coming out faster and faster and Terra was having a hard time understanding them.

Finally she'd had enough. "I want to *save* him!" She shouted.

Bell fell silent and smiled at the princess.

"I want to save him so I can save Diana! I want to save them both!"

"That, Princess is a most noble reason indeed." He smiled at Terra. It was as he had hoped. Her reasons for wanting to save the monster were pure. So long as she kept going the way she was, she would indeed be the key to his undoing.

"So I'm not crazy for wanting to help him?"

"Not at all princess," Bell said standing. "Now what do you say we start you're first lesson?"

"That would fantastic," she said relieved.

Bell got up to start with the young princess but stopped short.

"What's wrong?" She asked sensing the change in her teacher.

"Terra, how many times have you yielded white magic before?"

"White magic?" She asked.

"Just now, when you sent out that ring of magic and purified the shadows, you used white magic. Did you not notice?"

"No, not really. I was so caught up in the knowledge that if I didn't so something and soon, you would die. I didn't pay attention to the colors at all."

"That is *very* interesting."

"Why?"

"White magic is the rarest of all magics. Few people have ever even seen it yielded." When Terra continued to look at him confessed, he tried a different approach. "Well, let me ask you this, do you know what the colors in your magic mean?"

She pulled a face, "I know they mean different things, but . . ." Terra suddenly felt very ill prepared for her first lesson. Knowing the meaning of the colors was a very basic thing.

"Fear not princess," Bell reassured her. "This is our first lesson so let's start here."

"Ok," she replied, still not feeling any better.

"So why don't we start with your colors."

"Purple and sliver," she offered.

"Well your purple is a very dark purple. People with this color magic tend to be very spiritual and faithful. Intensely so. They love and believe stronger than any other people. They also have a tendency to be naive." He shot a very knowing look at Terra who blushed and turned away.

"Then there's your sliver."

"Diana said it's not natural," she offered glumly. "When you taught her years ago she told me that silver doesn't exist."

"Well she's a little right, but mostly she's incorrect. Silver magic is associated with people who have a mastery of magic. It is hard to achieve and not many people have ever been able to master it past just an accent color. People are not born with sliver magic, usually."

Terra thought over what Bell had just said. She understood that he was the master wizard and he knew more than her. But in this, he had to be mistaken.

"Master Bell," she started, "I don't mean to question your knowledge but I've always had silver in my magic."

"I understand that," he smiled, "It would seem that in many ways, you will be very unique student."

Terra didn't like the way that sounded. She didn't want to be unique. Anything about her that was ever different was cannon fodder

279

for Diana. If she was somehow special in magic? Diana would use it as a means to torment her for the rest of her life.

Seeing that the young princess was not especially pleased about the current conversation, Bell decided to try for a change. "Perhaps you can tell me this," he said, "At what point did you gain the ability to wear you magic the way you do?"

"You mean my aura?"

"Yes," he answered. He had noticed only once before that Terra's magic didn't seem to come from inside her the way it does for most people. Her magic she wore around her like a cloak of power, always there.

"I don't know . . . "she answered, thinking. "It was just there like that one day."

"Do you remember what day, exactly?" Bell pressed.

"Maybe after the night I was attacked," she said unsure. "I remember having to use the door that day you caught me in class. Then after I was attacked it was always there."

"Interesting," he commented, pondering.

"Is that bad?" She asked worried again.

"No, not at all," he reassured her. "I've just never heard of anyone being able to move past using the door before."

"So it is bad," she muttered hopelessly.

Bell reached out and placed a hand on her shoulder. "All this means is that you truly are the most remarkable person I have ever met." When she looked unconvinced he said, "How about we start our lesson? Let's test your magic levels, see where you're really at. How does that sound?"

Terra smiled, grateful for the subject change, "That sounds amazing!"

Over the course of the next hour Bell tested the boundaries and limits of Terra's power. Or at least he had intended to. After the first half hour Bell was finally starting to grasp the level of power the

Princess possessed. It was nothing short of amazing. He had never heard of a match for it.

At one point he had tested her ability to do spells without reciting incantations or invocations. It was something a person was able to do only after they achieved complete mastery of spell. There were some spells that even Bell needed words to complete. Terra, however, seemed to not need words at all.

No matter the type or difficulty of a spell, all Bell had to do was tell her what to do and she would do it. No words, no studying, nothing. After a while it became like a game for him. He would think of the most complicated spell he could and tell Terra what do. Then she would do it and he would laugh and sing her praises.

It was Terra who stopped first and pointed out the time to Bell.

"Diana will be here soon for her lesson," she said, a little breathless. She had just done a spell to summon a whirlwind into the room. It had blown around everything that wasn't nailed down, including Bell at one point.

"You are correct," he said, a little disappointed he couldn't continue.

"I should be going. You know how Diana gets if she's made to wait."

Bell looked around at all of the cracks and holes in the walls, evidence of Diana not getting her way, and decided Terra was right. "I do know of your sister's temper."

"Well I'll get going then. Is there anything you'd like me to work on before I come back tomorrow?"

He thought for a moment. "I think we're going to skip straight into element mastery. So I would like you to work on mastering the wind. Try to blow things around and lift things using only the power of the wind you summon."

"Ok," she giggled, grinning ear to ear. She couldn't believe that she would be able to do magic all by herself. No one could tell her to stop so long as she was receiving lessons from Bell. "I won't disappoint you."

She headed through the door and all but skipped down the hallway. She was just passed a corridor that lead to the old west wing, when something stopped her.

Turning back she saw her mother leaning against the wall of the corridor. She was wearing a flattering black dress that seemed to shine as though the light was directly on it. Her soft brown hair was piled high with a diamond encrusted tiara on her head. Her sharp blue eyes took in the sight of Terra in her pink dress, joyfully heading up the hallway and she laughed.

"Did you enjoy your first lesson my dear?" She asked with something akin to bitterness in her voice.

"Yes mother," Terra answered sinking into a deep curtsy. "I enjoyed it very much."

"Well you will have to be sure to thank your father, as it was he who convinced me to let you start at all."

"I . . . I will," she stammered, surprised at her mother's cold tone. She waited to see if the Queen would say anything else. When she turned away from her, Terra curtsied again and turned to leave.

"Terra," her mother called her voice suddenly soft.

"Yes Mother?" She asked, desperate to get away.

"I want you to know that I don't hate you."

"What?"

Her mother started toward her, stumbling slightly as she went. She understood now, her mother was drunk. Sure enough there was a large empty wine glass in her mother's right hand she hadn't noticed before.

"I don't hate you," Queen Elise repeated. "I just never *wanted* you."

Terra felt her mother's words as much as she heard them. It was like being slapped in the face and stabbed in the heart simultaneously. She had always known her mother didn't care for her. She had made that very obvious from the time Terra was born. Still, it was something completely different to hear her mother say she was unwanted.

"Mother . . ."she started, searching for something to say.

"I was only supposed to have one child. One!" Her mother leered at her for a moment and then turned and headed down the corridor to the old west wing, mumbling about having two children the entire time.

Terra was frozen.

She couldn't move or think. She kept hearing her mother's words, running in circles in her head, over and over again. She wasn't wanted. Her mother had never wanted her and now Terra knew it for certain. A small, dark place in her heart wondered if maybe it wasn't just her mother who didn't want her.

Grey was sitting at the table in his cell mindlessly flipping through some random book they had put in with him. He wasn't interested in whatever it said. He was still going over everything that had happened the night before with Terra.

It bothered him, more than he could say that she was right about him caring about her. There was this little spot; he could feel it, where she had somehow weaseled her way into his heart. It was like a painfully bright spot inside of him. Had he been outside of the box it wouldn't have mattered. His darkness would have consumed that bright spot and been done with it. Trapped as he was, his darkness was slower to respond.

A sudden strange feeling seemed to waft into the cell. Grey stood and rolled his head around as he tried to understand what was going on. It was Terra, he could tell that much at least. He moved to wall and put both hands on the glass. Through the magic there he could almost sense her, even though she was too far away to read.

Something was wrong. There was this strange feeling of despair and shock. It was hard to get a clear read from so far away. His heart throbbed painfully as he strained to see what was going on, but to no avail. She was too far away.

His little bright spot throbbed as he started to worry about what was going on. At least he knew that if something so bad had happened, then that useless guard of hers should be there shortly. It pained him to think so, but at least someone would be there for Terra.

'Even if it's him and not me,' he thought.

Shocked and appalled at his own thoughts, Grey walked away from the wall and threw himself onto the bed. He needed to get this damn bright spot dealt with now, before he started to feel more. He couldn't let his emotions tangle up his plans for the princess. He needed to keep his head clear. He would just wait until the feelings passed and keep going.

He shook his head. Grey was not a man to just lie down and wait for things to get better. He decided he needed to take action.

Eric watched as Jones circled him slowly, sword up, ready to strike any weakness he could find. Eric knew well enough how to fake his old friend out. He shifted his left foot slightly and Jones leapt on him. He dodged right instead and parried the blow from Jones. He then rolled on the ground and came up behind his friend, the point of his sword poking him in the back.

"I believe that's my victory," he laughed.

"Well played," Jones conceded. A few onlookers of the sparing match hooted and called to the two men. Eric ignored them and shook hands with Jones.

"I've gotta say, beating you so easy makes me nervous for you as the new Captain," Eric teased jokingly.

"Hey I was going easy on you, what with your cushy new job. You don't get out too much and that's gonna make you soft. I was just trying to be nice to an old friend."

"Soft?" He asked. "I'll show you soft!" He was about to leap at Jones when the sound of thunder rumbling through a perfectly clear day stopped him. Clouds suddenly swept in from the ocean, covering the sky. In a matter of seconds a perfectly bright sunny fall morning had become cloudy and grey. Thunder rumbled again and lightning danced across the sky.

"What the hell is going on?" Jones demanded.

"I have no idea," he replied, "But I've got a really bad feeling about this."

A second later rain began to pour down on their heads. People cried out and ran for cover as the rain started to pour. Eric grabbed his practice shirt off the ground and shook the hay from it. He motioned for Jones to follow him and together they headed back in through the main door to the castle and directly to the right where the Kings Guard kept their inner barracks.

As though nothing had changed, Eric walked through the strong wooden door into the barracks and then straight back through the main waiting room past a few soldiers who saluted Jones and Eric, and finally through the door in the back where the Captain of the Guards personal office was located. Eric walked through the door and leaned against the small humble desk in the corner as Jones closed the door behind them.

"This isn't natural weather," Eric said firmly.

"You could say that again," Jones said. "What do you think caused it?"

"I'm not sure, but I know it's not good. Weather like this could mean big trouble for everyone if it goes on too long."

"Floods?"

"Not just floods. This kind of weather can ruin crops and wipe out whole harvests if it persists. We have to find out who or what started this and stop them."

"Isn't it a little early to set up a man hunt?" Jones asked. "Couldn't it be someone messing with magic they don't understand? It doesn't have to be something evil or sinister."

Eric gave him an are-you–kidding-me-look. "Jones I don't need to tell you how bad this will be if it turns out my suspicions are correct and it comes out that we sat on our hands in the beginning. It's best to act now and cut down the risk."

"I suppose you're right," he conceded. "What do you have in mind?"

"Nothing too much for right now," Eric said. "Take a few men you trust and do a sweep of the castle. I want to know where everyone is and what everyone is doing. We'll decide what to do after that."

"Out of the sash but still can't let it go can you?" Jones asked jokingly.

"Old habits and all that." He pushed off the desk and headed for the door.

"Wait where are you going?"

"To check on Terra, I have bad feeling about her."

Terra stood in the hall, even as the rain outside started to pour down. She felt frozen to the one spot, as if she would never move again. Her mother's words had cut her so deep she wasn't sure she could manage to go on. How did a person go on after learning their mother didn't want them? How do you just brush it off and keep going?

Terra didn't know she could.

Lighting stuck outside the nearby window and made the shadows in the room dance around. It had gotten very dark very fast. She knew she should be worried, or at least concerned about the strange weather. She felt neither. All she could feel was the cold of her mother's words.

Terra caught a glimpse of movement out of the corner of her eye. Without having to look she knew it was a shadow. She could sense its dark presence. Part of her wanted to run and get away to safety; most of her simply didn't care. If her mother didn't want her why would a shadow bother with her? She wasn't worth the time.

As it approached Terra turned her head to stare at it. Curiously she noticed its eyes were closed. She couldn't even see where the slits for eyes would be. Well it was as she assumed, the shadow wanted nothing to do with her.

With a distant sense of curiosity the princess watched the shadow approach. It stopped about a foot away from her and hovered. She watched it knowing in the back of her mind that the behavior of this shadow was nothing short of bizarre.

It still wasn't enough to make her care.

The shadow reached out with what Terra assumed was an arm and touched her right between her eyes. A moment of freezing pain so intense that it burned, and then the world went dark.

Eric felt a searing pain in his forehead and stumbled, falling down the flight of stairs he had been running up. He managed to roll for the most part and only hurt his right wrist where it smacked against the granite floor of the main hall. He lay there for a moment, too dazed to move. His head was spinning and his vision had decided to join in.

He heard the sound of approaching footsteps and was able to get his vision to focus long enough to see John and Jack come running up to him. They shouted things at him he couldn't hear and helped him to his feet. Carefully they dragged him up onto the stairs and sat him down.

"Guard Reynolds!" John shouted, "Can you hear me?"

"I can hear you John, you can stop shouting," Eric assured him. He shook his head to clear away the last of the confusion but couldn't seem to shake the ringing in his ears.

"What happened?" Jack asked.

"I'm not sure," Eric answered truthfully.

"We saw the whole thing," John told him. "You were running up the stairs and then suddenly you were flying down them. We were afraid you would kill yourself rolling down the way you did."

"I'm alright," Eric surmised, rolling his wrist and wincing painfully. "Except for this I guess."

"What do you suppose happened?" Jack asked.

A terrifying thought struck Eric. He reached out through the bond and tried to find Terra.

He couldn't feel her at all.

Just like the night she'd gotten her scars.

She was gone.

Panic started to well up inside him as his mind raced through all the possibilities of what could have happened. She could be dead, or dying somewhere. He had to find her and he had to do it now. He looked up at Jack and John. He knew John well and trusted him; he was a damn good man and a better soldier. Jack, on the other hand, he didn't know well at all.

"I need your help," he told them both. "I think something is wrong with Princess Terra, but I don't know for sure. I need to search for her without inciting a panic. Jack I need you to go and check on Princess Diana, she should be in her lessons with Master Bell. If she's not there check her room and if you still can't find her report to Jones and tell him to sound the alarm.

"John I need you to help me search for Princess Terra. I'm going to check her room I want you to go with Jack and start looking around the school room; she had lessons earlier with Bell. If you can't find her or Bell tells you he hasn't see her all day, you come find me and we'll raise the alarm. Can you two do this?"

Both men nodded and saluted. Together they took off running down the hall as Eric got to his feet and headed up to check Terra's room. The last time he couldn't find her she had been hiding out in her room. Hopefully he wouldn't have to kill anybody this time.

Diana looked up from the book Bell had her reading when she heard a strange sound come from the master wizard. His shoulders had come up and he looked nervous.

"What's wrong with you?" She asked, annoyed that she was being disturbed during her reading.

"The airs changed," Bell said quietly. He walked to one of the four windows that ran the length of the classroom. He pulled the shutter open and slid the glass up. Wind howled in bringing with it the cold dank smell of rain as it beat on the castle roof and walls. Lightning struck and thunder rumbled overhead as rain began to pour down on the castle harder and harder still.

"Something's wrong," Bell said pulling the window closed. "Our lesson for today might have to be put on hold."

"On hold?" Diana asked trying to sound like it bothered her, even though it didn't. In fact, the thought of being able to skip this today sounded like a damn good idea to her. "What's going on?"

"I can't be sure," he answered walking away from the window and pouring over a large leather bound volume on his podium. "It seems something has caused the weather to shift and to do so suddenly and violently."

"So," she asked. "Why does that matter?"

"It matters," Bell said, annoyed by the Princess's lack of concern, "because I'm afraid something may have happened to you sister."

"Terra?" She laughed. "I'm sure whatever is wrong she's fine. She's always fine in fact." Her words had come out much more bitter than Diana had intended.

"What does that mean?" Bell asked, his keen mind picking up on something in Diana's voice that made him worry.

"It doesn't mean anything Wizard," she replied warningly. "Mind your own business."

Bell stared at the princess. She was so different from her sister it would almost be comical if there wasn't something dark about her. Bell worried Diana might have done something intentionally to hurt her sister. If that was the case, there was little he could do about it. As a princess of the realm and the savior, unless Diana was caught killing her sister red handed, there was nothing anyone could do.

A few moments later the door flew open and two young guards came spilling into the room. Both out of breath and looking grim. They bowed to Diana and to Master Bell.

"Master Wizard," the younger of the two said. "I'm looking for Princess Terra, have you seen her?"

289

"Princess Diana, Guard Reynolds has ordered me to stay by your side and escort you to your room," the other said.

"Jack what's going on?" Diana demanded incredulously.

"John and I just met with your sisters Guard. He believes something may have happened to her and he's ordered me to take you back to your room and await further orders."

"And I'm to make sure Princess Terra attended her class today and see what time she left," John said.

"It is as I feared," Bell worried. "Young man, John is it? Terra was here but twenty minutes ago. She couldn't have gotten far. I'll help you search."

"Thank you Master Wizard," John said genuinely grateful for the help Bell offered. "You know the princess better; I'll follow your lead."

"Let's get going," Bell headed for the door without so much as a backward glance at Diana.

"Excuse me!" She yelled, "You can't just walk away from me, we're in the middle of a lesson!" Diana didn't really care about the lesson, but she would be damned if Terra took one more thing away from her. "John can search, you stay here!"

Bell turned and looked to Jack, "make sure she gets to her room as soon as possible." He bowed to Diana and then was out the door before she could say another word.

Diana felt her temper flare wildly out of control. How dare he treat her this way?! She was the next in line for the throne, not to mention she was the princess in the prophecy. People don't just treat her this way. She would have him fired, if not his head for this insolence.

"Princess," Jack asked hesitantly. "Did you want to get going? Or did you need a minute?"

Diana turned to Jack, eyes blazing with anger.

Jack shrank back away from her as she glowered at him. He and the princess had become rather close over the last month, or so he thought. They had snuck off several times and lain together. She was beautiful woman well versed in how to please a man. Now, however, she was terrifying and Jack wished he had been assigned to look for Princess Terra instead of John.

Terra's head was killing her as she rolled over in bed. It felt like the blacksmith was using her head as the anvil. She rolled on her side and buried her head in a pillow. She had been dreaming something just a moment ago. Something about herself and Grey, she thought. There had been a field a red flowers and a cave nearby. She couldn't recall the details but she knew that she and Grey were having an important conversation.

Her head throbbed painfully and she put her hands up to try and quell the aching. A hand touched her shoulder and she froze. Someone was in bed with her? Slowly she opened her eyes. Everything was foggy and blurred, like looking through an old looking glass. She couldn't really focus.

Still she could tell that someone was lying right next to her with their hand on her shoulder. She blinked and squinted, trying to get her eyes to clear. To no avail, her eyes were still foggy and she still couldn't tell who was there.

Quietly she sent out a small stream of magic to see who was across from her.

"You don't have to do that," Grey's voice whispered from in front of her.

"Grey?" She asked squinting. "Is that you?"

"Yes . . . can you not see?"

"Not really," she admitted. "Where am I? How did I get here?"

"I was hoping you would know that."

"I don't know what . . . oh," she suddenly remembered the conversation with her mother and the words she had spoken. Her heart sank and suddenly nothing else seemed to matter. Not the fact that she couldn't see, or the fact that she was somewhere, in bed, with Grey. Nothing really mattered right then.

"Terra what's wrong?" He asked alarmed.

"I . . . I . . .," she struggled to make the words to tell he what had happened.

"I can't see into your head or heart at all right now," he admitted quietly, more to himself than to her. His bright spot throbbed again, aching to make her better somehow.

Completely unaware she was doing anything, Terra grabbed Grey's hands and placed them, one on each side of her head. She thought over everything her mother had said and how it had hurt her so. Just thinking about it hurt her.

Grey's breath caught in his throat. It wasn't just her memories she was sharing, it was her emotions. It was a rush of more emotion than he had ever dealt with. He could feel the sorrow she felt that went beyond words thanks to her mother's callousness. He could feel just how upsetting it was too her to know that Eric had lost what he felt for her. While simultaneously he could feel how relived she was that he didn't care the way he had. Then he could feel what she felt for him.

Grey could see plainly how she cared for him as a friend and how there was the beginnings there of something more. He could feel it then, the crack he had made in her, it was widening. It had nearly doubled in size by the time he felt it calm.

"Terra," he muttered, overcome by her emotions. "I'm so sorry . . . I don't really know what I'm supposed to say or do here."

"There's nothing to say," she whispered, feeling her eyes start to water. She blinked rapidly, trying to clear the tears. As she blinked the tears themselves seemed to wash away whatever was blinding her and she could see again.

Grey was lying on the pillow next to her staring at her looking very concerned with his hands on either side of her face. They were in his glass cell. She wasn't sure how she'd gotten there but she didn't really care. Maybe they had put her in here because no one wanted her.

"Hey," he said, shaking her face gently, "people want you. Don't think like that."

"My own mother doesn't want me," she whimpered. "I doubt anybody else will."

"People want you," he argued, not liking where this conversation was going or the fact that he couldn't break away from the princess. "Lots of people."

Terra just stared at him, blankly. "Ok."

"Damn it Terra don't make me say it!" He grumbled, losing more control every second.

"Say what?" She asked blankly. She had been going through the list of people in her mind, each one she knew didn't really want her. Not her mother or her father. Not Diana or Bell or even Mammy. Certainly not the kingdom or the people, they all wanted Diana not her. Not even Eric or Grey . . .

"Hey!" he shouted now. "Don't you think like that!"

"Ok," she replied, her train of thought continuing despite her not wanting it too.

"Damn it Terra!" He all but growled. "I want you ok?! I want you around!"

Something about what he said or how he said it struck her. She looked to him and for the first time her eyes seemed to focus on his face. He looked younger again, like he had in her dream. Not as young as she was of course, but not as old as he normally looked. She would have guessed he was only a little older than Eric right now, instead of being closer to her Father's age like normal.

"You?" She said her brain still foggy.

"Yes me," he stated, frustrated. "I need you, more than you know."

"Grey?"

"Shut up," he said pulling her toward him and holding on to her. "Stop thinking like no one wants you or needs you because that's insane. I need you. You're the only good thing about being trapped in this stupid glass box. I couldn't make it if it wasn't for you. And what about Reynolds? That idiot wouldn't know what to do with himself if something happened to you. He may not care about you like he used to but he does care."

Terra hesitated for a moment. The whole situation was so awkward she wasn't really sure what she should do. Grey had wrapped his arms around her and was holding her against him. He was warm and he had said that he wanted her. Not just wanted, but needed. He said he *needed* her.

No one had ever said that to her.

Giving in, Terra nestled her head into his chest and cried. She was starting to really hate the way she constantly cried lately. It seemed to her that every time she turned around she was crying about something else. She wasn't weak like this, not normally anyway.

"Don't worry about tears," Grey soothed.

She nodded and her mind started to wander off to something, anything else except her mother. She thought about her lesson with Bell and how she'd had so much fun working with wind and doing all of these really complex spells. It was hard at first with all the shadows but after that got worked out things were great.

"Shadows?" He asked? He was still in Terra's mind, watching her memories float by. "You fought shadows today?"

"Yes," she replied, "Master Bell summoned them to test the limits of my powers. But it got a little out of hand." As she spoke she remembered and Grey saw.

"Wow," he muttered, seeming uncomfortable.

Terra, sensing that Grey wasn't enjoying this line of thought, moved on to thinking about yesterday and turning sixteen. She thought about going to see him in the morning and the dancing and then, before she could stop it she was thinking about the premonition she had about Grey kissing her. She tried to stop but her thoughts had taken on a life of their own and she couldn't stop them.

Grey stiffened slightly around her and she cursed herself for thinking about that. She tried to think about something else, like the exceptionally long dress fitting she had to go through that morning, her horrible pink dress, anything.

Sadly, he would not let her change the subject so easily.

"Hold on a minute," he said, "what was that?"

"Nothing," she replied quickly.

"Was that the premonition you had? You had a seeing that I was going to kiss you?"

Terra felt her face flush. She suddenly wanted to be anywhere but where she was. She had never intended for Grey to know about what she had seen. After she had learned he hadn't seen anything the first time she had been so relieved. Terra had sworn to herself then that she would never let Grey know what she had seen that day in his arms. She hadn't been thinking straight, she was depressed and had almost no control over the steam of her thoughts. Even now the scene kept playing in her mind.

"Terra," he started, trying to push her back so he could see her face.

She kept her head down and refused to look up at him. She couldn't look into his grey eyes and tell him that she had seen them kissing and she had run away. Worse than that, in the state she was in if Grey tried . . . if he tried to . . . kiss her, she might let him and she can't let that happen. She wouldn't let that happen.

"Terra look at me," he asked, sounding a little frustrated. "Don't cover your thoughts now, it's too late. Look at me and talk to me about this premonition."

"Can we not?" Terra pleaded weakly. "Can we just pretend you didn't see that?"

"No," he laughed. "You saw that and ran out of here like the building was coming down around you. I want you to talk to me."

"Grey," She whispered. Slowly she looked up at him. He was staring down at her so intently that his grey eyes seemed to sparkle inches from her face. "I can't talk to you about this."

"Why?" he asked. "Terra we're literally in bed together right now, what could you possibly not be able to tell me?"

Terra blushed up to her hair again and looked back down. She hadn't really given much thought to her current situation when she'd

295

woken up. Everything had been blurry and she didn't really care at that point in time. She hadn't cared about anything. Grey could have grown a second head and eaten her and she still, probably, wouldn't have cared.

"Grey, please understand. I know that we spend a lot of time together and that as the time goes by that, well, feelings may develop," Terra tried to explain awkwardly.

"Feelings?" He asked doubtfully.

"Yes, feelings," she repeated. "These feeling can't be allowed to grow. It could be catastrophic if . . . if things don't play out right."

"So what you're saying is that I can't fall in love with you, or you with me, because I have to kill you sister. Or be killed by your sister," he asked practically laughing. "Do you know how ridiculous that sounds?"

Terra was struck. "It may be ridiculous for you," she said, unable to keep the hurt out of her voice. "But not all of us are emotionally stunted and incapable of having actual feelings!" She pulled away from Grey faster than he could grab a hold of her.

"I should be going," she snapped walking toward the glass wall.

"Wait, Terra," he called, "What the hell just happened?"

She stopped, hand on the glass. "I get it," she whispered, tears making her voice sound off. "I'm just me, just the shadow princess. I'm not Diana and I don't look like her. I understand that. Still, you don't have to act like someone loving me is the most ridiculous thing in the world." She pushed through the glass and hurried from the room, ignoring Grey's calls.

He had been cruel and unkind. She knew she shouldn't have been surprised; Grey was the bad guy after all. He was the monster who had haunted her nightmares since she was child. Foolishly she had allowed herself to become close to him and now was paying the price. He was no better than the other people in her life. No one really wanted her and no one really cared.

With a heavy heart, Terra walked slowly through the castle to her room.

Grey stared at the door.

Moments ago he and Terra were talking over what had happened with her and the premonition she had about them kissing. Then she had flow from the room like he was trying to kill her. He sat on his bed and went over everything he had said to her and everything she had said in return.

Like lightning it dawned on him then.

What he had said about them loving each other, and the way he had said it.

He could have slapped himself he felt so stupid. She had completely misunderstood his meaning and who knew what she was thinking now.

Terra was essential to everything he had planned. He couldn't very well use her against her sister if she hated the very sight of him. It was going to take something extreme to fix this mess.

Terra made her way slowly to her room. She had just reached the top of the stairs and was staring at Eric's door and the spiral stairs that led to her room. She was almost there. Just a few more stairs and she could collapse in her room and shut out the day.

There was a sound of footsteps coming down from her room. Not wanting to deal with Mammy right now, she ducked into the alcove of Eric's door and waited for her to pass. It wasn't until just before she saw him that she realized it was Eric.

She watched him walk down the rest of the stairs and start down the set that lead to the castle. She wanted to call out to him, to ask for him to help her, to make her not feel this way. Even if he lied, she just needed to hear some kind words right now. After what Grey had said she wasn't sure she would ever feel like a person ever again.

Eric stopped at the top of the stars. He could feel her again. She was close and she was hurting, He almost couldn't breathe there was such a strong pain in his chest. He doubled over and held on to the railing to keep from falling down the stairs again. Whatever had happened to her was bad. He needed to find her.

He turned and there she was.

Standing in front of his door, looking like she might break down at any moment, the princess stared at him. She had on a strangely pink dress with her dark green cloak wrapped around her. Her hair looked mussed, like she'd been lying down and her eyes were red from crying. She looked at him and he could see how badly she was hurting inside.

"Terra," he asked quietly, "What happened?"

"I can't . . ." she stammered. "Not now. I just want to go." She looked around for an avenue of escape. Eric knew he couldn't let her run; he needed to know what was going on if he was going to protect her.

There was something else too. He cared about her, she was his friend and he didn't want to see her hurting. He knew that before everything had happened with Bell and his magic he had cared about her more, but he didn't feel that way about her now. It was possible that in time he might again. It just wasn't how he felt right now.

He knew that information hurt her, and it pained him to no end to know that. He couldn't fake it though; he respected her too much to lie to her that way. Still, he couldn't let her hurt like this. So he decided to do what he had to do to help her.

"Terra I don't know what happened but talk to me, I can help." He walked toward her slowly with his arms open. She looked at him and just shook her head. She didn't look like she was going to run anymore. She looked broken, defeated. When he got to her she looked up at him and shook her head. He wrapped his arms around her and held her. She stood there, stiff and unmoving.

"Terra please," he pleaded. He wasn't good with the bond and magic but he tried to show her how much he cared. He poured all of what he felt for her into the bond. He needed her to know that she was important to him and that he cared.

298

Terra made a small noise and then she seemed to melt into him. She started crying and holding on to him like he was her life raft and she was drowning.

They stood in his doorway for nearly fifteen minutes. Terra cried, sometimes she spoke but mostly it was garbled and hard to understand. Eric would shush her and hold her until she stopped. It was a while before she stopped shaking from crying so hard.

"Eric," she ventured, her voice slightly muffled from his shirt. "Thank you, but I'm alright now."

"Are you sure?" He asked pulling away so he could see her face. "You don't look ok."

"I'm alright," she reaffirmed. She wasn't feeling better, but at least she was past the crying. Eric put his hand under her chin and lifted her face so he could see her eyes. Reaching up with his other hand he wiped away her tears. He could feel her broken heart through the bond and it made his feel like breaking too.

"Terra, tell me what happened?"

"I can't," she repeated. "Not because I don't want to, but because if I talk about it, I'll . . . I'll . . . I just can't ok?"

Eric nodded; he understood she couldn't tell him just yet.

"What do you want to do now?" He asked her.

"I don't really know," she replied. "I wanted to go to bed but it's not even noon yet and the last time I went to lay down this early, things went bad."

"Right," he agreed, not sure if she was making a joke.

"So I guess I can go study for a while, or practice what Master Bell taught me today."

"What did he teach you?" Eric asked seizing an opportunity to turn Terra's attention to something positive.

She smiled, just a little, but it was still a smile. "Well you'll never believe how he chose to test me today," she started, her smile widening just a fraction.

Eric smiled and her and gestured for her to start up the stairs to her room. "What did he do now?"

Terra and Eric sat in her room and watched the rain fall as they talked about her lesson with Bell that day and all that she had learned. A few times he would stop her and question if she was serious. Terra would laugh and assure him that she wasn't lying. After a while she was laughing and smiling as she talked with him. She didn't even realize at first how much better she was starting to feel.

Near to one a knock at the door pulled the two out of their little world. Eric got to his feet and walked to the door. "Who's there?" He called.

"It's John, sir."

"Oh no," he whispered turning back to the princess. "I sent him out looking for you over an hour ago."

Terra's face matched Eric's. "That's not good."

He grimaced and opened the door.

John stood to one side and Bell stood at the other. Both looked concerned as they scanned the room and found Terra sitting in bay window.

"I take it you found the Princess then?" Bell asked.

"Yes," Eric replied sheepishly. "I'm sorry I didn't come find you sooner. But when I found her . . ." he trailed off; he wasn't sure how to explain the state Terra was in when he had first found her by his door. "It wasn't good. Let's just leave it at that."

"Is she alright?" Bell asked quietly.

Eric stepped forward and said equally as quiet, "She seems ok now but I can't be sure. Whatever happened must have been bad. That's all I know."

"Is she injured?" John whispered.

"I'm fine," Terra called from her seat. "And you all don't whisper as quietly as you think you do."

"Princess," John greeted, bowing with his fist over his heart.

"I apologize if we were excluding you Princess," Bell explained. "I'm simply trying to ascertain if you are well."

"I'm fine, as I said."

"May I ask what happened?"

Terra looked at Bell. He was one of the most intelligent people she knew. So she knew she didn't have to speak to convey the fact that she really didn't feel like talking about what was going on right then. He met her eyes and gave the slightest nod. He understood.

"Well I'm glad everything's ok," John added, still confused about what was going on. "But the weather is getting worse and a kitchen maid named Jenny is looking for the princess. It's time for lunch to be taken down to the prisoner."

"Very well then," she sighed, standing. She brushed her dress off and walked to the door. "Thank you Eric, for everything. Master Bell I apologize for making you worry and pulling you away from your lessons with my sister. I'm fine now and I'll find my sister and apologize to her as well.

"John, thank you for caring enough to help them search. I won't forget your kindness or your loyalty. Thank you all so much."

"I'll walk with you," Eric offered as they headed down the stairs.

"I will return to my lesson planning," Bell stated.

"I suppose I should get back to post outside the prison," John added making a strange face. He was walking down the stairs with the Master Wizard, the Princess and Her Royal guard. Big name people walking with little ol' John.

Terra thanked Eric for escorting her and headed through the door into prison. She kicked it closed behind her. She didn't know what was going to be said between her and Grey but she knew she didn't want an audience for it.

Keeping her head down, she walked across the room and set the lunch tray on her table. She moved a few things around, prolonging the inevitable.

"I brought your lunch," she mumbled pushing the tray through the glass. She didn't look up to see if he was close enough to take the tray, she just hoped that he was. She felt a pull on the tray so she pushed it the rest of the way through.

Grey grabbed her wrist and pulled her through the glass before she could think to stop him.

She heard the tray clatter to the ground, throwing food and drink everywhere as was pulled into the cell. She went straight through the wall into Grey's arms. In less than a heartbeat she wrapped in his arms with her head resting against his chest.

"Terra, I'm sorry," he whispered into the top of her head. "I didn't mean for you to get hurt by what I said. I didn't even mean it the way you took it. I'm sorry I made your day harder."

She was frozen.

Terra had walked down into the basement thinking over all the things Grey might say or do when she got there. This was not even close to what she had anticipated.

It certainly wasn't the first time he had held her, it had happened so often of late. But it was the first time he held her the way he was holding her now, tightly against him so she was literally pressed into him. It was most certainly the first time he had apologized and sounded so sincere about anything.

For a moment she couldn't process what was happening enough to formulate a reply.

"I didn't mean to say that being with you would be ridiculous. I mean to say that the two of us falling in love when I'm fated to fight your sister to the death sounds ridiculous. Being with you and loving you wouldn't be ridiculous . . ." he trailed off.

Terra didn't know what to say. He was saying things that sounded like things he shouldn't be saying. They should not be standing in each other's arms talking about love. She couldn't let things like this happen. She needed to keep her head clear.

It was no use, her head was all fogged up, and she couldn't have thought straight if she wanted to.

"Grey," she started. "I don't know what to say."

302

"You don't have to say anything. I just needed you to know what I meant. I didn't want you to think that loving you was crazy. I felt how much it pained you to think that and how little you wanted to be in here with me. I told you, I need you."

"Grey, we can't . . . we can't say these kinds of things," Terra said pulling away a little. He let her back up a bit, but not much. Her hands were against his chest and his arms were around her waist. She was looking up at him with tears in her eyes and he was looking at her as his control slowly slipped away from him.

"I'm not saying anything, not yet," he explained. When she opened her mouth the question the "yet", he continued. "I just wanted you to know what I meant and that I need you and I want you. So don't go start thinking that people don't care."

"I won't," she promised smiling slightly. "Thank you Grey."

"Don't worry about it." He reached up and wiped the one stray tear that had managed to escape. "You should probably get going; Reynolds is getting twitchy out there waiting for you. He's wondering what's taking so long."

"Ok." She moved to break away from Grey but found that his arms were locked around her. "Grey?"

"I'm sorry for this," he whispered quietly as he pulled her toward him again. Terra thought he was going to hug her again, but at the last second he shifted her to the side and kissed her. Her mind exploded into white light and every thought in her head disappeared. For a moment she wondered if this was another premonition. At least until Grey pulled her closer, and deepened the kiss.

Terra could feel a strange power flowing around them and she could sense a change in Grey. He made a strange noise and held her tighter somehow. Terra felt like she was melting into him and he into her.

Finally, they managed to break away from one another. Terra's heart was racing and she felt like her head was swimming. Her breathing was shallow and rapid and when she looked at Grey, he seemed to be feeling the same as she was.

"What was that for? She asked, still breathless.

"I know that after today you'll be feeling better and your walls will go back up and I'll never get another chance to do this again."

"You would want to do this again?"

"I don't know," he replied. "I know that as soon as I saw it in your head I haven't been able to get out of mine. Reynolds is coming," he said suddenly. "We'll talk tonight?"

"Yes," she stammered, turning for the glass. Grey grabbed her wrist and pulled her back in, he put his hand behind her neck and laced his fingers through hers. He kissed her once more, quick and simple and then pushed her toward the wall. She had just managed to get through the glass when the door opened up and Eric walked in.

"Is everything alright?" He scanned the room taking in Terra at the glass and Grey with his lunch tray on the floor. "What's going on?"

"Grey dropped his tray," she blurted. It was the only thing she could think to say.

"I can see that, why is that taking up so much time?"

"Because Terra was apologizing for it, over and over again," Grey complained. "She seems a little off."

"Excuse me?" She demanded as she turned to face him.

"I'm just saying, a little off. Maybe right here." He whispered to Eric and pointed to his head.

Terra stared at him like she couldn't believe what he had just said. She was going to fly through that glass and hurt him, not much, but enough that he won't be saying and doing crazy things like this again.

Eric, seeing Terra's reaction, interceded. "Ok we need to go. It's time for lunch and I don't want to have to explain to your father why I let you break your fists on the glass prison cell."

"Oh I'll break them on something" she growled shooting murderous looks at Grey as Eric dragged her from the room.

"I'll see you at dinner," he called with a smile as she was pulled through the door.

"You should have let me stay, I have unfinished business with that man," she grumbled.

"Come on Terra," Eric said as he continued to pull her along toward the spiral staircase. "You can deal with him at dinner."

Terra and Eric had lunch in the grand dining hall with her parents and her sister and then she had other lessons to attend and Eric had training of his own to go to. As they went about their day the rain continued to pour down from the sky. Bell continued to watch, weary that there was something more going on than what he could see.

Somehow it was tied to the princess, he knew it, he just didn't know how. One thing he did know was that if he couldn't talk with Terra and figure out what was wrong, this rain wouldn't stop. He needed to talk with her sooner rather than later.

Grey knew before Terra ever entered the room that he would kiss her. Ever since he had seen it he couldn't stop seeing it. He told himself it was the perfect way to break her. She would never see it coming. That was the only reason he was doing it.

She put the tray to glass and Grey grabbed her. He tossed the food to the ground, he didn't need it right then. He pulled her in and held her. He apologized for what he had said. All the while watching the crack he had seen earlier.

As he had hoped, he could feel it weaken as he spoke.

"I'm sorry for this," he said as he pulled her in.

Grey had anticipated every reaction Terra might have to his kiss. From rage to love, he was prepared.

What he didn't anticipate was his own reaction.

When Terra's lips met his the feeling that spread through him was like nothing else he had ever felt. It was like a bright light emanated from where their lips met and spread through the two of them until he couldn't differentiate between Terra and Grey, there was only light.

Feeling like he never had before, Grey pulled the princess closer and deepened their kiss. He held onto her like he would never let her go.

Suddenly there was voice in the back of his head. Reminding him that he had a job to do and he couldn't allow himself to get lost in some petty kiss.

After another few moments he was finally able to pull away from her. Breathless, with his heart racing, he looked down into her emerald green eyes and for just a moment, a fraction of a moment really, all he could see was her. Not the crack he was trying to widen, or the girl he was going to use. All he could see was the beautiful woman in his arms.

"What was that for?" Terra asked.

Like the snapping of fingers, whatever spell Grey was under broke. He knew then he couldn't allow something like that to happen again.

He couldn't afford to lose control like that.

He had a job to do.

Dinner time came almost too quickly for Terra. She wanted to talk to Grey; she *needed* to talk to him. At the same time she was terrified of having to go talk to him about what had happened earlier. She knew she couldn't have feelings for him, not the kind of feelings that went with the way they were acting toward each other currently. She couldn't let herself feel this way about him.

Grey was waiting patiently on the other side of the glass with a stack of trays ready to be taken back to the kitchen. He smiled awkwardly at Terra as she walked in and she felt the smallest bit of relief that maybe he was a nervous as she was about all this. Not that it was a good thing; she had to be firm and unwavering in how she handled this situation. These incidents with Grey had to stop before feelings developed.

"Evening," he said as she set the tray down at the table.

"Good evening," she replied simply, starting to sort the food.

306

"Terra?"

"Yes?"

"I'm sorry about earlier."

Her head shot up. "Sorry?"

"Yes. I allowed myself to get caught up in a moment and I crossed a line." He paused for a moment, considering how much to say to her. With a sigh he continued, "I'm not sorry that I pulled you in here, I needed to tell you what I meant. I'm also not sorry about the kiss. I'm sorry that I crossed the line but I think the kiss was necessary."

"Necessary?" Terra asked confused. Done sorting she put the tray to the glass and Grey pulled it through. He set his tray down and handed her back the two trays from earlier. She sat them on the table but made no move to sit and eat.

"Yes, necessary. I understand what you said earlier about us and unwanted feelings. No matter how things play out between your sister and I, things can't and won't ever work out in favor of us caring about each other. Either way this goes down, once I'm out of this cell, I can't be the man I was in here again."

"I understand that," she confirmed. "I know that the person you are now isn't the same person who exists on the outside. Once you're out everything will change and we'll go back to being enemies, you on the side of darkness and I on the side of light. If you think about us even being friends . . . it's dangerous."

Grey nodded. He had thought for a long time about how to deal with this. He couldn't pull completely back from the princess, he still needed her. On the other hand he'd lost control too many times when she was around for him to be comfortable with the rapid way things were accelerating with her. He needed to pull back to slow things down so Terra didn't scare off and his plans didn't go to hell. Also so he can work on his own control where she was concerned.

"I don't think I could not be your friend at this point," Grey observed. "I think we've already invested too much into each other to just be . . . I don't know what we would be if we weren't friends."

"Enemies?" She offered, unsure.

"One day," he replied grimly. "But not now and not here in this room."

"Agreed," she sighed. "What happened earlier, the kiss, you said you weren't sorry about it. Why not? If I can ask that, as a friend."

He smiled. "Well for one thing I think it needed to be done. After you saw what you saw I don't think either of us could have moved on, as friends, not knowing what that would have actually been like."

She considered his words. "You're right. I would have wondered about it."

Grey smiled again. "The other reason is, honestly, I enjoyed it. That for me is what made me really stop and think about what you were saying.

"I didn't think I was capable of having feelings like that. Since I had never been presented with the opportunity to feel that way, it didn't matter if I could or not. In the past month I have learned a great deal about myself as a person. I know now that I can feel and probably fall in love if presented with that opportunity. Which is something that I can't allow to happen, at least not here and now."

Terra nodded. She understood what he was saying and she agreed with him. They needed to be more careful about what they did and said to each other. She especially needed to be careful when it came to Grey. He seemed kind and caring on the outside but she knew that every second she was down there he was throwing darkness and dark magic at her in the hope to break her resolve and her will.

"Can I ask you something?" Grey asked.

"Of course."

"If given the opportunity, would you stop having dinner with me?"

"No," she answered before she could think to stop herself. "I wouldn't. I enjoy our time together. Which I know isn't helping matters much."

"I wouldn't either."

Terra smiled and blushed. "Can I ask you something now?"

"Seems only fair."

"If you were given a chance to be with me, as more than friends, but it meant giving up the fight with my sister, would you?"

"I don't know," he replied before he could shut his mouth.

"Ok" She kept her face impassive but smiling inwardly. There was still a chance she could help him. "So we're agreed then. Only friends, no more funny business and . . . ." Terra searched for the words she was looking for.

"And no more talk of love," Grey finished for her. "If we keep talking about it, it might just show up to see what all the fuss is about."

She nodded. "Agreed then?"

"Agreed. So as your friend can I tell you something?"

"Of course," she said, concerned about what else he might have to say.

"As your friend, that dress looks hideous on you. Pink is not your color."

She scowled at the glass. "It would be a shame if I had to come through the glass and beat you up all on account of this dress." She grumbled jokingly.

"Hey I was just being honest."

"Yea, well, shut up and let's eat already. I'm starving." Terra smiled and Grey smiled with her, both thinking they could break the other and change where their loyalties lie in the coming war. Neither one realizing the effect they were having on each other.

Bell watched the skies from his room, worried about what the continued down pour might mean. He knew that at this stage in the harvest, rain like this could be more than detrimental, it could mean the difference between life and death.

Using magic he had tried to send the storm away.

To no avail.

Somehow it was all tied to Terra.

As a Master Wizard Bell knew what weather manipulation like this could mean. While Terra was by far the strongest child he had ever seen, something like this was simply not heard of.

Still, as the rain poured down, despite his attempts to stop it, he had to consider the fact that maybe Terra was stronger than even he had anticipated.

Then, just as suddenly as it had stared, the rain stopped. Dark grey storm clouds gave way to stars and night sky. In the span of less than three minutes the storm was completely gone. Bell turned to small book he had dedicated to Terra and what she could do. Carefully he noted the time and made a note to confer with the princess to see what she was doing at this exact moment.

Eric paced slowly outside the prison. Lewis was eating and pretending he wasn't paying attention to anything going on, but Eric could tell he was watching him. He had been pondering about a strange feeling he had when he sat with Terra today. It was familiar but alien at the same time. It had taken him nearly all day to figure out what was going on. Now he paced back and forth not sure if he should tell her or leave it as it was.

He should tell her.

She'd been having a day and maybe if he told her what was going on she would feel better and maybe even tell him what happened to her earlier. It seemed like every time he had to leave her alone for even the shortest period of time, terrible things happened. While that wasn't *all* his fault, he certainly felt like most of it was. It was his job to protect her and he wasn't doing a great job so far.

On the other hand, if he told her it could bring up things from the past that might just make her feel worse and make him feel like an idiot.

It was a risk either way.

After close to an hour in the prison, Terra pulled the door open carrying three trays. She looked like she was in a much better mood now than before, although she did look very tired. She smiled at Eric when she caught his eyes on her.

"Can you give me a hand?" She asked.

"I'd be happy too," Lewis interjected, jumping up in front of Eric. He grabbed the trays from her and thrust them at Eric who caught them by reflex. He wrapped a hand around Terra's waist and pulled her close so he could pull the door closed behind her.

Eric stared at him with his jaw on the floor and his hands full of silver trays. He couldn't believe the nerve of him! He tossed the trays onto the nearby table and started forward to grab Lewis and teach him a thing or two about respecting the Princess.

He cried out suddenly and jumped away from the princess, who was once again encircled in purple and silver flames. She stared at Lewis like she was thinking about seriously hurting him. Lewis stared at her wide eyed. To shocked to make words.

"I will tell you one last time," she threatened, "do *not* touch me."

Lewis nodded and backed away as Terra walked over to the table. She flashed a brief smile at Eric and started walking toward the spiral staircase. Eric, doing everything he could not to laugh, grabbed the trays off the table, nodded to Lewis, and then took off after her.

Once they were out of sight and earshot, Terra's flames disappeared.

She and Eric burst out laughing.

"Did you see the look on his face?!" She exclaimed! "I thought he was going to keel over and die of shock!"

"I definitely don't think you need to worry about him touching you ever again," Eric laughed as they reached the metal doors that lead to the west wing.

"Well it serves him right," she snapped. "I'm tired of him leering at me and making excuses to press up against me. It drives me up a wall!"

"You know, I didn't know you could just turn that fire thing on and off," Eric observed.

"Well I had to use it earlier with Bell, remember? After I did it then I knew how to kind of call it on when I need it."

"That's a very handy self-defense tool," he calculated, his mind working like the strategist he was. "It provides light and heat, not to mention it burns anyone you don't want near you."

"I suppose that's true," she agreed. They were nearly to the kitchen now so Eric decided to wait to talk to the princess until after they were on their way up to their rooms. He didn't want to chance them being overheard and having to deal with the repercussions of that. Once they were already up the main stairs and turning down the fifth floor hallway, he decided it was as good a time as any.

"I think the feelings I used to have for you might be coming back," he confessed. He had said it much more bluntly than he had intended, but he also didn't want to dance around the subject. He wanted to tell her what he was feeling without all the stress and hype that came from amping it up.

Terra kept walking. She was shocked to hear him say what he had said, but it didn't really surprise her. When she and Eric had sat and talked earlier she had felt through the bond that something was changing in him. She couldn't really say she was happy about it. As much as it pained her to say so, it was good for Eric to not care about her. After what had happened today with Grey, she had already way underestimated the effect he had on her. There was no way to tell how long she could withstand the amount of darkness he combated her with every time she was in there.

Part of her, despite what she said to herself, was glad that Eric cared. It was nice to have him back to speaking terms with her, but she felt that her relationship with him still wasn't close to what it had been before. On a purely friend level of course.

"Terra," he queried tentatively, "say something."

"I'm glad," she started. "I'm glad that you're starting to get back some of what you lost."

"There's a 'but' in there isn't there?"

"But," she added. "I meant what I said to you that day in your sick bed. It's not safe for you to care for me the way you did. It nearly killed you, after a day of being my guard it nearly killed you."

"Terra," he started as he reached down and took her hand. She tried to pull it away at first but he laced his finger through hers and she sighed and stopped fighting. They came to a stop outside his bedroom door.

"I'm not saying that I love you, all I'm saying is that I care for you as more than a friend."

"I don't know what to say Eric," she replied honestly. "I'm glad that you care for me as I do for you, but I also don't want to think about your feelings for me being used against you some day. I don't know what will happen in the future and . . ."

"Exactly," Eric cut in. "You don't know what will happen tomorrow or six months from now. So for now, accept that I'm telling you how I feel and let's not worry about things like love or people being turned against one and another until the situation requires that we do so. Does that sound like something we can do?"

"Yes," she sighed, conceding his point. "But you have to be honest with me about how you feel. If things get close to how they were before you have to tell me. Ok? Promise me."

Eric smiled down at the princess. He wouldn't tell her tonight, but loving her didn't seem that far away at the moment. So he nodded and said, "I promise."

"Thank you," Terra said with a sigh.

"But until then," he asked, pulling her closer. "Are we allowed to . . ." He bent to kiss her and Terra stepped back and away.

"We can't," she said. "The point is to not encourage feelings like that. If we start sneaking around kissing in hallways, we'll be doomed before months end."

Eric smiled at the thought of being "doomed" to love someone like Terra. Still she seemed quite adamant about what she was saying so he released her fingers and nodded. "We'll do things however you see fit *my* princess."

"Thank you," she whispered, her voice raw from even more tears threatening to fall, "For now let's call it a night, shall we?"

"Yes," he agreed with a yawn. "Goodnight Terra."

"Goodnight Eric and thank you."

"I'll see you in the morning. Mammy has more dresses for you to try on." He laughed at her sudden horrified face and slipped into his room before she could argue with him about it. With the door closed and safely latched, Eric started wonder what he was going to do if he did fall in love with the princess. Other than the obvious stature issues, she was right about the darkness in the prison.

Some days it was all he could stand to just be outside the doors. Terra was strong but he worried how long her strength would hold up against evil that dark. Even she would break in time. Even if his love for her made him a target on the day when her strength finally failed, he would still choose to love her that day, as he had all the days before.

Terra pushed her door closed and let out a long exasperated sigh. Today had been the strangest day she'd ever had. So far at least. She thought over everything that had happened and wondered for a while how she would go on from here. How could she go on being friends with these men when she knew what it would mean for all three of them? How could she ever trust herself around them?

Slowly she got ready for bed, letting her hair down, putting on her shift and pulling down the covers. She climbed in and lay down. Her mind raced with thoughts from the day and all the conversations she had. Most prominent among them were thoughts of Grey and the kiss. She had been kissed before by Eric, but nothing like this. When Eric kissed her it was sweet and kind and gentle. When Grey kissed her it was deep and passionate and completely unexpected,

Terra felt her face flush red again. She pulled the pillow next to hers up and covered her face. She screamed in frustration. A month ago her life was simple. She would get up go to lessons sneak into

314

Diana's magic lesson, read, work on magic with Diana and sleep. She'd wake up the next day and start again. It wasn't perfect but it was easy.

Now she was a young woman with responsibilities in the castle and more to come in the kingdom soon. She was the sole gate keeper for the most dangerous man on the face of the earth, who she just so happened to be friends with. She had her own personal guard who had fallen in love with her once already and was dangerously close to doing so again. Not to mention that Diana had been cold to her since her birthday and Terra was worried that maybe she'd done something to upset her sister again.

Then there was the fact that her mother didn't want her. Hadn't ever wanted her it seemed. A fact that called every other relationship she had into question. Tara started to wonder what the future held for her now and whether or not she could survive what was coming.

Chapter 8

Four Years Later

Terra gazed into her looking glass. It was getting older and had just started to fade around the edges where the sun touched it. It was hard to believe she'd had it for almost four years now. It was part of a set she had received for her sixteenth birthday from her father.

So much had changed in such a small amount of time.

Terra was full grown now and a woman. She was just over five foot seven, a full two inches taller than Diana, not that it was a good thing. Diana begrudged her for so many things now, her height included. Terra had fallen into the habit of slouching in her sister presence. If she didn't look any taller than Diana would leave her alone about that at least.

She found other things to get mad at her for. Terra had grown up and grown quite lovely. Her green eyes, which at one point had seemed too large for her face, were dazzling now with their deep color and the slant they had taken on as she aged. Her hair was a dark and thick as ever and the freckles on her face had become part of her natural beauty.

She had stayed slim in her waist but her chest and hips had grown and filled out. She had taken on a classic hourglass shape like Diana had. With a few stark differences. Diana was still very slim she had kept her pre-teen thinness. They were both lovely, but as far as Terra was concerned, Diana would always outshine her.

She stood and straightened out her deep purple dress. She could sense Eric coming. They were still bonded, somehow. It baffled Bell to no end that their bond had managed to persist for so long. He had told them that some bonds can last for lifetimes, but usually only in family members or spouses. He had theorized several times that the reason they were still bonded was because of their frequent use of it. They were always reaching out to one another for different reasons.

Terra was glad she had the bond with Eric. She never felt alone, unless she asked him for privacy, and he was always there when she needed him. It didn't matter what she needed him for when or where they were, he would come. It didn't help that the bond kept them close as the years went by. She could tell that his feelings had grown for her as she'd grown.

Eric was very good at keeping quiet about how he felt about her. There had been a couple of instances where they had gotten too close and Eric had tried push past the line Terra had drawn. It didn't take much to get him to back off, but those situations had started occurring more and more frequently over the last year. It was all she could do to step back before things went too far. Another great thing about the bond was that he could usually tell when she needed him to back off.

The best thing about their bond was that it kept Grey out of her heart.

She needed what she felt there to stay secret and to stay safe. If someone, anyone, ever found out what was in her heart, if they could see the things she felt and who she felt them for . . . they would hang her for treason.

Eric knocked once on the door and came in. He could already tell that Terra was ready to go down to dinner. She felt her heart skip at the sight of him, as it often did. He was so handsome now, not that he hadn't been before. His face was more chiseled and his hair was longer. It wasn't much of a difference, but Terra certainly enjoyed it.

"You look beautiful," he remarked as he leaned in the doorway. She flushed awkwardly.

"Thank you," she smiled. He was looking at her like he did when he was pondering about them being more than friends.

It happened a lot.

"Are you ready for dinner?" he asked.

"Yes," she replied heading toward him and the door.

"How were you lessons with Bell?" He asked as they headed down the spiral staircase.

"Amazing," she gushed. She loved her magic lessons and the way that Bell would push her to explore everything she could do. It was the constant good thing she'd had to turn to over the past few years. With the rise in shadow activity and the new rules her father had laid down as a result, Terra needed good things to keep her busy. If she sat around too long doing nothing her mind would wonder. Since it seemed to always wander toward the future she was rushing to a full speed, she tried not to have any down time if she could help it.

"What are you guys working on now?"

"Well, he's teaching me about sending my conciseness out over long distances. I reached as far as the castle wall before our lesson was over and Diana came in."

Eric grimaced, "How are things going with her?"

"Not great," she admitted as they started down the grand staircase. "She still hardly talks to me." In the last year or so Diana had gone from tolerating her around and insulting her as they passed to not talking to her at all. Sometimes Terra would catch her staring at her, scowling at her was really what she was doing, but she didn't see it that way.

"What do you think is going on with her?" Eric asked, opening the door to the grand dining hall.

"I don't know," she sighed. "I wish I did, but I can't figure it out." She and Eric paused their conversation and bowed to the King and Queen. Her father nodded his permission for her to continue on, her mother didn't even bother to look at her. As they hurried on to the kitchen men and women would salute or curtsy as she passed. Terra would wave and thank each of them, often referring to them by their name.

When they finally made it to the kitchen Jenny was waiting with the tray of food for her and Grey. Terra smiled her thanks and headed back toward the west wing and the prison. It usually took them less than ten minutes to complete the entire circuit, from her room to the kitchen down to the basement. They had gotten good at making their way around with the tray of food. After four years, dinner this way had become routine.

Eric pushed the large wooden door in and held it open for her. "I'm going to head up and eat. Think of me when you're ready to go."

"I will," she promised. She squeezed past Eric who had decided to hold the door a little more close tonight. Making it harder for her to get in and out without pressing against him, he was having one of those nights. One of those nights meant that he was once again reevaluating their relationship and trying to find a way to take it beyond what it was.

318

It was less than six months after he had told her his feelings were coming back, that Terra felt the sudden change in him. He loved her. At first her heart soared to feel him realize that. Then, like a rock thrown at the sky, it came crashing down. If he loved her . . . really loved Terra . . . than he could be hurt, or worse, and it would be all her fault. She couldn't let him know she knew. He had promised not to love her and as long as he never said the actual words, she was sure she would be able to keep it together around him.

Still, on some days, like today, she could feel him staring at her, weighing the options of telling her how he really felt. For three and a half years he had decided the best thing was to keep his feelings quiet. At least until such a time as she could hear him and really tell him how she felt as well.

Not that she would ever admit to herself how she felt.

Terra waited until the door was closed before she started across the room to the glass cell. It looked ever the same, large, imposing, glass that hummed with her power. It seemed that time had no effect on the glass cell where they kept Grey. In truth, it didn't seem like time had much of an effect on Grey either. As she aged and changed, he remained the same. He looked the same now as he had the day she met him.

Except for those few time when his face would change.

There were rare moments where Grey would suddenly seem so much younger to her. He denied it, said it never happened. Terra knew the truth.

She looked at Grey who was leaning against the glass waiting for her, like he did so many nights. He smiled at her and her heart leapt uncomfortably in her chest. The wicked grin that spread across his face told Terra he was aware of her hearts current gymnastics.

She shot him a warning look and he laughed.

"Good evening Princess," he said as she set the tray on the table.

"Good evening prisoner," Terra mocked, matching his overly formal tone.

He laughed and said, "You look lovely tonight Shadow."

"Thank you," she replied, trying to sound off hand while her heart leapt again at the mention of his secret name for her.

"So he's having one of those days, hu?" Grey asked scanning the door. "What fun for you."

"Grey," she warned. "You promised not to bring up the things you see in Eric, remember?" Terra had run from the room one night, nearly a year ago, when Eric had also been having a day like today. He had lingered outside the wooden doors and Grey had picked up on what he was feeling. He had then tried to explain to Terra exactly how Eric felt about her and what he thought about her.

She had responded by clapping her hands to her ears, singing loudly and running away.

After that she had made him promise to not talk about anybody's feelings while they were having dinner, not even their own.

"I remember," he recalled, "I was just remarking on how it must have been a long day for you, that's all."

"Well it was actually a good day," she explained reflectively.

"Are you eating in here or out there?" He asked. Unbeknownst to everyone but the two of them, Terra had started dinning with Grey inside his cell. It was easier than being separated by a wall and it seemed to keep him from flying into outbursts as often. Also, not that she would ever think it or say it out loud, but she enjoyed the closeness with him.

"I'll eat with you," she answered, knowing that it was what they both wanted. She knew deep down that she should keep her distance and not put herself in so many situations where things could so easily go out of hand. Sometimes she listened to that little voice deep down inside herself, most of the time she didn't.

Grey's eyes sparkled for the briefest second. He gave her his little half smile, something Terra always took as a good sign, and extended his hand to the glass.

"Let me help you with dinner," He said.

She nodded and put the tray up to the glass and pushed. It slid through as easy as ever with Terra along behind it. Grey quickly switched the tray to his other hand and took Terra's left hand up to his mouth and kissed it gently before turning it over and kissing her palm. Carefully he would fold her fingers over the fresh kiss so she could hold on to it.

Terra's heart always went crazy when he did that. He held her hand and looked down into her eyes intently. She could tell, despite his actions, he was trying to see into her heart. He did so every time they were alone together. She knew why, and she was determined he would never find the answer he sought there.

"We should eat," she stated breaking away. "It's been a long day."

"Tell me about it. What did you do with yourself today?"

"I went and visited the children's home today."

"How is going?" He asked, genuinely interested.

"It's going very well. They've almost finished the construction on it and the Master Builder says it could be ready for occupants by the end of the week." Terra had been struck by the idea to build a home for the orphaned children in the castle town almost a year ago. She had gone to her father the next day and asked for permission to begin working on such a place. Her father, so pleased to see one of his daughters taking an interest in the kingdom and its people, agreed. With the condition that Terra was in charge of all of it.

She needed to find a place, work with the Master Builder and Carpenter, and help draw up the plans for the building itself.

Terra had exceeded all expectations set for her by her father and every other man she worked with. She had drawn up beautiful plans and found the perfect location to build the home. At her insistence, the Master Builder hired only men from the castle town to handle the construction. With an influx of new jobs and the promise of a new home for orphaned children, the people in the town started to notice Terra for the first time in her life.

"Next week?" He asked threw a mouthful of chicken, "That's amazing."

"I know," she smiled, her face practically glowing with pride. "I can't wait until we can start getting these kids the things they need."

Grey looked at Terra and let out a quite sigh. She still amazed him, even after all this time. Her selflessness and her insane need to help others, two things about her that had originally grated against him, now they were some of the things he admired the most about her.

It was too bad those things would be ceasing soon.

He had been waiting for four long years. Patiently using anyone he could to slowly manipulate Terra. She would have to love him, he had realized a few years ago. The only way he could get her to help him do what she was going to have to do was if she loved him. Not just love, she had to love him implicitly and without the shadow of a doubt.

He was so close now. Her feelings for him grew stronger every day and what had started as a crack in her resolve was now a giant spanning chasm of doubt and darkness in her heart. Soon he would be able to push her past that last bit of resistance and break her. Then she would be his and his plan for her sister could finally start to unfold.

After nearly two hours of talking and laughing Terra could feel Eric get anxious through the bond. He always worried if she was gone too long. She sighed and turned to Grey, he would already know that she had to get going, he was always in her head when he could be. He made his usual it's-too-early face, but didn't say anything.

"You know he's only going to wait for so long," she reminded him as she started to gather their plates and silverware onto the tray.

"He can wait a little longer," Grey muttered irritably. "He has all day with you out there; he doesn't need to be cutting into my time as well."

"Your time?" She asked. "I didn't realize I was rentable."

Grey shrugged. "For the right price, I find almost all women can be "rented."" He was smiling wickedly again.

Terra stood and walked to the wall without so much as a look or word of parting. She had a hand on the glass by the time he got to her. He grabbed her shoulder and pulled her gently away from the wall, a mixed look of concern and doubt on his face.

"Come off it now, you know I was only joking."

"Oh I know," she smiled. "You and I both know you couldn't afford my rates."

Grey froze, a look of pure disbelief on his face. He couldn't believe what he'd heard her say. Terra didn't talk about things like that. Ever.

"You should see your face," she laughed. "I didn't realize saying that would break you. I'm sorry." She laughed harder as he continued to stair.

After another second or so Grey finally managed to pull himself together, scowling at Terra as she continued to laugh. He shook his head and folded his arms across his chest.

"So we can't talk about feelings but you can talk about how much it would be to rent you out?" he asked accusingly. "How is that fair?"

Terra's laughter died out. He had a point.

"I'm sorry," she apologized earnestly. "I was just trying to counter your joke, I didn't really think before I spoke."

"No need to apologize to me. If we're gonna talk about emotions and other such gooey things, I'd just like a forewarning is all."

"A forewarning?" She asked confused. "Why would you need a forewarning?"

Grey smiled and his eyes twinkled with desire and something a little darker. Terra cleared her throat loudly and stepped back away from him. He could get a little intense when he looked at her this way. Not like a little girl or a young lady or even a princess, he looked at her like a woman he would have in his bed.

Terra felt a small shudder of desire go through her as her mind suddenly wandered down the path that wondered what being bedded by a man like Grey would be like. Would he be passionate? Or would he be gentle with her since she was still a maid? Her mind wondered what it would be like to be bedded at all. She was twenty now and most other women her age were married and on their fourth child. She and Diana were still unmarried, due largely in part to the fact that Diana was still being groomed into a savior for the people.

She didn't have time to court or marry anyone right now. Especially if things didn't go her way during the final battle between, a battle she dreaded with a cold pit in her stomach. Everything would change that day. One person she . . . one person that she . . .

Terra shook her head.

She wouldn't allow herself to think it. Not here or now in the cell with Grey. She wouldn't allow herself to think about that at all.

She looked up and almost screamed.

Grey had taken advantage of her momentary reverie to step in closer, pinning her in the corner of the cell. He had a hand on the glass on each side of her and was looking down at her intently. All traces of desire were gone from his eyes, replace by something that Terra thought looked a little like impatience.

"Don't mind me," he said, "by all means, finish your thought."

"Grey," she started with an annoyed sigh. "I have to go, Eric will be here soon and I need to be on the other side of the glass when that happens."

Looking like he'd much rather be pressing her for answers, he stepped back so Terra could grab the tray. "You know you could just be honest," he added.

"Honest?" she asked, feigning stupid to buy time so she could get away before the conversation went too far.

"With me. You can be honest with me." He reached out and put a hand on her shoulder. Terra, still gathering the dishes, ignored the contact and how it made her feel. "Just tell me how you feel. You can say those words to me."

324

She stopped and turned, looking him in the eyes. "I don't know what words you mean," she lied badly. "I'm going on my way now. I'll see you for breakfast in the morning."

Terra was through the glass before Grey could respond. He watched her walk to the door and pull it open. Once on the other side, she set the tray down and grabbed the door to push it closed. A heartbeat before she was out of sight, she looked up and her eyes locked on Grey's. They both knew how the other felt, though neither could say it out loud.

Terra feared that if she said it out loud, she would give life to those feelings and never be able to take them back. Once they had a life of their own, those words could destroy her and everyone she cared about. She couldn't risk it. She had to keep how she felt a secret to everyone. Even herself.

Grey watched the door close, locking eyes with Terra just be for it did. He could tell his plan was working, he just couldn't tell how far along they were. He needed her to tell him how she felt about him. His heart gave a painful leap at the thought of her loving him. His mind knew it was all part of his plan, but his damn heart. It wouldn't listen to his mind, it did whatever it wanted. There were times over the past few years where he and Terra would be talking and the next thing he knew he had her in his arms, inches from her face. He would be breathless and it would take all he had to keep from pushing the line Terra had drawn for them.

He needed to find a way to force her to tell him the truth.

Reynolds.

That fool hadn't been utilized in a while. Maybe it was time for him to prove his usefulness.

Diana strode back and forth along the large, very expensive, rug in her room. Jack should have been back by now. Damn fool probably got lost somewhere. She swore if it wasn't for his particular set of skills in the bedroom, he would be completely useless. She had sent him to go fetch the wretched old hag from town nearly an hour ago. She couldn't be seen outside the castle at this hour. She needed Jack to get the woman and hurry.

A soft knock at the door pulled Diana from the thoughts of what she would do to him if he failed her. She slid the bolt and opened the door. A very old woman came shambling in, followed closely behind by Jack.

"You're Majesty," she said, bowing to Diana. She was old, well into her seventies, even though to Diana she looked nearly one hundred. Her robes were old and dirty and they smelled of fifth and her foul dealings. Her face and hair were just as dirty and the robes she wore, if not more so. What few teeth she had were black and rotting away.

It made Diana queasy just to think of such a woman standing on her fine rug in her fine room, surrounded by all of her fine things. She wanted this over with as soon as possible.

"Do you have what I need?" She demanded.

"Yes m'lady," she responded, her voice horse and her accent thick.

"Give it to me," she demanded.

"Payment first, highness."

Diana scowled at the old hag, but she snapped her fingers at Jack who produced a small bag of silver and bronze sols. He shook it once and threw it at the old woman. She caught it in the air quick as a cat. She jingled the bag a few times then, satisfied, reached into her robes and produced a small glass vial filled with a dark black liquid.

Jack snatched the vial out of her hand and passed it to Diana. She held it up to the light and tried to see through the thick liquid.

"Will it do what I need?" She demanded of the woman.

"Aye, that it will," she answered. "It will remove the child inside without damaging anything else m'lady."

"Good. You're excused." Jack opened the door back up and both he and the old woman turned to leave. "Oh and old hag, if you're wrong, I'll kill you," she added without looking up.

Old though she was, the woman knew that the Princess wasn't kidding. She nodded and followed the young man back out into the hall. Diana pushed the door closed and slid the bolt in. She didn't want to be disturbed. She pulled the small cork out and dumped the liquid down her throat.

It tasted as foul as it looked and it burned on the way down. It hit Diana's stomach and she felt like she might vomit. Knowing she had to keep it down for the potion to work, she clapped her hands over her mouth and clambered into her bed. She pulled her pillow up over her face and waited for the trickle of blood between her thighs that signaled the potion had done as it was supposed to and the bastard Jack had gotten on her was gone.

Eric closed the door to his room and then banged his head against it. He didn't know what he was supposed to do anymore! For years he had been careful about how he felt about her and what emotions he showed her. He wanted to be good to the promise he had made all those years ago, but that was getting harder and harder as each year passed.

He loved her.

He loved her so much it hurt no to be able to tell her.

It was easy at first; she was so young it wouldn't have been right for him to love her then. Now though, now she was grown and easily the most beautiful woman he had ever seen. Not to mention the fact that she was kind, generous, sweet, funny, and did he mention beautiful? She was impossible not to love.

Yet he couldn't say it to her.

He couldn't grab her and tell her how he felt about her and he longed to hold her every day and how not being able to do so up until that point was killing him.

He couldn't say any of that.

He couldn't even think about it when she was around.

All he could do was be the best friend he could be until she was ready to be with him.

Terra stretched and rolled over. Light was just starting to bleed through the curtains on her windows. Dawn was breaking. Mammy would be just getting up and getting ready to come get her up. Terra thought about staying in bed and waiting for Mammy, but there was work to be done in town today and she had to be to the construction site early to overseen some of the smaller details of the children's home.

After that it was lessons with Bell and the new self-defense master her father had brought in from Pleiades Kingdom. She was supposed to be the very best anyone had ever seen. Father had paid a handsome sum to get her here to train them and Terra intended to make sure it was worth every sol. After that she needed to head back to the construction site and talk with the other men about the completion of the building and her father's approval for a party the day it's completed.

 Then back to the castle to wash and change for dinner with Grey.

It would be a very full day, but Terra liked it that way.

Deciding that waiting would only put off what needed to be done, and give her time to ponder on things she didn't want to ponder on, she decided it was time to rise. She threw the blankets off and got up. After a few minutes looking through her wardrobe, she decided on a simple dark grey dress. It had a beautiful cut to it, corset, square neck line, cap sleeves and a simi full skirt. It would look nice on her and it would be appropriate for what she had to do that day.

Not waiting for Mammy, Terra dressed and washed her face. She combed through her long locks of hair and then fought with it to make it stay up on her head and look nice. Half way through her struggle Mammy came in.

"Up already?" She asked, an amused smile on her face.

"Yes," Terra replied, still struggling with her hair. "I have a lot to do today and I wanted to get an early start. Except that my hair absolutely refuses to do anything I want it to. Maybe if I had some scissors I could fix it."

"Don't you dare," Mammy scolded laughing. "Here let me help." She came up behind the princess and with deft nimble fingers she soothed the mess that had become her hair and twisted some and braided other parts. In less than two minutes Terra's hair was up and looking beautiful on her head. She even had little ringlets framing her face and at the base of her neck. Mammy was amazing.

"I don't know how you do it," she muttered appreciatively. "I don't know how to do anything with it."

"You don't need to know," Mammy replied. "If you would just let me hire you some ladies in waiting you wouldn't ever have to worry about things like your hair."

Terra rolled her eyes; she'd heard this argument before. When she turned sixteen it was customary for her to take on at least three ladies in waiting. She had decided not to do so. Something her mother still found unforgivable. Every proper lady had ladies in waiting.

Terra just didn't like the idea of a group of women whose sole purpose was to follow her around and do what she said. She could find her own dress and lace her own corset; she didn't need a gaggle of women to do it for her.

Mammy sighed, knowing she wasn't going to win that argument today. With a few last adjustments, she stepped back and let Terra rise off her stool and get a good look at her hair. She couldn't understand how Mammy could do such an amazing job in so little time. She could barely get her hair brushed in that amount of time.

"Thank you Mammy," she whispered hugging her tightly for a moment.

"You're welcome child," Mammy replied. "Now hurry, Guard Reynolds is at the base of the stairs waiting for you."

"He is?" She asked. Her heart fluttered at the thought of him up early and waiting for her. Her favorite part of the day was when Eric saw her in the morning. He always made her feel so beautiful.

"He is," she answered, smiling at the color that appeared on Terra's cheeks. "Now go on, shoo, get going."

"Bye Mammy," she called as she was playfully shooed from the room. "I'll see you tonight!"

"Eric! Where are you?!"

"Terra? Where are you?"

"I'm here, come closer."

Eric opened his eyes, he was surrounded by swirling grey mist and nothing else it seemed. He couldn't see land or sky, just billows of swirling mist. He couldn't see Terra, but he could sense her just a ways a head.

"Terra where are we?" He asked.

Suddenly she was in front him. She was wearing a grey dress that seemed to blend perfectly with the billows around her, making it near impossible for Eric to differentiate between the bottom of her dress and the mist swirling around.

"We're in your dream," she answered simply.

"My dream!?"

"Yes. It's the only safe place I can talk to you."

"What do you mean? Why isn't it safe?"

"Grey. He's always watching me. I can't risk talking to you where he might hear me."

Terra closed the distance between them and grabbed his hands in both of hers. She looked up at him sad and scared. There was something about her face that didn't seem right to Eric, her eyes didn't look right and her freckles were gone.

"I'm sorry to do this to you Eric," she explained, "but I just can't take it anymore."

"Can't take what?"

"Not telling you."

Eric's heart leapt up into his throat. "Telling me what?"

"That I love you. I've always loved you and I can't keep it inside anymore."

330

"Terra," he whispered. He had waited so long for her to say those words to him. To hear her say that she felt the same as she did, that she loved him. He wrapped his arms around her and held her close to him. He couldn't say how happy he was.

"Eric, there's something you must do for me," she instructed, her face against his chest.

"Anything for you," he replied simply.

"I need to know that you'll remember this outside of the dream."

"I will, I promise you Terra. I will never forget this."

"Dreams are hard to remember after we wake. I need you to prove to me that you remember having this dream. I need you to wait for the moment and take me in your arms and kiss me like you've always wanted."

Eric couldn't speak. He stared in disbelief at Terra's serious face looking up at him.

When he finally found his voice again he said, "You want me to do what?"

"Kiss me. Don't say anything don't warn me. I can't risk Grey finding out somehow. Just promise me you'll do this."

"I promise. But won't Grey just find out about the kiss and cause problems?"

"Not if it's spontaneous. Then it's just a heat of the moment thing and then we'll both know we remember this."

It made a kind of sense to Eric, he had to admit. Not to mention the thought of holding the princess in real life, kissing her like he'd wanted to for so long, it seemed too good to be true.

"When?" He asked.

"You'll know the moment," she assured him. Her image started to shimmer and fade. "I'm waking up I have to go. Please Eric don't forget."

"I won't," he called as she disappeared.

Eric's eyes snapped open. He was lying in bed and judging by the lack of light out his window, it was still very early. He sighed and ran his fingers through his long brown hair. That dream . . . there's no way that was real. It wasn't possible for people to share dreams. Was it? What if it was real? Could he really grab Terra and hold her the way he wanted? Or kiss her the way he'd always wanted? What about her father? Would he hurt Eric if he found out?

It didn't seem possible that such a thing could really happen. Could it be possible that Terra could somehow put herself in his dream? He had never heard of such a thing being done before. However, when it came to Terra, it seemed as though she broke through what was possible all the time. Bell was always saying that he didn't think there was anything she couldn't do, if she really wanted to.

He pondered for a while over what to do.

He didn't want to risk doing something to Terra that she didn't want. He also didn't want to entice the wrath of the King, who lately has been quite prone to anger when it came to his children.

So many people were demanding to know when Diana would be ready and when could the fight finally start. People were getting more and more nervous as the number of shadows being seen increased. All the signs from the prophecy were here, why wasn't anything being done to stop the Shadow King? Most people in the town now knew that he was held prisoner at the bottom of the castle. They wondered, angrily, why the King hadn't killed him yet. Why when he was a prisoner, had he been allowed to live?

King Sol was under a great deal of stress. Eric would greatly appreciate not exacerbating that stress by forcing himself on the Princess. There was no telling how the King would react to something like this right now. He could slap Eric on the wrist, or he could behead him. Either way, caution was called for.

Eric decided he would rise, get ready, and then judge, based on how Terra reacted to him this morning, if he should believe what he had dreamt or not.

As he pulled his door closed, Mammy appeared at the top of the stairs across from him.

"Good morning Mammy," Eric greeted cheerily. He liked Mammy, a great deal in fact. She was one of the only people in the castle that actually loved Terra and put her needs above her sisters. Most everyone cared only for Diana. Not that he blamed them, Diana was beautiful, she was the oldest, and she was the Princess of prophecy. It was hard to hate someone who was supposed to save your life.

Of course now he knew the real Diana, the cold, bitter, hateful princess that no one ever saw. No one except Terra, and by proxy himself and Mammy. They all knew what she was really like and how she treated people.

"Good Morning Eric," Mammy replied smiling at him. "What are you doing up so early?"

"Terra has a lot to do today, I just wanted to make sure I was up and ready when she rose. Are you headed up now?"

"I am. I'll get that lazy thing out of bed and send her down."

"Thank you Mammy."

With a nod, she started up the rest of the stairs to Terra's room. He could hear her talking to Terra; she was already up, like him. Maybe that was a sign she'd sent the dream. She was up because in the dream she said she was waking and that was before even he woke.

Eric shook his head. He couldn't let himself read too much into one thing. He had to be sure before he broke the promise he'd made her. So he waited at the base of her stairs while she and Mammy talked back and forth. It wasn't too long after she'd gone up that Eric heard the door opening. He stood up straight and adjusted his uniform.

"I'll see you tonight!" He heard Terra yell, then the door closed and he could hear her making her way down the spiral stairs.

A second later she came in to view.

She was wearing a stunning grey dress, nearly identical to the one she'd been wearing in the dream. A warm smile spread across her

333

face when she saw him standing there, waiting. She hurried down the rest of the stairs and stopped in front of him.

"Good morning," she said sweetly, her cheeks coloring slightly.

"It is indeed," he agreed. "You look beautiful today."

"Thank you," she said, her cheeks getting redder.

"I like your dress," he offered. He was hoping she would say something that would tell him she'd chosen it on purpose for today. Anything that might lead him to believe that is was this dress he'd seen her in during their dream. He so wanted to believe that it was real.

"Thank you," she repeated. "I wasn't going to wear it at first. But as I looked at it I felt like I needed to wear it today." Terra hadn't realized until talking to Eric that she hadn't intended to wear this dress today at all.

"Today?" He asked, not sure he could trust his own ears.

"Yes," she confirmed, considering. "I just felt like I needed to wear it. Is that strange?"

"Not at all," he answered smiling. He knew. She was trying to tell him she wore it so he would know she was in his dream. It was real. The day he had been waiting for, the day that he had imagined every day for the last four years was finally here. He could finally tell her how he felt about her and hold her as he'd always wanted to do.

"Are you ready?" She asked.

"I am," he answered offering her his hand. "Let's get going."

Terra walked through the door's to the prison carrying Grey's breakfast. She was getting down later than she had intended. She had gotten to the kitchen so early they weren't done with his breakfast yet. She had been sure that as soon as she went through the door, Grey would be waiting impatiently for his breakfast. He was always cranky in the morning.

When they rarely fought it was almost always in the morning.

So when she came through the door to find that he was still in bed, she was more than a little surprised. He was always awake when she came down. Honestly she'd never seen him sleep before. He was awake when she left at night and up before she came down in the morning.

Not wanting to wake him, Terra pulled the door closed quietly. She took one step forward and heard the heel of her shoe make a loud echoing click on the hard stone floor. Careful of the breakfast tray, she slipped her shoes off and padded across the floor in just her stockings.

Once she got to the glass she could see clearly that Grey was still in bed and breathing softly. Apparently covers and shirts were too restrictive for him as he had neither on currently. He was rolled and facing the other wall. There was something about the way he looked laying there that sparked Terra's curiosity. She wanted to see him sleeping, not just want, she felt she needed to see his face.

She stepped through the glass carefully and set the tray down on the table as quietly as she could. Carefully she made her way across the cell to Grey's bed. He was still breathing in slow even beats as she stood over him. She was stuck by the realization that as he lay there sleeping he was vulnerable. That was most likely why he'd never let himself sleep so late as for her to see him, he was exposed and defenseless while he slept.

She smiled and wondered if it was possible he still didn't trust her. After four years of companionship, there was very little they didn't know about each other.

He made a small noise in his sleep and turned over onto his back.

Terra could see now why she felt she had to see him.

His face was changed again. He looked younger, more innocent. His face was absent all the hard lines that he bore from years of war and plotting. It was still Grey, same dark, wild hair, same face shape and she was sure if she could see them, he would have the same grey eyes. He had simply lost all of the things that made him look frightening.

"Terra," he whispered with a smile.

She froze.

335

Was he awake?

Could he see her?

Would he be mad that she had crept in and watched him sleep? It sounded creepy saying it in her head that way.

Grey let out a sigh and started to snore softly.

He was still asleep.

He was saying her name in his sleep?

Was he dreaming of her?

Terra felt her face flush at the thought. Could he really be dreaming about her? Sure she was the only person he really interacted with, but wouldn't that be more reason not to dream of her? Was it a good dream? What if he was dreaming about killing her or something else terrible? Maybe he wasn't as kind as she had been lead to think.

She was overcome by a sudden need to know what he was dreaming. There had to be a way to find out. She had magic and a brain; it shouldn't be that hard right?

Terra racked her brain for a way to see what was in his head.

It struck her then. Years ago, after she'd found out her mother didn't want her, she'd put his hands on the side of her face and he'd seen what was in her head. Maybe there was a way she could do that so she could see in his head. If she put her hands on Grey's face the way he had on hers, maybe she could see what was going on in there.

Terra looked at the way he was laying. He was on his back but still mostly facing the opposite wall. She walked around the bed and carefully crawled in next to Grey. She knelt down next to him and extended her hands. If she was right, she would be able to see what he was dreaming about her. If she was wrong the only things she would succeed in doing is waking him and putting herself in a situation that was going to require a lot of explanation.

Taking a deep breath she reached out and gently put one hand on either side of his face. She closed her eyes and focused on Grey and his dream. She tried to call forth the images in his head.

Terra opened her eyes.

336

She was standing in the middle of beautiful field of moonflowers. They were opened and turned up to the full moon overhead. A soft breeze rustled the flowers and blew Terra's hair around. If this was Grey's dream, it was one of the loveliest things she'd ever seen.

She heard laughter behind her and turned slowly. It was hard to move in a dream, she realized then. It was similar to walking through think mud. You couldn't really move fast at all. Once she managed to make the turn she saw Grey a few yards from her near a lake that glowed silver in the moonlight.

As she watched Grey spun slowly. He was dancing, with her.

It was the oddest thing she'd ever seen.

She stood in a dream surrounded by flowers watching herself dance with a man she was supposed to hate. Something in the way he held her and the way they were looking at each other struck Terra as odd. She'd danced with Grey before in the cell but it didn't look like that. He was holding her so close looking down at her like . . . well . . . like he loved her.

Terra felt ashamed for intruding on such a private thought. Grey was entitled to dream whatever he wanted, it wasn't for her to jump in and judge him.

She should go.

As Terra turned to leave she felt something behind her.

Moving slowly she turned to face the largest Shadow she had ever seen. It towered over her with bulging golden eyes. Not sliver like other shadows, but gold and menacing. Terra could tell that this was no ordinary shadow. Not just because of its size or because of its eyes but because of the amount of darkness coming off this shadow was unlike anything she'd ever felt in her life. It was pure black, dark, think and ominous. She felt like she was choking on the darkness. Almost as if the shadow was taking the air from her lungs.

It stared at her, eyes bulging.

'YOU DO NOT BELONG HERE!' A voice in her head boomed.

Terra clapped her hands to her ears. It was so loud it hurt.

'*YOU DO NOT BELONG HERE!*' It boomed again. '*LEAVE NOW OR SUFFER FOR YOUR INSOLENCE!*'

She staggered back a step, between the darkness and the sound of its voice in her head, she was starting to black out.

A scream from Grey's direction pulled her attention.

Dream Terra had vanished and the shadow with the golden eyes was attempting to pull Grey into itself. He looked at her with eyes wide, fear written plain across his face as he struggled to get away.

"Terra!" He screamed. "Help me!"

"Grey," she called back. She tried to run towards him, but found that she still couldn't move quickly. At the pace she was going, she knew the struggle would be long over by the time she got to him. She had to hurry.

Wind whipped across her face again.

Wind! That was it!

Not sure it would work in a dream, Terra tried to summon the wind to her as Master Bell had taught her to do. To her never ending surprise, the wind answered and came to her call. She encircled herself with wind and pleaded to the element to launch her at Grey.

Wind responded.

She went flying through the air and landed softly on the grass in front of him.

"GRAB MY HANDS!" She shouted.

Grey reached up and grabbed her wrists. Terra wrapped her hands around his and silently urged the wind to pull them up and away from the shadow, and the threat it posed to them.

Again, wind responded.

It lifted the two of them into the air and away from the golden eyed shadow.

It stared at Terra, golden eyes bulging out of its head. She met its gaze head on. She wasn't sure what this new shadow was, but she knew she wouldn't let it hurt Grey so long as she could help it. At her urging the wind took them away from where the shadow stood.

"Terra!?" Grey exclaimed. "You saved me!"

338

"Of course," she smiled, as the wind started to lower them back down. "You're my friend."

"Thank you," he said as his feet touched ground. He released her wrists and she slid down into his arms. Slowly he lowered her, never taking his eyes from hers.

"You don't have to thank me," she said awkwardly. "This is only a dream."

"I'm dreaming?"

"Yes," she answered guiltily. "I brought you breakfast and you were still asleep. I was going to leave, but you said my name."

"I see," he said, still smiling. "I should have known this was only a dream. That shadow wouldn't have been so easy to best otherwise."

Terra started to say something but stopped when things started to fade before her. "What's going on?" She asked alarmed.

"I'm waking up," he answered sadly. "Terra thank you for what you did, real or not."

"Grey wait!" She called. "Your face," she tried to ask, but it was no use. He and the world he was standing in faded away. For a moment she stood in an empty white void. There was nothing around, no sights or sounds. There was only her.

She opened her eyes. For a moment she couldn't understand what she was seeing. Somehow she was lying on Grey's bed, not sitting like she had been. Grey was half on top of her, pinning her right hand underneath him. His eyes were still closed and he was still breathing in a slow steady rhythm. It didn't appear that he had woken up yet.

Terra pulled slightly on her arm, trying to see if she could free it. Grey had been grateful in the dream, but awake Grey might not be so happy about the invasion of his privacy. Especially since the dream she had spied on, had been about her.

At the slight tug, his eyes shot open.

He looked at her with pure disbelief on his face. She was lying flat on her back and he was lying draped over the right side of her.

They looked like a couple who'd just woken cuddled next to each other. He opened his mouth but no sound came out. He just stared.

"Uh, good morning," Terra giggled awkwardly. "I brought you breakfast, but I should be going now." She tugged at her arm again. Grey looked down and understanding flashed in his eyes. Slowly the pieces were coming together for him.

"Why princess," he teased, enjoying his new found dominance over her. "Whatever are you doing in my bed? And trapped here no less? A lesser man might take this as an invitation."

Terra scowled at him. "Try it and I'll burn this bed to cinders." After so many years she was well versed in dealing with Grey.

He smiled. "You know I like a challenge."

"Grey let me go already!" Terra said impatiently. "Eric's outside and if I keep him waiting he'll come in to see what's going on."

"First tell me why you're in my bed."

Terra stared, "You don't remember?"

"Remember what?"

"Nothing," she said too quickly.

Grey shifted his weight and sprang up, grabbing Terra's left wrist as he went. He was now straddling her, one of her wrists in each hand. He pinned them back on the bed and brought his face down to hers. His black hair hung down and tickled Terra where it touched her face.

She squirmed and kicked, trying to get free. Grey was nearly a foot taller than she was and he had the weight to keep her pinned. Physically she couldn't best him.

"Tell me what I've clearly forgotten," he whispered intimately, hovering inches from her face.

"You have two seconds to get off me before I force you off," she countered.

"Go ahead and try princess," he replied smiling, "It's been a while since I've had a reason to go a few rounds in bed, but I think I'm still up to the challenge."

Getting more and more anxious as each moment passed she said, "Grey, Eric won't wait much longer, he'll burst in here and that'll be it. Supervised visits and no more dinner conversation."

He chuckled. "Eric is discussing with young John, the pros and cons of the newest sword they were all issued. He's been at it nearly twenty minutes and judging by what they're talking about now, it's going to be a good long while before he realizes how much time has passed."

He was right about one thing at least, Eric could talk about swords and crossbows all day. He loved weapons and all the ins and outs of them seemed to genuinely intrigue him. He could talk about a sword for hours if she let him. They were his passion.

"Grey, you're my friend and I don't want to hurt you . . ."

"Your friend," he cut in slowly. "That's right, I'm your friend." Terra could see in his eyes, he remembered the dream. "You were in my dream."

It wasn't a question but she still nodded. Grey jumped up and off of the princess. He slid easily from the bed to the floor and grabbed a shirt off the small wardrobe in the corner.

"You know it's rude to spy on other people's dreams."

"I wouldn't have spied if you hadn't said my name," she countered defensively. She carefully got out of the bed and used the glass as a mirror to fix her hair and adjust her dress.

"I don't talk in my sleep," he laughed.

"How would you know?" She asked. "How many people have ever seen you sleep?"

Grey froze halfway through adjusting the belt he wore around his shirt. "Hmm. I suppose none."

"So then how would you know?"

He considered this a moment. "I guess I wouldn't."

Terra laughed at the strange face he was making. Confused with a bit of deep thought, sprinkled with just a bit of sadness.

"I have to go." She walked over and put a hand on Grey's shoulder. "I'm sorry about the snooping in your dreams thing."

He looked at her and shrugged. "It's fine. I don't remember most of it anyway. Now get going. Your white knight has realized what time it is."

"White knight?"

"Here he comes," Grey repeated, pushing Terra gently toward the wall.

She stepped through the glass and kept walking, only stopping briefly to slip her shoes back on. "I'll see you at lunch," she called as the door swung open and Eric walked in. Terra didn't stop at the door; she walked past Eric and nudged him with her shoulder.

"Come on, we're already gonna be late," she said laughing as she passed him.

"What?" He asked. He scowled at Grey who waved at him with a smile. Pulling the door closed he ran after Terra who had already started up the stairs.

"Hey I'm not the one who's making us late," He said catching up.

"I know."

Eric waited.

When Terra didn't offer up a reason for being so late he asked, "So, what took so long?"

"He was asleep," she answered. She wasn't lying to him, but she wasn't telling him everything. A fact she hated herself for.

"Must be nice to sleep all day," Eric grumbled.

Terra ignored him as they hurried to get out of the castle.

Diana woke slowly. She rolled away from the sun and a sharp pain in her stomach stopped her. It was a hot angry pain that brought the night before back in even sharper detail. Diana opened her eyes fully and threw off her blankets. Her sheets were soaked in blood from her thighs down. Whatever that witch had given her had worked.

With a smile, Diana threw her head back on the pillow and thanked whatever power had been looking over her for getting rid of the bastard. When her ladies came in they would see the blood and think her courses had come. Judging by how much, they would think it was a bad course and she would be pampered and not have to go to her lessons.

Smiling wider, Diana cried out in pain and waited until her ladies came rushing in.

Bell stood in the presence chamber of King Sol, waiting for the King to come and meet with him. It had been several months since they'd last spoken about Terra and the prisoner. As the years had progressed, so too had their bond. It seemed that all of their original projections concerning the connection Terra was forming with the man she called Grey, fell drastically short of what the reality was. Terra had formed a bond with him that rivaled the bond she shared with her Guard.

If they were going to act on that bond, use it to their advantage, they would need to start putting those plans into motion now.

As he waited, Bell admired the room he was standing in. It was a great deal larger than the previous presence chamber the King had. There was a large fireplace directly across from the double doors that lead to the hall. A large fur rug adorned the floor directly in front of the fireplace. There were large cushioned chairs flanking both walls and small tables spaced intermittently between them. In the very center of the room there was a large oval solid mahogany table decorated with a beautiful pale white vase from the moon kingdom that was always kept full of fresh flowers from the Queen's garden.

It was a beautiful room.

"Master Bell," the King said, opening his large bedroom door.

"Majesty," Bell greeted, bowing with his fist over his heart.

"Rise Bell," King Sol commanded. "Tell me, what news do you have of my daughter?"

"The news is good, better than we had hoped in fact."

"And Terra? Tell me, how is her exposer? Is she being corrupted?"

"Terra seems to be the same bright happy girls she's always been. I can't sense any increase in darkness. Although she is harder to read than most, she has some very adept mental walls."

"That's a good thing isn't it?" King Sol asked.

"Yes. If I can't read her than its very unlikely that his darkness will be able to have much effect on her."

"Good," the King sighed, visibly relieved.

"My Lord, I've been watching things with Terra, monitoring her bond with the prisoner."

"And?"

"I think it's nearly time. Their bond has grown faster than we could have ever imagined. At this point if we wait too much longer we run the risk of damaging Terra in the process. Not only that . . ." Bell trailed off, not sure how to tell the King.

"What?" King Sol asked his eyebrows drawn together in concern.

"Majesty," Bell faltered, not sure he should have broached the subject.

"Master Wizard I am you King and your friend. Please don't force me to order you to tell me."

Bell sighed, "My lord I fear that there might be . . . emotions, between your daughter and the prisoner."

King Sol was quiet for a while. He pondered over what Bell had said. Terra had a big heart. It was something he always loved about his youngest daughter. She loved so easily and cared for all that she met. Sometimes he would ponder over what things would be like if she were to inherit the throne and not Diana.

Diana was strong and cunning; she had nearly all the traits a good ruler required. All she seemed to lack was compassion and caring. They weren't the most important traits for a ruler, but they were necessary. He worried that he was leaving the kingdom in the hands of a heartless ruler.

"My Lord?" Bell asked. "I know this news is bad but I believe that no matter what happens she'll be fine."

344

"How can you know?" King Sol asked.

"I believe that her bond with Guard Reynolds will protect her from most of the pain that might be associated with the prisoner's death. In time I believe she will be fine and she will find it in her heart to forgive us for our part in it."

"Very well then," he consented. "How soon should we begin our preparations?"

"Immediately."

Grey sat quietly on his bed thinking over the dream he'd had and the fact that Terra had somehow managed to put herself in it. Things like dream sharing weren't unheard of; it just requires a bond between the two people, or a seriously strong magical ability.

In this case it could have been either.

What Grey sat pondering about was the way Terra had faced down the golden eyed shadow for him. There was power and darkness in that thing the likes of which his little shadow had never seen. It was nearly impossible to breath in its presence. Let alone think or form any kind of thought that wasn't solely concerned with escaping.

Terra had flown over to him and pulled him away without any second thought. He called for help and she had responded. It was like it was the simplest of requests. It baffled him to no end. He stood and walked to the table. His breakfast was cold now but he didn't care. It wasn't food he was interested in today.

There had been a shift in the air.

Change was coming, he could feel it. For so many years all the different people who had some stake in the coming battle were building and waiting. Watching for the signs and preparing for their roles in the end.

Now things had changed. The last piece had fallen into place. Things would start accelerating quickly. The end was coming and Grey was looking forward to finally getting out of this cell.

345

Terra squinted her eyes against the bright light of the sun as she and Eric walked out of the castle gates and into the surrounding town. There was a smell of fresh baking bread and the sounds of families waking for the day. She loved the way mornings made everything seem so fresh. Every morning meant a new day and a chance to start over.

"You look happy," Eric remarked.

"I am," she replied.

"Good dreams?" He enquired.

"Good morning Princess," a woman called from the window.

"Good Morning Ruth," she called up. "How are the little ones?"

"As rambunctious as ever I'm afraid," she said with a smile. "Are you off to work on the home?"

"We are."

"Creator bless you and your kind heart," she called, before she disappeared back into her home.

"You as well," Terra called.

They started walking again. As they went the city seemed to come alive around them. Stores were opening and people were starting on their busy days. Everyone smiled and waved as they walked past. Women curtsied and men doffed their caps as they bowed. A few men who had known Eric growing up called to him and waved, laughing boisterously.

It took nearly twenty minutes to make the walk from the castle gates to the construction site. Already Terra and Eric were sweating in the heat of the day. As the sun rose it would only get hotter and hotter. She worried that it might be too hot for the men to work.

"Good Morning Princess, Guard Reynolds," the Master Builder said as he walked toward them. "A fine morning for building." He was a tall strong man. He stood over six feet tall and had the broadest shoulders Terra had ever seen in a person. His hair and beard were red and looked like fire with the sun shining through them. His eyes were

346

a light blue, like the sky or ice. He was good kind man, and his face showed that.

"Good morning Master Builder," Terra greeted him smiling. "How are you doing today?"

"Princess, how many times must I ask you to call me Harold? Or even just foreman would be better than 'Master Builder'."

She laughed. "I promise I mean no disrespect. Master Builder is a title hard earned and sorely fought for. I would feel remiss not addressing you with the title you deserve."

"It's hard to argue with logic like that," he said to Eric. "How about we agree on foreman? Still a title, full of respect, just not so long."

"Foreman it is then," she smiled. "So tell me then Foreman, how is our building looking?"

"Come see for yourself."

Terra and Eric spent the next hour with the Foreman walking all over the construction site and hearing about what was finished and would soon be. He explained that the only thing they still had to do was finish the work on the inside and take down the scaffolding they had built. They would be done before weeks end.

Thanking him for all his work, Terra made her excuses and said that she had to be leaving. Together they walked back to the castle making small talk and discussing the progress the home had made in such a short period of time.

"Can I ask you something?" Eric enquired as they walked through the main entrance to the castle.

"Of course."

They took the main staircase up to the third floor and then took the left corridor toward the east wing and the schoolroom. Eric was quiet for a while as he considered the best way to phrase his question.

"Why did you want to build the home?" He finally asked.

"You don't know?" She asked.

"No," he answered, thinking back to all the conversations they'd had about the home.

Terra stopped and grabbed Eric's sleeve to stop him too. "I'm building the home for you."

"For me?" He asked dumbfounded.

"Yes, you," she smiled. "The stories you told me about being an orphan and living on the streets and going from home to home never having a place to call your own. Or the way some of the people out there treated you . . . it broke my heart to think of you that way. That's why I wanted to build this home."

"You really did this for me?"

"I wanted to wait until the unveiling, but I suppose I can tell you now. The home is to be called "The Reynolds Home for Orphaned Children." They're putting the sign up tomorrow."

For the smallest moment Eric thought his heart might burst from his chest.

For him.

She was doing this wonderful thing for *him*.

Eric grabbed her and pulled her into an embrace. He wrapped his arms around her and held her tight against him. She rested her head against his chest and sighed. She loved the way he smelled and how safe she felt in his arms. He felt safe.

"Terra," he whispered, resting his head on hers and breathing the smell of her in. "Terra I love you. I love you so much I don't even know how to put it in words. I've loved you since I walked with you and talked of fireflies. I've watched you grown and I've seen the woman you've become and I can't imagine a woman I'd want to love more.

"You're the best thing that has ever happened to me and even if it means that one day I become a target for some kind of terrible evil, I wouldn't trade my time with you for anything. I love you."

Terra couldn't move. She had known for some time that Eric thought he was in love with her. She could feel it in the way he looked at her and the way he thought about her. She had wondered what it would be like to love him the way he loved her. To just love.

But she didn't have that luxury.

Terra didn't get love. She had to protect her sister and do all she could to help her prepare for the battle. Then there was her responsibility to Grey. She knew that he was still actively trying to corrupt her. There were days where it felt like he was winning, days where she could almost feel darkness in herself.

She didn't have the luxury of love.

Not right now anyway.

Possibly not ever.

"Eric," she whispered, feeling her heart break. She knew that what she had to now would nearly destroy her. Not to mention destroy the relationship she shared with her guard. There would be only pieces left at the end.

But she had to do it.

She had to keep him safe.

Terra pushed gently against Eric's chest, she need to be able to see him to tell him this. He let her pull away some, but kept her close. Tears in her eyes, she looked up at him and opened her mouth to say the words that would destroy all that lay between them.

Eric's face came down and he, without so much as a word to her, he put his lips to hers. At first the kiss was gentle and then the longer it progressed the more passionate it became. Eric pulled her closer and held her tighter. He pushed her back until she was up against a wall and the kiss became something more. Passion gave way to desire and everything shifted suddenly.

Terra's heart was racing as she felt Eric's hand slide down her neck to rest as the top of her bodice. She could feel the heat and desire coming off him in waves. In that moment he was no longer her guard, he was a man and she was a woman.

"Terra," he whispered when their lips parted. His voice was deep and heavy with desire. He pressed himself against her and she couldn't help the small moan that suddenly escaped her throat. It was a sound she'd never made before and it startled her. It seemed to drive Eric completely mad as he brought his mouth down on hers again.

He kissed her again and again each time holding his mouth to hers for longer and longer periods of time. Then he began to kiss down her neck, to her collar bone, to the top of her breasts.

Again a strange moan escaped from Terra's throat.

Things were getting out of control and she could feel all the reserve she had rapidly start slipping away. If she let this go on any longer she would lose control completely. She had to act now.

Summoning up the wind, she blew Eric back.

Caught off guard by the strong sudden wind, he flew backwards and slammed into the opposite wall of the corridor, thumping his head. Terra was instantly sorry she'd done it. She'd gotten too worked up and hadn't paid enough attention to what she was doing. All she wanted to do was push him away because she knew she'd never be strong enough to do it herself. Instead she'd thrown him across the hall.

"Eric," she started, wanting to explain. "Eric . . . I . . ."

He put his hand up so silence her. He was angry, more than angry he was hurt.

"I swear to the Creator Terra I don't know what to do with you!" He walked toward her and she shrank back against the wall.

"I don't understand!" He exclaimed the hurt of Terra's reaction plain on his face. "You told me this was what you wanted! You said you wanted me to tell you how I felt and I did!"

"When did I do that?" She demanded, her fear about hurting his feelings slowly fading.

"This morning in the dream!" Eric was beyond angry now. He had been so happy this morning when she'd told him that she wanted to know how he felt and that she wanted to be held and kissed by him the way he'd been dreaming about doing for the past few years. It was all he'd wanted to hear her say for longer than he could say.

He finally finds the perfect moment, a moment when he was overcome by the love he felt for her. She was building a home for orphaned children and not only was it going to be named for him, but it was for him. He'd talked with her so many times about this childhood and how difficult things had been being orphaned at such a young age. She'd always say how sorry she was that he'd had to suffer for so long, alone. She would hold him and tell him that he wasn't alone anymore.

There couldn't have been a more perfect time to tell her.

Now . . . she was acting like she didn't even know what he was talking about.

"What dream?!" Terra demanded.

"My dream this morning! You showed up wearing the same dress you're wearing now and told me to tell you how I felt! You said you wanted me to take you in my arms, hold you, tell you, and then kiss you!"

Terra's jaw dropped.

She had done no such thing.

She didn't even know how to do that!

"I *never* said that," she declared. "I *wouldn't* say that to you, not now anyway. Eric I don't know what you saw in your dream, or what you think you saw, but I swear to you that did not come from me."

Eric exploded! "How can you stand there in the same dress you were wearing in the dream and lie to me!?"

"I'm not . . ."

"Shut up!" He shouted. His shoulders were up, he was beyond anger, he was furious.

Terra stopped, he'd never yelled like this before. He'd never been this angry with her.

"I'm done," he roared! "I can't handle this anymore!"

"Eric . . ." she whispered.

"You can't treat people like this! You act like you love me, you let me hold you and kiss you. Send me dreams where you tell me that

351

you want me too. Then you turn around and use your magic against me!

"I can't take this anymore! I'm done with the games and childishness. Either you love me or you don't, I won't do this in between anymore!"

"Eric," she pleaded. She wanted to tell him how she felt, tell him everything he meant to her, but she couldn't. She couldn't put her wants and feelings above his safety. He knew that.

"Terra princess or not, I swear if you don't answer me . . ."

"I CAN'T!" She shouted. "Damn it Eric you *know* I can't tell you these things! I can't tell you how I feel. It's not about what I want! I can't put you in that kind of danger. I can't have feelings for you or for anyone! I told you this! You knew what this was from the beginning . . . I can't . . . I can't change that now." She had started strong, fueled by her anger and frustration. By the time she ended she was near tears.

"Cant' or won't?" He demanded bitterly.

"Both," she sobbed, feeling helplessly swept along by the torrent of emotions.

"Do you have *any* idea what I've given up for this, for you?"

"Eric."

"I'm a man, a man who has waited patiently for you to finally decide I was worth caring about. You told me once that you cared for me and since then you have hinted and insinuated that you loved me but you've never said it! Still, like an idiot I waited for you! And for what? For you to shove me away again and act like you don't know what I'm talking about!

"I'm done with the games and I'm done with the waiting. Either you tell me now, what I need to know, what I deserve to know, or I'm walking away."

She knew he wasn't bluffing, she could feel his resolve through the bond. He would leave, he would walk away and she would never see him again. Even knowing all that, knowing she could lose him, she still couldn't put her wants above his saftey. She hung her head and felt the tears start to run down her face. She couldn't say, not matter how much she wanted to.

"Say something goddamn it!" He shouted at her. "I'm giving up Terra don't you get that?! This is it, this is goodbye!"

She looked at him and met his stare. As much as he wanted her to say something, she didn't need to. He could see clearly in her eyes exactly what her answer was. When he started to shake his head disbelievingly, she hung her head again.

"I can't believe this," he groaned, the anger back in his voice. "For four years I have loved you and waited for you to be able to tell me you loved me. Four years I've waited!" He closed most of the distance between them in a quick step.

Terra was still against the wall and unable to shrink away from the anger she knew she deserved.

He put a finger under her chin and lifted her face so she was looking at him. "I'm done, Terra. I can't, no, I won't do this anymore." He bent and kissed her softly. He dropped his hand and stepped away. "I'm going to find your father and officially resign my duties as your Guard. Goodbye Princess." He placed his fist over his heart and formally saluted her before walking away.

Terra stood, still up against the wall, tears running like rivers down her face, and closed her half of the bond. It wasn't an easy thing to do by any means, and it usually left her feeling empty inside.

Not that it mattered now.

She would keep her side of the bond closed until it finally faded. At least now, she thought to herself, Eric would be safe. There would be no point in anyone or anything targeting him if he was no longer connected to her.

"Princess?"

Terra looked up, a wild hope in her heart that Eric had come back for her.

Master Bell was standing just outside the classroom door. When he saw her face his eyes went wide and he rushed over.

"Terra," he asked dropping her title. "Tell me what's happened? Are you alright?"

"Hello Master Bell," she whispered weakly. "I'm sorry if I'm late for my lesson."

"Terra," he sighed, wrapping an arm around her shoulders. "Why don't you come with me and we'll talk inside ok?"

"Ok."

Chapter 9

Bell led Terra into the classroom and closed the door. He sat her down on one of large benches and took the seat next to her. He had heard shouting out in the hall and had come to see what the matter was. Finding Terra the way he did made him worry. If she and Eric had a falling out right now it could be detrimental to the plans he and the King had for her.

She would need the strength of her Guard to keep her going and to deal with the emotional fallout that would certainly ensue after it was all over. Eric was going to be the only thing keeping her together. If their fight was bad enough, it could cost them everything they'd spent the last four years preparing for.

"He left," she muttered quietly, her voice rough.

"Who's left?" Bell asked, fearing the worst.

"Eric," she sobbed as her tears came down faster. "He left."

Bell considered this for a moment. "Terra, can you tell me what happened?"

She took a deep shaking breath and tried to speak. All she succeeded in doing was sobbing a little louder. Whatever happened must have been bad indeed for her to be reacting this way.

"Would you like some tea?" He asked. "It will help soothe your throat."

Terra nodded but didn't speak.

He stood and moved to the back of class room where he kept his desk. He took some water from a jar he kept in the room and poured it in to two glasses. He went to his herb cabinet and pulled out mint, chamomile, and lavender. He considered a few other herbs and finally pulled out a small vile containing essence of nightflower. It was a rare bloom that wasn't native to Sol. It came from the black woods in heart of the Ursa Kingdom.

A few drops of it in Terra's tea should calm her enough to be able to speak. It was a nearly tasteless liquid that would be undetectable when combined with the other ingredients.

Bell mixed the herbs into both cups and added a few drops of the nightflower to Terra's. He took both in his hands and summoned up fire as he had taught Terra to do. Fire sprang from his fingers and started to warm both cups. After just a few moments the tea was bubbling and ready to be served.

"Here you are," Bell said, offering her a cup.

"Thank you," she replied, blindly accepting the tea he offered. She put the cup her lips and sipped the tea, thankful for the temporary heat it offered her. She was so cold inside it was nice to feel the warmth flow through her.

Once the liquid hit her stomach, she started to feel better. It felt like the warmth of the tea spread throughout her entire body. It didn't take the pain of Eric's words away, but it did help with the aftermath. She stopped sobbing and her breath started to come easier. After a few more drinks her tears dried and she could feel her brain start to process things easier.

"Nightflower?" She asked.

Bell smiled, "You remember your herbs well."

"You taught me well."

"So it would seem. Are you feeling better?"

"I am feeling . . . more in control."

"Can you tell me what happened? I heard shouting in the hall but by the time I got there you were already alone."

Terra let out a long low breath. She needed to talk to someone about what was going on. Why not Master Bell? He'd proven in the past that he could be trusted and things that were told to him were not told to anyone else.

"Eric and I . . . I don't really know what we were, but he's done. He's gone to my father to officially resign his position as my Royal Guard."

Bell was shocked for a moment, but he recovered quickly. "What happened?"

"Master Bell," she whispered, not really wanting to get into things. While also wanting so much to talk to someone about it and talk to someone about her feelings and whether or not she was crazy for telling Eric what she had. Maybe she was making things harder than they had to be.

"Terra you know there is nothing you cannot tell me." He prompted.

"I know, it's just so much to tell and some of its . . . complicated."

"It might do you well to talk about it." He prompted again.

"I can't tell you everything."

"Then tell me only what you can."

With a sigh she started, "Eric has, for some time, had feelings for me. Strong feelings."

"He's in love with you," Bell said matter of factly.

"He told you?" She asked disbelievingly.

"He didn't have to. It was obvious in the way he looks and acts towards you."

"It is?" She asked, disheartened.

Bell nodded.

"Great," she croaked miserably. "So apparently last night Eric had a dream where I told him that I wanted him to tell me how he felt and hold me and . . ." she hesitated. "He seemed to think I sent him the dream. He thinks I sent him the dream because I wanted him to tell me those things. But I never did." Tears started flowing down her face again as she thought about the look of anger in Eric's eyes as he walked away from her.

"Did you tell him that?"

"Yes," she sniffled, drinking more tea. "He didn't believe. He told me I was leading him on and he was done. Done with me, done with being my guard, done with . . . everything."

Bell was quiet for a moment as he considered what to say to the young princess. Somehow they needed to mend things between Terra and her guard if plans were to progress. There was very little he could do right now, both were worked up and angry. They needed time to calm down.

"Terra, it is my belief that you and Eric will be fine. He cares a great deal for you as you do for him. I believe that he dreamed a dream he wanted to see, as we are all guilty of doing from time to time. He acted on that dream and created a rift between you two, a rift that looks larger than it really is."

She looked up and searched her teacher's eyes. "Do you really think it's not that bad?"

"I feel very confident in saying that things will work themselves out, in time."

"How much time?" She asked, "What am I supposed to do until then?"

"You both need time and some space to clear you heads and get perspective. Eric is already off cooling down. You should do the same."

"How? Where?"

"Why don't you go for a ride?" Bell suggested knowing she needed to be out of the castle today for plans to progress. "You haven't been out on your mare in months."

"I suppose I could do that," she considered, warming up to the idea of getting away for a while. "How though? With all the increases in shadow activity and the unruly nature of the people outside the city walls, Father would never let me go alone."

Bell considered for a moment. "Wasn't there a young man that Eric trusted a great deal, something with a J?"

"John," she answered quietly. "He was a new recruit when Eric was first assigned as my guard. He's been a good friend of Eric's for a long time now. Eric trusts him."

"Do you trust him?"

"I do," she replied without thought. "He's a good man."

"Why don't you go and prepare you horse and I'll send for young John to accompany you."

"What about my lesson?" She asked, not wanting to miss out on her favorite part of the day.

"We can have lessons tonight." He assured her.

"Thank you Master Bell," she said, "I can't tell you how much appreciate it."

"Don't think anything of it," Bell assured her as he was overcome by an overwhelming sense of guilt. He knew what was coming for her. He knew how much harder her life was about to become and a great deal of it would be at his owns hands. He put a hand on her shoulder and smiled reassuringly all the while knowing he would be the person who shattered her.

Terra had just finished brushing her horse with the curry comb when John came walking toward the stables. He smiled as he walked over and saluted her formally. He was wearing light armor today, with a chainmail tunic over his usual guard uniform. She was confused for a moment before she remembered he father saying something about how all guards, City and Castle alike had to wear armor when leaving the safety of the walls.

"Princess," he greeted rising, "the Master Wizard said you needed me to accompany you on a ride. Is Guard Reynolds unavailable?"

"Eric is . . . busy," she lied. "I was hoping to take a ride and clear my head. I was wondering if you could accompany me."

"Of course Princess," he replied smiling. "It would be my honor to go with you. I have heard tell of your riding ability. It would be nice to see if the truth measures up to the legend."

"Are you insinuating I can't ride sir?" Terra laughed.

"Not at all Princess," he smiled, offering his hand to help the princess into the saddle.

Gripping the pommel Terra stepped up onto John's hand and vaulted herself into the saddle. She settled in and made sure her dress was covering her legs and that her dark green cloak was spread out behind her. She reached up and stroked her horse's neck lovingly

"Who's a good girl, eh Venus?" She cooed to her mare. Venus shook her head and whinnied softly.

"Thank you John," Terra sighed as he came alongside her riding a beautiful chestnut stallion. "Are you ready?"

"I am," he said happy to be on a horse. "Where are we riding to?"

"I'm not sure," she answered feeling the wind rustle her hair. She wanted to be out and free for a while. She wanted to just be Terra. Not the princess or the jail keeper, just Terra. "Let's see where the horses want to go."

Eric stalked the halls for well over an hour before he finally felt himself cool down enough to think. He couldn't believe the way Terra had acted. After the dream and everything else that had been said today! He couldn't understand how she could stand there and act like she had no idea what was going on?! Even after all that she had stood there and kissed him the way she had.

Thinking about it made his blood turn hot. He had held her close and pressed her into him. He would have had her in that hallway if she'd been anyone other than the princess. He wanted her in a way that made it hard for him to walk.

He stopped and leaned against the stone wall of the castle.

He loved her so much it physically pained him.

That was done now, he reminded himself. He couldn't keep hurting himself for her. Not when there was no sign that things would ever change. As her guard he'd stood by her through so much. When her mother told her she wasn't wanted, when her sister had "accidentally" pushed her down the stairs to her room, when the shadows increased and her father had stopped spending time with her, and when she and Grey had that huge blow out over something stupid she wouldn't really tell him about. Through all of that he had stood by her and been there for her no matter what she needed. In all that time he'd only asked for one thing from her. That she be honest with him.

She lied to him today.

When she said she had no knowledge of the dream she sent him.

She lied and he could no longer take the pain that was associated with being her guard. He had meant to find the King but was too mad to face anyone right then. He would head to the weapons room and practice with his sword for a while. Anything to get his mind off Terra.

Terra and John rode down the lane that led from the gates of the castle town out into the kingdom. Woods on either side with the river that flowed passed the town and through the Queen's garden to the left. They rode past people coming and going in and out of town, some fresh from the lake with baskets of fish, others coming from nearby towns with vegetables and fruits. All called and waved at them as they rode.

Some people she knew and called to them by name. She enquired as to their lives and their family member's wellbeing. John could see in the people's faces how much it meant to have the princess remember their names. Everyone seemed to be glad to see a member of the royal family outside the gates again.

When they came upon the first fork in the road Terra let Venus decide their course. Going right would have meant taking the road to the town of Pisces. A small but prosperous town bordered on three sides by rivers, it was home to Sol's largest fish market.

Going left would lead them into the woods and eventually down the sloping cliffs to the beach. It was a long road that zigged and zagged through the densest parts of the wood. It did wind past a number of small lakes and streams and if you went deep enough in and far enough down you can see the water falls that were rumored to be home to merfolk and pixies. It was beautiful road when you had time to take it.

"Which way Princess?" John asked from her left.

"I've decided to let Venus choose our course," she explained, already feeling better. Being outside the castle walls in the fresh air with no one looking at her expectantly, it was the best she'd felt in a while.

"Your horse?" He asked amused.

"Yes, Venus tell us where we should go." At the sound of her name the mare's ears perked up and she looked around. She continued to the left walking toward the woods and what looked like some tasty grazing.

"It would appear we're going through the woods," she laughed bright and happy.

"Is that wise Princess?" He asked, a note of concern in his voice.

"It's not even noon yet," she said glancing up at the sun. "We have plenty of time to walk the horses before it gets dark."

"I suppose that's true," John muttered checking the sun. "So long as we aren't gone for too long."

"Not to worry," she reassured him, "everything will be just fine. Now what do you say we stretch their legs a little?"

"Princess!" John exclaimed in fake shock. "Are suggesting a race?"

"Me!" Terra exclaimed, matching his false shock. "Never I!" Then as quickly as she could get the words out, she shouted, "Mark, set, GO!"

She signaled Venus to run the mare answered happily. She threw her head back and started galloping toward the woods.

"Cheating will get you nowhere!" John hollered from behind her. Terra heard him urge his horse on and before she knew it they were neck and neck heading for the woods. She urged Venus on faster and faster. Together they started to pull away from John and his mustang. After a few seconds she realized that a war horse like that should have been able to out run her aging mare in a matter of moments.

She glanced behind her and stared at John. "Letting me win?" She demanded laughing.

"It would seem bad form to beat the princess," he called back.

"It would be worse form if I had to go back to the castle boasting to every person I could find of your inadequacies in riding. Not sure what that would do to your form, but I'd wager it'd be bad!"

John was suddenly passing her up and in just a matter of seconds he had reached the beginning of the woods and won the race. Terra slowed Venus down and came to a stop next to John. She clapped and bowed to him.

"I concede to your victory," she laughed. "Well played John."

"Thank you Princess," John replied breathless. "Am I now entitled to a prize?"

"I'm afraid I haven't a prize to give you."

"Well how about my prize is that you must answer me a question," John suggested.

"That sounds fair," she answered, weary. "So long as I can answer, I will."

"Good," John said still smiling. He made a noise to his horse and they started down the path and into the trees. Terra nudged Venus on and followed him down the road into the woods. She came up alongside him and waited patiently for him to ask his question.

"So my question for you is this," John said once they were well in to the woods. "What's really going on between you and Guard Reynolds?"

Terra felt herself go pale. She had just started to forget about that scene with Eric in the hall outside her schoolroom. She was starting to feel better and be happy. Eric was a distant thought. With one word, it all came rushing back.

"I'm sorry Princess," he said immediately. "It was not my place to ask such a question."

"It's alright John," she assured him weakly. "The truth is I don't always know what's going on between Eric and I. There are times when he's my best friend and times when I can't stand the sight of him. It's complicated."

"I see," he said thinking. "He speaks of you often. Of your strength and you bravery and how he admires the sacrifices you make for those you love."

She knew John was trying to cheer her up. He must have guessed that Terra and Eric had a falling out when he was summoned to ride with her. He was trying to tell her that Eric cared about her. She already knew that. Knowing how much didn't seem to make the hole forming in her chest feel any better.

"Thank you John," she whispered.

"What's that?" He asked looking ahead. The road sloped down and around to the left, just beyond the bend there was something on the side of the road. It was too far ahead to see clearly yet. Terra squinted but couldn't make it out.

"Let's go find out," she suggested, urging Venus on. Together they trotted down the road and around the bend. On the side of the road, nearly over turned, there was a large white carriage. There was no crest on the door and no markings to say what town or kingdom it hailed from. Two of the wheels were broken and as far as Terra could see, there wasn't another horse in sight.

As they approached someone cried out softly in pain.

"Hello?" Terra called.

"Princess maybe you should wait here," John whispered unsheathing his sword. He kept his eyes fixed on the wreck ahead of them so he didn't notice until it was too late that Terra had already slipped off her horse and was making her way toward the over turned carriage.

"Princess!" John called leaping down from his horse and running up alongside her. "You were supposed to wait on your horse."

Terra waved him off and kept walking toward the carriage. "Hello? Is someone there? We can help."

"Please," A man's voice called from the front of the carriage.

Terra ran forward followed closely by John. When they reached the edge of the road they could see a man lying under the carriage, pinned down by the weight of the vehicle. He was older with white hair and brown eyes. He was wearing some kind of livery Terra didn't recognize. Whoever he served they weren't from the Sol Kingdom.

"Dear Creator," she whispered as she rushed forward, down the small embankment that lined the road. She reached out and put a hand on the carriage for support as she precariously made her way to where the man lay.

"Terra," John worried, not sure about using her title. "Are you sure that's a wise idea?"

"He's hurt," she stated, "We have to help him."

"Thank you," the man muttered as Terra finally made her way round the empty yolk of the carriage.

"Don't worry," she reassured him, "We'll get you out of this."

"Who were you driving?" John asked, "And where have they gone?"

"John," she snapped, "Wait until we get him out of here to start questioning him."

John, looking unhappy about Terra's over eagerness to help, sheathed his sword and made his way down. He could see instantly there was no way they were getting that man out alive. By his guess, the man was the driver. Something must have happened and he was thrown from his bench seconds before the whole carriage was tipped. He had fallen flat on his back and the carriage had landed directly on top of him, pinning his right hand and everything below the chest.

Even if he and Terra were strong enough to lift the carriage, once it was up the man would die. John had never seen wounds like this, but he had heard of them. There was no way to save the man and judging by the way he was looking at Terra, he already knew he was beyond their help.

"Please," he coughed, blood coming from his mouth. "You must find my lady and help her. She couldn't have gotten far."

365

"Let's worry about getting you out of here first," Terra said trying to smile reassuringly.

"Terra," John whispered, grabbing her arm. He looked to the man on the ground and then back to her. Slowly he shook his head. "There isn't anything more we can do for him."

"There might not be anything more you can do for him," she countered, "but there is a bit more I can do." She pulled her arm from Johns and faced the carriage again. Closing her eyes she placed both of her hands on the white wood. "When I get this clear, pull him out."

John stared at her dumbfounded. How could she possible move an entire carriage by herself? It would take at least five strong men to get that thing to budge and inch. Terra was a beautiful woman, but not exactly strong.

Taking a moment to center herself, Terra breathed in and out three times. She felt the ground beneath her feet. She felt the sky above her. She focused on the wind that blew softly at first, but at her beckoning began to blow harder. Silently she called to the wind to help her lift the carriage in her hands. She asked it to help save a man's life and set the carriage right.

There was a sudden rushing of air all around her. It lifted the little hairs Mammy had curled and blew them around. Her dress was blown around and at times was pulled tight against her legs. Keeping her focus on the carriage, she started to push. At first it didn't move, and then she could feel the wind whooshing and swirling around her arms. She pushed again and this time the carriage began to creak and wobble. Slowly it started to roll back up the side of the road.

Terra's foot slipped in the mud and for a moment she was sure she would slide back down the embankment and the carriage would drop down again. A second later John was standing behind her pushing her back up. With her back now supported, she pushed the carriage again. It rocked up and out of Terra's hands and was almost back on its wheels when it lost momentum and came rocking back toward them.

"Brace yourself!" She shouted, seconds before it hit her hands.

Both she and John slid under the weight of the carriage.

John pushed against Terra and in turn she pushed the carriage. Summoning up all the wind she could, she gave the carriage one last push. It creaked and seemed to complain as it flew up out of the ditch and back up onto the road. John, unable to see the carriage with his shoulder squared against Terra's back, pushed again. She flew forward into the mud as John stumbled and joined her.

The princess didn't mind the mud; she kept her eyes fixed on the carriage. It rocked back and forth for a moment, like it was trying to decide if it would stay or if it should crash back down on the three people below. It rocked back down on the road and stilled. Covered in mud and leaning heavily, it rested.

Knowing time was against them, Terra rolled on to her side and slid back down the embankment, effectively covering her white stockings and bloomers in mud. She took no notice of this as she hit the bottom ran toward the man who had moments ago been trapped. She ran to him and then dropped to her knees to help.

"Thank you," the man wheezed, a strange rattle in his chest. "You must find my lady . . ."

"Don't speak," she whispered. "Just hold on." She pulled her cloak from her shoulders and balling it up, she placed it under the man's head to help make him more comfortable. She came around his side and placed her hands over his torso, leaving about two to three inches of space between them. She closed her eyes and tried to focus on healing the way Bell had taught her.

Terra had proven to be a fair healer, but with so much for her to learn, Bell hadn't spent long teaching her. He had covered the basics and when she proved she could do that, he had moved on to other things.

As she focused on the man's injuries, her hands began to glow with the familiar light of a healer. White light, colored here and there with flecks of purple and silver, emanated from her hands and seemed

367

to sink in through the man's clothes. He began to glow with the same light as Terra passed her hands up and down the length of him.

After less than a minute the light stopped and she opened her eyes. She looked at the man and whispered, "I'm so sorry."

"It's alright my dear," the man wheezed. "I knew before you arrived I was beyond salvation. I thank you all the same for taking the carriage away, Princess Terra of Sol."

"You know who I am?" She asked, shocked.

"Oh yes. Even so far away as Virgo at the edge of the Moon Kingdom, we have heard tell of a princess whose beauty is only comparable to the magic she possesses. She is Terra, Princess of Sol, marked by the Creator with white wings that spread across her shoulders as proof of her divinity."

Terra's jaw seemed to hang open. No one said things like this about her. People generally didn't even know who she was if she wasn't traveling with a banner that said she was royalty. People knew Diana; she's the one who's in the prophecy, the one that everyone loves. This man must have been mistaken in his names.

"Sir, while I am flattered, I'm afraid you have me confused with my sister Diana," she whispered gently, tears in her eyes as she heard him struggle to breath.

"Diana is the fair haired princess of prophecy," the man replied. "There is no confusion. But Princess please I need you to find my lady. She was pregnant when we set out from Virgo weeks ago, since then she had given birth to a strapping young son. Both were healthy after the birth but my lady hasn't had a restful night's sleep since then."

He stopped and started to cough violently. Blood sprayed out of his mouth. His body seemed to be racked with pain as coughed and coughed.

Unable to stand more, Terra reached out and placed a hand on the man's heart and on his head. Her hands began to glow again and he was suddenly still. He took his first unobstructed breath and seemed to visibly calm.

"I can't heal you," she whispered, silent tears running down her dirty face. "But I can take the pain away."

"Thank you Princess," he muttered with a faint smile. "Your reputation is well deserved."

"Shhh, rest now sir. You have served your lady well. We will find her and bring her safely from the woods. Her and her young babe. Sleep now and know that you have seen your task done. There is not to hold you here. Go and bask in the light of your creator."

As she spoke the man's eyes slowly closed. He smiled as his last breath escaped from his lips. Terra's hand's stopped glowing on their own, signaling that the man was dead. She sent up a quiet prayer to the creator to take this man's soul and show it all the kindness and love he deserved for a life lost in service.

She turned away suddenly and coughed roughly for a moment. She spit blood and quickly wiped it from her lips, hoping John wouldn't have noticed.

He noticed.

"Princess?!" He shouted alarmed. "Are you alright? What's happened to you?"

"It's nothing," she assured him.

"Princess you coughed up blood, which is not something that means nothing. What's happened?"

Terra sighed. "I took his pain," she explained. "You can't just take pain and make it disappear. It has to go somewhere. Very skilled healers can turn it into nothing but I am not that skilled."

"So you took his pain into yourself," he asked. "Wait, does that mean that you'll die?"

"No," she assured him, feeling herself start to fight off the pain. "I took only enough to make him comfortable in the end. I'll be fine in a few moments. Can you . . ."

Terra was cut off by the sound of the horses whinnying and stamping their feet. John ran up the side of the embankment in time to see a cloaked figure ride off on the princess's mare.

"Stop! Thief!" He yelled running down the road a ways. He stopped and ran back to the princess.

"Someone's taken you horse," he said quickly. "Can you walk?" He offered her his hand. She took it but found she could not make herself stand. Her legs shook violently underneath her when she tried. She looked like a new born colt trying to walk.

"It's no good," she told John. "I'll be down for at least the next ten minutes. Take your horse catch her. We can't let her get away."

"You think it's his lady?"

"I do. She's just given birth and gone through a terrible accident. She might not be thinking straight. We have to stop her before she hurts herself. You have to go."

"I won't leave you here, unprotected and unable to defend yourself."

"We don't have much choice."

"Yes we do." He ran back to where his mustang was shying nervously away from the tree John had left him near. It took a second to calm him enough that so that John could grab the reigns and lead him back down to where Terra was still trying to stand. He left his horse on the road and slid back down the embankment.

He pulled the cloak gently out from under the man's head and draped it over this body. He then turned to Terra.

"With your permission Princess," He said.

Confused, she only nodded.

John bent down and scooped her up his arms like a baby. He turned and walked back up the embankment to his horse. Terra sat in his arms, mildly shocked. John was shorter than most guards, hardly taller than she was. He also didn't look terribly strong. However, the way he carried her up onto the road suggests that her previous assessments of his strength fell tragically short of the truth.

"I'm going to set you down, do you think you can lean against Zeus and stand?"

"I think so."

John set her feet on the ground and leaned her against the horse. Terra rested her head on his hindquarters and breathed in the sweet smell of horse as John vaulted up into the saddle. Carefully he reached down and offered her his hand. Grasping it, she was pulled up onto Zeus's back. John took less than a second to position her in front of him before he grabbed the reigns.

"Hold on," he shouted as he urged Zeus on. He leaned forward in the saddle and called out, "HUP HUP!"

Zeus took off like a shot out of a cannon. Terra was thrown into John who seemed to not notice at all as he took off after the stolen horse and its rider. Being on a young mustang chasing an older mare, it took very little time for them to catch sight of Venus just clearing the woods.

John leaned further forward, Zeus seemed to catch the meaning and put on a burst of speed. As they emerged from woods Terra was shocked to find that clouds now covered the sky. Dark clouds that threatened to rain down on them at any moment.

"We almost have her," John shouted over the sounds of wind whipping by and horse's hooves on the dirt road. "Wait, what are they doing!?"

Terra turned her head carefully and looked forward. She suddenly understood John's shock. As she watched, the huge wooden doors that lead into the castle town were swinging closed. At this distance she could just make out the soldiers on the wall, their armor glinting in what was left of the afternoon light.

Moments before the doors were closed a wall of shadows sprang up suddenly blocking the front of the gate completely. There was no way to get through now. There were at least two dozen shadows standing so close together there was no light visible between them.

Strangest of all, every one of the shadows had their eyes closed.

Terra watched as the hooded figure jumped suddenly from the horse's back, hit the ground and rolled. She was on her feet in a

371

heartbeat. Venus, scared and unable to stop in time, ran directly into the shadows.

Venus screamed in a way that made Terra's blood run cold. She watched, horrified, as her horse suddenly ceased to be. Still the shadows hovered in place, taking no notice of the horse they had just killed. Terra's heart ached for the loss of her old friend.

"Whoa," John called out to Zeus, slowing him down as the approached the front of the city walls.

"What's happening?" Terra wondered out loud.

At the sound of her voice, every shadow's eyes snapped open, zeroing in on her location so quickly it didn't seem possible. Lighting struck one of the guard towers that rose up off the wall and thunder clapped loudly overhead.

Zeus cried out loudly and bucked.

Caught off guard, Terra slipped from the front of the saddle and fell to the ground. She landed flat on her back and smacked her head against the packed dirt road with a sickening thud.

For a moment the world spun as she stared up at the dark grey sky.

She shook her head and the world came back in a sharp relief.

Zeus, still frightened by the presence of the shadows and the thunder booming overhead, continued to buck and shy as John fought to control him. Terra saw the horse's hooves land dangerously close to her leg.

Terrified, she rolled on to her hands and knees and scrambled to get away. A hand shot out in front of her suddenly. Not thinking, she reached out and grabbed the hand. There was the sound of grunting, and the Terra was pulled to her feet.

"Thank you," She said, finding herself face to face with the woman who'd moments ago stolen her horse. Her hood had blown back in the fall and her long red hair was falling in cascades down her shoulders. Her dress was dark blue and filled with intricate details. In her arms she was carrying a small bundle that stirred and cried. She shifted the bundle to her other arm and Terra caught sight of the babies little face.

He was adorable.

"Least I could do," she replied, a northern accent heavy in her speech. "After stealing your horse."

"Look out," Terra cried, pushing the woman behind her as Zeus bucked near them. Another lightning strike sent the horse running down the lane toward the woods again. John was thrown clear off the horse as he ran.

Terra rushed forward as he fell and managed to get under him before he hit the ground. Together they fell backward into the dirt. John wasn't too heavy so it didn't hurt badly when he landed on top of her. It did, however, manage to knock the wind out of her.

"Terra!" John cried rolling off of her. He jumped to his feet and pulled her up. "What in the name of the Creator did you do that for? I could have killed you!"

"You hardly scratched me," she grunted, accepting the hand.

"I hate to interrupt," the woman called running over, "But we have bigger problems right now."

Terra and John turned to see the wall of shadows was slowly progressing closer to them. It had covered nearly ten feet in the time it took Terra to catch John.

"Dear spirits," the princess whispered.

"I don't think they'll be much help right now," the woman remarked.

Taking a calculated risk, Terra looked up at their eyes. Even without pupils, she could tell they were all looking at her. She stepped right and then left. Where ever she went their eyes followed. They were here for her.

"Damn," she muttered. "John take this young woman . . ."

"Persephone," she interjected. "My name is Persephone."

"Ok, John take Persephone and her son and when I say, run around the wall of shadows. When the men at the gate see it's you they should let you in."

373

"Princess I will not abandon you here to die. Not only that, but the shadows would be on us in an instant if we get to close."

"No they won't," Terra countered. "It's me they want. I'm the only one they're after."

"It's true," Persephone added. "They didn't open their eyes or even start moving until after she started speaking."

"It doesn't matter!" John shouted. "You're my princess and I won't let you come to harm!"

"Damn it John!" She yelled, she could tell they didn't have much time. "I *am* your princess and I am ordering you to take this woman and her child to safety."

John looked insolently at Terra for a moment, ready to disobey. Instead he glowered at her and saluted. "As you wish *highness*." His voice was hurt and a little icy but Terra didn't have time to worry about his feelings right then.

"I'm going to run forward and then bank left toward the woods. When I do that they should follow me. Head right and slip around them."

"What about you?" He demanded.

"I can handle a few shadows. Now get ready." Terra took off running right at the shadows. She banked sharply left and cried, "Now!"

John grabbed Persephone's wrist and dragged her as he ran to the right as Terra had instructed. Just as she had predicted, the shadows paid no attention to either he or Persephone. They ran around and past the shadows, all the way to the gates of the city.

"Let us in!" John cried as he banged on the doors.

A few heads popped over the wall above the doors. There was a sudden shouting followed by the sound of the small wooden door, placed inside the larger door, opening up. A solider John didn't recognize ushered them in and promptly closed the door again, sliding the bolt all the way home.

"What are you doing you fool!" He shouted. "That's Princess Terra out there!"

Terra watched as John and Persephone slipped through the smaller door to safety. With a sigh, she turned back to the shadows. They had followed her to the edge of the woods. She knew to try and escape through the trees would be suicide. She had to lead them back the other way so she could get around them.

She started forward and stopped. They were beginning to circle around her, pushing her back to the trees. She was completely blocked off before she could formulate a plan of escape. They started to push in, forcing her back step by step. A sudden feeling of dread forced Terra to turn quickly and face the woods.

Another near dozen shadows emerged from the trees behind her. They closed ranks with others and formed a tight circle around her. There was no escape at all. With nearly forty shadows surrounding her, she knew she was out numbered several times over.

A few shadows she could purify and be safe. This many, however, this was more than she could handle on her own, still weak from helping the man pass on. She knew she was done for. Even if John had run straight to the castle for help, he would never be back in time to save her.

At least she had managed to save that woman and her child. John though, she knew he would blame himself for this. He would feel the guilt and responsibility of her death. She couldn't put that on him. He didn't deserve to carry that around.

Terra closed her eyes, not caring about her impending doom as it circled around her. She reached out with her mind and searched for John. Bell had taught her how to reach out with her mind and project her consciousness over distance. She didn't need to appear before him she just needed him to hear her.

She found him, running for the castle. He was still so far away; he wouldn't even make it to the doors in time.

"John," she said, knowing he would hear her in his mind. "I'm sorry John. I thought I could get away. I thought I'd have time and I was wrong. I need you to not blame yourself for my death. There was

375

nothing you could have done to prevent this. You did as I ordered and saved that woman and her son.

"Thank you for that. Thank you for being a good friend and doing what I asked of you in the end even though you didn't want to."

Terra hesitated for a moment. Taking another deep breath she continued. "John I need you to tell Eric something for me. I know he might be mad at first, but please I need him to know this before I'm gone."

'Tell him I love him,' Terra's voice echoed in John's head. *'Tell him I'm sorry I couldn't tell him before. He knows why. Please tell him how sorry I am that I couldn't tell him in person.'*

There was a pause and John feared what the sudden silence meant.

'And tell him that I took down as many of these bastards as I could before they got me.'

John pushed his legs to run faster. He screamed at people to get out of the way as he ran, screaming for Eric. He was almost to the doors when he felt the princess in his head one last time.

'Tell Eric he's the only thing that made my life worth living. He was the only person who ever saw me for me. Tell him how much that meant to me and how sorry I am I never told him. Thank you John, for everything and I'm sorry, again.'

Just like that the connection was severed and John could no longer feel the princess. She was gone. He slowed for a moment, tears in his eyes making it hard for him to see. He had known Terra for a while now and in that time he'd grown to respect her. She was more than his princess, she was his friend. The sudden loss of her hit him like a two ton weight to the chest.

He stumbled and fell to his knees, tears flowing freely from his face.

Hands he couldn't see grasped his arms and shoulders. They hauled him to his feet and helped him keep running toward the castle gates. He couldn't see who was helping him, but he was grateful for their aid.

"Hold on John," a familiar voice said gruffly. "We'll get you to the castle."

John blinked away his tears. Holding his right arm was the Harold, the Master Builder, on his left was a man he knew to be the Master Carpenter for the Kingdom, though he didn't know the man's name. Both had tears in their eyes and Harold had a few streaming down his face.

"What's going on?" He asked.

Harold shifted so he was now supporting John's weight as the carpenter jumped into a wagon tied to a horse. He extended his hands to John who took them without question. He was pulled into the wagon and the Master builder climbed in behind him.

Without a word, the other man grabbed the reigns and sent the horse flying down the main road to the castle gate.

"I don't understand," John shouted. "Why are you doing this?"

"We heard it too," Harold said grimly. "As you ran past it was like somebody tuned us into your conversation with the princess. We heard the whole thing."

"You heard all of that?" He asked, horrified that these men now knew how badly he had failed the Princess.

"We did," Harold replied. "When we saw your direction we grabbed the wagon and raced after you. We nearly ran you over when you dropped suddenly. We stopped the horse and grabbed you. Now we're headed to the castle."

He didn't say it, but John could feel him silently add "before it's too late."

Eric swung his sword down hard and sharp, slicing the top off the practice dummy. With a sword in hand there was very little he couldn't do. He knew how to cut, parry, slice, jab, and he could render a man headless in one swing.

This he knew and this he could break down, analyze and understand. Unlike everything else in his life it seemed. He would never understand things like women.

Women made no sense at all.

He attacked the dummy again.

Women act like they love you, lead you on until you love them too. Make you feel like you're the only one they'll ever love. Lie to you and make you feel like your entire world revolves around them. Then they act all shocked and shaken when tell them how you feel like they asked you to!

Eric brought his sword down in a deadly arc, splitting the dummy in two.

He sheathed his sword, panting heavily. Using the sleeve of his practice tunic, he wiped the sweat from his face and walked over to the nearby window. He opened the shutters and stuck his head outside. The wind blew past gently, cooling his face and carrying the scent of coming rain.

Suddenly the door he had closed for privacy burst open.

Bell came rushing in followed closely behind by John, Harold the Master Builder, and Thomas the Master Carpenter.

Shocked Eric just stared.

"Eric there is not to explain," Bell panted, "Terra is in trouble and you're the only one who can save her."

Eric's heart began to race again. He took a breath and tampered it off. He wouldn't allow himself to jump back into something that might have nothing to do with him.

"What's wrong?" He asked coolly.

"Damn it boy this is not time for you to coddle your wounded pride. She could die!" Bell burst out, his usual calm demeanor gone at the sight of Eric's indifference.

Like a bucket of cold water to the face, Bell's words and appearance snapped him out of his mood. "What's happened? Where is she?" He demanded.

"There's no time to explain," Bell reiterated. "She is just outside the city gates. You need to open you half of the bond and help her. She needs your strength to survive. Without your help she will die!"

Eric was too stunned to speak.

Frustrated, Bell grabbed him by the shoulders and shook him violently. "I don't care if you're feeling hurt or feeling like she betrayed you. You are the *only* person who can help her. Now open you half of the bond and help her!"

"I c . . . can't," Eric stammered. "I didn't even know it was closed."

"Of course it's closed. Your anger and resentment toward her closed it. You have to let all that go if we're going to save Terra. Do you understand? You have to let it go or she will die."

Eric felt suddenly like a child being scolded by a father.

"I don't know how to let it go," he answered timidly. "I don't know how any of this works.

"You have to let you feelings go! Focus on Terra and the bond. Try to connect with her through the bond. Once it's open she can pull strength from you when she needs it." Bell explained as slowly as he could. He knew Eric knew little about magic, but there was no time to coddle him now.

He tried to do as Bell had instructed him. He tried to reach out to Terra through the bond but when he tried he couldn't feel anything. He tried again and again but the result stayed the same. He looked up helpless at Bell who seemed to tower angrily over him.

"I can't reach her," he cried, defeated.

"You cannot fail!" Bell shouted. "There is no more time. You have to do it! DO IT NOW!"

Terra spun around exhausted.

She had managed to take down six of the nearly forty shadows that surrounded her. She was breathing heavily and she could feel her strength start to wane. She didn't know how much longer she could keep going. At this rate she would be dead before the next two shadows fell.

Each time she would purify a shadow, the others would close the circle around her faster. Every few seconds a shadow flew from one side of the circle to the other. Sometimes Terra could dodge it, other times she would purify it as it got close. With each passing action Terra felt herself get closer and closer to the end of her strength.

A shadow came at her from the right, she jumped backward and avoided it, but she stumbled and fell to her knees. She was panting now and her chest was getting tight. She couldn't go on much longer.

She tried to push off the ground to stand, but she was upright for less than a second before her legs gave out. She sank back down to the ground and had to throw herself violently to the left to avoid another shadow. She rolled to the center of the circle and stopped, flat on her back. She was done. Her strength had failed her and there was nothing more she could do.

Around her the shadows slowly moved in closer.

Terra tried to sit up. A sharp pain under her ribs brought her back down. It hurt every time she tried to take a breath. Tears in her eyes, Terra resigned herself to her end. She stared up at the dark grey sky. She could hear thunder somewhere nearby and every so often she could see the faintest light from lightning. She wondered if she would get to see the rain again before she died.

As if the sky were answering her, the rain began to come down. In a few seconds she was soaked. Terra smiled, glad to feel the rain one last time.

Shadows were absorbed by other shadows as they closed in around her. It wouldn't be long now. Terra wondered if John had gotten to Eric. What would he say when he heard she died? Would he happy or sad? Would he blame John for her death? Or would he know that John had done as she had asked him to? She tried to use the bond to reach out to him, but again there was nothing on the other side.

Terra stared at the sky as her tears mixed with the rain.

Grey.

What would happen to Grey if she died? Would he be set free without her magic to hold him in the box? Or would he die in there without her around to pass the barrier? She wondered what his reaction to her death would be. She would never admit it out loud or even to herself, but she would miss him. She had really started to care for him. Terra knew she had been so close to purifying him, she could feel the change in him.

It was too late for all of that now.

There was sudden crackling in the air. Terra looked around to see the shadows were close enough now that should could have reached over and touched them if she wanted. As she waited for death, she could feel something shift suddenly around her. She looked up in time to see lightning strike the ground directly in front of her.

Around Terra the wind picked up suddenly. Swirling around her and blowing the rain around in odd directions. She was suddenly overcome by a huge influx of energy. She could feel it, swirling around her pouring through her. It took the pain from her rips and the exhaustion from her muscles. There was suddenly breath in her lungs and energy enough to stand.

Slowly she rose to her feet, knowing despite this new found energy, time was not on her side. Carefully she took stock of her situation. There were still eight shadows around her closing in fast. She couldn't' get them all one by one, there was no way. They were moving too fast for her to attempt that. She would either have to take them all on at once or this new energy wouldn't change a thing.

Terra thought back to Bell in the classroom. She had done something then that had enabled her purify every shadow in the room. There had been fewer shadows then but the same principles should apply to now. She just had to figure out what she had done.

Taking a few deep breaths she closed her eyes. She could feel a tether; one end attached to her the other to whoever was providing her with their energy. She silently asked the person to help her just a little bit more. She just needed a little more energy and she knew she could take them. She felt another rush of strength as the shadows closed the distance between them. There was only six now, the same as the other day.

"Please," Terra whispered.

She brought her hands up and laced her fingers together like she was praying. Quietly she sent up a prayer of thanks for the person who'd helped her and focused all of the energy she had on the light she always saw when she purified a shadow.

She willed that light to come now, begged it to come forth and saver her again as she had before. There was a strange moment of silence, where Terra could hear nothing, not the rain, not the thunder, not even her own heartbeat.

Then came the thundering boom and the circle of white light exploded out of her hands and rapidly expanded around her, purifying everything around. Each shadow exploded into their own beam of blinding white light. The combination of the ring of light and the shadows exploding made a light around Terra so bright she couldn't see anymore.

Bell, John, Harold, Thomas, Eric and a nearly half the town stood in the arch of the gateway, watching as the dark afternoon lit up like midday. Where the Princess had been standing seconds before, surrounded by shadows, a light suddenly exploded from the earth, blinding everyone who had been watching. In a sea of mixed emotions the people watched as the light began to fade and Terra stood on her own, surrounded by flecks of grass and leaves that had been caught up in the explosion of light.

She stood there, hands clasped under her chin, like she was in prayer. Her dress had been washed clean by the rain, though the sheer cap sleeves had been destroyed and her hair, which had come down during her struggle, blew around her in dark black ringlets soaked by rain. Her shoes were gone too he notice, they could just see the pink of her toes from this distance. She looked like one of the old Goddesses the people in the hills talked about some times.

Terra raised her head and looked up at the people standing on the wall and pouring out of the opened gates. She smiled, seeing everyone was safe. Eric felt more than saw when her eyes met his. She looked like she wanted to say something, but the next second her eyes rolled back and she dropped to the ground.

Everyone cried out as Eric, Bell and John raced forward.

Eric ran and hit the ground sliding on his knees and coming to a stop at Terra's side. He scooped her up in his arms put his ear to her chest. He tried to hear a heartbeat, but there was nothing. He couldn't hear a thing. Her heart wasn't beating.

"I can't hear her heart beat," he cried miserably as Bell and John came running up. "I think she's dead." There was an outcry from the town as they heard what Eric said. He could hear the news spread through the small collection of people like fire through dry grass.

"Let me see her," Bell demanded, lifting her carefully out of Eric's hands. "John, take hold of her legs." John nodded and wrapped his arms around her knees. Bell supported her upper body in one hand and put his other hand over her chest. He could instantly feel her heart beating. It was a little slow, but that could easily be explained by her lack of energy.

"She's not dead," Bell explained loud enough for everyone to hear. "Eric, give me your hand."

Standing Eric extended his right and to Bell.

Bell grabbed his hand and placed it directly on Terra's chest. "I need you to breathe," he said. "Breathe and think of Terra breathing. Think of her opening her eyes and looking at you. When you feel something pull at you, let if pull. That's the bond trying to pull energy to wake her up. Let it take what it needs."

Eric nodded, not trusting his voice. He thought about Terra's big green eyes, with their circle of gold around the pupil and the ring of blue around the outside and how they could convey so much

383

emotion. He thought of how it made the pit of his stomach flutter whenever she looked at him with her eyes shining.

He loved her eyes.

"Open your eyes," Eric pleaded, "Please open your eyes."

There was a sudden pull, like suction, on the palm of his hand. He resisted for a moment and then simply let go. He could feel the energy flowing from him, through his arm, into Terra. After just a few moments Terra began to stir.

"That's enough," Bell said removing his hand.

Terra's head rolled around for a moment before her eyes opened slowly. She looked up at Bell, then John and finally to Eric. She held his gaze for a long time.

"What happened?" She asked.

"You depleted all of your energy," Bell sighed, "again. How are you feeling?"

"I'm alright, I think." She guessed, she made a mental check of everything. Nothing seemed to be broken or damaged.

"Can you stand?" Bell asked.

"I think so," she answered with a nod. Carefully John lowered her feet on to the ground as Bell straightened her out. She stood for a moment and then nearly toppled to the ground. Eric was at her side in a second. He wrapped her arm around his neck and supported her.

"Thank you," she said, feeling a rush emotion as Eric smiled at her. "I'm ok now," she said standing up on her own.

"Are you sure?" Eric asked.

"Yes, I feel just fine now, thanks to you all."

"Terra," Bell whispered. "I know this is going to seem odd, but there are a lot of people behind me who are waiting to see if you're alright."

"Oh . . ." she stammered, not sure what to do about masses of people waiting for her.

"When we turn around you should wave to everyone, let them know you're alright. Everything you just went through was seen by everyone on that wall. They need to see you turn around triumphantly. Do you think you can do that?" He asked. "Can you walk through the gates? We can carry you if need be."

"No," she assured them, strengthening her resolve. "I can do this, let's go."

"Eric, stay on Terra's left, John stand at her right. I'll follow you in and keep the crowd from following too closely. Remember, no matter what really happened, this is a victory for Sol."

Terra nodded as the boys took up their positions on either side of her. Bell nodded too, pleased by what he saw. He stepped back and behind Terra.

Once the people caught sight of their princess, battle worn but still standing, they erupted into shouts and applause. It seemed like the entire town had emptied out of the gates to see what was going on, despite the torrential down pour.

"Dear spirits," Terra muttered.

"You can do this," Eric encouraged her, taking her left hand.

"We're right here for you," John added taking her right hand.

"Ok. Let's go."

Together the three of them walked hand in hand toward the city gate. People cheered and called to them as they walked through the archway. Every one parted around them as they walked through. Terra kept her head up and smiled at everyone whose eyes she met.

"Princess," some called as she walked past. Others just smiled. Some thanked her for what she had done.

One woman, who Terra had never seen before, reached out and touched her on the shoulder. Terra, Eric and John came to a stop. She smiled at the princess and said, "Bless you Princess. Blessed by the creator." A mummer went through the crowd at the woman's words.

"Her wings," someone shouted from the crowd. Terra looked around confused. John and Eric both started walking and she was pulled along with them.

As they made their way slowly through the throngs of people more and more they started reaching out to touch the scars on her shoulders. A hush fell over the crowd as they gathered closer around them, each reaching out hoping for a chance to touch the princess. She tried very hard not to be alarmed.

Terra glanced to John and then to Eric, both had smiles on their faces, both looked proud to be leading her through the crowds of people toward the castle.

Diana rolled over in her bed. It was getting cold. She could hear the rain and thunder outside her windows. Rain meant the sun was gone and that her room was getting colder. She could have pulled up the spare blanket at the foot her bed but she was "sick" and she didn't feel she should have to do anything.

"Sarah!" She shouted, calling for one of her ladies in waiting.

When no one answered she started to get frustrated.

"Sarah! Jane! Rose! Someone answer me!" She bellowed.

There was the sound of footsteps running in the hall and Diana sat up on her bed, waiting for her ladies to come running in. She would make sure they think twice before making her call twice again. Foolish girls, she could replace them so easily. They should be more careful not to try her patience in the future.

She heard the footsteps run passed her room.

"Excuse me!" She shouted as a group of people ran past her door. "You!" She called as a young man ran passed.

He stopped and looked around. "Me, highness?" He asked pointing to himself.

"Yes you!" She snapped. "What is going on!? Where is everyone going? And where are my ladies?!"

"Haven't you heard Highness?" He asked. "There's talk of a shadows outside the city gates and something's happened to Princess Terra."

"Terra?" She asked, amused. "Has she died?" She asked, unable to keep a thread of elation out of her voice.

"I don't know highness. I was going to find out."

386

"Do that then," she waved him off dismissively. "If you see my ladies send them to me at once!"

"Yes highness," the boy said pulling his cap off and bowing. He backed out of the room slowly and then took off running down the hall.

Diana lay back in bed, considering what it might mean if Terra had died.

By the time Terra, John, Eric and Bell reached the gates to the castle, everyone seemed to have heard the news about the princess. Including her father, who was standing at the gates waiting for them.

She stopped in her tracks when she saw the look on her father's face.

"Don't stop now," Eric encouraged under his breath. "It'll only get worse if you wait."

"You can do this," John added with a smile.

With a nod they continued forward again. Just before they reached the gates, King Sol's stern face broke as he rushed forward and grabbed Terra. He held her for a moment looking down into her eyes. A single tear rolled down his cheek as he took in the sight of her. He wrapped his arms around her and held her tightly.

"My baby," he whispered holding her in his arms. He rocked back and forth holding her for several moments while he whispered to her how much he loved her and how worried he was about her.

"Papa," Terra whispered. "Papa I'm so sorry. I just when out for a ride and there was this over turned carriage."

"I know," King Sol assured her, "I know about the carriage and the shadows at the gate but what happened after that? How did you get away?"

"It's a very long story, Majesty," Bell cut in. "Perhaps a story best left for private."

King Sol glanced around at the mass of people who had followed Terra to the gates. They were all staring at her in a way the King didn't really understand at first. Then it dawned on him.

Reverence.

They were looking at her like she was their Queen. In this moment, they worshiped her as their ruler. It was a kind of respect that was hard won. Especially in times like these.

"You're right," King Sol agreed. "Let's go inside."

"Father," Terra asked as he turned to leave. "Can we wait, for just a moment?"

"Of course," he replied. "Is everything alright?"

"Yes," she smiled," Just one minute."

Terra stepped back twice and then turned. She walked back to the gates where the people were still gathered around watching. Eric and John followed her down and stood on either side of her. Terra walked through the gateway and back out into the throngs of people. They circled around her and the boys and waited to hear what she had to say.

"Thank you," she called loud enough for everyone around to hear. "Thank you to all of you for caring about me so much and for seeing me safely back to my father. I can't tell you how much it means to know that I have all of you looking out for me."

"Princess," someone called, "how did you do it? How did you use light to drive the shadows away?"

"I did what I had to do to keep this city and this kingdom safe," Terra called over the sound of the rain. "I can't say exactly how I used the light. I only know that I was fortunate enough to be able to use it to save my life and lives of my friends." She reached back grabbed John's hand. She squeezed it and then let it go again.

"But princess," A woman near the front called to her. "Won't the shadows come back?"

Terra shook her head. "No. I believe those shadows were here for a specific target and purpose. Now that they're gone I'm nearly certain they won't return."

"What were they after?" Someone called.

"Who was their target?" Another voice from the left.

She turned to look at Eric. He nodded, it would be best to be honest.

Terra sighed and explained, "I was their target. They were coming after me. I don't know what they wanted from me, but I do know that they were unsuccessful in getting it. I know . . . I know . . ." she faltered as she felt the world start to spin.

Eric was at her side as soon as started to faint. Her knees buckled and she went down. He caught her and scooped her up in his arms. He swung around and started back toward the castle.

As he carried her away the people outside the gate got down on one knee, bowed their heads, and placed their fists to their hearts to Terra as she passed. Even after Eric and the rest of the group were walking up the castle steps, the people stayed on their knees. It wasn't until she disappeared from sight that they rose again and saluted her. It was the most respect they could pay a person, and they paid it to Terra.

Diana stood in a window near the front of the castle. She watched as her sister was carried in and as the people around the gate fell to their knees to honor her. She felt rage then like she could not believe. It was stronger than anything else she had ever felt. Stronger than any emotion she had felt ever.

Watching her sister be honored in a way she never had before made her consider, not for the first time, that maybe Terra was going to be a bigger problem than she had originally thought. She was usually just nuisance, a bother, easily ignored and often forgotten about. However, Diana had stood in the window, and even from here she could see the blinding white light that she assumed had come from Terra. Whatever it was, it was powerful and that made her little sister more dangerous than she had previously considered.

If she wasn't careful, Terra might just find herself in Diana's way. Now that right there, that was a dangerous place to be.

Deciding she needed time to think over this new information and what it meant to her and her plans for the future; Diana turned on her heel and walked back to her room.

Chapter 10

At Master Bell's insistence, Terra was taken directly to the infirmary in the north wing, closest to main doors and Bell's personal room. Bell didn't want to waste any time getting the princess to the healers. The princess had come around before they had crossed the main hall. Insisting she could walk, Eric set her down but was at her side the entire way up. John stayed glued to Terra's other side, with Bell and King Sol making up the front of the party.

They reached the infirmary and Terra was instructed by Bell to lay back on the bed in their while he and the healer on staff examined her. They each put held their hands just over two inches from her body and moved them up and down, checking for injuries or internal damage. She stared at the healer for a moment. Their white robes with the strange white hoods had always creeped her out as a child.

Age hadn't changed that effect much.

"So explain to me again what happened," King Sol asked.

"I wasn't feeling well," Terra explained, "so Master Bell suggested a ride might clear my head and make me feel better." She snuck a glance at Eric; he was staring at her with a mix of emotions on his face. Terra could make out a few, but not all. She could see guilt quite plainly, relief also. Aside from that she wasn't sure what was there.

"Then?" The King prompted.

"Then, as John and I were riding we came upon an over turned carriage."

"Why weren't you with Reynolds? He's your Guard," King Sol demanded.

Terra looked at Eric and he looked at her, neither sure what to say next.

"Excuse me my Lord," Bell cut in. "May I have a word?"

"I'm trying to ascertain what happened to my daughter," King Sol replied curtly. "Whatever your news is, it can wait."

"My Lord," Bell insisted, trying to communicate the importance of the information he had through his eyes. "This cannot wait."

"Then just tell us," Eric interjected rudely.

"Yes Bell," King Sol agreed. "Out with it."

Bell looked around and the all the healers dropped what they were doing and exited through a door at the back of the room. He turned and looked at John and Eric. He raised an eyebrow and waited.

"I'm not going anywhere," Eric stated. "I let her out of my sight once today and look what happened." He looked down and put a hand on her shoulder. "I won't make that mistake again."

Bell turned his gaze to John.

John squared his shoulders and stared at the wizard.

"I would like John to stay," Terra said quietly. "He's been with me since the beginning of this ordeal. And besides that, he's a trusted friend."

"Is that so?" King Sol asked, staring the young man down.

"It is," John replied not backing down.

King Sol leaned in further, looking like he hadn't decided to hurt the young man or hug him. John stood his ground and stared back at the King, respectfully of course.

"Very well then," King Sol declared finally. "Go and stand at her other side." John saluted the King and then went to stand on the left side of Terra's bed.

She looked to John who smiled and patted her shoulder reassuringly. Then she looked to Eric who reached down and took her hand in his. He squeezed it and all three of them turned to the Master Wizard.

"So be it," he sighed. "I was first made aware of Terra's situation when John, along with both the Master Carpenter and Builder, came barreling through the main entrance in a wagon. They explained to me what was going on and together we went in search of Guard Reynolds.

"When we found him I informed him of Terra's situation and told him the only way to save Terra was to open his end of their bond and allow her to draw on his strength."

"Why was his end of the bond closed in the first place?" King Sol demanded.

"That's my fault Father," Terra answered. "Eric and I fought and I closed the bond." She looked up and met Bell's eyes.

"There was no way for Guard Reynolds to open the bond. Not without physical contact," Bell added.

"Wait," Terra cut in suddenly. "That can't be right. I felt a rush of energy. Someone gave me the strength to keep fighting. They saved my life. It could only have been Eric. I don't share a bond with anyone else."

Bell looked to the King who nodded.

"What?" She asked. "What is it?"

"You do share a bond with one other person. It isn't a normal bond, and we certainly don't understand all about it yet, but you do have a bond with one other," Bell explained as gently as he could.

"No," she whispered shaking her head. "There's no way, it isn't possible."

"I'm afraid there's no mistaking this magical signature," Bell explained. "Look within yourself, and tell me I'm wrong." His face was solemn as he watched her close her eyes for half a second before they flew open again.

"That makes no sense, why would he try and save me?"

"Who?" Eric asked, not sure he was following the whole conversation.

"I am sure," Bell stated. He looked to the King. "There can be no mistake."

"I see," was all King Sol said. "Bell, perhaps we should adjourn to the war room and discuss this more."

"Agreed," he nodded. "Princess," he added turning to Terra. "Rest up for now and I'll come find you later for that lesson we missed."

Terra could only nod as her mind started to race. How could it be possible? There was no way he would do what he had done and then try to save her. It made no sense. She nearly died, her horse did die! Not to mention he endangered John, Persephone and her young son.

King Sol and Bell took their leave and left Terra, Eric and John alone in the infirmary. Each confused about what was going on in their own way.

"John," Terra asked, "What happened to Persephone and her baby?"

"I'm not sure," he answered. "I entrusted her to the city guard. They should have brought her up by now. I can go find out what's going on with her if you two need some . . . time."

"Can you please make sure she's alright?" She asked.

"Of course," John smiled and bowed to Terra. He stopped and saluted Eric before he disappeared out the door.

"Was it Grey?" Eric asked. "Is he the one that saved you?"

Terra shifted uncomfortably on the bed. "It would seem so."

"I don't get it," he muttered frustrated.

"Me either!" Terra shouted. "Those shadows had to come from him. He's the Shadow King! So why would he send his shadows after me and then try and save me!?"

Eric looked at her; she was angry and frustrated and tired. He could talk to her later he supposed. Right now they needed to find out what Grey was up to before more people got hurt.

"So you're sure then?" He asked. "You're sure about where the energy came from?"

"I'm positive," she confirmed. "It came from Grey."

Grey flopped down onto his bed, exhausted. That had been close, much too close.

He had no idea where those damn shadows had come from but they had nearly killed Terra. He didn't even know he had shadows in those woods right now. Let alone any that were hell bent on his ticket outta here's destruction. Worse than that, when he had tried to command them to disperse, they hadn't listened.

Grey had been certain he would have to stand there and watch as Terra died.

When he felt the reach it was all he could do to keep from crying out. He had happily given her all the energy he could spare. Through the eyes of the shadows he could see her stand and fight again. As he watched her climb to her feet again he felt like the largest weight had been lifted from his chest.

He could breathe again.

Except that now he was exhausted. To channel that kind of energy through this damn box and into Terra had nearly tapped him out. So he lay back on his bed and pulled a pillow over his eyes. He would try and get as much rest as he could before Terra, inevitably, appeared before him demanding answers.

Answers he didn't have.

"It was a reach my Lord," Bell whispered as they walked the halls to the war room. "There can be no mistake. Terra reached to the prisoner and he responded."

"This is a good thing isn't it?" King Sol asked, confused by Bell's worried expression.

"It is and it isn't," he explained. "It is very good for us and our plan that when Terra reached to him he responded. It is, however, troubling that he could reach back and channel so *much* energy to her from such a distance and through his glass cell that should prevent him from doing anything like that."

King Sol nearly stopped in his tracks. This was troubling noise indeed. "I seem to recall a conversation with you, many years passed, where you assured me that the cell you had constructed would hold that monster no matter what."

"I'm afraid I wasn't factoring Terra's part in all this. She is so much stronger now than she was four years ago. She is the one who reached and she is the one who allowed his energy to slip the confines of his cell."

"So what does this mean for us Bell? For the plan?"

"I'm afraid I don't know yet sire. I shall take time now, before Terra's lesson to ponder on these things and decide the best course of action."

"Very well then," King Sol said, dismissing Bell. "I shall be in the war room if you have need of me."

Bell bowed, fist over his heart, and then turned back up the stairs. King Sol walked on to the west wing, unsure how to feel about the information the day had provided. With a tired sigh he headed down the long corridor to the War room.

Eric helped Terra out of the infirmary bed and over to the door. "I'm ok," she assured him. "I can manage walking."

"You say that now," Eric laughed. "But I haven't always known that to be the case."

"Oh wow, really?" She asked laughing. "Taking cheap shots when I'm half dead? That's nice. Very gentlemanly too."

"Well I do what I can," he replied laughing.

Terra laughed and made her I'm-gonna-kick-your-butt-face. "You know I would smack you right now if it wouldn't drain what little energy I have left."

"Oh you mean that energy you took from me?" He asked, holding the door open for her.

Terra straightened up and walked through the door and into the hall. She looked around for a moment and stopped.

"What's wrong?" He asked still smiling.

"Nothing," she lied, not giving Eric the satisfaction of knowing she wasn't sure where to go.

"Lead on Princess."

Terra sighed. "I'm not sure where I should go."

"Why ever not?" He asked mockingly.

"I'm not really sure what time it is."

Eric laughed and walked forward. He was going to put his hand on her shoulder when he stopped and thought better of it. He was beyond relieved that Terra was ok. He was thrilled that she was fine, but that didn't change anything that happened between them. There was still the issue of the dream and her lying to him about it. He couldn't just act like none of that had happened.

Terra could sense the change in him as soon as it happened. She knew things wouldn't stay playful like this. Things were said and a line was drawn in the sand. She could tell things had to change if she was going it keep Eric in her life. After everything that had happened she knew she needed him.

"Eric," she started.

"Terra I can't do this right now. I want you to be safe and I can't tell you how horrified I feel to know what you went through because of me."

"That wasn't your fault," she explained turning to face him.

"It was. If we hadn't fought then you wouldn't have been outside and you wouldn't have been out there when those shadows showed up. You would have been safe."

"If that had happened then Persephone and her baby would have died. I was in danger, but I wouldn't put my safety above their lives. In a way our fight saved them."

"That doesn't make me feel any better," Eric said flatly.

"Well it should," she insisted. "I know that things are . . . hard right now with us, but I want talk to you about that."

396

"Terra I don't need to go over the same things over and over again. I heard what you have to say . . ."

"You haven't heard all of it," she interjected. "Things have changed."

"Changed," he asked, a glimmer of hope in his eyes.

"Changed," she confirmed.

"Changed how?"

"Are you the Princess Terra?" A voice called from behind her.

Terra and Eric turned at the same time to see a large blond woman come walking toward them. She was the largest woman either of them had ever seen. Taller than Eric, and possibly even Grey, she had shoulders as broad as Terra's arm. Her light blond hair was cropped short and only added to her overall manliness. She was wearing a dark black tunic and dark black pants.

Eric, knowing it was impolite to stare, tuned his eyes downward.

Terra walked up, extending her hand. "You must be Merope, from the Kingdom of Pleiades." She didn't remember all of Pleiades customs, but she did know that they don't bow, they shake hands. When you shake the hand of a warrior, and Merope was that indeed, then you had to shake hands firmly.

"I am," the big woman replied taking Terra's smaller hand in her own. "But you may call me Mer."

"It's very nice to meet you. I can't tell you how much it means to me and my family that you agreed to train me and my sister."

"I was honored that your father thought I might be able to help." Mer looked over Terra's shoulder. "And you are?"

Eric stepped forward. "Eric Reynolds, Royal Guard to the Princess Terra." He put his hand out and shook Mer's hand firmly.

"Well to be honest Guard Reynolds," Mer noted taking in the sight of Terra, half soaked, dirty, torn dress, hair down, barefoot and a number of cuts all over her arms and shoulders, "You don't appear to be doing a very good job."

Eric's chest puffed out as he walked toward the large woman. "What did you just say to me?"

"Ok I think it's time for our first lesson right?" Terra asked Mer, stepping up between her and Eric.

"It is time," she replied laughing at the sight of Terra blocking Eric. "Unless you'd like some time to change?"

"No I'm fine," Terra assured her quickly, knowing she needed to get Eric away from Mer. "I'll be right there."

"Don't take too much time," she laughed and heading back down the hall.

"What did you do that for!?" He demanded as soon as Mer was out of earshot. "She insulted me! You should have . . ."

Terra leaned against Eric, and pushing up on to her tip toes she kissed him.

A quick and simple kiss.

Every thought in Eric's head vanished. He looked down at her and she smiled up at him. She had actually kissed him. That had never happened before. He had always instigated anything romantic between them.

"Changes?" He asked.

"Changes," she confirmed smiling. "Will you meet me in the Queen's garden before dinner?"

"I can . . . yes I'll be there."

"Good," Terra sighed, her smile widening by the second. "I'll see you then." She pushed herself up on her toes and kissed him again. This time he caught her and kissed her back.

"I'll see you tonight," she whispered breaking away.

"Uh hu," was all he could manage.

She smiled and started down the hall. Completely forgetting about her appearance.

Eric watched her go, feeling for the first time in years, like things might actually be getting better.

Terra caught up with Mer before she made to the girl's practice room.

"So you look like you've been through quite a bit today Princess," Mer remarked as Terra came up alongside her. "I heard something about a wall of shadows and a blinding white light?"

"Yea," she replied sheepishly. "That was me. Thought I'd take a ride into the woods earlier. Not my best idea."

"It would seem not," Mer said neutrally. "Did you really take on that many shadows at once?"

"I did," she admitted, not feeling like it was something you brag about.

"If you can do that, Princess," Mer commented, considering. "Then I'm not sure there's much I can teach you."

"I've heard all about you and what you can do," Terra explained. "I know that you're the strongest warrior anyone has ever seen. And it isn't all about your strength either, although your strength is formidable. It's about the way you think and the way you analyze a situation to make the most use of your available resources and time.

"That's what our father wants us to learn."

Mer nodded. "You certainly know a lot," she conceded. "Do you really think this is something you can learn? I don't want to be rude Princess but training like this, is a hard, difficult struggle that not many people can handle."

Terra silently considered what she had said. It was true that her father had her and Diana in defense training from the time they were little. He had people brought in from all over the world to train them in self-defense. Defending against people and against shadows, but they were not taught any kind of offensive strategies. As a princess she knew that she should always try to solve her problems with words before resorting to violence. Since she was, as the kingdom referred to her, the "shadow princess", nobody had bothered to teach her much of anything.

"I know that it will be hard going," Terra agreed as they rounded the last corner before the double doors that lead out to a small practice yard the girls used for weapon and physical training. It wasn't a huge space, as Diana would often complain, but it was isolated and easy to keep safe.

"If you don't wish to receive the training Princess," Mer started.

"No I do," she assured her. "I want to be trained."

"Good," Mer smiled. "You have to want it."

"Oh and Terra, please."

"Not Princess? Or Highness or Majesty?" Mer asked with a raised eyebrow.

"No titles, please," she insisted.

"You may be the first royal I've ever met who didn't love the sound of their own title," Mer observed.

"You may also call me crazy if you like," she added with a laugh.

"I'll take that under advisement."

They spent the next hour learning the commands Mer would use while they trained. If she made this noise it meant duck, this one meant jump, this one meant run. It wasn't until the last twenty or so minutes that she started to train Terra.

"You have to turn off the voice that says fear and the voice that says panic. You need your mind to be at peace, calm, tranquil. Or you'll be struggling to keep up the whole battle. This is the first and hardest thing to learn. Once you can calm you mind, even in the face of great danger, then you'll be ready to learn what I have to teach."

"Princess," John called, poking his head through the door.

"This isn't a great time John," she explained, indicating with her head toward Mer.

"Terra I found Persephone."

"That's great," she sighed, relieved.

"Do all your guards call you by your first name?" Mer asked from behind her.

"I'm not her guard," John corrected.

"Just a friend," Terra corrected him. "So where is she?"

"In jail."

"How did this happen!?" Terra exclaimed as they ran to the city guards barracks in the courtyard. The main gate that lead to the courtyard in front of the castle was flanked on either side by large round turrets. Each one housing barracks for the guards who patrolled the city surround the castle. The one directly to the left from the castles main door was where the King kept his personal jail.

"I have no idea," John replied as they raced down the hall. "I left her with the city guards but then I had to get Eric and everything happened with you."

"Why would they arrest her?" She asked out loud. "They can't possibly think she had anything to do with it."

"I guess we'll find out."

They ran across the courtyard, the rain still beating down on the kingdom, until they reached the far left side. There were soldiers loitering outside the three wooden doors that spanned the length of barracks. The doors were simple but they were made of thick strong wood from the King's forest.

As Terra and John approached, the five or so soldiers who were joking around outside fell to their knees and formally saluted them.

"Princess," the man closest to her said. "How may we be of service today?"

Terra stopped short.

She had never been treated so formally by the soldiers. They were always respectful but never so formal.

"I . . . uh," she stammered.

"May I say, Princess," a solider off to the left said. "We heard about what happened outside the city walls."

"Oh."

"We were so amazed to hear how you handled the shadows," a man to the right added.

"Yes, we just wanted you to know that we are honored to be able to say we have served you and would be happy to help you in any way."

"That's good," she started "Because I have been informed by John that the woman who was brought in by him an hour or so ago, right before the shadows attacked, that she has been placed under arrest."

"She has," the solider in front of her said, getting to his feet.

"I would like to know why." Terra said trying to sound as much like her father as she could.

"Per the Kings orders, no one is to enter or exit the kingdom without consent of the King or his advisors. She raced past a check point without stopping and led the soldiers there on a wild chase through the countryside."

"She also stole your horse," another man offered. "She endangered the life of a princess of the realm."

"I was never in danger," she countered.

"I'm afraid that's not up to us," a dark haired man at the back said. "It's up to the judgment of the King."

"I see," she thought for a moment. "Then I'd like to see her please."

"I don't know if we can do that," the man near the front remarked.

"Jesse," John started. "This is princess Terra; she just took on over three dozen shadows and walked away. She just wants a few minutes with the woman she saved."

Jesse looked to the other soldiers. After a few seconds of whispered conversation, he turned back to her and said, "We can let you see her but not for long."

"That's all I ask," she sighed gratefully.

Together the seven of them made their way through the main part of the barracks that had the kitchen and a number of tables and chairs. Through the sleeping area that was wall to wall bunk beds. Through the weapons room where they housed the swords, maces, shields, and the armor that the soldiers used, and finally to a large metal door that lead to the prison.

Jesse turned to the group at the door and said, "I'll take them down. You guys make sure we aren't disturbed to soon." The other four men nodded and headed back out into the sleeping area. "You won't have long to talk, and if anyone catches you in there in could be a lot of trouble for all of us."

Terra paced a hand on Jesse's shoulder. "I promise no blame will fall on you. I'm your princess and I ordered you to do this."

"Alright," he said with a nod. He pulled a key from under his shirt and put it in the door. After a few rotations there was a click and the door popped open. Jesse pushed it in and motioned for John and Terra to follow.

He led them down a long spiral staircase that at first was made of wood but as they went deeper they appeared to be cut from the same stone as the walls of the castle. Torches were placed in brackets intermittently along the walls as they went down. Creating light but making the air smell of smoke so badly it burned Terra's eyes. Deeper and deeper they went until she was beginning to wonder how far down the prison really was. One thing was certain, the princess was starting to wish she'd grabbed shoes.

John, seeing the look on Terra's face said, "They cut the prison down deep into the stone under the castle to ensure that no prisoner could ever escape and get to the King. It's deep but it's safer this way."

"Right, safe," Terra muttered.

After another few minutes they came to the bottom of the stairs and another large metal door. Jesse knocked on the door three times, then two times and then finally four times. There was a sound of a key in the door on the other side and then it swung open to reveal a man in his late forties with dark brown hair and blood shot brown eyes.

He eyed Jesse, John, and Terra for a moment and then turned to Jesse. "Who are they?" He asked jerking his chin in their general direction.

"Princess Terra and her guard John. They need to see the woman they brought in a while ago."

"Can't do that," he grumbled.

"I need you to do this," Jesse told him. "I'll explain it all later, but for right now, let them pass."

He considered Terra and John a moment more before saying, "You'll owe me Jesse."

"That'll be fine," he sighed, "Now let us pass."

"Not my head on the block of it goes sour," he grumbled as he shuffled back and pulled the door all the way open.

Terra rushed through with John and Jesse on her heels. There was only one row of cells with maybe six cells all together. It was dark, barely lit at all. But the air, that's what nearly stopped Terra in her tracks. It was thick and smelled of foul things. She couldn't believe they would keep anyone in a place like this.

"Persephone?" She called.

"Terra?" Persephone cried, her arms sticking out of a cell down on the left. "Terra is that you?"

"Oh dear spirits," she muttered rushing forward. "I'm so sorry I didn't realize they would arrest you." She faltered for a moment. The "cell" was nothing more than an eight by eight opening cut in the stone underground. There was no sit or rest and as far as she could tell, the floor doubled as a bathroom.

"I figured they might," Persephone remarked bitterly.

"Persephone . . ." she started.

"Seph," she cut in. "The only people who call me Persephone are my parents and my old instructors."

"Seph then," Terra corrected. "Why would they arrest you like this?"

"I'm a runaway princess," she explained.

"Princess?" Terra and John asked simultaneously.

"Yes," she sighed. "I am Persephone of the Moon Kingdom. I am the youngest of five siblings and a wanted fugitive in my own county."

404

"Wanted? Why?"

"I fell in love," she answered simply.

"Last I checked love wasn't a reason to arrest someone," John observed.

"When you loved someone who's a Shadowed Man, it is."

"A what?" Terra asked.

"A Shadowed Man," Seph explained, "Is a man or woman who supports what the Shadow King is trying to do. They believe that the world has gone wrong somehow, twisted. They think the darkness the King brings will purify the world and set it back on the right track."

"That's insane," John laughed. "How could anyone think what he does is a good idea?"

"People, generally, are insane," Seph commented.

"I've never even heard of such a thing as a Shadowed Man before," Terra murmured.

"Neither have I," John added.

"Me either," Jesse chimed from behind them.

"So what happened?" Terra asked.

"I fell in love," Seph sighed, "his name was Darien and he was the most beautiful man I had ever seen. He was tall with dark hair and blazing blue eyes. He had the kindest face and the most amazing smile. He worked with my father and my two older brothers on a castle for my older sister. She had just gotten married.

"He was around all the time, working on plans helping select materials. He was everywhere, I went every time I went there. One day I was in our garden playing in the stream that ran through there when I slipped on a rock and fell."

Seph pause and smiled at the memory. "He was there. He helped me out of the stream and tore his tunic to wrap my ankle. He carried me all the way back to the castle and stayed with me until a doctor could be summoned.

"After that we were inseparable. Everywhere I went, he went and vice versa. Before I knew it we were in love."

Seph stepped away from the bars and paced back to the end of the cell. Terra had seen tears in her eyes before she had turned away. Whatever she was about to say must be very painful for her. She walked back to the bars, tears gone, and continued.

"One night he asked me to marry him. I said yes of course and we went to my father for his blessing.

"As it turned out my bothers had been looking into what was happening with Darien and me. They began to look into who he really was and what kind of past he had lead. It was then they found out about his connection to the Shadowed Men."

"Connection?" John asked, "Was it a connection or was he actually one of these Shadowed Men?"

"He was one," Seph confirmed. "They followed him one night to a meeting that was being hosted just outside of Luna, our capital city," Seph added noting John and Jesse's blank faces. "They were meeting in some of the woods near there. My brother's men hadn't anticipated on the shadowed men's paranoia.

"They had traps set and warning systems in place. When the men got close the shadowed men knew. What they had hoped would be a simple arrest tuned into a blood bath. In the end my brother's men won and arrested everyone there who was left alive.

"A lot of people died that night.

"Darien managed to escape somehow. He came to me and explained everything. He told me that his father had been a Shadowed Man and he had just been raised into it. He stayed active with them out of respect for his father. We both knew that no one would ever believe him. So we ran.

"We married in secret while we ran and found out less than a week later that I was pregnant.

"So we settled into a small town near the border and waited for the baby to be born. Until one day a guard passing through town caught sight of Darien and arrested him." Her voice broke as she continued to speak. "I watched as they put his head on a block and beheaded him in the square."

Tears streamed silently down her face as she remember the way Darien had looked up and met her eyes just before the axe came down. He had managed to convey to her a lifetimes worth of love in those last few seconds.

"Once I saw how quickly they killed him, I knew my baby wasn't safe there anymore. So I left. Darien's manservant found us an unmarked carriage and we ran. It took a few weeks to get out of my country and then once we had enough money we tried to buy our way into Sol.

"We nearly made it, but we were spotted by some guards and they chased us. We managed to hide in a nearby farm when I had the baby. It wasn't the easiest labor but we got through ok."

"Wait where's the baby?" Terra asked looking around.

"With the king's men," Seph sobbed miserably. "They took my baby boy. My little boy. They just took him right out of my arms." She breathed out sharply, the tears in her eyes flowing faster down her face. "I have to keep him safe. No matter what happens to me he has to be safe. That boy is all that's left of the man I love. I have to know he's safe."

"I promise you Seph," Terra said reaching through the bars and grabbing the woman's hand. "We'll make sure he's safe. We'll make sure both of you are safe."

"Thank you princess," Seph smiled, "But I don't know that you can keep me safe. I saw my brother's carriage when they were leading me down here."

"Your brother?" Terra asked. "What will he do?"

"If Charles is here," Seph answered, looking grim. "Then he'll go before your king and insist that I be turned over to him to be taken back to my own kingdom. They'll prove that I had a baby with Darien and I'll be shamed and beheaded."

"What?!" John burst out.

Terra put a hand on his shoulder and nodded. "What grounds will he use?" She asked turning back to Seph.

Seph thought for a moment and then said, "He'll say that I'm a runaway princess and that I need to be returned to my family. I've broken no laws here, except racing passed the guards at the border."

"That's not enough to hold you here," Terra observed. "Even if my father wanted to, he wouldn't be able to keep you here."

"If they take me now they'll know I had a baby. I'll be killed and my poor boy will be killed along with me." Seph whimpered, her words dissolving into sobs.

"Can't we do anything to stop them?" John asked Terra.

"Even if we can stop them today," she replied, "We couldn't stop them forever."

"I don't need forever," Seph cut in. "I just need them to wait a little longer, maybe a day or two. By then they won't be able to prove I had a baby."

"That we might be able to do . . .," Terra pondered out loud. "What would two days change?"

"I had the baby weeks ago now. Everything's pretty much back to the way it was, except my milk is still flowing."

John and Jesse both looked away awkwardly.

"Will two days really change that?" She asked.

"I only nursed my son the first night of his life, after that we made do with bottles or wet nurses. Whatever we could find where we were. I'm confident that in a few more days the milk will completely dry up."

"Maybe we can find a way to buy time, just enough so that by the time you got home there would be no proof of the baby," Terra said thinking out loud.

"So what happened after that?" John asked. "How did the carriage turn?"

"Shadows."

"Shadows?" The three outside the bars asked in unison.

"As we made our way down the road a huge group of shadows came out of the woods in front of us. They didn't stop or try to hurt us, but they did spook the horse. It bucked and bucked until the yolk broke on one side. It tried to run, but the carriage was still attached and it took this corner too fast and we tipped. All the weight and pressure on one side tipped the carriage and broke the other side. Before we even had to me to react to the shadows, we were free falling into the embankment.

"Tom . . . he . . . got pinned. I tried to pull him out but . . ." Seph's voice broke and her tears started again. "Did he . . . is he . . . gone?"

Terra looked to Seph, her own eyes full of tears, and explained, "We found him under the carriage. We managed to set it back on the road and free him." Her voice shook and she wasn't sure she could go on.

John set a hand on her shoulder and gave her a warm smile. He looked to Seph and said, "Terra held him in her lap and took his pain away. He passed comfortably into the next world, his final thoughts of you and your son's safety."

"He didn't suffer then?" Seph asked.

Terra shook her head, "No, he didn't suffer in the end."

Seph slipped her hands between the bars and offered one to both John and Terra. "Thank you both so much," she whispered as they each took her hand. "I would have died if not for him. I can't tell you what it means to me to know that he wasn't alone or suffering in the end."

"It was right after that when you took Venus," John remarked.

"Oh," she blanched, "I am sorry about stealing her and about her dying." She pulled her arms back into her cell.

"I know," Terra said smiling at her, "You were just doing what you had to do to save your son. I couldn't fault you for that."

Seph gave Terra a small tight smile. "So what can we do to keep me here? You seemed to be thinking something earlier."

"I'm not sure yet, but I have a few ideas. But Seph what happens to your son when your brother eventually takes you home?"

Seph looked like she might dissolve into tears, again. "He'll have to stay."

"Stay?" Terra asked confused. "I thought you had to keep him safe?"

"What do you think I'm trying to do?" she snapped. "The safest place for my son is as far away from me as he can get. He'll stay here and I'll be forced to deny him."

"What exactly does that mean?" Jesses asked.

"It means they'll bring him before Seph and demand that she say he's hers. Most likely they'll hurt him and see if she reacts," Terra explained, her voice dripping with disgust.

"What person wouldn't' react to child being tortured?" John asked disgusted.

"I don't know," Seph replied. "But first we have to find a way to keep me here."

"Well," Terra started, "maybe we can . . ." A sound of boots on stone pulled everyone's attention back the way they had come.

Jesse jogged to the door and looked up, his face when pale and he ran back to them. "The King's guards are coming down the stairs right now," he whispered panicked. "You two can't be down here, we have to hide you. Follow me."

Terra and John followed Jesse down to the last cell on the left. He fumbled with the keys for a second but finally got the door open. He motioned for the two of them to get inside and quickly. Terra, trusting implicitly, hurried in. John, however, stopped at the door and turned to Jesse.

"Don't worry I'm not going anywhere," Jesse assured him. "You two can't be down here, especially not the Princess." After only another second of hesitation, John stepped over the threshold of the cell and Jesse closed the gate quietly. He had just enough time to run over to the door before the King's Guards became visible on the stairs.

Terra walked to the corner of the foul smelling cell and listened as the guards came down and started talking to Jesse and the other prison guard. John leaned against the cell wall near to where the metal bars connected with it. He leaned back and gave her sheepish grin. Terra, understanding his meaning, retuned the gesture.

410

There was a sound of bars being opened and Seph started to shout.

"What are you doing?! Unhand me! Do you have any idea who I am?!"

Terra started forward, ready to jump to Seph's defense and stop the guards.

John caught her around the waist before she could reach the bars. He pulled her over so her back was against him and put a hand over her mouth. He shushed her quietly when she started to try and talk through his hand. She quieted, although somewhat begrudgingly.

There was another sound of footsteps, going up now. Terra struggled against John as Seph's voice started to fade away. They were taking her to the King and if she didn't get there soon she wouldn't be able to help Seph or the baby.

Satisfied it was safe; Jesse came back and opened the door to their cell. Terra burst away from John and ran to Jesse.

"Where are they taking her?!" She demanded.

"To the King, for judgment."

Terra and John raced up the spiral steps as fast and as safely as they could. They raced through the barracks and passed some very confused looking guards. Back out into the courtyard and the pouring rain they ran. Terra was starting to tire, she had had used all of her energy and borrowed energy form two other people already. She was starting to feel light headed and her legs were getting heavy. Still she pushed on. Through the main hall, tracking mud and dripping water, straight up the grand staircase and into the throne room.

Together they burst through the normally open ornate double doors and into the room. King Sol was standing at the edge of the small landing that raised his and Queen Elise's thrones off the ground there was an unfamiliar man standing next to him talking to him behind his hand.

Seph was standing at the edge of the worn red carpet, shackles on her wrists with chains that led to the King's Guard

411

standing next to her. Her head was hung and she was soaked from head to foot. Terra couldn't see it but she was sure there were still tears streaming down her face.

At the sight of Terra, dress torn, hair down, muddy, soaking wet, barefoot, and out of breath bursting through the door, the King's jaw hung open.

His shock was short lived as he rounded on his daughter, his face getting red and the vein on his forehead sticking out.

"Terra," he asked gruffly, "What is the meaning of this?!"

"Father," she panted. She sank into a deep curtsy as John formally saluted the King next to her. "I must speak to you about the prisoner. It's urgent."

King Sol motioned for Terra to approach him. She waked toward her father with all the dignity and grace she could muster in her battered state. John followed behind Terra, making sure he kept a respectable distance away from the Princess in the presence of the King.

"My Lord," Terra said, curtsying again as she approached him. "I need to talk to you about the prisoner you have here."

"Daughter," King Sol said, a warring in his voice. "This is Prince Charles of the Moon Kingdom. He's come to collect his little sister. Prince Charles this is my youngest daughter Princess Terra. You'll have to excuse her appearance; she's been through a great ordeal today."

"Your highness," Terra and Charles said in unison as they each bowed or curtsied to the other. Terra looked up and studied the prince. He was as tall as Eric, with dark blond hair and dark blue eyes. His face was chiseled and gorgeous, and it seemed to Terra that his body was as chiseled as his face. As she stared at him she could see the darkness behind his eyes. There was something black inside him and she was worried. She couldn't allow him to take Seph.

"Might I just say," Charles add, taking Terra's hand in his. "I was at the gates to the city earlier; I witnessed your impressive display of power." He pressed his lips to the back of Terra's hand. "I was most impressed by what I saw."

Terra smiled politely, as she was raised to do, and said, "Thank you."

"You must tell me how you managed to accomplish such a thing." Charles asked, still holding Terra's hand.

"I assure you, your highness, it was nothing," she replied. She kindly pulled her hand from his and turned back to her father. "Father I must speak with you immediately about the prisoner."

"I'm afraid Persephone will be coming home with me," Charles said. "She has a doctor waiting to examine her and pass judgment over her for her crimes." Seph's face went white and her brown eyes found Terra's pleadingly.

"Father you can't let her go!" Terra shouted.

"Terra," King Sol demanded, surprised. "What's gotten in to you?"

The princess racked her brain for a thought, any thought that might help her get Seph free. She only needed to buy a few more days to keep her safe.

She had it.

"I'm sorry father," she said, trying to sound convincing. "I'm still a little shaken from the day."

"After what you did today princess," Charles mused, "I wouldn't be able to stand."

Terra smiled kindly at him, he was helping her case. She was planning to convince her father that Seph had threatened her life somehow and that she would have to stay for a few days while they investigate. She just needed to look exhausted, which wouldn't be too hard at this point. Her vision was starting to swim and her head seemed to be buzzing.

She looked at her father and tried to keep her vision locked on him but that got harder and harder to do the longer she tried to force it. "Father I need this prisoner to stay while I investigate her claims." She tried to explain as the buzzing in her head started getting louder.

"What claims?!" Charles demanded.

Terra tried to shake her head, to clear away the buzzing but it only made it worse.

"What claims is she speaking of?" Charles demanded of the King.

"I assure you sir I do not know," King Sol warned, "But I'll remind you to whom you are speaking."

Charles put his hands up and said, "I apologize uncle, I meant you no disrespect, I simply need to know what your daughter is speaking of. Not that it matters. King Sol, my sister and I should be going before this storm gets any worse."

"No," she stressed. "She claimed she knew a way . . ." her vision started to tunnel, "to defeat . . ."

"Princess," John shouted. He ran up and caught her as she started to fall.

"Terra!" King Sol shouted. He quickly closed the gap between himself and John. Carefully he lifted his daughter out of the young man's hands. He held her close against her chest and gently pushed the hair out of her face. Her eyes fluttered open for a moment and he knew she was fine, exhausted but fine.

"Is she well?" Charles asked.

"She is," King Sol said, lifting Terra off the ground. "I'm afraid I must attend to my daughter. This will have to wait until tomorrow."

"King Sol I'm afraid I must insist we conclude our business here first," Charles insisted, his temper coloring his tone.

"And I'm afraid I must decline," the King responded, his voice dangerous. "My daughter is unwell and must be tended to. This can wait until tomorrow."

King Sol turned to leave, making every guard in the room jump to assume their positions around him.

Terra reached up and touched her father's face. He stopped immediately and turned her slightly so she could see his face better.

"Terra, what is it?" He asked.

414

"She's a princess," Terra breathed, "we can't put her in the prison. It would insult mother's . . . family . . ."

King Sol pulled his daughter up again and turned to face John. "You, guard. What is your name?"

"John, your Majesty."

"Who are you named for?" King Sol asked, purely out of curiosity.

"Uh, your father, sir," John answered awkwardly.

"Good man. You are to take Princess Persephone to Princess Diana's old room on the fifth floor. You will then find Jones, tell him what is happening and post a guard outside Persephone's room. Instruct him to find appropriate accommodations for Prince Charles and then come find me. I'll be in the infirmary."

John, having finished relaying all the information the King had asked him too, headed to the infirmary. He ran the whole way there, afraid to keep the King waiting and wanting to know if Terra was ok. She was probably the best friend he had in the castle, aside from Eric. Originally he and Jack were great friends, until a few years ago when he suddenly stopped hanging around. He wouldn't tell John where he was or why he didn't want to hang out anymore. He was just always busy.

Come to think of it he hadn't seen Jack in a while. Not in at least a day or so. He hadn't even reported for duty. John would have to figure out what was going on with him. Defecting was not something the King took lightly.

He reached the door of the infirmary and took only a moment to collect himself before he knocked and entered.

King Sol stood over a bed holding Terra's hand. Bell stood at the head of the bed holding his hands over the princess's head. There was a healer at the foot of the bed holding his hands over her feet. Terra was breathing steadily but her feet twitched every so often.

"Your Majesty," John said, saluting the King. "I have done what you requested and everything has been arranged as you asked."

"Good man," King Sol repeated, not looking up from Terra.

"If I may ask my Lord, is the Princess alright?"

King Sol looked up and stared at solider for a moment.

"You're concerned about her." It wasn't a question.

Still, John answered. "I am my Lord. She is a friend, as well as my princess."

"I see," the King considered.

"Papa," Terra mumbled waking, "what's going on?"

"It's alright Terra," he said, "you're alright."

She tried to sit up. "What happened to Seph? Is everything alright? You didn't let her leave did you?"

"Calm down," he said, a hand on his daughters shoulder. "Princess Persephone is in your sister's old room, under guard, and her brother is put up in mine and your mother's old room."

"Thank the spirits," she whispered, sinking back into bed. "I was so worried."

"My Lord," John asked, still in the doorway. "I was wondering if there was anything else you need me for?"

"Yes," King Sol said, finally looking away from Terra. "Today you protected my daughter. You put her life above your own and, if what I've been told is true, you are the only reason my daughter made it back to the castle and the only reason Guard Reynolds was able to reach her when he did."

"My Lord it was . . ." John started.

"It is a service I can never repay," the King explained, raising a hand to silence John. "For that service, I would like to extend to you the offer of being my daughters second Royal Guard. Despite it being her sister in the prophecy, Terra seems to have a knack for finding trouble.

"It would ease my mind knowing that there was a man with your convictions at her side."

John found he couldn't speak. He wasn't even a captain. He was only slightly above the lowest rung on their totem pole. A promotion like this was unheard of. However, Terra was his friend and it would mean that he could spend more time with her and Eric.

He bowed formally to the King and said, "I would be honored to be so trusted by you my King."

"Terra?" King Sol asked. "How would you feel about that?"

She looked to John and gave him a warm smile. He was a good friend. "I would like that, very much Father."

"It's decided then," King Sol said beaming. "John I will leave my daughter in your care and send Guard Reynolds along in a while to explain to you the details of your new duties. Terra, get rest and I'll send Mammy to your room to draw you a bath so you can bathe before dinner. Will you be alright without me?"

"I will papa," she assured him smiling at her father. "Thank you and I'm sorry about earlier."

"You don't need to apologize to me," the King said. "But you will explain yourself to me as soon as Bell tells me that you are well."

"I know father," she answered, feeling guilty. "I promise I will explain everything to you soon."

"Look after her," King Sol said, looking to Bell and John. "I will expect to see her well rested and cleaned up at dinner."

"Yes my lord," John and Bell replied together, bowing to the King.

King Sol, satisfied that his daughter's needs were being met, headed out the door, a line of guards following him. Bell smiled at Terra and slipped out the door after the King.

"Majesty," he said, "might I have a word in private?"

"Give us a minute," the King said, waving his small army of guards away. "What is it Bell?"

"Things with Terra," he started.

"I know," King Sol cut him off. "Still, she survived and so long as she's ok, then the plan will still work."

"Majesty, I know it's not my place, but maybe it's time to consider a different plan? To awaken Terra, just enough to get her to open her eyes, not enough to fully revive her; it took nearly all the energy the two of us could muster. If she depletes all of her energy like that again, there's no way to know how long it might take to awaken her.

"I think it's time to consider a new plan."

"We can't do that," King Sol replied. "We've come too far. There isn't time to start again."

"As you wish sir," Bell answered reluctantly. He waited for the King to turn and walk away before turning back to the infirmary door and slipping in.

Terra watched as Bell headed out the door after her father. Once the door had closed she sat up and slowly swung her legs over the side to the bed. Her head was still swimmy but the longer she sat up the better she started to feel. She slipped down to the floor and, as soon as she was sure she wouldn't fall, she waved John over.

"Royal Guard hu?" She asked, "That's amazing!"

"I can't believe it," John agreed. "I think I just passed nearly a dozen different ranks"

Terra smiled and threw her arms around him. "I'm so happy for you!"

"P . . . princess . . ." he stammered awkwardly, "what's this for?"

"I'm saying congratulations," she explained, "and thank you. For everything you did for me today."

John put his arms around the princess and hugged her back. "I think this is going to make every other soldier and guard I work with jealous," he laughed.

Terra pulled away and smirked at him. "Jealous of all the perks your new position comes with?"

"Jealous that I got to hug a princess," he said mockingly.

"Ha ha ha," she joked. "What do you say we head up to my room? I don't want to keep Mammy waiting."

"Especially if she heard about what happened today," John observed. He put his arm around Terra's shoulders and helped her walk to the door.

"Oh I don't even want to think of how frantic she's going to be if that's the case," she muttered laughing nervously.

John reached for the handle just as the door was pushed open. Bell walked in and eyed the two of them. He looked at Terra and she could tell there was something he wanted to say, something in the way he held her gaze made her feel like he was on the verge of speaking to her.

"Princess," he remarked nodding. He pushed the door open wide and stepped back so they could pass through.

"Master Bell," she asked. "Our lesson?"

"Ah yes," he replied, the faint trace of a smile on his lips. "If you have time before dinner, meet me in the school room. The lesson I have for you is short so it won't take long."

"Alright," she grinned, glad at the chance to keep her lesson. "I will see you shortly."

John helped Terra walk up through the castle and up to her room. Mammy was pacing back and forth outside the door. At the sight of her, she exploded into tears and rushed forward to help John.

"Terra, oh my dear Creator! Baby what happened?!" Mammy was blabbering and tears were streaming down her face as she took up Terra's other arm and helped them the rest of the way to her room.

There was a large porcelain claw foot tub in the middle of the room filled with water so warm Terra could see the steam rising from it. She stopped, halfway through the door. Her normal tub was a barrel that they rolled up from the closet in Eric's room. She had never had a tub like this. She couldn't even figure out how the tub got all the way up to her room in the first place.

"Your father sent it up," Mammy said, catching Terra's gaze. "He said that after the day you had you deserved to be able to bathe comfortably."

419

"How?"

"Master Bell," Mammy answered simply.

"Oh."

"John you should go now," Mammy said, "I know you have other responsibilities."

"Actually I don't," he smiled.

"What does that mean?" Mammy asked. She stepped away from the two and pulled a screen around the tub.

"You tell her," he whispered, setting her down on the padded stool in front of her dressing table.

"Are you sure?" She asked, whispering too.

He smiled and nodded.

"John has been assigned as my new Royal Guard," Terra explained still smiling at him. "Effective immediately if I'm not mistaken."

"Two guards?" Mammy asked walking back over to Terra.

"Apparently I'm some kind of lightning rod for trouble," she replied with a shrug.

"Who knew?" John asked sarcastically.

"Well Guard or no," Mammy said smiling kindly at him. "You'll need to head out while the Princess bathes."

"Oh, of course," he said blushing. "I'll be right outside if you need me." He bowed to Terra before turning and walking out the door.

"So then," Mammy sighed, "Tell me about today."

Bell walked slowly back to the school room. He mind was racing and he walked mindlessly forward. What he had seen Terra do today went beyond anything he could have ever imagined. It changed everything that he and King Sol were planning. If only he could get the King to see that.

Terra being as strong as she was meant that it might be nearly impossible for them to manipulate her the way they had intended. She would be able to detect and deter any magical advance Bell might make. If it got out, before their plan was complete, exactly what he and the King had been planning for the last four years, it would destroy Terra. Her trust in them would be shattered and they would lose any advantage they had over the Shadow King.

It made Bell nervous to think about her being isolated and alone due to his poor planning. If she became estranged from her father and from him she would be weak to any advance the Shadow King might make. She needed something to protect herself with, something to keep her safe from him and what he can do.

A thought struck Bell then. Years and years ago he had taken a small crystal from a locked cabinet in the schoolroom. He hadn't known then why he had taken it out and what he was going to use it for. Now, however, he was beginning to think he had figured out why he pulled the thing in the first place and maybe, a way to help Terra.

Terra sat on the padded stool again.

This time Mammy stood behind her pinning her hair up.

She was fresh from the bath and she felt wonderful. All the dirt and sweat from the day had been washed off, leaving only a clean shiny princess behind. It had taken a while though. Terra had soaked in the tub for nearly half an hour. By the time she finally rose from the water, (kept nice and toasty warm by her mastery of fire), her fingers and toes and gone past wrinkling and looked to be turning in on themselves.

"What's wrong dear?" Mammy asked with a mouth full of pins.

"Nothing," she sighed, not really sure what it was about her appearance that unsettled her.

"Terra, you know I know when you're lying to me."

"I know," she admitted. "I just don't know about this dress."

"Why is that dear?"

"It's such a pure white. I'm terrified I'm going to ruin it."

Don't be ridiculous. You look stunning in the dress and besides," Mammy explained placing the last pin, "this is the dress your father specifically requested you wear."

"Why is that?"

"I think it has something to do with what happened in town today. Although it could have something to do with the prince in our castle too," Mammy observed pointedly.

Terra made a face at Mammy through the looking glass. "Oh no Mammy," she explained, "he is not a good man. There is some kind of darkness around him. Not to mention the fact that he's my cousin."

"Second cousin," Mammy corrected.

"Still," she insisted, standing. "I don't like him. More importantly, I certainly don't like the way he was looking at his sister today. I'm worried about her Mammy."

"You've spared her so far," she reminded the princess, "let's just see how things go from here, alright?"

Terra nodded as she appraised herself in the looking glass. Her dress was completely white. Not off white or an eggshell color, it was white. It had a very tight corset that made Terra feel like her waist was gone and her hips were wide. There was some kind of beading and lace work done throughout the entire dress and the skirt was a full poufy skirt. It was beautiful, but more like a wedding dress than a dress you wear to dinner.

"It seems like too much," she remarked.

"Not at all," Mammy assured waving away Terra's fears. "Now off to dinner with you."

"Not just yet," she said, "I have to go see a few people."

Terra knocked quietly on the door to the schoolroom and waited.

"Come in," Bell called from beyond the door.

Terra walked in slowly and closed the door. Bell was back at his desk holding up something that glinted in the light of the setting sun like a blade. He was rolling it over in his hands as Terra walked up.

It was in fact a knife.

A dagger to be exact.

It was a beautiful steel weapon with some kind of engravings on the blade and on the hilt. Terra couldn't read it but she could feel the magic coming off the object as Bell held it reverently in his hands. He turned to her and extended the knife for her to take.

She hesitated.

Terra didn't enjoy fighting or violence, and she especially didn't enjoy death. Still, Master Bell didn't do things for no reason, so she carefully lifted the blade from his hand and examined it.

She was struck as soon as she touched it buy the odd feeling that circulated through her. It was clearly a magical blade, quite powerful in fact. Although to her that power seemed to be limited. At the end of the hilt there was a beautiful polished purple stone. Amethyst, she thought.

"What do you make of this blade?" Bell asked.

"Its old," Terra answered, her eyes fixed on the blade. "Steel I think?"

"Steel handle, silver blade," Bell informed her. "What else?"

"Well I can't read the language the inscriptions are in, but I can tell its powerful, though that power seems, to me anyway, limited somehow. Leading me to believe that this dagger was created for one specific purpose only."

"You're mostly right," he confirmed. "What can you tell me about the hilt?"

"Well, its grip is wrapped in leather and there's a sizable piece of amethyst in it." She touched the purple stone for a moment as she tried to nail down what it was about that stone that felt different. Then she realized it was that it felt different at all.

"This stone, it wasn't originally part of the blade was it?"

"No."

"It feels like it has power too and I can tell you it's different than the blade."

Bell reached out and took the dagger from Terra. "This knife is the only one like it in existence. It was specially made and crafted to stop the Shadow King. All of these words," he indicated with his hand to the hilt, "they are each a kind of disappearing spell. And these," he pointed to the runes on the blade now, "they mean vacuum and hold.

"When this blade is thrust into a person of substantial magical power, the hilt disappears. Not only that, but the blade pulls all the magic the victim has and keeps it pinned in one place in their body. Rendering all of their magical powers innate and making them defenseless."

Terra looked up into the eyes of the man she had known all her life and for the first time she saw a hardness in those blue eyes that she didn't recognize. "This was made to kill Grey, to kill the Shadow King." It wasn't a question.

"Yes. After the prophecy was first translated your great-great-great- grandfather contacted my master's master, Master Atlas, and had him construct this blade. When I was contacted by you father to by the Master Wizard of his kingdom, my master entrusted the blade to me."

Terra was silent as she considered all that Bell had said.

"You're giving it to me, aren't you?" She asked.

He nodded. He picked up a black sheath from the table and careful slid the blade inside. There was a small clasp at the top that prevented the blade from slipping out. He fastened it and handed it, hilt first, to Terra.

"After everything that happened today, I don't think we can ignore the threat the prisoner poses to you."

"Master Bell if you are suggesting what I think you are suggesting . . ." she started.

"I am only suggesting that you carry this knife with you. That stone in the top, it's has the ability to project your conscience out of your body."

"What would I need that for?"

"When you're in Grey's presence, so long as you have the knife, he can no longer read your mind." Bell explained. "Even if you don't project your mind it will coat it in a sense. Making it impossible for him to know what you're thinking."

"So he won't see it coming," Terra said flatly.

"So that you are safe," Bell sighed. "I know that you have developed some sort of feelings for him and while I can't say what those feelings are, I know that they exist."

Terra opened her mouth to argue with Bell but the hard look in his eyes stopped her.

"Your feelings for him tend to cloud your judgment. I just need you to be safe and you carrying this blade ensures that."

"I can't say what I do or don't feel about Grey," she replied honestly, "But I do know that my judgment isn't clouded. I know that he's the enemy and I know that he is evil. There is darkness in him and it's a threat to every living thing on this earth.

"I also know that the prophecy says that Diana must be the one who kills him. Who knows what might happen if we start changing things."

"I'm not saying that you should kill him. I'm only saying that it would make all of us feel better knowing that if he tried something you could protect yourself."

Terra looked at the knife. There was a feeling in her gut that she couldn't shake. Something about this knife made her very nervous. There was fear and hatred attached to that blade and she wanted nothing to do with it. Looking to Bell, she knew that she didn't have much in the way of options. He wanted her to take the knife and she knew that it would be good to have a way to keep Grey out of her head, especially after today.

"It could help Diana," she sighed. "In the end."

"Will you take it then?"

Terra sighed, "If it'll help Diana, I will take the knife."

Bell sighed and he seemed to visibly relax. "Thank you Princess."

Eric stood in the center of the Queen's garden as the sun set over the ocean beyond the cliffs at the edge of the castle grounds. Queen Elise had the garden specially made when she and the King had first married. She had brought over hundreds of different flowers from her home in the Moon Kingdom. Some bloomed during the day, but most only bloomed under the light of the full moon. It was a magical place to be on nights like those.

Eric glanced up at the sky.

He was almost certain tonight wouldn't be a full moon, but it might be close and it would still be beautiful.

It seemed only fitting that tonight would be the night he and Terra finally expressed their feelings to each other. Or she expressed her feelings for him seeing as how he had already vocalized his.

This morning seemed so long ago now. He had talked with her and explained how he felt like she had wanted, or like he though she wanted. After that fight he was sure that it was over between them. He couldn't think of life without her but he also couldn't handle living the way they had been.

He paced back and forth, thinking of all the things he would say.

As the sun slid down the sky, it shone its fading light on the garden and made the water in the fountains and streams sparkle. Eric stopped and admired the beauty of the things around him. He loved the way the light would wash all the pale flowers in oranges and yellows. Twilight was his favorite time of day.

"Eric?"

He turned to see Terra standing under the archway behind him. Her dress seemed to glitter and glow in the fading light of the sun. She was beautiful.

"Terra," he said breathless. "You look amazing."

"Thank you," she blushed, walking forward. "And thank you for meeting me here. I know after everything we talked about today and after all that was said it wasn't easy for you to come. So I want you to know how much I appreciate you being here."

"Terra," he started, walking up and taking both her hands in his. "I need you to tell me honestly what's going on with us. I love you, I've told you that and you completely shut me down."

"Eric . . ." she started.

"Let me finish please," he interjected. "Terra, ever since the night I stood in the dark with you and watched the fireflies I have loved you. And I know that you were young then and it wouldn't have been fair to put that kind of emotion on you. So I waited. Then you told me that we couldn't have these feelings for each other and I knew then that it was too late.

"Still I waited, silently, until a time came when I could hold you without fear and tell you how I feel. And maybe today wasn't supposed to be that day, and I'm sorry for the way I acted earlier but I need you to understand that I only acted that way because I love you and not being able to tell you how I've felt all these years has been the hardest thing I've ever done.

"So please, if you can stand here and tell me you love me too then tell me because I need to hear you say it. Otherwise . . . you . . . you have to let me go."

There were tears in his eyes as he continued, "If you can't be with me than you can't. I know you have your reasons and I respect that you have conviction enough to stick with them. If that's the case then you have to break our bond and let me go."

Terra, tears in her eyes waited until she was sure he was done before she spoke. "Eric . . . I've been through so much these last few years. All the changes I've made and all the changes that have taken place in the world. Some good, most . . not. Still, no matter what was going on I knew that you would be here, at my side, no matter what.

"You're right, I do have reasons why I think we can't be together, reasons that I still believe are valid. I do think that you're a

427

target based on your proximity to me. Just as my Father, Mother, Sister and now I suppose, John are.

"But today . . . today I stood surrounded by shadows knowing that I was going to die. I laid flat on my back, looking up at the sky and I knew I would never see your face again. Never again would we joke or play around like we used to. I would never get to tell you how I feel.

"I know you know how I feel, but I would never get to *tell* you. Certainly I had reasons. A lot of reasons actually, more than I needed and more than I wanted." She paused as she considered how to tell Eric what she had to say. She felt like she would need all night to properly tell him how she felt.

"I stood there and realized how stupid those reasons were. No matter what I say to you, you will always be a target. What did my being honest with you change? Nothing. Except perhaps how happy we are. I decided then that if I ever got out of that mess I would bury myself in your arms and tell you exactly how much I love you."

Eric started. He opened his mouth and closed it several times as he searched for the right thing to say. Terra said she loved him. He wasn't wrong she had said it.

"I love you Eric," she said again. "I can't tell you how sorry I am that you have had to suffer for my short comings all these years. I can't promise that we'll be together forever because I don't know what's going to happen, for all we know I could be dead tomorrow. And I can't promise you anymore than my heart. Even after everything between Diana and Grey is settled, I'm still a princess. Which means I have little to no say in who I'll marry.

"So if you can accept the limitations of my love, accept me knowing that I can only give you so much, then . . . then stay. Because I don't know if I can do this without you here . . ." she was cut off when Eric, having heard all he needed to hear, scooped her up in his arms and kissed her.

She laughed and cried as he lifted her off her feet and spun her around, kissing her.

He spun her, both of them laughing and crying, kissing her until they were both to dizzy to stand without leaning on the other.

"Of course I'll stay," he laughed when he set her on her feet. "All I want is to be with you for as long as I can. Even if it's only until tomorrow, I'll take it. I love you Terra and you've made me happier than I ever thought possible."

Terra smiled, tears still in her eyes, "I love you too." She smiled at how amazing it felt to finally be honest with Eric. To be able to tell him just how much he meant to her and how much she cared, it was beyond what she thought it would be. It was the greatest moment of her life.

A sound of music coming from inside the castle signaled that it was time for dinner. Terra made a sound and buried her face in his chest. Eric, understanding her frustration, sighed. He put a hand on each of her shoulders and pushed her back so he could see her face.

"What are you going to do?" He asked.

He didn't say it, but Terra could hear the "about Grey?" at the end of his question. She sighed and fidgeted with the tip of the sheath that Bell had given her. She felt odd standing there in her mother's garden, telling a man she loved just how much she loved him whilst wearing a very old, strangely powerful dagger around her left thigh.

"I have to go talk to him," she answered finally. "I don't want to but I have to know why he did what he did. And then I'm going to tell him that I will no longer be keeping him company at dinner. I'll still have to bring him dinner since the box is keyed to me. Still, no more conversations between him and me, no more me being his friend. I'm done."

"Do you want me to go in with you?"

"No. I need to do this alone. He focuses better if it's just us. I just have to go in there hand him his dinner and tell him I'm done. He'll argue I'm sure, but I can handle that. After everything today, I can handle this too."

"If you're sure," he asked, "Then let's go get this over with."

Chapter 11

Grey sat up in bed and looked around, unsure what was going on. He ran his hands through his long, unruly, black hair and searched his thoughts for a moment. He remembered the shadows attacking Terra, and the feeling of helplessness as he watched them circle her, completely beyond his control. Then . . . then he had sent every ounce of energy he had to help her. He'd sat back on his bed then, exhausted and waited for Terra to come bursting through those doors, demanding an explanation and furious about what had happened.

Not that he would have blamed her. He was the Shadow King and shadows tried to kill her today. It only made sense for her to be mad at him after that. He sat down wanting to rest so he could explain things to her, get her to understand that it wasn't him who had sent those shadows after her. It would take some convincing but he was sure Terra would believe him.

He must have fallen asleep.

As far as he could tell hours had passed between now and then.

Yet somehow there was no Terra.

She was going to be furious when she came down here, she wouldn't have walked away just because he was asleep. She might come through the glass and shaken him awake demanding answers, but she wouldn't have just let him sleep. He glance over at the table, there was no tray from lunch. Just the tray she'd brought from breakfast.

She hadn't been here since then?

An image of her underneath him flashed in his mind.

He stopped for a moment, thinking over all that had raced through this mind at that moment.

She was beautiful in her grey dress, with her hair slightly out of place after he had rolled on top of her. She looked up at him with her green eyes full of anger, fear, and something he thought could have been desire.

Not for the first time in his life, Grey nearly lost control looking down at her that way.

He was glad she had threatened him with the fire like she had. It had snapped him out of the crazy thoughts that had been racing in his mind.

He stopped and focused for a moment.

Reynolds was coming down the spiral staircase, which must have been what woke him.

Not just that, he was coming alone.

Grey focused harder. There was no trace of Terra, although she did seemed to feature predominantly in Reynolds mind as he walked across the floor now. He couldn't tell all of what he was thinking form this distance and the way his mind seemed to buzz around a million different things didn't seem to help.

Could she have sent him in her stead to argue with him?

No. Terra wasn't the kind of woman who let a man fight her battles for her. If Reynolds was on his way down here, alone, than it was because he wanted to get his two cents in before she came down and said her piece.

He stood and stretched. Reynolds was fool if the thought he was going to come down here and argue with him. Grey was a King in two different rights and in two different worlds. Reynolds was less than an insect to him. If he pushed it too far, he would just kill him.

431

'Terra would never forgive me if I killed Eric,' a small voice in the back of his head whispered.

A sudden flash of anger at the voice had Grey's temper up and his patience down. He stalked back to the end of his cell and leaned against the wall. He thought about reaching out and darkening nearly all the torches so when he walked in, Reynolds would be surrounded by darkness. If he did that however, then it was possible that Reynolds would just close the door and bar it. He would never get a chance to explain anything to Terra if that happened.

Not that it mattered what she thought of course, he just needed her to get her sister was all.

So Grey decided the best course of action.

He would release enough dark magic into the room to make it nearly impossible for anyone to be in here. It would swirl and build in the room, completely unseen, until there was no clean air left. Eric would walk in and start chocking. He would be lucky if he managed to get two words in while Grey stood in his cell and laughed.

Reynolds was now at the table with the other guard, the one who had the . . . interesting thoughts about Terra. He was stopped and talking so Grey knew he had time. He had just started to flood the room when the door opened and Terra stepped in carrying the dinner tray like she always did.

He stared shocked. He couldn't detect her at all. She stood at the door and met his gaze. Her eyes were set and hard and there was something so different about her face. There was a kind of determination there he hadn't seen in her before. She still looked the same, although she was beautiful in her white dress with her black hair.

He realized suddenly she wasn't just furious she was outraged, appalled even. He had never seen her so mad. Terra was not the kind of person prone to anger. She was the person who took the crap that everyone dished out and told herself that it was her fault, even though it rarely was. Terra didn't get mad, not like this anyway.

"Terra," he started, knowing it would take more than just explaining to get her to understand now.

Terra walked into the prison room, carrying a tray laden down with some of the best foods the kingdom had to offer. Her mother had spared no expense when preparing dinner for Prince Charles and Seph, even if she was in custody.

As soon as she was through the door she was struck by how much dark energy was circulating in the room. It seemed to be pouring out of the cell and lingering on the floor. Like a lake of black clouds surrounding the cell and lapping toward the door. She looked up and met Grey's eyes, knowing this might very well be the last time she ever spoke with him.

She could see the shock on his face as it registered for him that he hadn't seen her coming. With Bell's knife strapped to her thigh she was literally invisible to him. Still not sure about having a knife on her, Terra was incredibly grateful for the protection it offered her thoughts and feelings. If Grey could see in to her head and her heart he would know how much she was hurting inside at the thought of what she had to say to him. He would be able to see the way her mind raced for different explanation other than the obvious one.

Weapon or no, she was glad Bell had made her take it.

"Terra," he said.

With a sigh, she started forward. As she walked into the darkness she felt its icy cold curl around her ankles like a cat. She shuddered against the cold and felt the darkness at her feet tremble for a moment, before it vanished all together.

"Terra," he repeated, more shocked this time. "How did you . . ."

She set the tray on the table and turned back to face he. He'd walked down to the corner closest to the table and was leaning against the glass. He met her gaze with a mix of emotions swirling behind his eyes. She could have stopped and figured out what each of those emotions was, but that would only make what she had to do all the harder.

"I'll keep this simple," she started, more grateful than she could say that her voice sounded steady and strong. "Today a man died because you were trying to get to me. A good man who was only doing what he knew to be right. . ."

"Terra let me explain," he interjected.

She put her hand up, "This will go so much easier if you just let me talk first."

"Only if you listen to me when you're done," he countered hotly.

"Fine," she agreed.

"Go on then."

Terra took a breath and forced herself not to be swayed by the hurt in Grey's eyes. "Today I held a man in my arms as he died. I didn't know the man personally, but I know now that his name was Tom and he was from the Moon Kingdom. I know that he was a good man trying to protect his princess, even though it meant his life. He died protecting her.

"His death, though caused by your shadows, is my fault. Something . . ."

"How could it possibly be your fault?!" He demanded suddenly.

"It's not your turn yet," she shot at him.

Grey scowled but motioned for Terra to continue. "His death is my fault because those shadows were after me. They came for *me*. He had the unfortunate luck of getting caught in the middle of your plans for me. The guilt of his death I will carry with me for the rest of my life.

"I have always known who and what you are," she was quieter now, the heat of her anger fading quickly. "For a time I told myself I could heal you. I thought I could take the darkness in your heart away. Make you better I suppose.

"I was young and I was stupid. I was sure if I could heal you than I could save you and Diana. Because if there was no darkness in you, than neither of you had to fight. Neither of you had to die." Terra paused for a moment as she considered what to say next. There was so much she needed to tell him before she walked away that it was hard for her to keep track of it all.

"For years I tried to be here and help you, even though the whole time I knew you were trying to corrupt me. You started the very first day I was in here." Grey made a noise like he was going to argue, but again she held up her hand to silence him. "I know you've been trying Grey, don't try to lie. I actually understood why you were doing it. I was so blind by my own simple ignorance that I justified it. It was only logical for you to do all you could to escape here."

"Terra I. . ." he started.

"I can see your darkness."

Grey nearly fell out of the chair he was trying to sit in. "You can do what?! How?"

"I don't know how," Terra sighed exasperated. "I don't know how I do half the things I can do! But that's not the point!"

He stopped, words on the tip of his tongue. Thinking better of it, he waited for her to go on.

"My point is I knew what you were doing and who you are and what you're capable of. Still I let myself think . . . I even let myself feel . . ." Terra's words trailed away. She took a long shaky breath and said, "It doesn't matter now. What matters is that after today I know how wrong I was about you. I know that you are the monster I tried to pretend you weren't all this time.

"Today you tried to kill me, tried and almost succeeded. So I have to know, why did you help me? Why send your monsters to kill me and then save me at the last second? What good does that do? What is the point of putting me through all this? Is it all part of your little game to corrupt me? Why, just tell me why?"

435

Grey waited a moment before he spoke, wanting to be sure she was done. "Terra I didn't send those shadows."

She scoffed, "Of course you didn't. I'm sure there's someone else out there who can control shadows right? That makes perfect sense." Terra's tone was bitter and sarcastic. Tears were in her eyes and threatening to spill down her face. She had to blink rapidly several times to keep from crying.

"Terra I gave you a chance to speak, you have to pay me that same respect," Grey growled getting heated again.

"Fine!" She exclaimed irritably. She had absolutely no desire to hear what he had to say, but she sat down in her chair and motioned for him to continue.

Grey was starting to get angry. Terra was looking at him the way everybody else looked at him, like he was something less than people. She had never looked at him that way, and she sure as hell had no right to do it now.

"Damn it Terra listen to me!" He shouted, slowly losing control. "I didn't send those damn things to kill you! I don't know what happened but they weren't listening to me! I tried to stop them but I couldn't! I was just sitting there watching them as they advanced toward you; it was all I could do to send you energy when you reached for it!"

"You control them!" She shouted jumping out of her chair. "You're the only one who controls them!"

"Damn it Terra that's what I'm trying to tell you! I couldn't control them! I'm slowly losing my control on them and that's YOUR FAULT!" He was yelling in full now. He had lost all sense of control as he fought to make her understand what was really going on.

"How *dare* you!" She yelled, sounding more like her sister than herself. "How can you stand there and blame *me* for the shadows *you* sent! How is this in anyway MY FAULT!?" Terra was at the glass yelling at Grey as loudly as he was yelling at her.

"BECAUSE I'M IN LOVE WITH YOU, YOU IDIOT," Grey shouted not thinking.

Terra stumbled back a step, away from the glass. "What?" she asked, all the fire gone from her eyes.

Grey cursed himself and his lack of control. He had never meant for her to know how he felt. He had discovered just over six months ago how he really felt about her. Much to his own dismay, he had realized that the feelings he was faking to corrupt her had stopped being fake. For a time he told himself that it wasn't that he loved her. How would he even know if he did? He knew nothing about love personally. He had seen some of the things people did in the name of love and some things people tried to pass off as love.

When he had found out he was shocked and disgusted with himself. He knew that there would never been anything between himself and the princess, nothing real anyway. Grey had planned to use a number of fake emotions to manipulate Terra once she was under his control. In all his plans and schemes, he had never planned for love.

Mostly he blamed that wretched little bright spot in his heart. For years he'd tried all he could to return it to normal. But to no avail. Once he knew what he felt for her he knew it was all because of that.

Now he had told her how he felt and the aftermath of that confession could change and devastate everything he had spent the last four years working towards.

"Terra," he started, not sure where to go from here. "I . . . I'm sorry."

"You're sorry?" She demanded, her anger coming back. "You nearly killed me today and then you tell me you love me? What kind of sick game are you playing at?"

"It's not a game!" He shouted, getting angry again too. "You think I want to feel this way? Do you think that this is fun for me? Do you have any idea what loving you has done to me?!"

Terra stopped. She was so mad and so enraged at his fake declaration that she felt she might explode. To stand there, today of all days, and act like he was in love with her. As if he even knew what love was. She felt her resolve weaken suddenly as the tears she'd been fighting broke free and started to run down her face.

"You aren't capable of love," she finally whispered, surprised at how bitter she sounded. "So don't stand there and make excuses about what happened today. If there was even a shred of humanity in you, you would tell me why you did what you did so that I can go."

Grey, stuck by a pain in his chest at her words, said, "Terra I couldn't have sent those shadows after you if I wanted to. I don't understand how it happened or even when it happened for certain. All I know is that I do love you. Despite what you or I might want. That's why when you reached to me today I gave you all I had.

"It's why when you ask me not to do thing or to stop, I stop. Even if I don't want to. If you ask me to do it, I will.

"I convinced you to start having dinner in my box because being that close to you without being able to touch you was more than I could stand. Over the years, this last one in particular I think, I have bent and broken to your will, and yours alone. Not for some damn plan or to manipulate you."

He took a deep breath, unable to stop the words that flew from his mouth. "I did it because I love you. Even though I've fought that love every step of the way. Even now I would fight it if I knew how."

Terra's mind raced. It was just over a year ago that the number of shadows and shadow attacks skyrocketed. If what Grey was saying was the truth than his feelings for her meant that he was losing his control over the shadows. Which had to mean that she had been right all along, she'd been slowly purifying him.

Still, if she was willing to believe that then she couldn't dismiss his claims of innocence out of hand. She would have to consider the fact that he was telling the truth. She would have to consider that he actually did love her.

"No," she whispered. "I can't do this." She turned for the door. If she had to start thinking about him loving her it would . . . it would lead to the conversation of how she felt about him.

She had taken anything she felt for him and locked it away inside herself. She didn't want to know, she didn't want to think about it. All she wanted to do was save him and her sister from a fight that could claim both their lives. She couldn't allow herself to even think about . . . feelings . . . for him with this kind of weight on her shoulders.

"Terra wait!" He shouted. "Don't go!"

She slowed to a stop, halfway across the room. She hated herself for stopping, hated that the pain in his voice had caused her to stop.

"I know that today was bad, and I know that you don't want to hear this, but I do love you. I've told you that, the least you could do is tell me how you feel about me. I feel like my heart might die if I don't know. And don't worry; I hate me enough for the both of us for saying so."

"I can't," Terra sighed still facing the door.

"Can't what?"

"Can't talk about this, not after everything that's happened."

"Terra you know I'm telling the truth. I know that you know this, even though I can't detect your heart or your mind, because you're trying to run. You know what I'm saying is true and you're trying to run from that truth."

"Grey," she whispered, her voice breaking. "What good would it do to tell you how I felt about you or if I felt anything about you? In what world would that make things better?"

"Terra," he started, not exactly sure what to say. "Tell me this one thing. Tell me this and I will tell you anything else you want to know about me or the shadows or the plans that I was making. Anything, just tell me how you feel so my stupid heart will stop hammering in my chest."

She turned slightly and regarded Grey out of the corner of her eye. There were many things they didn't know. If she asked the right question than it could tip the scales in their favor. It could change the tide of the coming battle.

With a sad and defeated sigh, she turned and faced him. Tears still silently flowing down her face she said, "Grey . . . you are this piece of me, this part of my heart that . . . that I wish I didn't need. I tried for so long to keep what I felt about you locked away inside of my heart. I knew that what I thought and what I felt were treason and would destroy me if I voiced them.

"So there," she finished, stating to get angry again, although this time she wasn't sure why. "You are the piece of my heart I wish I didn't need. Because our love would destroy worlds. Maybe just our own, or maybe Diana's or John's or even Eric's. Our love would be a . . . tragedy of unheard of proportions." Terra had spoken from her heat and said everything she had been thinking for so long.

She looked at Grey; he seemed too shocked to speak. So she gathered her long skirt in her hands and headed for the door again. It would be best if she just left now. She would speak with Bell in the morning and ask him what one piece of information would be the most beneficial for them to know. Then she would ask Grey and be done. She wouldn't come back for anymore conversations.

"If our love is such a tragedy then why are you the one thing that's healed me?!" He shouted, seconds before Terra's hand found the door knob.

She turned, confused, and faced him again. "What did you say?"

"You heard me," he all but spat. "If our love is such a terrible thing, such a great tragedy, then why is it the one thing that has healed me? Why is it the thing that clears away the fog in my mind and makes me wonder if I've been right to do what I've done?! How is that tragic?!"

Terra stared, unable to speak.

Her heart sang to hear the words Grey said. To know that there was a part of him that wasn't convinced that being this man, this Shadow King, was a good. Could he really be telling the truth?

Terra cried out as the sensation of the second heartbeat in her chest returned, as it did sometimes. She put her hand to her chest and leaned against the door. It didn't hurt per say, it was just intense and sometimes knocked the wind out of her. As she stood she noticed how much more intense it was this time. Usually she would wait and it would be over.

Now it held on and made Terra feel like she couldn't see straight.

A sound across the room drew her attention back to Grey. He had one hand on the glass and the other on his chest. He had felt it too. He looked up and their eyes met.

"You?" Terra asked. "This *is* you?"

"This isn't me," he grunted. "I have no idea what this is or why it happens."

Terra shook her head. This was the grain that tipped the scale, she couldn't take anymore. She looked at Grey one last time, yanked the door open and ran.

Eric stood, dumbfounded, and watched Terra run from the prison and up the stairs. She didn't stop and say a word to him as she went. She hadn't even looked to see if he was there. He felt for her through the bond, but forgot about the knife that she wore. He couldn't feel her so long as it was on. He glanced into the brightly lit prison and saw the prisoner on his knees at the edge of the glass.

For a moment he went back and forth, trying to decide if he should chase after Terra or if he should go and demand to know what happened.

He knew Terra well enough to know that there were times when she needed to be alone. On the other hand though, today was a very special day for them. He didn't know exactly what they were to each other, but he knew that if she needed him, he should be there.

Even if it meant that he had to come back down here in the wee hours of the morning to find out what that monster had said to her.

He shouted over his shoulder for Lewis to close the door and not let anyone pass except him, then he ran up the stairs and started trying to figure out where Terra might be.

King Sol slowly made his way to the west wing. He needed to go over some things where the Moon Kingdom was concerned. With two of the five royal children here, it wouldn't be long before he found his Brother-in-law at his front door demanding to know what was going on. If it were at all possible, he would like to avoid that confrontation. His brother-in-law, the King of the Moon Kingdom, was not a reasonable man. He would not take interference from King Sol lightly.

He opened the door just as Terra came barreling through.

"Terra!" He exclaimed as she ran into his chest. "What on earth is going on?"

She looked up at him, tears in her eyes, and sobbed something he couldn't quite understand. Instinctively he wrapped his arms around her and waved his guards off. All but Markus bowed and took up positions outside the door to the west wing.

"Markus get the door to the war room," King Sol told him as he helped Terra walk back down the hall. He wasn't sure what had happened but she was coming from the prison and that usually meant trouble. He led her into the war room and sat her down in his large ornately carved throne.

"My Lord," Markus said from his side. King Sol glanced up to see Markus holding a handkerchief he had produced from his uniform.

"Thank you Markus," he said. "Go and wait by the door, I don't want any interruptions." With a slight bow, Markus turned and walked to the door. He stood facing away from King Sol and Terra, out of respect.

"Terra tell me what's happened?" King Sol asked. He tried to keep his voice concerned but fatherly.

Terra looked up at her father; she could tell he wouldn't handle any of the news she had very well. It seemed the only thing she could do was lie. She couldn't tell her father that she and Eric were in love and had spent part of the evening wrapped in each other's arms in her mother's garden. Even worse than that she couldn't tell him that Grey loved her and that . . . she . . . she might feel something . . . similar. How could she tell her father any of that? How could she expect him to understand when she still didn't understand any of it?

So she did the only thing she could thing to do.

"I'm sorry father," she started, trying to steady her voice. "It just gets so hard having to deal with the prisoner. Especially after everything that happened today to me and John and Seph. It was just a little more than I could handle."

King Sol smiled kindly down at his daughter. She was never raised to be a queen or to handle the pressure that came with ruling. Everything that had happened today and in the last four years had really put a strain on her. She had borne the weight of all her responsibilities so well that King Sol had often wondered what kind of Queen she would be. It only made sense that after everything that had happened that she would start to strain under it all.

He cupped her face in his hands and used his thumbs to wipe her tears away. "I know it's been a hard day, and I know you never wanted to be involved in all this. But I want you to know how proud I am of your for taking all this on. You stepped up to save your sister and saving her is the same as saving everyone. It's a hard road to travel, being royalty, but you have trod it well and you have made me proud. So know that going forward."

Terra smiled. "Thank you Papa. I'm sorry I let myself get worked up this way."

"We all have moments of weakness my dear, but at least you can recognize that and move forward. Just remember you are stronger than you think you are."

"Thank you Papa," she repeated. "I'm fine now I just needed a moment to collect myself."

"Good, that's good." King Sol made a face as he pulled back from his daughter.

"What is it Papa?" She asked, recognizing the face her father was making.

"Don't worry about it tonight Terra, we can talk in the morning."

"Papa you can talk to me now. I could use the distraction to be honest."

King Sol considered for a moment. "Very well then. What did Persephone say to you that was so important we had to hold her here? It looks bad to not release her to her brother, you must know that."

"I do father," she assured him. "When I spoke with Persephone earlier she informed me that she might have information prevalent to the fight between Diana and the Shadow King. I was going to see what the information was and then if it was relevant I had planned to come to you with it."

"So what was the information?" King Sol asked his interests peeked.

"I don't know," she stalled, running out of lies to tell her father. "I was trying to talk to her earlier when the guards came in and took her before you. That's why I stopped you before you could send her away."

King Sol silently considered what he daughter had said. It seemed unlikely that a princess from a neighboring kingdom would have information that they could use. But any information that could be provided was always taken and considered. She was family and that meant that extra considerations had to be made. He knew that her brother wouldn't leave without her, but a few days certainly wouldn't hurt. Especially if that meant help for Diana.

"If what you're saying is true than I'll send the Captain in to talk to her in the morning," King Sol decided.

Terra's eyes went wide. Seph had no idea about the lie she had told to keep her here. If Jones went in to question her, and she

444

told him that she didn't know anything the house of cards Terra had been building with her lies would crumble around her. She needed to get to Seph before anyone questioned her.

"Father, do you think that's wise?" She asked, "To send in the Captain of the Guard in to question one of our cousins? Won't Uncle Lusin take that as an insult? He's very . . . particular that way."

"You make a valid point," he agreed. "What would you suggest, were you in my shoes?"

"I would send me in," she answered simply. "I'm her cousin so her and I having a conversation is just two girls catching up, and she's already opened up to me about this today so it warrants the thought that she would do so again."

King Sol considered what Terra said. It made a good deal of sense to him. It kept Lusin off his back and made it possible to get the information from Persephone. It was a very good idea. King Sol swelled with pride at the thought of his daughter being so diplomatically inclined.

"I think that is an excellent suggestion," he said. "Will you let me know as soon as you speak with her?"

"I will thank you father, for helping me and for trusting me," Terra said standing and curtsying to the King. "I will speak with my cousin as soon as possible."

Terra knocked on the large wooden door that had once belonged to her sister. Jones was standing on one side of the door and another solider Terra didn't know very well was there too. She felt better about having Jones there. She didn't know what the protocol was for housing a princess who was a runaway, but it made her feel better to know she had a friend outside Seph's door.

"Go away Char," Seph shouted from behind the door. "If they didn't let you in before they aren't going to let you in now."

"Seph it's me, Terra." There was the sound of walking followed by the sound of the bolt being drawn on the door.

Seph poked her head out of the door. "Are you alone?" She asked.

"Yes," Terra replied, "it's just me. Can I come in?"

"Yes," Seph whispered, pulling her in by her arm. "Just hurry."

"Seph are you alright?" She asked, "You're acting a little . . . paranoid."

"I'm sorry Terra but with Charles down the hall I can't be too careful. I'm telling you he will stop at nothing to prove to my parents that I had the baby."

"Why?" Terra asked. "What has he got against you?"

Seph scoffed. "It would be easier to list the things he doesn't hate me for."

"Why?" She asked again.

Seph sighed and said, "I'm the youngest. When I was born my mother almost died. She was sick in bed for nearly three months. During that time my father had me with him everywhere he went. It was unheard of and people thought he might be going mad. We bonded during that time I suppose. After that he was always around. He and I went everywhere together. If he had to go to a different kingdom to discuss anything, I was with him.

"Needless to say I got a lot of special treatment. Most of my siblings resent me for it. Before everything happened with Darien, I was always by my father's side. Once there was a risk of Darien being a Shadowed Man, my father completely turned his back on me. Leaving me completely exposed to my siblings wrath."

"Oh. So your brother is . . ."

"Trying to oust me as my father's favorite," Seph said with a nod.

"That's terrible."

"That's why I can't thank you enough for stopping your father from letting him take me."

"That's also why I'm here," she explained. She pulled Seph over to the small sofa and sat her down. "I spoke to my father tonight and I told him that the reason you had to stay because you have information prevalent to the battle my sister has to fight."

"I don't have any information about that!" She shouted starting to panic.

"I know!" Terra sighed. "But it was the only thing I could think to say. It was the one thing I knew would give my father pause."

"So what happens when he realizes that I don't have any information for him?"

"Um . . ." she stammered, "best case scenario, he sends you back to your brother that second and he locks me away for treason."

"That's the best case scenario?" Seph asked, her jaw hanging open.

Terra rolled the thoughts around in her head for a moment and then said, "Yea that's the best."

"So then what do we do?"

"I don't know . . . make something up that sounds good?" She suggest at the end of her rope with all the lies.

"Like what?"

"I don't know!"

"Ok, we can do this," Seph nodded. "We are young intelligent women. We can think of something."

"Ok, yeah, you're right. We can do this . . ."

"What about the prophecy?" She asked, "What does it say exactly?"

"I don't know," Terra admitted. "I've never seen it."

"Wait, really?"

"Yeah," she grimaced. "I could give you a general run down but that's it."

"I thought you guys would have it here to look at, in case it helped your sister."

"I think it's at the Great Library," she guessed.

Seph stopped and thought for a while. She knew so little about the prophecy itself. Her one hope was that it was here and there was something on it she could use to help herself out of the situation she and Terra were now in.

"Wait I've got it," Seph exclaimed with a laugh. "The prophecy is the answer! Tell your father that I told you that there's more to the prophecy than what we know. Tell him another sign showed up in my kingdom and I came to tell you. By the time he sends a rider and it comes back and they go through the entire thing, weeks will have gone by and there'll be no more proof of the baby."

"That's genius! Seph you may have just saved us!" Terra leaned forward and wrapped her arms around her cousin's neck and hugged her. "Thank you so much I was terrified that everyone was going to find out we lied."

Terra's thoughts shifted to her cousin's newborn son and her smile faded. "What about the boy?"

"He'll stay here," Seph sighed again. "Once I've denied him he'll be named an orphan and sent off to a home." It was clearly all Seph could do to not break down crying.

"Well then he's in luck," Terra stated, smiling kindly at her cousin.

"How do you figure?"

"Because in a matter of days I will be opening a new orphanage in Castle Town. A bigger, better and safer place for the orphans of the kingdom to come. He'll be safe there."

"You're sure?"

"I am."

This time it was Seph's turn to hug Terra. "Thank you. I can't tell you how much better that makes me feel."

She hugged her cousin back and said, "It is the very least I can do."

Seph nodded and pulled away. "So when do we tell your father?"

By the time Terra was finally climbing the stairs to her room, she was exhausted. She had left Seph's room and tracked down her father. After explaining everything to King Sol she volunteered to go in the morning and examine the prophecy herself. Citing that sending anyone else risked compromising the mission and the quality of answers they received. She had to meet with her father and Bell in the morning to discuss what they should do.

She was really hoping that he father would let her go. She needed to get out for a while and she hadn't ridden out past the local farms in years. Plus the ride would give her time to think about Grey and Eric and clear her head. Something she sorely needed to do.

"Terra there you are," Eric sighed walking down the last few steps to her room. "I've been looking everywhere for you."

"I'm sorry," she apologized. "I forgot that with the knife you can't tell where I'm at."

"Or if you're ok," he added. He walked up the last few steps to her room and stood with her at the door. He reached up and brushed a few stray hairs away from her face. Terra smiled and leaned her head into his embrace. She sighed contentedly at his closeness.

Eric put a finger under her chin and lifted her face up to his. He leaned down and kissed her, soft at first and sweet. He wasn't sure how far he could take things with her before she would pull away. When she kissed him back and made no move to back away, he wrapped his arms around her and pulled her into him. He turned his head and deepened the kiss.

Terra reached up and wrapped her arms around his neck. She knew it was a bad idea. She knew that things with Eric could only go so far. After the day she'd had and everything that had happened, it was nice to just be Terra in the arms of a man she loved.

Eric made a noise in the back of his throat. He pushed Terra against the wall opposite him and kissed her harder. He pulled her hands up and pinned her wrists above her head with his left hand. He took his free hand and ran it up and down the sides of her body, carefully skirting anything thing that would make her shy and pull away.

He kissed her down her neck and to the top of her collar bone.

449

Terra shuddered under his touch, completely surprised by her own reaction. She wanted him to touch her everywhere; she liked the way his lips felt on her skin. Still part of her wanted to run away, surprised by the way she felt and a little afraid. She wanted to turn and run.

"Terra," he whispered against her skin. "Oh Terra let me show you how much I love you."

Something in his words pulled her out of her hot and foggy train of thought. "Eric," she panted. "Eric, stop. I can't do this, we can't do this."

Eric groaned and stepped back. "Are you sure we can't do this?" He asked, his voice deep and gravely.

"I am sure," she told him, trying to sound firm.

"Alright," he muttered sounding sulky.

"Good night Eric," Terra said smiling at his sulkiness.

"Good night Terra," he replied bowing to her.

He straightened up and turned for the stairs. Not trusting himself if he stood there and stared at her breathless and up against the wall. He knew he would lose control.

"I love you," she called as he stepped down.

He stopped and turned, a huge smile spreading across his formally sulky face. "Say it again."

"I love you."

Eric rushed back to her and scooped her up in his arms he spun her around kissing her saying, "I love you," over and over again. He set her on her feet and kissed her again.

"Good night Princess, I love you."

"Good night Guard, I love you too," she replied laughing.

By the time she managed to get into her room and into her shift, Terra seriously thought her legs might give out. She crawled into her large four poster bed and pulled the sheets up to her chin. Today was the single strangest day she had ever experienced. Two men had confessed their love for her, she had met her cousin for the first time, she had nearly died, and she got a new Royal Guard, lied to her father, lost her horse, and nearly finished an orphanage.

It seemed like some if it had happened weeks ago.

She was so tired

She stared at the purple canopy over her bed and waited for sleep to find her. At first her mind wouldn't settle. It wanted to run over everything Eric and Grey had said. Line by line and syllable by syllable until it made sense.

Terra considered, for a moment at least, staying awake and thinking about it. Then she closed her eyes for a second and the world fell away as she finally nodded off.

Chapter 12

Diana wandered forward in the strange swirling black mist. She didn't understand where she was or what she was doing. She simply needed to walk forward.

So she did.

Until she got frustrated and stopped.

"Hello!" She called, "Where the hell am I?! Hello?!"

'Hello Princess,' A voice in her mind echoed.

Diana spun around quickly searching the mist for the source of the voice. "Who's there?!"

A swirling in the mist directly to her left pulled her attention. A huge shadow rose up before her. Bigger than every other shadow she'd ever seen, it towered over. Its eyes were huge and gold and they bored into her very soul.

"What are you?" She asked.

'*I am the darkness.*' It replied. '*And I have a message for you.*'

"What kind of message?" She asked as her eyes narrowed.

'*You must not let your sister read the scroll. If she reads the words, all of this will change. Nothing will be as it was.*'

"What is that supposed to mean!?" Diana shouted. Slowly the world started to fade away as the princess stood and shouted at the shadow that had already melted back into the mist around her.

Diana shot up in bed like a bolt.

She was covered in sweat and her heart was racing.

What kind of dream was that?

What was that shadow?

What kind of scroll was he talking about?

Diana ran her hands through her long blond hair as she pondered about the dream and the warning the shadow had given her. She wondered what kind of scroll Terra might have found. What kind of trouble could it cause her?

Feeling restless and displeased about what her dream may have meant, she stood and bellowed for her maids. She had might as well get dressed and start the day.

Terra woke early, not able to sleep for too long. She got up and pulled her deep purple dress with the sliver accents out. It was her favorite dress and by far the most intricate. If she had to go as far as Titan to find the scroll than she had might as well look good. Creator knows it would make her mother happier to know she was going somewhere looking like royalty for once.

By the time she had dressed and started in on her hair Mammy was up and coming in.

"Good morning my dear," she said coming in, eyeing Terra's dress approvingly. "Would you like some help with your hair?"

"Yes please," she replied smiling. "I'm going to Titan today. To the great library."

"Is that so?" Mammy asked, going to work with on her mass of black hair. "What are you going there for?"

"I'm going to see the prophecy, to check it against signs my cousin has seen in her kingdom. If she's right, then it could be we missed something before, something that will help Diana in the final fight. Or at least that's the hope."

Mammy was quiet as she finished putting the princesses hair up. It was beautiful and the little flowers she placed here and there really made it match the dress. Terra thought she looked really pretty.

"When is this little expedition set to take place?"

"As soon as I'm up and ready to go."

"Well, you be careful," Mammy remarked going around the room cleaning up as she went. "Will you take John and Eric with you?"

"I expect so, unless they have other things to do."

"Don't go alone!" Mammy cried, suddenly and passionately. She turned and grabbed Terra by the shoulders. "Please child, after everything that happened yesterday, don't go alone."

"Mammy," she asked, surprised by her sudden change in behavior, "I promise I won't go alone. Is everything all right?"

"Yes, dear," she sighed. "I just worry about you so much."

"I know," she smiled. "I promise you I'll be careful."

Bell paced back and forth slowly, once again waiting for the King. This time he waited in the throne room and waited for not just the King but for Terra as well. According to Terra the princess from the Moon Kingdom was under the impression that more signs had popped up which could change the course of what fork to follow on the prophecy.

He had never seen the prophecy himself. It had been locked away in Titan's library years before he was born. It made sense that it would be time to look at it again. Make sure that nothing new has come up.

"Good morning Bell," a cold voice drifted across the throne room. "Aren't you here early?"

"Good Morning Princess Diana," he greeted, bowing formally to the princess as she sauntered across the room. She looked stunning in a sky blue dress filled with intricate gold detail on the bodice and sheer cap sleeved. She had a darker blue cloak wrapped around her shoulders and tied at her throat with a rope as golden as her hair. Her hair was swept up in a braid that wrapped around her head like a crown with the remainder trailing down her back. She had pulled fresh flowers from her mother's garden and had them laced through her hair along with a ribbon the same color as her dress.

She looked quite beautiful.

It was a shame her eyes were cold and filled with malice.

"What are you doing here?" She inquired.

"Waiting for your sister and your father."

"Why?" Dina asked, her eyes narrowing.

"Your sister is going to Titan today, to the Great Library there."

"Why on earth would she do that," she scoffed. What a complete waste of time, going to a library.

"She's going to look at your prophecy. To see if maybe there was some information there that might help you in your coming fight. She'll actually be the first to look on the scroll in some time."

"Scroll?" Diana asked, the warning she'd gotten in her dream fresh in her mind. "It's a scroll, the prophecy?"

"Yes, of course," he answered, confused by Diana's sudden interest.

She considered this for a long time. If the shadow from her dream was to be believed, something terrible will happen if Terra is allowed to look on the prophecy. She couldn't deny her sister the right to go, not if her father was already involved. Even if she insisted to go instead of Terra, they would never let her just kick her sister off her little quest. Her only real option was to go with her.

As much as she hated the idea of being stuck in a carriage and then a library with her sister all day, there was little else she could do

454

to make sure everything went her way. She would volunteer to go with her.

"Good morning Master Bell!" Terra called as she came in through the same door as Diana. "Oh, good morning Diana," she added tentatively.

"Good morning Sister!" Diana replied brightly. "How are you doing this morning?"

"I'm well," she answered cautiously. This was the most she had spoken to her sister in nearly three months. "How are you feeling, I heard you were feeling unwell yesterday?"

"Oh I'm fine," Diana assured her, waving Terra's concern off. "I was just hoping to speak with father about possibly going out for a ride. I think the fresh air would help my health."

"Really?" Terra asked, excited about possibly getting to spend time with her sister. Their lives had grown in opposite directions for so long that she rarely had the opportunity to spend time with her. "I'm on my way to Titan today as it happens."

"Yes, Master Bell was just telling me that. So you're going to look at the prophecy?" Diana inquired, trying to sound light and casual.

"I am! I heard from our cousin that there might be more to the prophecy that could help. You know Diana, the prophecy is about you, you should come with me. It would give you a chance to get some air and you know how to read prophecy much better than I do."

"Oh I don't want to intrude on your plans," she sighed smiling sweetly. She knew her sister well enough to know that she would fall into her trap like the gullible naïve fool she was.

"It's no intrusion at all," she all but shouted cheerfully. "I'd love for you to go. In truth I'll probably need your help figuring the prophecy out."

"Well that sounds like a great plan," Diana muttered through gritted teeth, not sure how much longer she could force a smile.

"What sounds like a great plan?" King Sol asked entering the room.

"Oh Good morning Father," Terra greeted curtsying.

"Father," Diana remarked, curtsying to match her sister.

"Your Majesty," Bell said formally saluting him.

"Father Diana was telling me that she wanted to go and get some air and I was telling her about how I was going to the library so she offered to come with me. Which is a really good idea since I can't actually read prophecy."

"An interesting proposal," King Sol considered. "Who would you take with you?"

"My Guards," Terra offered. "Eric and John."

"We can take what's-his-name, too," Diana offered. "The captain of the guard."

"Jones?" Terra asked. "I think he might have work to do here."

"Indeed he does," Bell offered. "I'm sure that Terra's guards should be enough for a trip to Titan. It's less than a half days ride. So long as they don't take too long in town they should be back before it gets dark and there's any real threat to their safety."

King Sol silently considered what Bell and Terra had to say. Diana stood near the back of the group looking indifferently out a window. She knew if she looked at her father he would see that little sparkle in her eyes that meant she had ulterior motives.

"Is this what you would like Terra?" He asked her.

"Yes father," Terra replied earnestly. "Diana and I so rarely get to spend time with each other. I miss my sister. And again, I kind of need her to read the prophecy."

"Very well then," The King said smiling kindly down at her. "But you must promise to be safe and not dawdle while in town."

"I promise Father."

"Well go and gather your gloves and cloak, find those guards of yours and meet your sister out by the stable."

"I will, thank you father," she called as she curtsied again and back out of the room. She disappeared through the door all but skipping as she went.

"Diana," King Sol said, turning to face his oldest child. "I'm glad to see you wanting to spend more time with your sister. Please be mindful of her limitations as well as your own. Neither of you had an easy day yesterday."

"I'll be careful father," she assured him, "You don't need to worry. I'll take care of Terra."

Terra rushed up the stairs toward her room as fast as she could. She was so excited to get out of the castle and spend some time with her sister and Eric and John that she could barely contain her glee. She needed something fun like this after everything that had happened to her in the past few days. It might get a little awkward with Eric there and the secret they shared between them. Still, she was sure that everything would be ok.

She stopped, struck by a sudden thought.

They should have a picnic!

If she stopped in the kitchen on her way back to her room she could have Jenny get it all ready for her. By the time she found John and Eric and got her cape and gloves, Jenny would have it ready to go. Jenny was good and she was quick. Terra would have to go a little out of her way to swing by the kitchen but it would be worth it.

"Jenny?" She called, walking into the kitchen. "Jenny I know it's early but I need a huge favor!"

"Princess?" Jenny called emerging from the large pantry room at the end of the Kitchen. She yawned and rubbed her eyes. "It's early for breakfast isn't it?"

"Oh," she muttered suddenly deflated. "I completely forgot about breakfast."

"If you're not here for breakfast than what can I do for you Princess?"

"I need a lunch basket made up, if you can," she asked sheepishly. "My sister and I are going out to Titan today and I wanted to be able to stop and have a nice lunch with her along the way."

"That sounds lovely," Jenny said smiling. "I can have something made up for you if you like. When do you want it ready?"

"Um soon as you can I guess," she considered. "It'll take me about twenty minutes to round up the boys and get them ready. Oh and I've got to take breakfast down to Grey." Terra made a face at Jenny who laughed goodheartedly at her obvious discomfort.

"Things not going well with the caged man?" She teased.

"Is it ever?" She asked glumly.

"I suppose that's true," Jenny smiled. "Do you want to feed him or shall we just starve the mean out of him?"

Terra laughed. "We'd have to starve him for a long time."

"Forever would do it I'd say," Jenny remarked. The two girls burst out laughing as they considered how hilarious it would be trying to starve the mean out of Grey.

"I guess I have to feed him," Terra sighed when she could finally talk. She wiped a tear from her eye and said, "Can we just toss something simple together? I really don't have time for much."

"He won't like it," Jenny said warningly.

"Well as it happens I'm not super interested in what he likes right now."

"Alright then," Jenny smiled genuinely enjoying the drama that always ensued between Terra and Grey. "Just give me two minutes and I'll have something ready for you ok?"

"Thank you Jenny."

A few minutes later Terra had a tray of toast with jam and some sliced ham form the night before on a tray for Grey. She had requested some extra food for him since she would be gone at lunch time. As she had hoped, John was standing at his post outside the door.

"Hey," he said smiling. "You look . . . good."

"Thanks. Hey I wanted to talk to you about something."

"What's going on?" He asked, pleasantly.

"I'm going with my sister to Titan, to the great Library and I was hoping that as my newly appointed guard, you would be ready to do some guarding . . .?" Terra stopped and thought about rewording what she had said, but by then it was too late.

John laughed and said, "Some guarding?"

"Yeah, I know."

"I'd be happy to come. Not that I have much choice though. I think when my princess summons me I have to go."

"Well then consider yourself summoned," she mocked, trying to sound like a royal.

"Yes Princess," he replied with mock civility, "Right away Princess." He formally saluted her, laughing then entire time. "I will go and let the Captain know."

"Thank you," she called as he walked past. "Hey do you know where Eric is?"

"I think he's still sleeping, something about a really long day yesterday," he called to her as he walked toward the door. "Wouldn't know anything about that would you?"

Terra blushed up to her eyebrows as she stared at John wide eyed.

"Meet you at the stables," he called as he ran off laughing.

Terra shook her head and set the tray down. She grabbed the door and pushed it open, picking the tray back up she headed in to the prison.

As she had been hoping, Grey was still asleep. It was early enough that he wouldn't be expecting her and with the knife strapped to her thigh there was no way for him to detect her. She could slip in, leave his breakfast on his table, and slip back out without him waking up and bothering her about what was said last night. She was planning on using the long ride to think about everything that had happened to her yesterday and everything that was said to her. She needed the space and time to think.

She also needed to get away from Grey before he had time to wake and start talking.

Terra walked up and looked into the glass prison. He was rolled facing the door. He must have passed out. He was lying on top

459

of the blankets and he was still fully clothed. She stalked quietly over to the glass and pushed her way through. She set the tray quietly down on the table and slipped back toward the wall. She glanced quietly back at Grey, still sleeping soundly. He looked sad and she couldn't help but wonder if that was her fault.

Knowing it was unwise, she crept forward and knelt next to the bed in front of Grey. She watched him sleep for a minute while thinking over all that he had said to her.

"Oh Grey," she whispered quietly. "Why do you have to be you?" She reached out and brushed a few stray hairs from his face. Like a ripple effect, his face changed and once again Terra was staring at a young Grey.

Well a younger Grey anyway.

Knowing she had to leave, Terra leaned forward and kissed him gently on the lips. "It's an odd thing," she remarked to the sleeping man, "loving and hating someone at the same time. It complicates so much. I'm not sure I can do it anymore," she reached up and brushed away the few remaining strands of hair on his forehead. "Fate is a cruel and fickle thing."

She kissed him on the forehead and stood. She pulled some paper from his writing desk and scribbled him a quick note. She tucked it under the tray and headed to the wall.

With one final look at the sleeping Grey, she slipped through the glass and out the prison, pulling the door closed behind her.

A pounding on the door pulled Eric up and out of bed. "Uh . . . what's . . . going . . . who?"

"Eric!" John shouted through his door, "Eric get up we have to go, Terra needs us."

"What about Terra?" He asked suddenly more awake.

"We have to go. Terra and her sister are leaving for Titan and if you don't hurry up they're going to leave without you."

The door jerked open suddenly and John, caught off guard, nearly fell through the doorway into Eric.

"Where exactly are you going now?" He demanded.

"To Titan, with the princess," John explained slowly. "They need us since we're Terra's guards."

"Oh," Eric yawned, still half asleep. "Just the two of us?"

"As far as I know."

"Too light," he muttered consideringly. "Where's Jack? We'll bring him along with us. Three of us plus a driver should be good."

"You haven't heard?" John asked in disbelief.

"Heard what?"

"Jack, he's deserted."

"He what!?"

John nodded. "He didn't report for his night time duties a few days ago and no one has seen him since. We sent riders to his parent's home but he hasn't been there in over a year."

"How do you know something hasn't happened?" Eric called, pulling on his guard uniform and grabbing his armor from the chest at the foot of his bed. Since the shadows had become more active and the King had set down stricter rules about where and when he daughters could leave the castle, Eric hadn't had much opportunity to use his armor.

"We don't, I suppose," John admitted, concerned.

"Did he take anything with him? Any of his personal effects or things like that?"

"No It's all still around his bunk. Do you really think that something might have happened to him? And we've been acting like everything was fine."

"There's no way to know," Eric remarked, quickly pulling all his hair back into a ponytail at the base of his neck. "But we'll deal with it later. Let's go."

It took less than fifteen minutes for Eric to finish cleaning himself up and getting ready to go. He had wanted to shave that morning, seeing as the stubble on his face was rapidly progressing toward beard. But he knew the ride to Titan could be a long one and

461

with just himself and John to guard the Princesses, it was best they get back before nightfall.

By the time he and John got to the stables the carriage was already sporting two of his majesties noble grey hunters with Lucas, her father's personal driver. He was incredibly strong and quick, not to mention he was a force to reckon with when he had a club in hand.

"Morning Lucas," Eric called brightly.

"Good morn' young guard," Lucas called back, his accent thick in his voice.

"Eric, John," Terra called from the seat next to Lucas. "Glad to see you finally made it."

"What do you think you're doing?" Eric called up to her.

"Sitting, obviously," she replied snarkily.

"Not up there you're not," he countered climbing up the side of the carriage. "Here give me your hand and I'll help you down."

"You can't be serious," she laughed.

"Terra you can't sit up there, it isn't safe," he explained taking her hand. "I'll help you down."

She pulled her hand out of his and leaned away from him. "I'm fine up here."

A frustrated look passed over his face. "Terra," he muttered irritated.

"Don't let him speak to you that way," Diana called as she approached the carriage. "He's your guard and he can't tell you what to do. You tell him what to do."

Everyone stopped what they were doing and bowed to Diana. She smiled and soaked it in as they worshiped her. It was things like this that she loved. Things like this also terrified her. One day, when that idiot of monster in the basement was dead, all of this would end. They would still love her, she was a princess after all, but not like they worshiped her now.

Terra climbed down the opposite side of the carriage and, with a hand from John, she stepped in and sat down. Diana was helped in next and sat on the opposite side of the carriage. She stretched out and settled in. It was only after she was all but laying down that she looked up at Terra.

"I would fire him," she remarked casually.

"Eric?"

"Whatever his name is," she yawned dismissively. "If you let them talk to you that way they'll walk all over you."

"He just cares," Terra explained awkwardly. "He's not trying to boss me around or walk all over me. He just cares."

"That's even worse!" she shouted outraged. "Don't' let them care about you! He's a guard Terra. A *guard*! He's nowhere near good enough for royalty. If he cares it's even more reason to fire him."

"It's not his fault," she started, "It's our bond; it makes things crazy and blows things out of proportion. That's all."

Diana scoffed but didn't say anything else. She glanced out her window and didn't seem all that interested in Terra anymore.

"Princess Terra," John called. She turned and glanced out the window. John was riding Zeus again and looked ready to go. "Are you doing alright in there? It looks like we're ready to go when you are."

"Oh John! When did you find Zeus?"

"He made his way home once the storm subsided. He's a good boy that way," he answered patting his mustang's neck. "So are we ready?"

Terra glanced to Diana who kept her eyes out the window. "I guess we're ready."

"Alright I'll let Eric and Lucas know." He nudged Zeus forward and the carriage jerked forward suddenly. Diana grumbled something under her breath but didn't' say anything more. Slightly disappointed, she leaned her head against the wall of the carriage and started out the window.

In a couple of minutes they were moving through the courtyard and out into the city. Terra's spirits lifted as she saw people rushing out to greet the carriage. She smiled as they waved from the sides of the street, women curtsied and men doffed their caps as they passed.

"Princess! Princess!" Children called as the raced alongside the carriage. "Where are you going princess? Can we come along?"

"No not today I'm afraid," she called reaching out and touching the children's hands as the raised them toward her. "I'll be home before dark, we'll play then."

"Awwww," the children exclaimed, disappointed that the princess couldn't play.

Terra watched as the children fell away and as the people of the town continued to wave and salute the carriage. Happy and feeling loved by the people of her kingdom, she turned to see if her sister was enjoying the ride so far.

Diana's eyes were closed and she was leaning against the wall of the carriage, her color was bad and she seemed to be in some kind of pain. Every time the carriage hit a bump in the road or a dip her sister cringed.

"Diana," she asked, her worry for her sister making her feel brave. "Diana what's wrong? You look like you're in pain."

"I'm fine," she lied, cringing as the carriage hit a particularly large dip in the road.

"You're lying," she countered, "Tell me what's wrong."

"I said I'm fine," Diana replied more firmly. "Just leave me alone."

Terra, not letting anything alone, carefully reached out with her magic, trying to carefully asses her sister. A shock went through her body as her magic came in contact with her sister's aura. It felt like it had burned her, like her sister's aura had become fire.

Confused she looked up to see Diana glaring at her.

"I said leave me along," she repeated bitterly.

"Not until you tell me what's wrong!" Terra insisted. "Now, either tell me what's the matter or I'll keep poking at you until I find a weak spot. One way or the other, I'm going to find out."

"Why do you care so much?" Diana shot at her.

"Because you're my sister and I love you," she replied as though it was obvious.

Diana scoffed. "Love," she muttered the word like the very idea disgusted her. "What a waste of time."

Terra laughed, "Don't be so weird. Let me see what's wrong? Maybe I can help. My healing isn't great but it's better than suffering through the whole trip."

She regarded her sister with cool eyes. "Fine," she sighed. She didn't really like the thought of opening herself up to anyone else or their magic, but there was no way she would survive the ride all the way to Titan and back feeling the way she did.

Terra smiled, glad to be able to help her sister. She stood as much as she could and shot over to the other side next to her sister. Carefully she placed one hand just above her sister's head and another above her stomach. Taking a few deep breaths she focused on the area of Diana's aura that was stressed and angry.

She could see almost instantly the point of pain.

Diana was having her courses, and painfully at that. It looked like she was suffering a great deal in the carriage. It broke Terra's heart to think of her sister going through so much pain just to spend some time with her.

She closed her eyes and focused on healing and calming the angry parts of her sister's aura. It didn't take long for Diana to start to visibly relax. All the strain went out of her face and her shoulders drooped. She sighed contentedly. Terra felt so happy she could cry. Diana had so much weight on her shoulders and so much pressure on her all the time from everyone. It made her happy to know that she could do this one thing to make her sister feel better. Even if it was as simple as taking away the pain she felt from her monthly courses.

Diana lounged comfortably in the carriage as Terra slowly took away the pain she was feeling from the potion the old hag had given her. She'd been having pain for over a day now. That was to be expected though. This wasn't the first time she'd had to deal with things like this. Things were a little different this time, the pain was stronger and it seemed to be hanging around longer. Thankfully

Terra's idiotic need to help her was making that pain seem like a distant memory.

  She snuggled down into the thick blankets and furs that lined the seats of the carriage and felt herself drift off.

  Grey sat up in bed slowly, stretching and yawning as he went.

  He looked around the room, it was empty. He couldn't detect anyone around him, just a guard at the other side of the door. It wasn't the usual guard, what's-his-name, the one always pinning over Terra. This was the lecherous one that usually hung around at night thinking things about Terra that made Grey want to burst out his cell and commit some homicide.

  Another glance around the room and he noticed the silver tray on his table, piled high with food. He got up and walked over; under the tray there was a small piece of paper that read:

Dear Grey,

  I'm afraid I will be unable to bring you lunch today as I will be in Titan visiting the library there with my sister. I will see you tonight for dinner.

Terra Elisabeth Sol

  Grey read the letter several times before folding the paper carefully and sticking it into a pocket on his belt. If Terra was in Titan with Diana, something was going on. What, he couldn't say for sure. But he knew enough to know that it wasn't going to be good.

He had banked on her avoiding him today, maybe even the rest of this week. He hadn't wanted to say what he'd said to her. Unfortunately the unusual shadow activity yesterday had expedited his plans. Terra's trust in him, something he had worked very hard to build over the course of four years, was suddenly shattered. If he didn't do something, and fast, to fix it, he would have lost her forever.

Grey simply didn't have time to go back to the drawing board and figure out another way to come at Diana. He didn't need to be outside to see the signs or read the stars to know that the end was coming, and coming quickly. He could sense the change in the air all around him, most especially around Terra. She seemed to radiate change.

Still, catching her off guard the way he did might actually do more good than harm.

She wasn't expecting anything like that from him. She was expecting something angry or some kind of fighting. Catching her off guard made it all the more shocking. Hopefully she was sitting somewhere thinking about him and wondering if he really loved her.

Terra leaned out the window watching the rolling green hills of the country side as they sped past. Every so often John would ride up next to her window and see how she was doing. At first she was fine. Diana was sleeping soundly stretched across the other bench and she loved having the wind in her face. After a while though she started to feel cooped up in the carriage and she longed for lunch time so she could stop and stretch her legs.

After a few hours on the road John road up alongside the carriage again.

"Princess," he called.

"John, do I really need to tell you again?" She asked.

"Sorry, Terra," he corrected smiling. "Are you two ready for lunch?"

Terra glanced at her sister, still sleeping soundly. Her stomach rumbled and she longed to be out of the carriage and move around. Diana looked so peaceful, and she had been hurting before, she didn't have the heart to wake her yet. She needed rest.

"I don't think so," Terra answered, sounding a little disappointed.

"Why on earth not!" Diana shouted. "I'm starving."

"Oh you're awake," she cried elated. "Do you feel like stopping for lunch? I had Jenny pack us a nice basket so we could stop on the road."

"Then let's stop," she said irritably.

"I think we're ready John."

Lucas found a nice shady spot along the bank of the Hailey River. There was a large group of trees that cast the entire side of the bank in shadows. Hailey, which usually ran as fast as the deer that frequented it, was slow in this spot, making it a perfect place for the royal carriage to stop.

Terra bounced anxiously on the seat as she waited to get out. When Lucas finally called the horses to stop, she burst from the carriage and ran out onto the grass. She knelt down and rolled over onto her back smiling and laughing like a crazy person.

"Are you alright Terra?" John asked, dismounting Zeus and tethering him to a tree.

"She doesn't like to be cooped up for too long," Eric called hitching his horse next to John's. "She gets all squirrelly and crazy if she's forced to be contained for too long."

Terra, so happy to be out of the carriage, she forgot all about being angry at Eric for being bossy. "I don't know what he's talking about," she called at John. "He's crazy. I'm just enjoying the grass. It's lovely in this part of the kingdom." Together the three of them laughed.

"Terra, really?" Diana scoffed as she emerged from the carriage. "Can't you at least act like royalty for a few minutes?"

468

"I am acting like a royal," she laughed. "All good royals love their land. That's all I'm doing. Just loving the land."

Diana rolled her eyes but didn't say anything else. She stood and waited for Lucas to set up the folding chairs and table for the princess's. Then she sat down leered at Terra, Eric, and John. She needed to bring better company next time.

John walked over and set down the picnic basket on the table and quickly set up lunch for Diana. There was ham and grapes, plus some cheese and bread. Diana took the best of everything and the turned away from the group to face the water.

"Terra, are you going to come eat?" John asked walking over.

"Soon," she replied, still lying on the grass in the shade. "You guys eat, I'm ok right now."

John laughed and lowered himself down next to her. He looked up at the blue sky with its few wisps of clouds passing overhead. "So why are you laying on the grass?"

"She needs to stretch," Eric answered feeding the horses.

"Hey John," she stated, "Did you know that Eric has changed his name to Terra and now answers to Princess?"

"What?!" Eric shouted as John and Terra laughed. "What did you just say?" He walked over to them and stood, towering over their heads, hand on his hips.

"*You* don't even answer to Princess most of the time," he mocked.

"I don't know to what you are referring to," she scoffed with mock indignation. "Now be gone servant, you're blocking my sun."

"Oh really?" He asked flopping down on Terra's other side. He turned and lay down, folding his arms behind his head.

"This is surprisingly comfortable," John commented as a breeze blew over them, ruffling their hair and clothing.

"Yup," Terra sighed happily.

"Someone should get the food," Eric commented.

"Yea," John and Terra agreed in unison.

Feeling much more at ease, she sat up and stretched again, hearing loud popping sounds coming from her back, she smiled.

"Dear creator was that you?" Eric asked sitting up.

"Yea," she laughed getting to her feet. She brushed the grass off her cloak as both the boys hurried to their feet. "I'm starving. Let's eat."

Together the three of them got food and spread out in the shade to eat. They passed the hottest part of day blissfully cool under the tall sweeping oaks that grew along the river bank. Diana sat in her chair and regarded her sister and her guards like they were some nuisance that she couldn't be rid of. For a while Diana wondered if it was a wise idea to have come.

When she had the dream she was sure she needed to be with Terra all day to ensure that her cryptic warning didn't come to pass. She hadn't realized at the time that it would entail being dragged across the kingdom to a library or being stuck with her idiot sister's guards all day. She hated the way things were between Terra and her Guards. People that served you needed to respect and to fear you, that was the only way to keep them in line.

Looking at Terra and the way she laughed and joked with them, Diana realized that they didn't fear her at all. Quite the opposite actually. It seemed that these poor fools actually loved her sister.

Idiots.

She almost felt bad for them.

Almost anyway.

For a moment all Diana could think about was how to destroy the three of them. How could she take their happiness and rip it away in a way that would hurt the most?

No. She shouldn't destroy them, that would be to obvious and she'd had a hard enough time dealing the last man who had crossed her, and there was only one of him. She couldn't be so easily rid of Terra. Not that she really wanted to, Terra served several purposes for Diana.

Firstly, she was the best scapegoat. Anytime Diana knew she was going to be in trouble she would go to Terra with some completely dramatized story and tell her she needed her help. Terra would jump up to do anything for her. She loved her, and that made her weak. Her love and the way she loved made her weak and made it easy for Diana to exploit her.

Secondly, as she'd proven today, she was handy when Diana was hurting. As much as it pained her to admit, she was good with her magic. It made her useful.

So she would just make a mental note of Terra and her two guards and the feelings they shared, it might just come in handy later.

After lunch Terra packed everything back up into the basket and hauled it back over to the carriage. She took the plates and silverware down to the river to wash them off. Jenny would give her an earful if the plates and forks came back gross and sticky. She kneelt down carefully and rinsed them in the casually running water.

"I'm sorry," Eric apologized walking up behind her. "About earlier, I was out of line."

"I appreciate you apologizing," Terra said not looking up. "But I would be much more interested to know why you reacted that way."

"Truth?"

"Always," she answered looking up at him and smiling.

He sighed and said, "I had this dream last night, a nightmare really. About you and today and this trip."

"What happened?"

"I don't really know," he answered honestly. "I remember you being there with me and I know I was terrified for you. Part of the dream, the only part I can really remember, was you telling me about the trip you were taking. You didn't say where you were going or when but when John woke me I knew it was this I was dreaming about this trip."

Terra considered this for a moment, "So you thought that I might get hurt like in your dream?"

"Something like that."

She shook the water off the last of the plates and wrapped them in a towel. She stood and looked at Eric. He was clearly sorry and he felt bad about what he did. Which she appreciated. Her only concern was that he was getting more and more comfortable acting less like her Guard and more like her intended.

She loved him and he loved her and that made her very happy. However, if anyone else were to find out about them and the way they acted together, he would be hung for treason and she would be sent off to live in shame somewhere as the house pet of a lesser Lord or Duke. Assuming her mother didn't just have her completely exiled.

"Eric you know you can't do things like this," Terra tried to explain kindly. "If people know about us, or what we felt for each other . . ." she let the sentence fall away. He was more than aware of what would happen to them if they were found out.

"I know," he sighed. "It won't happen again. It's just hard being your guard and feeling like this. But it's only because it's so new. Things will get better with time."

A sudden chill ran down Terra's spine. Something about what Eric had said, something about time the two of them, something bad. She couldn't' put her finger on it but the princess was sure this sudden shadow that passed over her heart was a warning of some kind.

"Terra are you ok?" He asked, concerned by her sudden change in demeanor.

"I'm fine," she replied, shaking the last of the dread from her mind.

"Are you sure you're alright? You're very pale," he observed.

Terra could hear Lucas getting the horses ready to go, it was time to head out. She turned to Eric and forced a smile. "I'm fine, I promise." Together they walked back to the carriage and piled everyone in. Terra laughed as Eric and John fought momentarily about the best way to get to the library while Lucas barked orders at them like they were children.

Diana scoffed and said something about men under her breath as she went back to lying in the carriage. Terra just laughed, pure and happy.

It was only an hour later when they rolled up to the city gates. Diana sat up and leaned out the window. She had always like Titan. It was the biggest city in the Kingdom. It sat in the flat planes area nestled safely inside Aries Bay. All the tall hills around the bay kept the harsh winds from the sea away from ships seeking the safety of port. It was a huge trading city. People from all over the continents came here to buy and sell. It made the city so large that it had to be split into districts.

There was always a party or a huge event going on somewhere within the city. It was the place to be for anyone under the age of fifty. Naturally Diana frequented the city as often as her mother would allow.

Which sadly wasn't often.

Diana wondered if she would able to slip away from the library and see what was going on elsewhere in town. She doubted it but at least she could try.

Terra watched the city pass as they drove on through first three districts and on to the fourth where the library was located. She didn't really care for Titan. It always seemed too busy to her. There was always something going on somewhere and it all seemed so loud. She preferred the quiet peace that came from being up against the forest the way the castle was.

Thankfully it took very little time to get to the library.

Terra was shocked at the sheer size of the building.

It had to be nearly the size of the castle. Except that the castle had turrets and towers whereas the library seemed to be one huge rectangular building. Filled with books and scrolls and knowledge. She couldn't wait to get inside and get started.

When the carriage came to a stop Terra had her hand on the door ready to fly out and up the side set of steps that led to the large wooden doors. They stood nearly ten feet tall and were at least as wide. She couldn't wait to get a look inside at all the books and scrolls, all the knowledge of their kingdom was stored there and she couldn't wait to see it.

Just before she could fly out the door, a hand on her arms stopped her.

She turned to see Diana looking at her annoyed and frustrated. "Terra you can't go flying out of the carriage like some common idiot. You're royalty and you have to act that way."

"Oh," she stammered, not sure what was wrong with the way she was going to get out. "What should I do?" She asked not wanting to upset Diana.

"I will exit first, and you will slide to my side and exit behind me. Then together we will walk up the steps like the princesses we are."

"I guess we can do that," she agreed as her door opened up and Eric poked his head in.

"Princess," he said smiling offering her his hand.

Terra smiled and looked at Diana. With a roll of her eyes she waved her away. Smiling she grabbed Eric's hand and stepped out of the carriage into the warm afternoon sun. She could hear John on the other side helping Diana out and commenting about her dress. Together the four of them walked up the long flat steps as Lucas took the carriage around to the stable near the side of the library.

As they got close to the top of the stairs, the doors opened and three men came strolling out toward them. One was very old with long grey hair and a long grey beard. He wore a simple brown robe with a dark green belt tied around his waist. He walked with a slight hunch in his back but the use of a large staff seemed to help him.

Directly to his right was a slightly younger man, maybe in his late fifties, his hair was salt and pepper and the black of this moustache was the only thing that spoke to his original coloring. He was thin and tall and wore all black with only a thick gold belt around his waist.

To the left there was a much younger man. He was maybe as old as Eric, but no older. He had dark red hair and eyes so blue Terra could see them before she even got close. He wore pale blue robes with a purple belt.

"I heard once that the guardians of the library must wear colors that correspond to the colors of their magic," Eric whispered into Terra's ear.

Once they reached the top step the old man with the staff stepped forward and together the three of them bowed.

"Princesses Diana and Terra," the oldest man greeted. "My name is Arthur and this is Dominick," he indicated to the man in black, "and Alexander," now the man in blue. "We were most pleased to hear that you would be joining us today. What can we do to help?"

Terra stepped forward, "We've come to see the scroll that concerns my sister and the Shadow King. Our cousin from the Moon Kingdom has seen signs that we believe may lead us down another fork and aid my sister in her coming battle."

"Princess Terra," Alexander said stepping up next to Arthur. "We have heard stories of your power; we're honored to help you in any way possible."

With an exasperated sigh Dominick stepped up next to the other two men and said, "We three are the guardians of the library. Nothing comes in and nothing goes out without our expressed say so."

"If you will please follow Alexander he will take you to the section we have set aside for prophecy," Arthur said kindly. "It may take some time to find it though. As I recall that prophecy hasn't been looked at in nearly a decade."

"Over, sir," Alexander offered. He smiled brightly at Terra who blushed and shifted her weight from side to side. Eric took notice of his gaze and scowled. He started forward, deciding that the best course of action was to lead Terra in, keeping this Alexander as far from her as possible.

He slammed into something.

Looking bewildered, he turned to stare at the three men before the door.

"I'm afraid the Library has denied you entrance," Dominick said smirking. "The weapons you carry prevent you from entering."

"What is that supposed to mean?"

"I'm sure you have heard that the library was built upon a naturally occurring magical well." Dominick remarked.

"What's that?" John asked leaning in to ask Terra.

"A magical well is a deep reservoir of magic that occurs in nature," she explained, remembering the book she had read about this kind of thing very well. "No one knows exactly how they were formed or where the magic comes from. They're very rare and most are hidden under buildings. It's not exactly something you advertise if you've found one."

"Exactly," Alexander said his smile for her widening.

"This particular well is unusual in that it causes physical changes in the world around it," Dominick explained. "Sometimes it simply alters the coloring of a person's clothing." He gestured to Alexander and Arthur. "Other times it won't let certain people pass its bounds. Usually it has to do with the weapons a person carries. So I suggest stashing the swords or get comfortable waiting."

"You can't be serious," Eric demanded exasperated. "I'm Princess Terra's Royal Guard. It's my duty to protect her. How can I do that if I'm unarmed?"

"She is perfectly safe within the walls of the library," Alexander offered.

"Outrageous," he complained pulling the sword off his belt. He reached down and grabbed the two daggers he kept hidden in his boots. He set them on the stairs at his feet and tried to walk forward again. Still he couldn't pass.

"I'm sorry my lad," Arthur said, "The well doesn't seem keen to let you pass. You will have to wait out here."

Eric took a deep breath, like he was preparing to say something, loudly.

He stopped, let the breath out and turned to Terra. "I don't enjoy the thought of you going in there without me. However, I know that this is very important. So I will wait out here if that is what you want."

Terra couldn't help the grateful smile that spread across her face. Eric was keeping it under control. Even though through the bond she could tell that all he wanted to do was scoop her up and leave this place. He was keeping his temper under control for her.

"Thank you," she whispered, "I do need to do this. I need to go in and try and find a way to help Diana," she glanced back at her sister, love clear in her face, "she has so much on her shoulders that I have to do all I can do to help. Including this."

Eric's face remained passive but she could feel his disappointment. "Then I'll wait here."

Terra nodded gratefully and walked forward with Diana who was already making her way leisurely up the steps.

Diana, intent on ignoring her sister and her guards, continued forward. There was a moment when she hit the invisible wall of the well. She pushed against for a heartbeat, not being able to move. Finally, after less than a second of resistance, she pushed through the wall and blew past Terra and the three guardians.

"Let's go," she hollered.

"I'll stay out here with Eric," John offered.

"Thank you," Terra said. "I'm ready to get going."

Alexander nodded and said, "Follow me."

Terra nodded to Arthur and Dominick as she passed and they bowed to her.

As she passed through the double doors of the library she came to a stop. She looked up at the large celling, sitting nearly forty feet above her, made entirely of fractured glass. Each pane was different size and shape but they all fit together making beautiful patters above her. Some panes were angled just right so that they caught the sun and shone brilliantly. It was one of the most beautiful things she had ever seen.

"It's an amazing celling, right?" Alexander asked.

"It's breathtaking," she whispered.

"Yea," he agreed. "So the library is split into different sections, sort of like how the city is split into districts. There are two major sections, one is for books and the other is for scrolls. Each major section is split into two smaller sections. One for current and new additions up to twenty years ago and the other one is for anything older than that."

"Won't that make finding the scroll we need difficult?" She asked as they walked to catch up to Diana who, having gotten lost, was waiting for them up ahead.

"It won't be easy," he admitted.

"Alexander," she started.

"Alex," he said smiling at her.

"Alex," she corrected herself. "Do you know, approximately where the scroll is?"

"I wish I could say that we did but there was a problem a few weeks ago and things have been a mess ever since then."

"What kind of problem?" She asked, curious.

Alex made a face. "Someone broke in and messed up a number of things. Books got moved all over and scrolls were unrolled and everywhere. The prophecy scroll was hanging up in the middle of the library in a room were we keep the most valuable of all our editions, it was gone when we came in the next morning."

Terrified, Terra reached out and stopped Alex. "Is it possible that it was stolen?"

He smiled and patted her hand where it was still holding his arm. "It is impossible to take anything from this library without Arthur's consent. His staff does more than aid him as he walks, it's imbued with a kind of magic that gives him control over the entire library. Everything in here is magically linked to the staff and only that staff can allow things to pass.

"So we know it's in here somewhere, we just don't know where."

"How long is this going to take?" Diana asked irritably.

"I can't say princess," Alex admitted sounding genuinely upset that he couldn't answer her. There was a brake in the thirty foot book cases that made the walls. Alex took the left and led them down a hallway made of shelf after shelf of scrolls. After about fifty feet of solid shelves there was a break, a kind of clearing amidst the tall shelves with a large round table and a dozen chairs. There were already scrolls rolled out on the table and some stacked off to the side. Next to that there was a very comfortable looking sofa with a large fur rug rolled out in front of it.

"So somewhere in this area," Alex said, "We've been searching for it for a day or so now. This is the only section we haven't checked."

"You two have fun," Diana sneered walking toward the clearing. She sauntered slowly down the aisle and then flopped down on the sofa and covered her eyes with her arm.

"She's not feeling very well," Terra explained sheepishly to Alex.

"I understand completely," he said smiling. "So how about I take left and you take right?"

"Sounds good to me," she agreed. She turned right and stopped. "What does it look like, the scroll? What does it actually look like?"

"Oh," he laughed, "I forgot. Its rolls are gold with intricate carvings on them. If you find one you think it might be, pull it out and it will say what it is on the front. Just be careful, these shelves stand thirty feet tall. If you fall it could be fatal."

479

"I will, thank you," Terra said as she turned and headed into the forest of book shelves off to the right. If the celling hadn't been glass, she was sure that she wouldn't have been able to see at all. It seemed like there was so many scrolls on so many shelves that it would nearly impossible for her to search all of them in one day. Even with Alex's help and help from everyone else in the library, there was no way to search half of where she needed to in the time she had.

With a sigh bordering on defeat, Terra approached the first humongous book case before her. She glanced up, leaning all the way back trying to see if anything looked gold or even gold-ish. As far as she could tell she would need a ladder and literally the next week to look everywhere. Something inside, something she didn't understand or fully comprehend told her she didn't have a week.

Bell paced nervously back and forth in his room. King Sol had excused himself from their meeting to see his daughters off and then to deal with his nephew. Prince Charles had proved to be more of a handful than anyone had expected. Bell understood why he needed to go, but he still needed quite desperately to talk to his King.

Something was coming. It was something huge and dark and terrifying.

He had felt things stirring for some time. Nothing huge or major at first, just little things here and there, until Bell woke up this very morning and was so overcome by the sudden and terrifying feeling that he was unable to move. He had wondered out into the hall, shocked and amazed that no one else seemed to feel it.

Whatever this impending darkness was, it was coming soon, possibly even today.

Terra and Diana seemed to be at the heart of this coming storm. There was darkness swirling around the two of them. For Terra that was normal. Her exposure to Grey every day left a strange residue on her. She was still as bright and pure on the inside as ever, or as far as he could tell anyway. Still, there was something that seemed to hang on her, even hours after she'd left him.

Diana thought, that was something that worried Bell. She was usually a little dark and not quite right. Most of the time she just seemed slightly off or off colored. Today however, she was dark, darker than Terra. It worried him that she was out with her sister and only Eric and John to keep her safe. It was more than unsettling, it was quite harrowing.

Bell knew it was preposterous to be concerned about Terra when she was with her sister. Diana was meant to save the world. Surely she could be trusted with keeping her sister safe. Bell knew she had a dark side, and had even run into it from time to time, but it wasn't anything that was dangerous. She certainly wasn't a danger to Terra, who was one of the single most gifted people he had ever met.

Perhaps he had seen darkness swirling around the princesses because this terrible darkness that was coming, this thing that set the hair on his arms and neck standing upright, maybe it was the final battle. Diana was of age now and her training had made fair progress over the years. Granted she wasn't where he had hoped she would be, but she was strong. With Terra by her side, Diana could take him.

She could end this.

Not today, but she could start the process.

All the death and destruction that monster had caused could be ended.

So why couldn't Bell shake this terrible feeling of dread when he thought about Terra alone with Diana today? Was he so immersed in his studies of Terra and the man she now called Grey that he was seeing the darkness everywhere?

That had to be it.

It was the only explanation that made any sense to him.

After forty-five minutes Terra was starting to lose hope. She'd made so little progress searching the shelves. At thirty feet tall, each shelf took over ten minutes to search and that was just when she searched with her eyes. If she had to get up and search them by hand she would be here forever.

"Are you having any luck princess?" Alex called from somewhere to her left.

"Not much," she called feeling frustrated. "There has to be a better way to do this Alex. I can't be here all night."

He was quiet for a moment as he considered what she was saying. "Princess may I be frank?"

"I would appreciate it."

Terra could hear him walking over to her. "I have heard that you have some remarkable magical skills. Why not simply try to seek it?"

"Seek it?" She asked confused. "I don't know what you mean."

"A seeking spell. Their easy I believe," Alex explained as he came around the corner. "I don't have much magical skill, but I think I could do a seeking spell with your help."

"Alright," she agreed, happy for the small glimmer of hope. "Just tell me what to do."

He closed the distance between himself and Terra and said, "Give me your hands and close your eyes." She did as he asked. He took both her hands in his and said, "Take a deep breath and relax. Keep breathing deeply and focus your mind on the scroll we're looking for."

"I don't know what it looks like," she pointed out not opening up her eyes.

"You don't have to," Alex said calmly. "I know what it looks like. You just have to focus on what it's about. Focus on the content."

Terra took another deep breath and focused on everything she knew that the scroll said. Everything about Diana and her being chosen and the shadows and the signs. She didn't know any passages by heart, but she knew generally what it said. As she focused she could hear a strange kind of humming.

"What's that sound?" She asked.

"What sound?"

"It's like a loud humming. Like a large hive of bees is nearby."

"That's the spell working," he assured her, "focus on the sound. When the humming gets high pitched open your eyes and look around. You should be able to find it."

Terra nodded and closed her eyes. She could feel the humming more than hear it. It vibrated everything in her, even her teeth seemed to be vibrating. After a few more minutes the humming became more of high whining. She opened her eyes and looked around.

There was this faint band of light that seemed to be hovering above her head. It vibrated with the whining she heard. Not needing anymore instructions, she released Alex and started to follow the light. It led her down and around several cases, left here and a right there, over and over until Terra was lost in the isles of scrolls.

Finally the light came to a stop in a book case, all the way at the top. It shinned there for a split second and was gone. Terra looked around for one of the mobile stair cases she could use but found none. With no other option and feeling like time was against her, she grabbed her skirt and tied it in a knot at her side. She kicked off both of her shoes and started to climb.

At first it was hard to find her footing with all the scrolls around, but this section seemed to be comprised entirely of new scrolls so they moved for her feet with ease. After a few seconds it seemed easy to keep going. When she got about halfway up the height of it started to get to her.

"Keep breathing," she whispered to herself. "You can do this Terra, you *have* to do this." She clung to the case and made her way slowly up.

Around twenty feet the case started to creak under her weight. Terra thought she could feel it start to sway under her. She clung to the case, feeling like the biggest idiot in the world for trying to climb a thirty foot case all on her own. Now she was frozen, clinging to her case like a fool. She needed to move and she needed to do it now.

"Princess!?" Alex called from bellow her. "Princess what are you doing?"

"I'm trying to get the scroll," she shouted, too afraid to look down. "It's just up a little further."

"Wait right there I'll get a staircase and come back!" Alex raced away, hoping Terra could hold on long enough for him to find a staircase and get back to her.

Terra sighed; happy she wouldn't have to climb back down. Still she needed to get up and get the scroll. She was close now if she could just climb a little higher she should be able to reach it. Then Alex would come back with the stair case and she could climb down and be done with the whole mess. Reaching out through the bond she found Eric and pulled from him. Strength came flooding through her with no resistance.

Her arms and legs stopped shaking and her breath started to come easier. She stretched her left hand up and grabbed the next shelf. Slowly and carefully she pulled herself up. When her body responded with little difficulty, Terra moved up quicker. In seconds she closed the distance to the shelf and found herself staring at beautifully ornate golden rollers. She knew as soon as she saw it that it was the scroll she had been searching for.

She reached in and pulled it toward her.

"You can't be serious," she muttered as she pulled the scroll and realized it was nearly four feet long! There was no way she could pull it out with one hand and hold the book case. She glanced around trying to find a way to get it without falling to her death.

"Princess I'm back," Alex called. There was a sound of something being scrapped across the floor and then the whole case shuddered and swayed as something hit it close to her feet. "Just hold on Princess I'm coming," he shouted as he started to climb up to the stairs he'd just brought.

"I found the scroll," Terra called, "I just can't get it out. It's too long for me to grab and still hold on to the case."

"Ok," he said, "Princess I'm right behind you, with your permission I will uh . . . put my . . . hands . . . on you . . . and help you down."

Terra, ignoring the obvious discomfort in Alex's voice said, "I'm going to grab the scroll and pass it to you first, is that ok?" She turned as much as she could comfortably and looked at Alex. His face was red and his eyes were huge as he stared at her legs. "Alex," she sighed, I need you to pay attention."

"Right," he agreed, his attention snapping back up. "Pass me the scroll I'll get it and then you."

Terra nodded and grabbed the ornate rollers again. She pulled it out as far as she could. It teetered nervously half of its weight in Terra's hand and the other half still balanced on the shelf. Just as she feared it might fall, she felt a hand overlap hers and pull the scroll from her hands.

"I've got it," he assured her. He pulled the rest down and set it carefully on the step in front of him. "Now you," he said reaching up awkwardly. She took a deep breath and leaned back as far as her arms would stretch. She felt Alex grab her by the waist and literally lift her off the case and set her on the step next to him.

"Wow," she exclaimed, "Alex you're incredibly strong!"

"Not exactly," he admitted blushing, "my magic manifests as physical strength. So I'm not exactly that strong."

"You are strong," she told him reassuringly. "Now let's get this scroll to a table." Alex nodded and scooped the scroll up off the stairs and followed behind Terra as she carefully made her way down to the bottom. Once safely down she stepped into her shoes and smiled up at Alex.

"Let's go tell Diana we found it," she smiled, pleased to have finally made progress.

"Follow me, she's just over here," Alex told her, lifting the scroll onto his shoulder. "This way."

Diana yawned and stretched out. This small couch was quite comfortable and if she didn't' move too much her stomach didn't hurt so badly. That damn woman had given her something too strong! How was she supposed to function and keep her secret if she could barely

485

move for two days? It was outrageous and if the woman wasn't already rotting in the ground, Diana would kill her again.

"We found it!" Terra called obnoxiously chipper as she ran around the corner followed by the library attendant carrying a large gold scroll. "We have it, come and see!"

Suddenly Diana's stomach pain faded away as she looked at Terra. It was as though the very sight of her sister holding that scroll filled her with a dread so powerful that all other pain seemed to vanish.

She stared as she realized that she had her skirt tied up. Not only that, but there was a knife strapped to her thigh! Terra with a knife?! The very thought was preposterous.

"Terra what in the world have you done to your dress?" Diana demanded.

"Oh," she muttered sheepishly, "I need to tie it up so I could get the scroll." She started to untie her skirt quickly.

"And the knife?" Diana asked. "Did you need that for the scroll as well?"

"Uh . . . no." She stopped untying her skirt and pulled the knife off, holster and all. "Master Bell gave me this, for protection."

"Let me see it," Diana insisted sticking her hand out. Obediently Terra handed the knife over to her sister. As soon as her fingers touched it, Diana could feel the power of the blade. It was a dark kind of power that left burning sensation in her hands. At the end there was a particularly lovely purple stone. It shone brilliantly in the light streaming through the glass ceiling. Diana was fascinated by the blade. She loved the way it seemed to hum with energy.

"It's for Gr . . . the Shadow King," Terra corrected herself. "The blade is magic. Master Bell told me it creates a vacuum inside a person, sucking up all their magical power and holding it there. Then the hilt disappears and blade burrows so deep that there's no way to get it out. You die . . . slowly . . . and painfully."

"Really?" Diana asked, liking the sound of what this knife can do. "It can do all that?"

486

"Yes," she answered, her voice growing forlorn.

"Why did Bell give it to you?"

"To protect you during the final fight between you and the Shadow King," she answered, sounding as thought she might cry.

Diana turned her attention away from the knife and stared at Terra long and hard. A knife like this could kill not just the Shadow King, but anyone. A knife like this could kill her. If she doubted her sisters steadfast loyalty for even a second she would take the knife and never give it back. Something about the heartbroken forlorn look on her sister's face comforted Diana.

If Terra had plans to use the knife against her, she wouldn't look so unhappy. She would be shifty and uncomfortable. Instead she was sulking because she was going to have to kill that idiot in the basement. Satisfied that Terra was not a threat to her, Diana handed back the knife.

"You think you can do that?" She asked her.

She looked up and met Diana's gaze, her dark green eyes hard and unwavering. "I can do whatever I have to do."

Diana decided that was all she needed and said, "Let's unroll this and see what we can find. I want to be home by dinner."

Terra nodded and took one roller as the boy, Alexander she thought, took the other. They started to spread across the table. Except that it was too large for the table. Confused Alex stared at Terra and raised his shoulders.

"Take it to the floor," she said stepping around to the side of the table. Alex walked with her and the rolled it out. After it was all rolled out on the floor it sat nearly ten feet long and four feet wide, every inch covered in writing.

"Dear creator," Terra whispered, "this whole thing is the prophecy?"

"I'm not surprised," Diana remarked, "I was told once by the man who taught me how to read prophecy that this one was lengthy."

"How will we even know where to start looking?" She asked.

Diana laughed. She'd been trained to read prophecy and could very easily see past the false forks and the things that had already come to be. She marveled for a moment at all the things that had to come to pass for her to be born who she was when she was. All the signs that had been read and all different pieces that had to fall exactly into place.

She truly was an amazing human being.

As her eyes traced down the forks that had already happened, the dread set back in. Like a rock in the pit of her stomach it sat with her. She traced the lines down and down. Here it talked about the sign of the goddess and the golden princess and . . . she froze.

There was a fork branching off here, where it talked about the sign she was born under. It was never fully explored, she could tell by the fact that there were no notes scrawled next to it. It was a fork that stopped her heart and made her blood run cold.

This fork talked about what changed if two princesses were born under the same sign. It read:

"If two princesses born under the sign of the
Goddess subsist,
One shall be of light while one shall be of night,
Only one to save the world,
With one to cause its fall
Two sides of the same coin battle for dominance
Gold corrupts
Night embraces
Things are never what they seem."

It was about Terra. Both she and Terra were born under the sign of the Goddess. She couldn't be sure but it seemed like this fork was saying that one of them would save the world and one would destroy it. Diana looked up at Terra, she was watching her sister very intently as she realized that the love she felt for the monster, for the man she called Grey, that's what would corrupt her. He would turn her against not just herself, but the world.

She could tell her parents, tell everyone. They would lock her in the box right along with the man she loved. It would be so much of what she deserved that Diana nearly shouted it out right there.

"Princess," Alex asked walked over to Terra's side. He was looking at her shoulders, no at her scars. Those damn scars were such a nuisance. People were fawning over her and those scars before everything had happened yesterday. Now everyone stopped and stared at them, a lot of people actually touched them.

Diana had tried to squash the rumors about Terra having been touched by the creator as soon as she heard them. Still they somehow managed to persist. If she went to the King and Queen and the people of the kingdom with this information now, no one would believe her, especially not after what happened yesterday. They would look at her like she was crazy.

Worse than all of that, they would look at her like she was the princess who would bring the world down. No one would believe that Terra was capable of anything like that. Hell Diana didn't even believe it.

She couldn't let anyone see this scroll. Not until everything from yesterday blew over.

Terra watched as Diana studied the scroll. Her face seemed to fall slack. She was just about to ask what was wrong when Alex walked over to stand by her.

"Princess," he asked timidly, "can I ask you something?"

"Of course," she said still not taking her eyes off Diana.

"Is it true?"

"Is what true?"

"Did you truly defeat an entire field of shadows all by yourself?"

"Oh," she sighed looking up. "It wasn't like that. There certainly wasn't a field of shadows."

Alex looked at her shoulders again.

"You can ask," she said kindly.

"Is it true? Were you touched by the creator?"

"I'm afraid not," she explained. "Just an old scar."

"Still," he observed, "it's lovely."

"Thank you," she smiled turning back to Diana. "Have you found something?"

Diana glanced up at her, eyeing her slowly. She blew her breath out and stood up straight. "I'm afraid I can't find anything that will help us."

"Are you sure?" Terra asked, sure she had seen a look on her sisters face.

"I'm the one who knows how to read prophecy, not you. If you think I've missed something . . ."

"No," Terra said cutting her off. "I didn't mean to say that you missed something. I just can't believe that we came all the way out here for a dead end."

"Well I can only read prophecy so well," she explained making an excuse. "I'm going to find Lucas and get him to get the carriage ready. We're leaving." Without another word she stalked off toward the door, leaving Terra and Alex to stair off after her.

Disappointed, Terra walked to one end of the scroll and said, "Will you help me roll it up?"

"Of course," Alex replied. "What will you do now?"

"I'm not sure," she answered honestly. She had been banking on finding something, anything, in the prophecy. She had wanted to buy more time for Seph, at least a couple of days. This would buy her less than a day. She needed more time. There had to be a way to prolong her stay.

"I wish you guys had found something," Alex commented as he rolled his end towards her. "You could have stayed longer that way." He added almost too quiet to hear. "Maybe if you came back with the Master Wizard he might see something?"

"Master Bell?" Terra asked quietly to herself. A master wizard could easily read the prophecy. He would see anything that Diana might have missed. With everything going on at the castle and everyone preparing for Diana's battle, Bell would never have time to come all the way out to Titan to look at the prophecy.

If she could somehow get the scroll to him, he could look at it then. It would buy more time for Seph and it might actually help Diana. She just had to get the scroll out of the impressively guarded library, into the carriage, and all the way home without anyone seeing it. If she could convince Arthur to let her borrow it . . . maybe then.

If Diana saw it though, she could take it the wrong way and explode at Terra. She had blowup at her for so much less before. She would think Terra was questioning her abilities, and fly at her in a rage. She really didn't want to start a fight with Diana right now. She had too much on her mind to worry about a fight with her sister and they had just made up. She just needed to keep it hidden.

Except that the scroll was four feet wide, there was no way she could smuggle that thing out of here past her sister. However, if she said it was a different scroll. Maybe she could borrow a different scroll and then trade it out for this one. There were so many scrolls in to choose from here, she just needed to find one that was the same size as the prophecy.

"Alex I need your help," Terra told him taking the scroll and setting it up on the table.

"Whatever I can do princess," he said.

"I need to get this scroll to the Master Wizard."

Alex made a face, "Princess . . ."

"I know there's no way Master Bell will have time to get down here so I have to get the scroll to him."

"Princess this scroll hasn't left the library in well over a hundred years. I don't even think Arthur would let it leave."

"I know," she sighed. She grabbed Alex's hands and held them in both of hers. "I have to help my sister fight this battle and I can't shake the feeling that this scroll is instrumental in my being able to do that.

"So I know I'm asking a lot of you and I know that I don't' hardly know you. But I'm your princess and I'm asking you for your help. Not only would be helping my sister and the kingdom but you would also be doing me an enormous favor. I would literally be in your debt."

Alex let the thought of having the princess owe him a favor sink in. He could call on her at any time and for anything. She was beautiful and if the rumors were true, she was also kind. There were so many things he could think to ask her for. There was one thing that more than anything else he needed.

"I'll help you," he agreed. "But I want to call my favor in now if I can."

"If it's something I can do for you now I will be happy to," she said, relieved that he was willing to help.

"There's a girl . . . a woman I mean. Whom I love, greatly. I've been wanting to ask her to marry me for so long but . . . being a guardian is a calling, not really a job. So I have very little money to purchase a proper ring."

"Is she about my size?" Terra asked.

"I . . . don't know," Alex stammered. "I suppose."

She smiled and pulled the sliver ring from her finger. A diamond sat in the center of the setting flanked on either side by emeralds. It had originally been Diana's but she found the diamond in the center too small for her taste and had passed it off to Terra.

"Here," she said handing it too him. "I've never really cared for the ring. Honestly I didn't even know why I put it on this morning."

"Princess," Alex said breathless. "I can't accept this. It's too much."

"Then sell it and buy a better ring and a whole wedding."

"Still . . . it's so much . . ."

"Honestly I'm happy for you to have it. So long as you promise to help me."

He took the ring and slipped it into a pouch at his waist. "Ok here's what we can do. I'm going to grab a scroll that's similar in size to this one and ask Arthur if you can borrow it. Then we'll find a way to wrap this one so no one can know."

"Here," she offered, pulling her cloak of her shoulders. She handed it to Alex and together they wrapped the scroll as best they could.

"This would be easier if you weren't so short," he commented.

"Ha ha ha, you're so funny," she laughed mockingly. "Still, you are right. My cloak can't cover it completely."

"What do you want to do?"

Terra thought for a moment. "I'll wait until everyone is loaded in the carriage and then load it in to the chest in the back. That way no one will see it."

"That could work," he agreed smiling. "I'll go and find a scroll, you wait here."

Ten minutes later Terra was closing the trunk on the back of the carriage and making sure it was secure. John was talking to Lucas and Eric was making sure his horse was saddled properly. Arthur came walking slowly toward her smiling and waving at people as they passed by.

"Princess," he said smiling. "You'll be sure to take good care of our prophecy?"

She froze. "You know?"

"Of course. I'm old, not daft," he joked with a twinkle in his eye. "Just make sure she finds her way back to us, won't you?"

"Of course. And I'm sorry . . . I just didn't know . . ."

"No need to explain," he assured her, turning to leave. "Just take care."

"I will, thank you." She watched Arthur walk back up the stairs as Eric came over.

"Everything ok?" He asked.

"Yea," she replied. "Just ready to get back."

"Good, me too," he said smiling. "Hop in and we'll get going."

Terra nodded and climbed in. Diana had already stretched out across the opposite seat and was actively ignoring everything she started to say to her. With a sign, Terra leaned back against the wall of the carriage and wondered what the scroll, tucked safely away in the chest behind her, might tell them. Maybe it would tell them how to save Diana and Grey.

Maybe it would help Diana win.

Maybe it would change everything.

Chapter 13

By the time the carriage rolled through the gates to the castle most of the day was already gone. Terra looked up at the blue sky starting to turn slightly gold as the sun approached the cliffs to the south west. There was only a few hours left of daylight. Still, it was enough time to find Master Bell and show him the prophecy before she had to face Grey for dinner.

Diana continued to snore on the bench across from her. She had slept the entire way home, leaving Terra with no one to really talk to and nothing to do but look out the window and think about the scroll in the back. She thought about Grey for a while. All the things she had said to him and most importantly what he had said to her.

After a while she had stopped thinking about Grey. In truth she began actively not thinking about him. All she managed to do was think the same things over and over again. She knew what he had said and what she had said to him but none of that seemed to help her decide what to do or what to say.

So pulling up to the castle should have made Terra feel better. She could start to make a real difference in things with her sister.

It didn't.

She didn't feel happy or even excited.

Instead she felt this terrible sense of foreboding. It seemed to her that there was something terrible, just around the next corner. She could feel it there, she just couldn't see it yet.

Not sure what was making her feel this way, but sure that she needed to get to Bell before anyone put together that the scroll she had wasn't the one she was supposed to have, she decided to waste no time. So as soon as the carriage stopped Terra flew out, not waiting for anyone to help her step down or open a door. She didn't even bother to stop the carriage door from swinging round and slamming into the side of itself.

She ran around back and started to undo the buckles on the back chest. Once it was open she pulled the scroll out, not thinking about the cloak covering it. She didn't have time to worry about it, she needed to get it to Bell now.

Diana was awakened by the sound the door crashing into the carriage. She started awake and nearly fell off the bench. Sitting up quickly she straightened her dress and stood. Lucas was at the door waiting to help her down.

"M'Lady," he said bowing his head as he helped her down the stairs.

"Thank you Lucas," Diana said, her head held high. "Where is my sister?"

"Runnin' off that way," he answered inclining his head in the direction of Terra, running across the yard.

Diana watched, in disgust, as she ran like a common slut through the yard. Just then a man walking one her father's hunters, darted in front of her sister causing her to stumble and nearly fall over into the dirt.

'*Would serve her right*,' she thought smugly, stepping away from the carriage and toward the main entrance to the castle.

It was then she saw it, tucked under her sister's arm, half hidden by her cloak was a scroll. A huge scroll, nearly as tall she was and Diana would wager nearly ten feet long.

It couldn't be.

Terra had left almost immediately after Diana had, she would have had no time to get a scroll out of there, especially not *that* scroll. It wasn't allowed to leave the library; she'd heard that one boy say so. No one could remove anything from the library unless that really old guy said they could.

So there was no way.

It wasn't possible.

Still Diana found her eyes fixed on Terra like a hawk. She watched as her sister recovered her balance by swinging quickly to her left and bouncing out of the way. As she jumped back, part of her cloak caught in the late afternoon wind and blew off the top of scroll. There, glaring in the suddenly harsh light of day was the ornate golden roller that belonged to only one scroll.

Terra had the prophecy.

Suddenly frantic Diana turned to Lucas, "Where is my sister going?!" She demanded.

"I couldn't say," he replied, ignoring the frantic undertones in Diana's voice.

Outraged that Lucas would brush her needs off so dismissively and feeling every second tick by like a physical pain, Diana grabbed the man by his shirt collar and released enough magic into him to get her point across.

"I asked you a question," she threatened through gritted teeth. "Do *not* make me repeat myself."

Lucas winced as the magic hit him, causing him sharp pain with every syllable Diana uttered. "I think she said somethin' about

496

needin' to see the Master Wizard," he panted, "that's all I know, I swear it."

Diana dropped the man and turned back to find her sister. She had to be stopped. Once Bell saw that scroll it was all over. No one would ever believe that she was the still the golden princess. Not after the way Terra had been parading herself around the Kingdom lately. If Bell saw that he would call a tribunal and put her side by side with Terra and then let the people of the kingdom choose which princess they wanted for their savior.

No one would choose Diana.

Terra was gone.

In the time it had taken her to question Lucas, Terra had slipped away. She had to catch her, she had to stop her sister. She was an excellent liar and Terra a gullible fool. She could think of something to say to stop her sister from showing it Bell, at least for now.

Diana raced forward, knowing she had no time to lose. She would run and check the school room. Bell was usually stalking around there somewhere.

It had taken less than five minutes to run to the school room, but to Diana it had felt like a lifetime had slipped past her. She ran to the door and shoved it open.

It was dark and quiet, not a living thing in sight.

Neither Terra nor Bell was here.

Diana sank down into a chair near the door. She had no idea where to look for her sister next. No idea if she was in her room or down it the prison with that idiot. Even if she did find her what would she say? How could she convince Terra to wait to show the scroll to anyone? How long would she even be willing to wait?

It dawned on Diana then, what she had to do. There was no way to protect herself from her sister as long as Terra had that scroll. She might be able to convince her to hold off on showing it to Bell for a time but that wouldn't last long. Soon Terra would ignore her sister and show the scroll to anyone she thought might be able to read it. When that happened Diana was done for.

The only way to properly ensure that her sister and that damned scroll no longer threatened her was to take them out of the equation.

Terra would simply have to die.

It made sense the more Diana thought about it. If the scroll was right then Terra would be a threat to her one day soon enough. It only made sense to deal with it now. Nip it in the bud as it were. It would take care of so many problems she had. No one would love Terra more than they loved her, no one would question who the princess in the prophecy was and she would finally be done with all of Terra's insistent goodness all the time. Most importantly of all, she could finally get her hands on the so called Shadow King in the prison beneath the castle.

Terra being dead was starting to sound better and better.

Still, how would she do it?

It could never come back to her.

People could never know it was Diana who had ended her.

Suddenly the room pitched around her and she flew out of the chair onto the floor. Diana shot to her feet as the room around her was plunged into darkness.

Spinning and frantic, she called out. "Who's there?! Who dares to treat a princess of Sol this way?!"

'*Diana, Princess of the Kingdom of Sol!*' A voice inside her head boomed.

"Who's there!?" She shouted again. A soundless thunder rumbled through the room dropping Diana to her knees.

'*Be not afraid Princess. We have come to help you.*'

Diana scrambled to her feet and braced against the wall. She scanned the darkness trying to see anything that might tell her who was after her and why. It was so dark that her attacker could have been a hair away from her nose and she wouldn't have been able to tell.

"I demand to know who is there!" She screamed, happy to hear that her fear wasn't apparent in her voice.

Suddenly all the darkness in the room seemed to swirl into one spot. In a matter of seconds a huge shadow stood looming in front of her. It was taller than any shadow she'd ever seen before with huge golden eyes. It bent down and put its face inches from hers and hovered there.

It took her a second but then Diana realized that it was the same shadow she had seen in her dream.

She would have shrank away from the intense gaze of the shadow, but she was already up against the wall. So she kept her chin up and stared back. If it was going to kill her at least she would die like a princess.

'We have come to help you with your . . . problem.' A voice in her head echoed.

"I don't know what you are monster, but I have no problem you can help with." She spat at the shadow in front of her.

As odd as the thought sounded in her head, Diana would have sworn that the shadow was smiling at her.

'What of your sister then?" It asked, almost mockingly. 'What will you do with her and the scroll she carries with her? How will you handle that situation?'

Diana scowled at the face of the shadow. She wasn't sure how this thing knew what was going on with Terra. No one could have found out in the little time they had been back. At first she wanted to spit in the monsters face and tell it to go back to the hell it came from.

Then she stopped.

If this monster somehow had knowledge of her predicament, it might do her well to hear it out. Even if it didn't know anything useful, she didn't have any better ideas right now.

"What would you suggest then Shadow? How best should I solve my issue?"

It pulled away and looked down at her in a way that made her veins run cold as ice. For a brief moment Diana greatly regretted not

499

attempting to destroy the monster and be done with it. Now it was too late.

'We will give you the power to handle the situation your sister poses to you, permanently.'

Diana eyed the shadow up and down. Scrutinizing it and what it had said. If what it had said was to be believed, then it would be the solution she was looking for. Terra had to die, that much was decided, but if it was a shadow that killed her, this shadow. There would be an outcry from the kingdom the likes of which had never been seen. It would be perfect.

Too perfect.

Keeping her chin high she stared the shadow down and said, "What exactly do you get out of this?"

'We would simply request that after you receive the power we will bestow on you that you allow us to continue to live in your realm.'

"That's all? You just want to stay here?"

'Yes. Give us your word that we will be allowed to stay. Servants, if you will, in your kingdom. Then we shall grant you the power to destroy your sister and any enemy who would stand against you.'

Diana considered the offer for less than a moment before she nodded and said, "If you can do all that you say then prove it. If I can destroy my sister and the scroll she carries, as you say I will be able to. Let me see this power of yours in action. If I am happy with the outcome then I will accept your terms."

'Very well. We will grant to you our power and the ability to locate your sister. We assume you will want to handle this situation personally.'

"Indeed I will," Diana said smiling at her luck. "Indeed I will."

Terra raced down the hall. She knew based on the time that Master Bell wouldn't be in the school room, but if she hurried she might be able to find him in his room meditating. He liked to spend a little time in the afternoons by himself. She just needed to hurry and she would be able to catch him on the way out. *

She rounded the corner that lead from the main hall into the servant's hall that ran along the corridor that used to house her and her family's old rooms. Down at the end of the hall Master Bell still stayed in his old room. He had passed on an opportunity to move with the royal family stating that he and his room had a connection he enjoyed.

Terra was nearly half way down the hall when she fell.

As she went down she rolled carefully, making sure she fell onto her shoulder and not onto the centuries old scroll she was carrying. She hit the stone of the hall hard, sending shocks of pain through her shoulder and down her arm. She cried out instantly and then bit down on her lip to keep from making any further noise. If people came out into the hall to see what the noise was and found her on the ground she would never be able to get away.

She scrambled to her feet quickly but was thrown down again. It took her brain a few seconds to process the fact that it wasn't her feet that were tripping her up; it was the fact that the ground was moving.

Making her way to the wall she got to her feet. The floor continued to shake as she stood there, terrified. It was a gentle shaking at first but as she stood it started to shake harder and harder. A chunk of ceiling, roughly the size of Terra, broke off and came crashing down a few feet to her left.

Like a slap in the face, the celling crashing into the floor woke her out of her frozen fear induced stupor. She ran back the way she came, careful not to fall again. She wasn't sure where she was going but she knew she needed to not be standing where she was.

"Terra!"

Turning she saw Eric running toward her.

"Terra we have to get out of here," he shouted grabbing her wrist and started leading her down the stairs.

She only nodded and let herself to be lead away from the danger. Half way across the main hall she stopped dead in her tracks, nearly pulling Eric to the ground.

"Terra what are you doing we have to go," he said, panic coloring his voice.

"Diana," she stated simply, as though the one word would be enough to convey to Eric what she needed to do.

"Terra we don't . . ."

"Help!" Someone shouted off to their left.

A woman ran toward them, wobbling due to the shaking and bleeding from a huge cut on her forehead. "Please," she shouted grabbing Eric by the sleeve. "You have to help me, my son is trapped and I can't get him out!"

Eric looked to Terra, clearly not sure what to do.

"Go," she told him, "I have to find Diana and make sure she's safe. Help him."

He nodded and said, "I will meet you by the stables, wait for me there!" He took off with the woman in tow and head back toward the main dining hall.

Another violent shake sent Terra to the ground again; the scroll fell out of her hands and rolled away. She went to get it but a sudden rush of people, frantically trying to escape the castle, caught it up like the tide and swept the scroll out of the main hall and away. She watched it go, knowing she should go after it, but also knowing that she had to save Diana.

What good was a scroll without Diana?

With a shake of her head she got up and ran toward the kitchen. It had been a few minutes since she had seen Diana but her hope was that she was still somewhere near the kitchens and the stables.

Coming around another corner Terra's heart leapt as she sighted her sister running toward her.

"Sister!" She shouted grabbing her by the arm. "Diana we have to go! It's not safe here anymore."

"Terra what's going on?" Diana shouted as she let her sister lead her back the way she had come.

"No time!" She shouted. She pushed past the large kitchen door and pulled Diana out into the afternoon light. A crash behind her made both princesses turn to see the large stone archway that was once the largest doorway into the castle, crash to the ground.

Not wasting another moment, Terra dragged Diana away to the stables as more and more chunks of their home began to rain down from the sky around them. It was a quick walk, less than two minutes at a run. Still by the time they reached the stables most of the castle had come down and the only parts still standing didn't seem like they would hold up much longer.

Terra took Diana all the way to the far wall and pushed her down behind some of the hay bales kept on hand for the horses. It wasn't an ideal waiting spot but this was where Eric said he would meet her. She just had to keep Diana safe until he got there. As a former Captain of the Guard and a Royal Guard, surely Eric would know what to do in this situation.

Sensing the worst was on its way, Terra glanced around for something, anything she could use to protect their heads. With nothing in sight and time running out, she knew what she had to do.

She jumped down next to her sister and stretched herself out over the top of Diana as the shaking seemed to come to a head. She protected Diana as bits of rock and debris rained down on them. She knew it wasn't much, but she had to protect her sister.

Diana laid on the filthy smelling hay as Terra lay over her. She couldn't believe that she was now powerful enough to bring the entire castle down! Better than that, Terra, being the fool she was, had run right to her! Diana, who was currently planning the perfect way to kill her! Seeing the way everything was turning out so perfectly, Diana knew her plan was blessed by the creator. Even the almighty knew Terra had to die.

503

An incredibly loud boom tossed Terra off of her and nocked Diana to the ground. Terra was thrown to the wall, flipping head over heels as she rolled. Her skirt flew up and for a moment her bloomers were exposed and Diana caught a glimpse of the knife Terra had shown her earlier.

With a smile, she nearly laughed out loud. She now knew how she would handle her sister.

Terra's head hit the wall and everything seemed to swim around her. She shook her head clear as the last of the shaking seemed to finally stop. She scrambled up to her feet and rushed over to help Diana. She was lying on her side and didn't seem to be moving.

As she got closer Diana jumped up and looked at her sister.

"Thank the Creator," Terra sighed. "We have to go, it isn't safe here."

"Safe?" Diana asked laughing. "What makes you think anywhere is safe. If the shadows can do this they can do anything."

"Shadows?" She asked confused, "what makes you think this was the shadows?" Terra's mind jumped to Grey, sitting alone under the castle. With the way she ended things last night there was no way to know what kind of mood he might be in. Still she didn't know if it was possible for him to be this mad.

Mad enough to bring the whole place down? To kill all these people? Oh and the people! She hadn't even thought about that yet. There were so many people in the castle at any one time. If only half got out hundreds of people would be dead. Maybe more.

Could he have done that?

He'd killed so many people before she had met him all those years ago. A few hundred castle workers would be nothing to him.

Nothing.

"I saw the shadows," Diana stated standing and brushing the hay off. "Just before I ran into you I saw that King of theirs in the hall. I was coming to find you when you found me."

"Grey's out?" She asked more to herself than to her sister. "How is that possible?"

"I don't know," Diana said eyeing her sister completely confused. Seeing an opportunity she grabbed Terra by the shoulder and pulling her quickly behind a stack of barrels. "Quick!"

"What's wrong?"

Diana pushed her sister behind her and poked her head up over the rim of the barrel. "Shh," she said turning back. "He's right over there."

"He is?" Terra asked, thrilled and terrified simultaneously. "What's he doing?"

"I can't tell," Diana whispered turning back to her sister. "He's surrounded by those damn shadows of his."

"Oh," Terra whispered, deflated. As much as she hated to admit it, it looked like Grey might actually be the one behind all of this. It shouldn't have surprised her. Every day that went by took them closer and closer to the end. After everything he had said to her yesterday Terra was starting to think she could do it. She was so close to cleansing his heart!

Maybe that was what had prompted this.

Maybe he had felt the impending end to his darkness and took steps to ensure Terra was unsuccessful.

"Can you handle the shadows?" Diana asked looking back at her sister. "I know you handled some the other day, do you think you can do it again?"

"Yes I suppose so," she answered feeling hollow.

"Good. Draw the shadows off and I'll handle the rest."

"How?"

Diana had to struggle to not fly at her sister right then. She had a plan and she needed to stick with it. "The knife Bell gave you," she said recovering. "Give me the knife and I'll end this once and for all."

"Right," Terra whispered uneasily. She pulled her skirt up and removed the knife from its sheath tied to her leg. For a moment she hesitated. Something felt very wrong. Diana stood in front of her, her blue dress tarnished from the dust and debris floating around. Somewhere there was a fire going, she could see the Colum of black smoke behind her sister. From where she stood she could hear the cries of people either stuck in the ruble or those who had started searching it.

So many people would be dead.

Of course things felt wrong! Everything was so horribly wrong.

Diana looked at her waiting, her hand extended.

Taking a deep breath she pushed the hilt of the knife into Diana's palm and pulled her skirt back down. She knew this day was coming. Sooner or later people were going to demand action and Grey would have to die. Terra had always hoped that she would help him become better before that day came.

Now it was too late and Diana had the knife. All she could do was stand by her sister and do as she was told.

Diana looked her up and down and asked, "Are you ready?"

Terra nodded standing up straight. "I've got this." She turned on her heel, knowing that when she rounded the corner she would look upon Grey for the last time. Would he be happy to see her, she wondered. Would he feel the same as she did? Hollow and dead inside at the thought that this day had finally come? Or would he stand there and flash her that same wicked grin of his.

Caught up in her own little world of thought, Terra marched out past Diana to face her destiny. She had taken two steps past her sister when she felt Diana's hand on her shoulder. Before she could react her sister had spun her by the elbow and pulled her in against her, almost hugging her.

Terra froze as a sharp, unexplained, pain pierced her abdomen.

"Poor, stupid Terra," Diana whispered singsong in her sisters ear. "To dumb to see the snare set in front of her."

"Diana?" She asked convulsing slightly.

Slowly and smiling triumphantly, Diana stepped back to take a good look at Terra. She wanted to see her face, to fully grasp the pain and betrayal in her eyes. "Couldn't see the forest for the trees, could we?"

Terra looked down to see the magical knife Master Bell had entrusted to her, the knife she had just handed her sister, sticking out of her stomach with Diana's hand still grasping the hilt. For a moment she couldn't make her brain process what was going on. She could see everything happening but she couldn't make the pieces fit.

Then it all came together.

"You . . ." she started. Diana twisted the knife, spun her sister around and pushed Terra back. She cried out in pain and fell to her knees. Diana took a few more steps back, laughing the whole time. Once she was a few feet away she stood and folded her arms, content to watch her sister die. Not because she was evil of course, but because she had to make sure that the deed was done.

Terra reached out to grab the knife sticking out of her gut but before her fingers could touch the hilt it vanished, pushing the knife deeper into her abdomen. She coughed and nearly balked when she saw the dark red blood that came up from her throat.

"Why?" She asked, looking up at Diana. "Why would you do this?"

She scoffed and rolled her eyes. "You just don't get it do you? Poor simple Terra, there was only ever enough room in this kingdom for one princess. Once I knew that you were evil, it became glaringly obvious that you had to die."

"Evil?" Terra asked confused, clapping her hand to her wound as she struggled to stand. "How could you think I'm evil?! I'm your sister!" She was shouting now.

Diana looked around, startled. She had expected the knife to kill her almost immediately. If Terra could stand and talk she could tell

507

people what had really happened. Even if one person believed her it was one to many.

She looked around frantically, trying to find anything she could use to finish the job. She couldn't use magic because she was only really effective with physical contact and she didn't want to get to close to Terra just in case she decided to try for some retaliation.

Like a gift from the creator in her hour of need, Diana spied a barrow of oil for the kitchen right next to Terra. She took a step forward and kicked the barrel over. If fell on to its side and began to soak the hay spread across the ground. It rolled into another barrel and then into another. Within seconds the entire area was coated in oil.

Before Terra could make a move to stop her, Diana lit a spark in her hand and threw it to the ground.

With a deafening roar the fire roared to life around Terra. She tried to reach out with her magic and quell the flame but the knife in her gut pulled the magic from her body and made her defenseless. She backed away as the fire gained ground in front of her. Diana looked at her and smiled.

"Diana!" She shouted. Again the fire roared up around her and Terra stepped back.

She looked back up to yell at her sister. The words she had formed died on her lips when she saw Diana wasn't alone anymore. Her parents had run up to find her and they were flanked on either side by a handful of guards, Eric included.

"Eric!" She screamed! He looked at her and then to Diana who was suddenly in tears and leaning heavily on her father. Terra couldn't make out what they were saying over the sound of the fire. She stumbled back again as it roared toward her.

"NO!" She screamed. "I have done everything you ever asked of me! I have sacrificed all my life to better yours! Because you were the princess in the prophecy! Because you were the chosen one! And because I loved you!" Terra coughed and her body was racked with pain. Her vision was beginning to grow dark around the edges.

She was dying.

Whether by the knife stuck in her stomach or by the fire burning around her, Terra would be dead in a matter of moments. She looked at Eric and reached out to him through the bond. She tried to will him to feel the truth through the bond they share.

She couldn't even do that.

Again the fire roared closer and again she backed up, this time her back hit the wall of the stable. She was trapped, fire all around her as she bled out slowly. This was the end. So many thoughts raced through her head as she watched the fire dance before her. Diana stood wrapped safely in her father's arms as everyone looked down at Terra with disgust and shame.

She wondered about Eric, would he ever know the truth about what happened? Would anyone? What about Master Bell? Would he know the truth when he heard it? Oh and what of Mammy!? The news of Terra's death would be a devastating blow to her. What would she think? Would she know the truth?

The fire was closer now, so close it was singing the hairs on her arms. Not too much longer and it would all be over. Terra looked up at the sky, she prayed to the creator to take her quickly and not prolong the suffering.

Inexplicably her thoughts turned to Grey.

Knowing that all of this was Diana's doing meant that Grey had never left his cell. Her sister had used her connection to him to blind her about what was really going on.

Was he safe, she wondered? Was he still trapped under the castle? What would happen to his prison when she died? What would he think when he heard she was dead? Would it matter to him?

Terra screamed as her skirt caught fire. She slapped at it frantically, desperately trying to put it out. Her swinging sent another wave of pain through her body. Her knees went weak and buckled beneath her. She was going down and it was all over. For the second time in as many days Terra came face to face with the realization that she was going to die.

This time though, it wasn't the evil of the shadows that would claim her life, but the sister she had loved and admired all her life. She would succumb to Diana's deadly game having never known she was playing.

Seconds before she hit the ground, and arm came around her pulled her up and away from the deadly fire surrounding her.

It was Grey.

"How?" She coughed through the soot and the smoke.

Grey shook his head, and taking her face in his hands he said, "This place holds only death for you now, come with me and live."

She nodded. She could distantly hear Diana yelling something at her as Grey wrapped his arms around her. The fire roared a final time and closed the distance between them. She buried her face in his chest as the whole world went black.